The Girl Who Lived By The River

(A hilarious, heartwarming story of first love, friendship and family)

MARK DAYDY

MARK DAYDY

ISBN-13: 978-1537106960

ISBN-10: 1537106961

Cover design by Mike Daydy

CONTENTS

1977

1978

PROLOGUE:

THE VIEW FROM GREENWICH

The Present Day...

High on the hill at Greenwich, overlooking the sweeping Thames far below, it was easy to become lost in time. Things change and, as the past recedes, stories that seemed important have a habit of falling into the cracks between now and then, never to be told again.

But he was okay with that. After all, change was the engine of the world.

On a hot day, the breeze coming up from the river felt good. That never changed.

"Grandad?" said six-year-old Amy, seemingly with a thought in mind too.

"Yes, angel?"

His grand-daughter was drawing a picture of the view – an impressively detailed landscape that took in the Old Royal Naval College, *Cutty Sark*, the river, and the Isle of Dogs across the water.

"Did you draw pictures when you were little?"

"Sometimes, yes."

"Did you draw the same picture as me?"

He studied Amy's sketch of new apartments crowding the riverside, the glass towers of Canary Wharf pushing

1

upward, and a plane flying out of the nearby City Airport.

"It looked different when I was a boy."

"Why was it different?"

"Things change, Amy. When I was a boy there weren't any new riverside homes or tall glass office buildings. There wasn't an airport either. Back then it was all big dirty factories with big stinky chimneys and docks crammed full of ships coming in from all over the world. Until it all closed down, of course."

"Did you like it when you were little, Grandad?"

"Yes, I did. Very much so."

"What, even the big stinky chimneys?"

"Well, no, we're better off without those… and the chemical factory… and the lead works. It was just a different time, that's all. A time of big changes. Actually, there was a particular time down there that was very special."

"Why was it special, Grandad?"

"Well, one day, a teenage boy told a little lie that seemed so daft, it shouldn't have mattered. But it started something that changed everyone's lives. Not straightaway, but… well, like a magic spell, the whole future began to—"

"A helicopter! Shall I draw it in my picture, Grandad?"

"You can draw anything you want, angel."

Amy got to work with a red pencil, adding the aircraft to her exciting vista, while her grandad sensed a scene that had long since passed into memory. A time of teenage dreams writ large across a canvas of chimneys, factories and docks. A time of hope and the courage to try for what seemed utterly impossible.

1975

1 THE LIE

Perfect!

On a damp East London street, south of the oily Millwall Outer Dock, north of the murky, swirling Thames, Tom Alder was admiring his reflection in a grocer's shop window.

Start forming a queue, girls.

Yes, he finally had "the look": shoulder-length mousy hair, sunglasses perched on top of his head, crimson T-shirt, white Levi jeans, red Puma trainers and a pack of Benson & Hedges lodged pleasingly in the left hand.

Thank God he'd seen that cool bloke with "the look" in Chrisp Street Market on that sweltering Saturday afternoon in June. Pity it was now a dull Saturday morning in mid-September, where the "the look" felt less cool, more bloody freezing. Still, that's how long it had taken to save up for the Levi's. The main thing now was to use the power of "the look" to attract a girlfriend by his sixteenth birthday in two weeks' time.

'Tom!'

Crossing the road was Megan Vanderlin, a dark-haired, brown-eyed girl in the sixth-form at his school, who, despite living in a run-down block of flats, spoke in a self-taught middle class accent.

'Alright?' said Tom, projecting "the look".

'You look cold,' she said.

'Me? No.'

Her eyes peered directly into his. His eyes darted from her eyes to the purple jumper struggling to contain her promising bust and away to a boy kicking a ball around further up the street. It annoyed him, this shyness.

'What are you doing this far down?' he asked, forcing his attention back to her inquisitive gaze.

'Getting a loaf. They're all out up by me. My pain of a little brother refused to go out, so here I am. You're lucky not having a brother.'

'Yeah.' He did, in fact, have a brother once – a younger one – but it wasn't something the family discussed on account of it being too painful and complicated. It was one of those situations where Time had been handed the responsibility of burying the memories, but was doing a crap job thanks to Circumstances getting involved.

'I didn't know you smoked,' said Megan, eyeing his Benson's.

He didn't, although he fancied the *idea* of smoking, what with its cool, artistic French café society connotations. But should he admit that? Or would she think him a *poseur*?

'They're Mum's,' he said. 'She needs a top-up to get her phlegm going.'

Megan let out a queasy groan that turned to laughter when Tom, cottoning on to her interest, mimicked his mum's morning attempt to cough her lungs up.

'You're horrible,' she said.

'I'm not really.'

'No, you're alright.'

Tom glanced away again. 'You too.'

Further down the street, the boy's ball bounced over a corrugated iron fence to where century-old homes had been demolished to make way for modern housing.

'Do you like Bowie?' she asked.

Bowie? They rarely spoke at school, what with her being a year above him. Yet here she was, in Chapel House Street, talking about Bowie. Obviously, "the look" was working.

'Bowie's great,' he said. 'And progressive rock is great too. It kind of defines me. Musically. Sort of thing.'

Megan's intense stare flustered him.

'Genesis, Pink Floyd,' he said, trying to muster further useful information. 'Guitar... kind of thing. That's where I'm, you know, coming from. That's what gets me going. Er, musically, I mean.'

He wanted to ask her out. Although she was in the year above him at school, she was only a few months older. Only his heart rate shot up and made him feel ill. He'd never asked anyone out before. His date with classmate Sandy Smith to see *The Golden Voyage of Sinbad* had been instigated by Sandy. Only, she brought a friend called Midge – and left suddenly due to a mystery illness in order to set him up with the aforementioned Midge, who laughed like a machine gun at everything he said.

'Do you play, Tom?'

'Eh?'

'Guitar. You sound passionate about it. Do you play at all?'

'Oh... I dabble,' he said, unable to reveal his non-playing status to someone who was being tipped to be next year's Head Girl.

'I bet you look just like the Genesis bloke,' she said.

'Er, yeah.' Tom tried to imagine the "Genesis bloke" holding a battered Woolworth's acoustic with three strings missing.

'Ever thought of joining a band?' she asked.

'Er, yeah, it's definitely something I… you know…' His face felt hot enough to fry an egg. He didn't like telling lies to girls. He'd have to admit he wasn't a guitarist. His potentially amazing life probably lay in another direction anyway.

She raised an eyebrow. 'Ever thought of starting your *own* band?'

Oh God, he couldn't afford to lose a girl who was interested in music.

'Well…' His heart began pounding into his skull. 'That's the, er…'

'Plan?'

Tom gulped. 'Yeah.'

'Cool. First time we've talked properly.'

'Yeah…'

From out of nowhere, an intense silence settled on them. Tom tried to think of something to break it, but couldn't. He was too busy worrying about the big stupid lie he'd just told.

'Well, I'd better get that bread,' said Megan, turning to look past the fading poster of the West Ham Cup Final squad in the shop window to a rack containing the last loaf.

Tom shuffled. It was time to ask her out. An afternoon film, maybe? Only, his tongue felt like a slab of offal.

'Um… doing?'

'Pardon?'

'Doing anything… this afternoon?' The throbbing in his head indicated an imminent stroke followed by brain damage, dribbling and feeding through tubes.

Megan blushed. 'This afternoon? Nothing in particular.'

'Um…' Oh God. What if she said no? The embarrassment. The shame…

'Are you okay, Tom?'

'*Alan Freeman's Saturday Rock Show*,' he said, stepping back from the edge. 'It's the only chance to hear Pink Floyd and Genesis on the radio.'

'Oh, right. Well, enjoyed talking.'

'Me too.'

'We'll talk again.'

'Yeah, definitely. See you Monday, Meg.'

As she entered the grocer's, Tom sagged. Despite having "the look", he'd blown it. Worse still, Megan now believed he was a guitarist on the verge of forming a band – a fact likely to be shared with the entire school.

Essentially, he had five options.

1) Kill Megan Vanderlin

2) Kill himself

3) Move to Australia

4) Admit publically to being a fraud.

5) Buy an electric guitar, learn how to play, and form a band.

Walking past the old chemical factory on Westferry Road towards home, he tried to think of a sixth option, but it evaded him.

2. CONSEQUENCES OF THE LIE

All Saints School was founded in 1838. During its first century, it sat like a huge brick Buddha alongside the East India Dock Road – calm on the outside, busy on the inside improving the minds of local children as best it could.

Then, during 1939-40, the children of London's East End were whisked away to the countryside in anticipation of the bombs that the *Luftwaffe* duly dropped on a scale that appeared to make it personal. For every direct hit on the East and West India Docks, many more struck homes nearby, including those around the school.

On Victory in Europe Day, having survived Hitler's extended temper tantrum, the All Saints governors vowed to come back stronger than ever. This, they decided, would best be accomplished by fitting oak panels in the entrance hall and turning Grammar.

Thirty years later, in that entrance hall, beneath a carved wooden scroll bearing the school motto: *Te Nosce*, Know Thyself, Tom waited with a Genesis album under his arm. He just hoped his early arrival wouldn't be in vain.

With a mere twelve days left to deliver on his vow to attract a girlfriend by his sixteenth birthday, he'd decided to loan Megan Vanderlin *Selling England by the Pound*. The idea was to use her moment of pure delight to reveal that he wasn't really a guitarist starting a band. She wouldn't mind because they would have Genesis bonding them.

It was bound to work – as long as she didn't despise Genesis – and, frankly, he'd exhausted all the other methods of attracting women he could think of.

Certainly, attempting to become a karate expert like sixth-form stud Tony Cornish had backfired. Unlike Stratford *Kyokushinkai* black belt Tony, Tom's leg movements were only a danger to himself. On the plus side, a couple of girls at school had shown sympathy for his two black eyes and limp, although, sadly, not girls he wanted to go out with.

He looked to the entrance. Where was Megan?

Claire Cross came in and smiled at him. An unremarkable girl with National Health glasses. Despite being almost sixteen, she wore her mousy-brown hair in a ponytail and played cello in the school orchestra. He smiled back.

Fatal error. She came over.

'What's the album?' she asked.

'Genesis. But I'm guessing you're not a fan.'

'I might be. I mean I've never listened to them.'

Tom spotted Megan entering.

'Sorry, Claire. Bit busy, mate.'

Claire smiled and left.

Tom was slightly disappointed. Megan's buttoned-up blazer and school tie rendered her 25% less attractive. Still, in fairness, he was *sans* "the look", which probably meant a 50% reduction.

'Back here again then,' he said.

'Yes,' she said, adjusting her satchel strap. 'The weekend flies by, doesn't it.'

'Yeah.' He was finding her fake middle class accent ever more appealing. *Now give her the album and ask her out.*

'Doesn't seem that long ago we were talking,' she said.

'Yeah.' He could feel the album beginning to stick to his hand. *Give her the album and ask her out.*

'Well,' she sighed, 'Economics first. I don't mind that.'

In the name of God, give her the album and ask her out!

'Economics, eh?'

'What have you got?'

'English.' *Album... give... ask... out!* 'Actually, I was wondering if you—'

'Don't tell me the Royal Family's visiting,' said skinhead Micky Sullivan, bulldozing into view. 'Or is 'er highness lost?'

Megan looked to Tom then departed. Tom stared at Micky, the joint-youngest kid in their year, and projected with all his being the sentiment "tosser". He couldn't say it out loud, sadly, due to Micky being a psychopath.

Reaching his form room with the aim of finishing last week's English homework, Tom took a seat amid a swirl of chatter. His request to a couple of boys behind him to stop kicking the leg of his chair resulted in them shoving an upturned sports bag over his head and pulling the zipper. With their form master Mr Garner dallying in the corridor with Mrs Dorset (with whom, gossip had it, he was having a sado-masochistic affair) Tom guessed it was going to be difficult making any significant progress with "Structuring an Argument".

Removing the bag, he caught sight of Danny Collins entering the classroom with Micky Sullivan. Tom had grown up with Danny. They had been brothers until the age of seven, when Danny's real mum took him away.

Spotting Tom, Micky whispered something to Danny.

'Vanderlin?' said Danny. He swished back his long black mane and eyed Tom. 'Going upmarket, eh?'

Tom was annoyed. Megan Vanderlin spoke well – big bloody deal. Danny didn't exactly speak rough.

'Anyway,' said Danny, 'I thought you fancied Allbright?'

Tom shrank. Most of the class were listening, including Cheryl Allbright. It was true, too. He did fancy her. All the boys did. She had long blonde hair, green eyes, a pouty mouth, genuine cleavage, and she'd already turned sixteen.

'Is that right, you fancy me?' she asked. Before he could think of an answer, she leaned forward and whispered loudly into his ear. 'You should have said. I wouldn't mind letting you… y'know.'

Tom turned beetroot red and everyone laughed.

'Alright, back to your seats!' said Mr Garner, entering the room.

Tom sighed with relief. Then he looked down at his incomplete English essay. Not for the first time, he'd have to finish it in assembly.

The lunchtime bell rang and Tom, with his Genesis album under his arm, made for the usual spot. The usual spot being down by the school playground's fire gate, which wasn't visible from the main building.

First to join him was Polly – David Pollard – a gangly boy with red hair and freckles who was into Canterbury-scene prog rock and, since reading *The Ragged Trousered Philanthropists*, socialism. He was quickly followed by psycho Micky Sullivan's twin brother, Neil – a kid with round glasses under a thick blonde mop and a liking for metal Blakey tips on the heels of his shoes, possibly because their distinctive klik-klik told people he was approaching when they might not otherwise notice.

Both were curious to see if Tom's audacious plan to lure Megan Vanderlin with a Genesis album would get any further than a humiliating total rejection. And they didn't have to wait long, because Megan and her attractive but no-nonsense friend Sangheeta Sharma were coming into view further up the playground.

'Megan, alright?' called Tom.

He held up the Genesis album and they came over.

'You can borrow it if you like.'

'Great,' said Megan, taking it and admiring the genteel pastel painting on the front cover.

'It's worth playing a few times,' said Polly, supportively.

'At least seven,' said Neil.

'They've split up,' Sangheeta pointed out.

'No, they haven't,' said Tom. 'Well, not quite.' *Melody Maker* had reported Peter Gabriel's devastating departure from the band a few weeks earlier. 'I mean forget talk of Phil Collins taking over the vocals; that won't happen, but the band *will* carry on.'

Polly sighed. 'Hitler and Mussolini on the radar.'

Seeing Danny and Micky approaching, Tom felt like urging the girls to run.

'Guess what?' said Micky. 'Danny's starting a new school mag!'

'Leave off,' said Tom.

'I'm calling it *Devil's Advocate*,' said Danny. 'Get it? All Saints? *Devil's Advocate*? No? Well, if you do manage to fire up those tiny minds, I'll be welcoming contributions.'

'How generous,' said Sangheeta.

'The Head insisted,' said Micky.

Tom was surprised. 'Grimmo knows about it?'

'They'd never ditch *The Saint*,' said Neil.

Danny let out one of his long-suffering sighs.

'It's not instead of,' he said. 'Grimshaw says it should just be more informal than *The Saint*.'

'You've got a good opportunity there,' said Polly. 'You could introduce politics to the school. I wouldn't mind contributing.'

Danny scoffed. 'A stream of left-wing diarrhoea to frighten all the readers away? I don't think so.'

'You could do a piece about Tom forming a band,' said Megan.

Tom's heart rate shot up.

'How?' said Danny.

'Tom's a guitarist,' said Megan.

'No,' said Danny, 'Tom's a plank.'

'You're just jealous,' said Megan.

Tom desperately wanted to avoid admitting he'd lied to Megan. Luckily, she smiled at him and went off with Sangheeta and the album.

Polly turned to Neil.

'Is he really forming a band?'

Danny scoffed. 'Of course not! He's just trying to con his way into Vanderlin's knickers.'

Micky nodded appreciatively. 'Not a bad approach, to be fair.'

'The thing with you, Tom,' said Danny, 'is you don't amount to anything. There's more chance of Neil getting a girlfriend than you forming a band.'

'Hey!' said Neil, pointlessly.

'I'm starting a band,' said Tom, annoyed that Danny – seven months his junior – could talk to him like that.

'No, you're not,' said Danny. 'You don't have the balls. Or the talent.'

'Yes, I do.'

'No, you don't.'

'I'm starting a band. Fact.'

'What, with you on guitar?'

'Yes, with me on guitar.'

Danny laughed.

'I think he's serious,' said Polly.

'Seriously deranged,' said Micky.

Tom ignored them. If he wanted to keep his chances with Megan alive, he'd have to concentrate all his energies on forming a band. After all, you couldn't be a fraud if you started doing the thing you'd been lying about.

3. IT'S LENNON & MCCARTNEY ALL OVER AGAIN

The Alders rented an Edwardian terraced house in East Ferry Road by the fire station. Their narrow garden backed onto a contaminated dumping ground, while a nearby factory's giant chimney regularly pumped out yellow soot that covered Tom's dock-worker dad's tomato plants. Their landlord assured them that it was a perfectly safe environment and that the compulsory medical tests for any children living there were nothing to worry about.

Slumped in an armchair in the front room after tea, Tom was inured to the tobacco smoke that hung under the cracked yellowed ceiling and bonded with the fabric of a carpet that in terms of shade and condition resembled a mangy fox that had been run over by a lorry. He was busy wondering about bands and how they got going.

Perched on the edge of the peeling red leatherette settee, waif-like forty-two-year-old Rose Alder squinted over a ciggie at the *TV Times* magazine, clearly in search of entertainment beyond *Nationwide*, which was currently blaring out of the small black & white telly in the corner.

Tom's thoughts drifted from bands to a potential first date with Megan. Where would they go? What would they say? And would they snog?

He imagined snogging her.

'You alright?' said Rose.

'Fine.'

He switched back to thinking about the band. What would they aim for? Would it be all about "making it", whatever that actually meant. Would they aim for a record deal? A John Peel Session? Or would they, like ex-All Saints sixth-formers Westferry, settle for pub gigs and the Docklands Summer Dance?

'Well?' yelled Tom's dad from the kitchen. Obviously, forty-year-old Ted Alder's *discussion* with Rose wasn't over.

'It's coal, Ted. We have to have coal.'

'Four quid for two bags? He's taking the piss!'

'It's inflation.'

As ever, this kind of argument annoyed Tom. Sure, since the heyday of the docks came to an end, money had been getting tighter, but there was an answer. Rose would have been happy to get a job to earn the extra they needed. The only thing stopping her was Ted's edict that blokes who sent their wives out to work were an embarrassment to manhood.

'It's not just the coal!' moaned Ted. 'There's that new coat him in there had. Ten quid. Then them trousers. Six quid.'

'It was for school, Ted.'

'School? The blazer was twelve quid! Where do they make 'em? Savile Row?'

'School uniform's always dearer.'

'Gawd knows how the country's in a mess. I must be spending more than enough to keep it afloat!'

Doorbell chimes brought the discussion to a halt and Tom to the front door. It was Neil Sullivan.

'Come in!' said Tom, grabbing the sleeve of Neil's brown cardigan.

Up in Tom's pale blue woodchip-wallpapered bedroom, Camel's *Snow Goose* was soon on the turntable.

'Any news on Megan?' asked Neil.

'I only gave her the album today.'

'No phone calls then?'

'You make her sound desperate, Neil.'

'I meant you phoning her.'

'Bloody cheek!'

'Right… well… so you're forming a band then.'

'Definitely. I'm thinking of playing at next year's summer dance.'

'What, like Westferry?'

'Yeah.'

'Westferry are good.'

'I know.'

'They play in pubs.'

'I know, Neil. I know.'

From the gap between wardrobe and wall, Tom retrieved a battered acoustic guitar that, thanks to two minutes in the hands of Neil's destructive twin, had been missing three strings for most of the two years he'd had it.

'You won't be taken seriously with that,' said Neil.

Tom sat on the bed and rested the guitar on his thigh.

'I was having a practice earlier,' he said, suddenly wondering why some of the frets had dots on them. 'I'm not too sure of the advanced side of playing, though. Do you know anything?'

'You mean like how to tune it?'

'I mean stuff like "Every good boy deserves favour".'

'It's a mnemonic. Mr Lawrence taught it so we wouldn't forget it.'

'Yeah, but what does it mean?'

'I don't remember.'

'Fat lot of good you are.'

'Why don't you ask Craig Lycett? He plays piano.'

Tom studied the curve of the guitar body, the long elegant neck, the busy looking top bit where the ends of the strings spilled out like metallic spaghetti.

'Yeah, fair enough.'

He turned the record player off then resumed his playing position. Addressing the available strings, he pinged the skinniest and the fattest. The string between them wouldn't be required for this session. Using the skinniest string, he picked out a tune. This he followed with a more rhythmic sequence along the fat string.

'Know it?'

'Er...'

'It's Bowie.'

'Er...?'

Tom waved the query away. 'It's "Starman". It's neat how I can cover the guitar and bass bits with two strings.'

'Yeah,' said Neil, 'and it leaves you a spare string.'

'Yeah...' Tom looked down at his middle string and guessed that David Bowie didn't consider it spare. He also wondered if Bowie's fingertips hurt like hell after playing.

'Um, Neil...' An idea was forming. 'How about you play the bass lines.'

Neil's face drained. 'I haven't got a bass.'

'You can play it on a guitar using the fat string.'

'I haven't got a guitar.'

'Couldn't you buy one?'

'Leave off – I've only got a quid!'

'Blimey, Neil, what about showing some commitment?'

'Commitment to what?'

Tom sighed. There was no sense in getting worked up.

It was early days. Then again, if Neil wasn't going to play…

'It'd be great if someone sang.'

Neil's face turned purple. 'Can't you sing?'

Tom didn't feel inclined to mention that his own voice sounded like a cigar-smoking bloodhound.

'I have to concentrate on guitar, Neil.'

'Well, don't look at me. I can't sing.'

'Leave off – you were in the choir.'

'Yeah, when I was eight! Things have happened since then. I'm not a soprano anymore.'

'It's "Starman" – we don't need a soprano. Look, it's just the chorus.'

Neil looked horrified, but Tom strummed again, slowly building the single note drama. Then he changed the note, which was Neil's cue to sing. He didn't take it.

'Neil, how do you think Bowie got started?'

Neil said nothing so Tom tried again. Unexpectedly, Neil's mouth opened a little. Encouraged, Tom thumped the fat string for all its worth – until Neil made a noise like an under-powered whoopee cushion.

'Jesus, Neil, what was that?'

'I told you.'

'For God's sake, we're taking the first steps of something big here. At least give it some oomph!'

He began pinging the fat string again and Neil took the deepest imaginable breath. Tom ramped up the sound. This was it. *Sing Neil! Bloody sing!*

'*There's…*' But Neil froze, mid-note, mouth open, eyes bulging.

'It's alright, Neil.'

Neil drew back from the edge of a seizure.

'I've done it along with the record,' he said. 'It's just hard doing it here.'

Tom started picking out his skinny-string tune again. Only he stopped, gripped by an idea.

'Why don't I tape this bit then accompany myself?'

Neil brightened. 'Like a proper studio, you mean.'

Tom placed a fresh C-60 in his cassette recorder, simultaneously pressed "play" and "record" and started to play. He stopped though.

'Our first recording session,' he said.

Neil nodded. 'Yeah. Even Lennon and McCartney had a first time. Imagine if that recording was around now. It would be worth thousands.'

Their eyes moved to the cassette machine with its little wheels going round.

'Actually,' said Tom, 'if we had two tape recorders, we could record me and the taped bit onto a second tape.'

'Yeah,' said Neil, clearly enjoying the idea.

Then Tom had an even better idea.

'If we used yours and Micky's, I could leave you to record the vocals in your bedroom.'

Neil thought about that for a long time.

'Yeah,' he finally said. 'It's possible.'

'Let's go round your place. We'll record the music for "Starman" then I'll leave you to it.'

Tom felt good. Technically, he was no longer lying to Megan or Danny. He really was forming a band. Once he'd made some progress, he'd simply play Megan a song and she'd go weak at the knees and say inviting things to him in her fake upmarket accent.

'Just one thing,' said Neil. 'What if it goes wrong? I mean what if we implode and never speak to each other again, like the Beatles?'

'Don't be ridiculous.'

'Or what if we just fizzle out?'

'Neil, Golden Pyramid is going all the way. That's the

name of our band, by the way.'

'Okay. But the tape… we will keep it safe, won't we. I mean, if it ever got out, our lives wouldn't be worth living.'

Tuesday morning dawned dull and grey. Dragging himself out of bed, Tom yawned and stared at his brass LP rack. There was a gap where *Selling England by the Pound* usually sat.

Megan… he thought of pressing his fifth-form lips to her sixth-form lips. He even licked the back of his hand, closed his eyes and kissed the spot, just as Suzy Gray had shown them back in their second year at All Saints. And now he was thinking of Suzy. She was hungry for him. Oh boy, was she hungry. What a pity her boyfriend was seventeen-year-old Tony Cornish, who had given him two black eyes and a five-day limp at Stratford *Kyokushinkai.*

Hurrying out late meant catching a later bus. Worse still, the bus caught a bridger – the raising of the Blue Bridge to let ships in and out of the West India Docks. Watching the Blenheim ease into the enclosed waters annoyed him. By the time he reached school, the Fred Olsen Lines ship would be shedding passengers looking tanned from a cruise around the Canary Islands. This time tomorrow, it would leave with another batch of people with fat wallets and no concern for the poor sap on the bus trying to get to school.

A docker on the cobbles lit a fag. There was no hurry. It made Tom think of those who worked these waters. It seemed impossible that the Port of London Authority was considering the closure of the West India and Millwall Docks. The government claimed to care about working people, but said they wouldn't get involved. *Why not?*

Ultimately, he was so late he missed both registration and the start of assembly. Standing with three other boys in the entrance hall alongside Mrs Dorset and her Late Book, he wondered when the world would start treating him like a grown-up.

Staring up at *Te Nosce,* he recalled entering the building on that first day at All Saints back in September 1971. Aged eleven, he'd never felt so awkward. First there was the navy blue blazer with excess growing room. Had he turned into King Kong it still would have been baggy under the armpits. And then there was the crisp white shirt that, in cahoots with the school tie, cut off the blood to his head. Then there were the trousers with creases sharp enough to split the atom, shiny black shoes that shaved all the skin off his heels, and, as it was a grammar school, a plastic briefcase that rattled with pens, pencils, a geometry set, and an egg 'n' salad-cream sandwich in a Tupperware lunchbox.

Then there was the first time in the playground among older girls who looked like mums and older boys with broken voices and tatty blazers. Being shoved was just the start. Being asked for soap money in the toilets, being stabbed in the arse with a compass by an unknown assailant in the tuck shop queue and having an older girl open his briefcase, remove the lid from his lunchbox, close the briefcase and give it a good shake…

And then, just when he thought it couldn't get any worse, the most debilitating moment of all: seeing a boy he immediately knew to be Danny, his long-lost brother. And the recognition in his eyes. And the almost telepathic understanding that it was all too complicated, that too much time had passed, that there were still too many family pressures and that he and Danny would remain separate within this new world.

Assembly was over. They were coming out. The Head first, followed by the teachers with their baleful glances at the late-comers. Then came the kids, including Neil, who looked ill. Tom was pleased. It meant he'd done the deed.

'Alright, you can go,' said Mrs Dorset.

Tom headed straight for his band's lead vocalist.

'You did it then?'

Neil seemed scared. 'Yeah, all done.'

'Great. I can't wait to hear it.'

'No, not great, Tom. Not great at all.'

'Oh. That bad, eh?'

'No, it was okay, but um… it's gone.'

'Gone?'

'Yeah, you know, stolen.'

'Stolen? Not Micky? Not your stupid Neanderthal brother?'

Neil nodded.

4. HOW NOT TO HANDLE A POTENTIAL GIRLFRIEND

Sitting at the writer's bureau in his bedroom, Tom set aside thoughts of surviving on a desert island with Megan and thoughts of The Tape Incident to start on his History homework: The Battle of Cape St. Vincent, 1797.

Jervis and Nelson… Jervis and Nelson…

HMS Victory came up the Thames with an all-female crew. There were half a dozen women officers on the deck, all wearing the new regulation see-through blouses. They came ashore via a gangplank to Island Gardens where Tom was preparing to give an open air concert. Did he know any good pubs? Could he take them? He could see their erect nipples through the thin cotton…

He opened his eyes. He needed a distraction, a refuge from lust. He reached into the bin and grabbed the current edition of *The Saint*. Page four had Mr Garner in full flow.

"Do the docks dream of the past, of heaving quays full of ships from all parts of the Empire? Or of a future where weeds grow between…"

Boring.

He flicked past the school uniform advert to the Headmaster's column, where old Grimshaw was "thrilled" that ten former pupils worked in Whitehall. *Thrilled?* Jeez, they hadn't set foot on the Moon – they were stuck behind Ministry of Boredom desks wielding pens and staplers!

He needed to get out. A walk? No. His bike? Yes. He hadn't been out on his five-gear racer since the summer holidays.

Heading north on Manchester Road, he set a satisfying pace past the struggling riverside yards. If only he could turn back time and avoid what had happened at school: Danny holding aloft a cassette player blasting out something raw and uncertain to the class. Beginner-level guitar. A dodgy bass line. A voice like a sedated foghorn… 'Greetings pop-pickers!' Danny had cried over the economical Bowie tribute. 'I give you Alder and Sullivan!' Tom needn't have worried about the upcoming lead guitar bit causing further embarrassment – the unstoppable gut-busting laughter drowned it out.

Passing the Queen pub, Tom pedalled harder, increasing his speed over the Blue Bridge towards Poplar.

He started singing "The Fountain of Salmacis", recreating Peter Gabriel's Genesis tale of a young god's encounter with a sex-mad naiad nymph. Yes, he would educate Megan about the superior musical form known as progressive rock. He would be her guide, like that *Yogi* bloke who brainwashed the Beatles.

Turning into the neglected, rundown Poplar High Street, he finally slowed. Catching his breath, he wondered if to call in on Grandad Alder. He had a place just off the High Street. It would mean half an hour listening to someone grumbling, but this was an ex-docker in his sixties and you had to expect that kind of thing. Besides, he lived alone and might enjoy the company. Not that he would ever admit to being lonely, or any other imagined weakness. He was one of the rock-solid bomb-dodgers who worked right through the Blitz, ensuring that the West India Docks never lost a single day to the enemy.

Nonetheless, Tom felt sorry for him. It can't have been easy to go through all that while his son was evacuated to Gloucestershire and his wife worked as a first-aider. Not just cuts and bruises like nowadays, but whole limbs missing. Try sticking some ointment on that! Grandad's challenges didn't end there, either. The ciggies he and Nan smoked as a comfort killed her at fifty-five and forced him into early retirement at fifty-eight.

Not that Grandad was entirely alone. He occasionally referred to popping out to see the gang; very likely some old codgers he shared stories with over a cuppa. Maybe he was out seeing them now.

Tom decided against a visit. But definitely another day. *Definitely.* Ignoring the pang of guilt, he set off again, only slower than before due to his legs aching.

Feeling a distinct lack of stamina, he accepted that he needed to do this more often. Apart from games at Goresbrook sports fields on Friday afternoons, he tended to sit in school all day and in front of the TV or record player all evening. Surely, a man needed to be a fine physical specimen in order to easily attract women.

Pushing on, he was soon up to the junction with West India Dock Road where he swung left into Westferry Road. Heading south, he kept up a steady pace, passing one of Dad's mates coming out of Lenanton's timber wharf, his mate Darbs' mum leaving the Quarterdeck housing estate, McDougall's flour mills, the defunct oil wharf and the abandoned Scottish Church…

Up ahead, on the opposite side of the road, in a beige trouser-suit, Megan Vanderlin was standing at a bus stop with an LP-size carrier bag. Tom pulled in behind a parked Post Office van and peeked out. In his experience, you only took an LP out of the house to show it off to someone.

He wondered – would following her be a bit weird?

He decided – yes, it would, so don't do it.

Twenty minutes and three miles later, he watched her hop off the bus in Burdett Road, cross the road to St Paul's Way and, a couple of hundred yards on, enter a run-down housing estate. Who did she know among the grotty, graffiti-scarred blocks where a number of the homes were boarded up?

She stopped at a ground floor flat and rang the bell. A young bloke answered and she went in. Tom's mind was alive – was this a secret boyfriend?

No… no, no…

It had to be an A-level thing – English Lit, perhaps – and the LP was forty minutes of Shakespeare soliloquies. Except, he didn't recognise the boy from school and Megan did Economics, Maths and German.

Then Peter Gabriel's voice came through an open window. Peter Gabriel. Singing here of all places. Who would have thought you could improve your Economics, Maths or German by listening to prog rock with a boy in St Paul's Way.

Tom rode away.

He got as far as the main road then stopped.

What if he went back and waited? When Megan came out he'd just be "riding by" and in a brilliant position to stop and chat *and put her on the bloody spot*.

But, despite the undoubted clarity it would bring, he hated the idea.

Although… didn't he hate the idea of Megan playing his Genesis LP with another boy even more?

He imagined them together. By the time "Dancing

With The Moonlit Knight" ended they would be naked on the bed. By the time "I Know What I Like (In Your Wardrobe)" ended, they would be having it off. And by the time the big chords of "Firth of Fifth" crashed through the speakers, she would be quaking in a shattering climax. It wasn't lost on him that side one's closing track was "More Fool Me". Two quid that album had cost him. It wasn't fair.

The following lunchtime, in the school playground by the fire gate, Tom waited for Neil and Polly. He'd seen Megan earlier, but the only words to come out his mouth were, 'Hi, Megan'. He didn't know how to broach the tricky subject of infidelity.

While waiting, two fourth-form boys passed him on their way to the shops.

'That's why girls reaching puberty love Donny Osmond or the Rollers,' one of them was saying. 'It's because they sing directly to the girl. It's an emotional overload. The girl blows a fuse.'

Tom made a mental note. Maybe there was a thing about love songs. Maybe the Genesis track "More Fool Me" was a case in point. It wasn't sung by Peter Gabriel, but by Phil Collins, and it had an intimate quality. Maybe if he learned it and sang it to Megan...

'Are you really starting a rock band?' asked Cheryl Allbright.

He hadn't seen her coming.

'If you're about to take the piss...'

'You should ignore Danny and Micky. They're always being stupid.'

'Oh. Right.'

'So, a rock star, eh?'

Tom found himself warming to Cheryl. It was good to be cooler than his nemesis and ex-brother Danny for once – even if he was still expecting her to go "nah, just kidding – you're a dick.".

'Not quite a rock star yet, Cheryl. But that's the journey I'm on.'

'I think it's amazing.'

Tom gulped. 'Yeah? What really?'

Cheryl whispered in his ear. 'I wanna show you something.'

Tom's chest began to thump.

Cheryl turned and walked off.

'Tom!' It was Polly and Neil approaching. 'Coming down the chippie?'

'No, I'll catch you later,' said Tom, hurrying past them after Cheryl.

Show him something? What could she possibly want to show him? And yet every ounce of his being *knew*.

But what about Megan? Or did she no longer matter as she had a secret boyfriend up St Paul's Way?

Cheryl veered confidently into the science block.

Tom entered less confidently. She was going upstairs. What if they were caught? What if there were repercussions? No, it was time to start thinking like a man.

As he reached the top floor, the door to SC5 was slowly closing. The chemistry lab. Mr Singh's domain. But hang on! Singh would be over the pub having a ploughman's and half a lager with his assistant. The lab would be quiet for at least half an hour! Jeez. You could show someone a lot in half an hour. He wondered briefly if the biology lab might have been a more appropriate venue, but dismissed it.

Inside, Cheryl motioned him towards her. This was

great – so much easier when the girl clicked her fingers and said, more or less, hey you, come here.

Up close, with the warmth of her breath on his face, it was hard to think straight. Still, he couldn't just stand there saying nothing.

'Who's your favourite band?' he asked, regretting it instantly.

'Kiss me,' she urged.

Terror took hold, but he leaned forward and downward to offset the five-inch height difference. As their lips threatened to touch, he could see, out of the corner of his eye, the very spot he'd been sitting last week, listening to Singh drone on about Avogadro's Law. How easily schoolwork evaporated with plump lips on offer. Why didn't all the girls know this?

'Put you hand here,' she said, indicating the spot.

His heart was racing faster than a stolen transit van in Romford. He, Tom Alder, was on the verge of Contact – a feat that would guarantee him a place in the school's unofficial history. He placed his hand on the outside of her blazer as she hadn't specifically mentioned inside and he didn't want to get it wrong. He began a tiny stroking motion that he guessed was the right sort of thing, but his confidence wavered. He couldn't be certain, but the thing he was teasing through the heavy twill of her blazer was beginning to feel like a pencil case. He desperately wanted to move his hand inside, but what if she screamed?

'Inside, silly,' she said.

'Right.'

'Inside the blazer, not the blouse,' she added.

Good. Very good. No police action. No court case. No making friends in the showers at Wormwood Scrubs. He slid his hand inside her blazer. Except it slipped straight inside her blouse too and got stuck between the stupid buttons.

The door opened. Micky, Danny and Megan peered in.

Shit! Tom yanked his hand free, sending a blouse button skidding across the polished floor.

'Jeez!' cried Micky. 'He's tearing her clothes off!'

All became clear. Danny, Micky and Cheryl had set him up. Just to ruin his chances with Megan. The complete and utter bastards!

Megan fled.

Cheryl smirked. 'It was just a bit of fun.'

Tom hurried past a chortling Danny and Micky – the latter struggling to issue a public information announcement: 'Stand back, please. Sex beast coming through.'

Tom caught up with Megan in the playground, heading for the fire gate.

'I know I had my hand in her blouse,' he said, 'but you must understand it was only there by accident.'

'Oh grow up, Tom,' said Megan without stopping.

'It's like that song,' he said, trying to think of a song that might explain everything. But he couldn't name the song and Megan showed no sign of slowing down as she passed through the gate into the street.

Eating fish-fingers and chips for tea that evening, Tom pondered fronting a rock band – although probably not one with Neil Sullivan in it.

Later, sitting on the edge of his bed, pinging his skinniest string along to the Genesis album, *Foxtrot*, he wondered – was it possible to see a future rock star inside an ordinary person? Was it something visible?

Sneaking into his parents' room, guitar in hand, he opened their old Waring & Gillow wardrobe and tried a pose. And there he was in the door mirror displaying a satisfying degree of rock prowess. Yes, Tom Alder, the new Jimi Hendrix. Or better still, the new, improved Jimi Hendrix – the kind of guitarist Jimi would have become had he avoided death and joined a prog rock band.

A creak on the bottom step.

'Cup of tea, Tom?'

He didn't suppose Rock Gods drank tea.

'No thanks, Mum.'

He returned to his room. Not being able to play had brought him as far as it could. It was time to take the next step.

5. WORDS

Entering school, Tom didn't need to check his watch to tell him that he was late. Mrs Dorset standing there with the Late Book did that. Once she'd recorded his name, he took his place alongside two other miscreants beneath *Te Nosce*. In the main hall, the rest of the school was singing "Jerusalem".

Tom looked up. On the opposite wall, the school's Roll of Honour proclaimed the names of the Glorious Dead – old boys who had fallen during the two World Wars. He tried to imagine it: to go through all this schooling and then be handed a rifle and pack. Allen J, Barclay E, Bedford A, and co. of the 1914-18 column – maybe they too discussed music in a long-ago playground. Maybe they too took wrong turns with their potential girlfriends.

After assembly, Tom endured the glares of the Head and other masters leaving the main hall, and then the smirks of the pupils following them out.

'Okay,' said Mrs Dorset, 'don't let me see you here again.'

As he watched her hurry away, possibly for a sado-masochistic grope with Mr Garner, Tom spotted the pale, skinny pianist he wanted to talk to.

'Craig!'

Craig Lycett eyed Tom with suspicion, possibly because they so rarely spoke.

'You're a music man,' said Tom, pulling him aside so that they wouldn't be overheard. 'What does Every Good Boy Deserves Favour mean?'

'Why do you ask?'

'I'm interested.'

Craig Lycett didn't seem particularly enthralled by the news. 'We did it in music four years ago.'

'I know, but I wasn't interested then.'

'Okay. EGBDF are the lines on the treble clef. Every Good Boy Deserves Fanny. It's a mnemonic, lest we forget. Okay?'

Craig looked set to leave.

'Whoa, Craig. Every good boy deserves fanny. Like it. But what's it do? I mean, as a guitarist, how do I incorporate it?'

'Seriously, if you've learned the major, minor and seventh chords and a few scales for solos, you don't need to bother with it.'

'So I don't need to worry about every boy's fanny?'

'Only if you plan to read music. Of course, if you're going to write songs, it *might* be worth it.'

Light filled Tom's head.

'I do plan to write songs.'

'I'm impressed,' said Craig, sounding unimpressed.

'I haven't written anything down yet…'

'Look, seriously, I've heard Paul McCartney doesn't read music and he's done alright. Just write down your lyrics and note the chord changes in the right place above them. Maybe copy McCartney and write dopey love songs. Okay?'

Craig fled, leaving Tom to grapple with the magnitude of what had just happened. As far as he could tell, whether or not he incorporated EGBDF into his life, he was about to become a songwriter. Ha-ha! He'd sell bloody millions!

The first lesson was English Lit with Mr Reid. Tom and Neil took up their usual position at the back of the class by the bookcases, with Tom's chair tilted back against the wall to give the feeling of sitting in a deck chair. He was just glad that Cheryl Allbright was in the other English Lit group. Avoiding her had already become a bit of a chore.

'Have you spoken to Megan yet?' asked Neil.

'Every good boy deserves fanny,' said Tom, changing the subject.

'She said *that*? Wow.'

'No, you dipstick, it's the lines on the treble clef. I asked Lycett. It's all to do with writing songs.'

'You don't write songs.'

'Neil, you know absolutely nothing.'

But Tom had stated his frustration too loudly, because Micky, who wasn't allowed to sit at the back, turned to face them.

'Oi, tit-groper, I know a song… *All the nice girls love a candle, It's a girlie's pride and joy…*'

Mr Reid came in.

'Do carry on, Sullivan. I can't wait to hear how it turns out.'

Micky declined.

'Right,' said Mr Reid, 'Shakespeare's sonnets…'

The lesson went the way of all such lessons with some caring more about the contents of their nostrils than the fate of Shakespeare's Fair Youth.

Half an hour later, Tom yawned and stared out of the window at a plane high in the blue. Where would that be heading? New York? Paris?

'So, the third quatrain signals a change of tone…
would you agree, Alder? Alder?'

Tom became half-aware of his name in the ether.

'Alder? Are we keeping you awake?'

'Oh, sorry, sir. Just thinking of something.'

'Do share it with us.'

'I can't remember it.'

'Alder, I'm tired of your incessant day-dreaming. This
time next week you will stand before the class and recite a
sonnet of your own.'

'My own?'

'Yes, you will write a sonnet and recite it to the class.
Think of it as an opportunity to outshine the Bard.'

Normally, Tom, Neil and Polly wouldn't waste valuable
time queueing outside the grotty dinner hall for a plate of
some distant relative of edible food. But it was raining at
lunchtime, so queue they did.

While Neil burbled on about Isaac Asimov, Tom
spotted Megan with Sangheeta some way off. He
wondered if to attempt contact, but Darbs – Alan
Darbyshire, a dark-haired, half-Cypriot boy – barged into
him theatrically as he pushed into the queue.

'So what's the latest with Allbright?' he said. 'You, her
and Vanderlin going for a threesome?'

Tom looked for Megan again, but she had slipped out
of sight. Annoyed, he popped a Toffo into his mouth and
wondered how to write a sonnet.

'Tom?' It was Darbs nudging him.

'What?'

'Which one do you fancy shagging most?'

Tom sighed and turned to Polly, who was reading *The*

Chrysalids. Polly noticed he was being spied on.

'Yes, it's an O-level book.'

'Indeed – an O-level book about deviants,' said Tom, thereby reaching the full extent of his knowledge of a novel he too was meant to be studying.

'Not about Neil, is it?' said Darbs.

They were eventually seated at a table with a plate of shrivelled bangers, lumpy mash and sad peas. This was followed by industrial apple pie and custard.

'I hate this stuff,' said Tom, peeling off the thick yellow skin and hanging it over the edge of the bowl.

'Don't chuck it,' said Darbs. 'They make waterproofs for North Sea fishermen out of that.'

'Any early thoughts on your sonnet?' asked Neil.

'Yeah, I've narrowed it down to writing something that doesn't make everyone laugh at me.'

'Is that possible?' said Polly.

'What about David Essex?' said Darbs. 'You could recite "Hold Me Close" then break into song. You'd have every girl in that room going all gooey and demanding to have your babies.'

'What about Bowie?' said Neil.

'I can't just rip off some pop star's lyrics. I need to come up with something Shakespeare could have written.'

'Is that all?' said Polly.

Piss-Take Potential reared its head. Whatever he wrote, they would laugh. He could, of course, approach it like writing a song. After all, hadn't he decided to become a songwriter?

Yes, he had.

And a song-sonnet would negate Reid's punishment. He'd be able to read it to the class then re-use it as his first song lyric. It was probably just a matter of writing powerful words; basically something to make them think rather than laugh. The kids of All Saints were ready to grow up, weren't they? Of course they were. This wouldn't be pearls cast before swine. They would embrace the deeper meaning of his work. He then realised he was staring across two tables at Cheryl Allbright. Spotting him, she sucked on her beef sausage in what he considered to be an unnecessary manner.

At home, after spam-fritters and mash for tea, Tom decamped to his room to consider the act of profound thinking.

He'd heard about someone reading the philosophical book *Zen and the Art of Motorcycle Maintenance* and wondered whether he could learn anything useful from it. He'd also heard someone on the bus mention Freud and sex. And then there was that time Polly told him something to do with Jung and the meaning of life. In essence, was it possible to learn anything about human interaction from books?

In short, he had boldly promised himself he would have a girlfriend by his sixteenth birthday. That was just over a week away and he'd messed things up with Megan by getting himself into a mess with Cheryl – *and*, having shared double history with the latter that afternoon, it was clear that the end of the smirking phase was still some way off.

But what if he told Megan it was his fault and threw himself on her mercy? Didn't women like that sort of thing: a man who could say sorry? Or was it the opposite that women preferred: a strong, unapologetic man. It was all very confusing.

He wondered: would he dig out his library card and attempt to find answers in weighty books, or would he follow his mum's example and become a reader of "Dear Marje" in the *Daily Mirror*?

6. OH DANNY BOY

Sitting in his form room on Friday morning, waiting for Mr Garner to detach himself from Mrs Dorset, Tom's thoughts continued to flip-flop between his two current concerns: Megan Vanderlin and the song-sonnet. How would he woo her back? And what song lyric would he write to match Shakespeare in front of a class full of potential piss-takers?

Mary Dale patted him on the shoulder.

'Ignore them,' she said.

That was odd. He and Mary Dale never spoke. Not since last Easter's school trip to a snowbound hell-hole in West Wales where fourteen of them were verbally abused by a Hell's Angel on a moped. The teachers were in the pub at the time, but Tom was solicitous to Mary's concerns. Later, when they went to Aberystwyth to see *The Man With The Golden Gun* at a cinema with wooden benches instead of seats, she suggested he sit at the back with her. It was exciting being in the back row with a girl, but he'd been too scared to move his hand across to hers in case she wasn't ready to go that far.

Mary inclined her head towards Micky Sullivan by the door. Up until now, Tom had been ignoring the cave-dwelling half of the Sullivan progeny, but it was clear that Micky's fits of laughter were related to the batch of stapled papers he was carrying.

'Get yer *Devil's Advocate*,' he said, sounding like the *Evening Standard* vendor outside Mile End station.

'Hot off the press, eh?' said Tom, taking a copy with a feeling that something wasn't right.

'Page four!' said Micky, flinging out more copies.

Tom turned to page two.

"DEVIL'S ADVOCATE"
EDITORIAL TEAM
MR G. T. GARNER, Executive Editor
Alan PHILLIPS, UppVI, Editor
Terence FARMER, UppVI, Asst. Ed.
John FROBISHER, LowVI
Margaret SLATER, LowVI
Daniel COLLINS, 5G

Ignoring the growing cackle around him, Tom took a modicum of glee from the fact that Danny was very much the junior member. So much for starting his own magazine! That was so typical of Danny. Of course, Tom had no doubt whatsoever that within a few months his ex-brother would be in charge.

WELCOME
We hope you enjoy this inaugural edition of "Devil's Advocate". Whereas "The Saint" deals with school issues, this publication has the broader brief of an opinion-based Arts and Events magazine. So, whether your bag is poetry or Pink Floyd, Wimbledon fortnight or West Ham, Shakespeare or The Sweeney, you can hand your written thoughts to any of the editorial team

(deadline: Thurs lunchtime). Do join in and together we'll make "Devil's Advocate" the hottest mag in London E14!

Tom decided to never make a single contribution. Not unless it was to file a report on Danny having a fatal steamroller encounter.

'Page four,' Micky repeated. He was, by now, head of a small guffawing crowd.

Tom skipped "Ode to Autumn" by Jane Dobbs, 4B, on page three and turned over.

NEW SINGLES
A weekly round-up of the latest pop releases.

David Essex
'Hold Me Close'
Review by Don Byett
Already in the charts, the latest 45 from pin-up boy David will reach No. 1. That's it. Nothing more to be said. Apart from it being an insipid, dreary love song far removed from the effortless cool of 'Rock On'. Oddly, this has done little to diminish his appeal among the fairer sex. Indeed, the girls are palpably awash with enthusiasm. Prediction: Hit.

Now *that* was pure Collins. Aloof, cynical… but Tom caught sight of the next heading and froze.

Alder & Sullivan
'Starman'

Review by Terry Ball-Noyse

By the sound of it, this could well be a case of a truly talented guitarist and vocalist... not being involved, and thereby leaving us with Tom Alder, who can't play, and Neil Sullivan, who sings like a depressed duck.

Prediction: Hit... them with a bag of wet sand, you will demand.

Tom looked up. Micky was standing over him, grinning and proffering another copy of *Devil's Advocate*.

'Want one for Mummy to keep?'

'Piss off, Mick.'

'Ooh,' said Micky, feigning hurt, 'he's one of them *temperamental* rock stars.'

By lunchtime, Tom had muddied the waters with claims that the tape was a fake. Down by the fire gate, amid a small group, Neil didn't look too convincing in corroborating the lie, but he did his bit by following Tom's advice to keep his gob shut.

When Danny and Micky turned up, Tom put on an untroubled air.

'At least I've got the guts to start a band,' he said.

'So's Danny,' said Micky.

'What?' Tom's disbelief was quickly echoed by the others. 'And what sort of crud will you be churning out?'

'Intelligent pop,' said Danny. 'Keyboard and guitar based. Inspirational, cool. You know the sort of thing. Oh, silly me, you don't.'

'You don't even play,' scoffed Tom.

'*Au contraire.* I've been having guitar lessons.'

'Yeah?'

'Very competent would best describe my ability.'

'Yeah? I suppose your keyboard player's Rick bloody Wakeman.'

'No, Craig Lycett.'

'Lycett?'

Tom made his excuses and left the school premises. He didn't head for the shop. Instead, he went to Poplar Rec – the local recreation ground that provided a breathing space for those in need of it.

Strolling around the children's war memorial, hands deep in pockets, he mulled over the harsh fact that Danny's band had the East End Rachmaninov, while he, Tom Alder, the superior musical brain, had Neil the Laryngitic Frog. But the tide would turn. Oh yes. Tom made a vow to himself. To get ahead of Danny. To be better than him. To bloody well beat him.

Then he calmed down a bit and ditched the vow. He didn't want to beat Danny. He just wished they had never gone to the same school. They were in their fifth year together at All Saints and it just never got any easier.

He looked up at the names on the memorial. A bunch of little kids killed by a German bomb. He sighed. What use was the past? It was just a vessel for all of life's upsets. And not a quiet vessel; a bloody noisy one liable to go off at the slightest nudge.

Later, sitting on the coach with Neil, heading to Goresbrook for games, he thought back to the twentieth of May, 1967. Danny's seventh birthday. Tottenham were playing Chelsea in the F. A. Cup Final on the telly. They were just brothers watching football in their party hats. Then Danny was called to the front door. There was a fuss and a struggle. Tom came out to see what was happening. It was the only time he ever saw Danny cry. Well, Tom cried too. After all, it's not every day you lose your brother. It was four years before they saw each other again. By then they were strangers in brand new school uniforms. For Tom, being an eleven-year-old boy, the need to avoid awkwardness and embarrassment had been enough to sustain his distance. Now though, nearing the end of his fifteenth year, he feared a day of maximum awkwardness and embarrassment was coming. It had to.

7. ELECTRIC THOUGHTS

Late on Saturday morning, Tom was in Chapel House Street weighed down with a Puma hold-all packed with knickers, bras, boots, *Sta-Prest* trousers and a heavy catalogue. His mind was elsewhere though – pondering asking for cash instead of birthday and Christmas presents. That, along with pocket money, might get him close to buying a second-hand electric guitar and amp by Easter.

His mum, Rose, was a Freeman's catalogue agent. Dad Ted didn't consider flogging a few items of clothing a job that called his manhood into question. It wasn't dissimilar to other wives passing on a bit of bent gear and Rose's ten percent was legal, so no comebacks from the Old Bill. Not that it amounted to much.

This morning, Rose had a bit of a headache so it was Tom's opportunity to take over and scoop up a quid. In truth, she often had a headache after "a couple of stouts" on a Friday or Saturday night with their neighbour Mrs Cryer.

Middle-aged Mrs Samuels was his first call. Sometimes, while delivering a new item or picking up a payment, Mrs Samuels' nineteen-year-old daughter, Deirdre would slouch by in a skimpy nightie, leaving little to the imagination. No such luck today though. Standing in the Samuels' tiny hall, Tom could hear Deirdre upstairs, while, right in front of him, it was Mrs Samuels in the revealing nightwear. Worse still, she was the bra customer.

'It's definitely 38D?' she asked, studying the pack.

'Er…' said Tom, his eyes flitting from the pack to her ample bosom and away to Mr Samuels in the kitchen doing a spot of DIY on a cupboard door. Jeez, it had only been for a millionth of a second, but why had he looked at all?

Mrs Samuels squinted at the label.

'Only the last bra pinched at the side,' she said, indicating the exact spot.

Tom kept his eyes firmly fixed on Mr Samuels' knob-twiddling.

A few minutes later, he fled with his dignity intact and a quid off Mrs Samuels' new total of £8.75.

Approaching the main road with Basil Fawlty's builder problems of the previous evening fighting for headspace with voluminous middle-aged breasts, he spotted Tony Cornish in a driving school learner's car.

Tom was jealous. No doubt The Kyokushinkai Kid would soon be driving a red MG convertible with sexy Suzy alongside him. That was the annoying thing with Tony. He was one of life's lucky bastards. Back in 1971, his dad opened a scrap yard on the disused East India Dock quayside. Three years later, they moved from a flat in Thermopylae Gate to a Georgian house in Narrow Street. It made Tom think of money. Would he get a well-paid job if he left school at sixteen? Well, he'd stand a better chance if he had some O-levels.

O-levels…

He was over halfway through the two years it took to do them and so far he'd put in naff-all effort. Still, the mocks weren't until January so it wasn't too late to put in a late surge. Then he'd be able to leave at sixteen to pursue a career in…?

Reality swept in. Grammar schools churned out kids who went into boring banking or worked for the council in some godforsaken town hall. But he was destined for greater things, wasn't he? Yes, of course he was.

After a couple of routine encounters, his next customer was new: Mrs Green, two pairs of trousers. Tom wondered if she might be a young wife, see-through nightie, husband at work. He knocked. The door opened. Squinting over the cigarette glued to her bottom lip, a middle-aged hollow-eyed woman with peroxide-blonde hair invited him in. The old house might have looked okay from the outside, but, inside, the stench of unwashed bodies was deadly. Worse still, her decomposing husband said he'd try on both pairs. Tom was surprised when he dropped his rancid old strides in the hall.

Tom eventually escaped with a sale on one pair. The other pair had been rejected. This despite Mr Green's toxic lower half having been inside them. Tom shuddered. Freeman's would recycle them to some poor unsuspecting sod who would be exposed to a biological hazard.

Back on the street, he looked across to the old flats where Megan Vanderlin lived. This he knew from carol-singing for money last Christmas and her answering the door and claiming her parents were out. He thought about going up there and knocking. He could ask if she wanted to get a loaf of bread or something.

But what if she refused to speak to him? Or worse – her secret boyfriend was there? On the other hand, he'd be sixteen next Saturday. A man. And didn't *Dear Marje* advise against running away from responsibility?

He took a deep breath and crossed the road.

A man answered the door. Megan's dad, he guessed. With the sound of racing on ITV booming from inside, he had a betting slip in his hand and a tetchy look on his face. Tom wondered if he'd taught himself to speak nicely like his daughter.

'Hello. Is Megan there?' he asked, carefully enunciating each syllable.

'Nah,' said Megan's dad. 'Who the fuck are you?'

'Oh, no-one,' said Tom, departing hastily.

An hour later, with his round completed, Tom popped into the grocer's for his mum's ciggies. At the counter, Mrs Mason probed the same subjects she'd probed the previous week: Mum okay? Dad heard any more dock rumours? School alright?

Then a new one: 'Birthday soon, ain't it?'

'Yeah, next Saturday.'

'Let me know if you're having a party,' she said with a cackle. 'I'll be round.'

That struck him as a good idea. Not having Mrs Mason round, but the party bit. He'd be sixteen. Why not have a few mates over?

At teatime, in the Alders' smoke-filled front room, Tom was trying to ignore a) that he knew where Megan was when he copped a volley off her dad, and b) that she was probably still round there.

Perched on the edge of the settee, cigarette in mouth, Littlewoods coupon in hand, Rose was watching the end of the wrestling on *World of Sport*. She certainly shared commentator Kent Walton's excitement at two fat blokes trying to pull each other's heads off. Jackie Pallo, Kendo Nagasaki, Mick McManus – she didn't seem to care which of the regulars were on, as long as they were grunting and grappling.

'What time's Dad coming home?' asked Tom.

Ted Alder spent most Saturday afternoons relaxing with a fishing rod on the canal at Limehouse.

'When he gets to the point where he wants to kill someone,' said Rose, her eyes fixed to the screen, her body giving tiny jerks with each exclamation of pain. 'Go on, whack him!'

Tom hated wrestling. All that flesh and sweat and groaning. Barry Cohen at school said he saw a *Man Alive* programme that revealed Kent Walton's secret life as the producer of sex films, one of which was entitled *Lesbian Twins*. Nobody believed him though.

'Ooh!' gasped Rose as a body slammed into the canvas.

Tom wondered if there really was a film called *Lesbian Twins* and if he'd ever get to see it.

'Mum, do you think I could have a few mates round for my birthday?'

'What, a party?'

'No, just a few mates and a couple of Party Sevens.'

'You'll have to ask Dad.'

Yes! One down, one to go.

A few minutes later, as the wrestling gave way to the Results Service, Ted came home. Tom's mind quickly flooded with thoughts of giant tins of Watney's Party Seven Bitter.

'I'll make you a cuppa in a minute, Ted,' said Rose, spreading her Littlewoods Pools coupon on her lap.

'Disgusting,' huffed Ted, wedging his large frame into an armchair. He scooped his thinning swept-over hairstyle back into place then proceeded to take his boots off. 'Disgusting,' he repeated.

'What's disgusting?' said Rose.

'What Joe Shaw reckons about Tilbury.'

'Dad, do you think I could have a few mates round for my birthday?'

'What, a party?'

'No, just a few mates and a couple of Party Sevens.'

'Rose?'

'Oh let him, Ted. As long as they finish early.'

'It's next Saturday,' said Tom, as if his dad might have forgotten.

'Seven-thirty till eleven,' said Ted with finality.

Tom almost laughed with joy.

'Ooh, Man City and Man United two-all,' said Rose, placing a tick against an X on her coupon. 'So what did Joe say about Tilbury?'

'He's heard another rumour,' said Ted, clearly irked as he placed his first boot aside. He removed his sock to give his toes a wiggle. 'Well, same rumour, different source – about the PLA looking to open a deep water terminal at Northfleet Hope.'

Tom set aside his joy for a moment and considered how his life might change with a pools win. He imagined he would be very popular with women. God, he'd be fighting them off. Dad would be alright too. He wouldn't have to worry about the Port of London Authority's total disregard for the ordinary dock worker.

'It's just rumours, Ted,' said Rose, placing another tick on her coupon. 'I'll get tea on early. Mince and mash.'

'Good for you,' said Ted, taking his second boot off. 'I'm having a fry-up.'

Rose huffed and scuttled out to the kitchen. This was clearly unfinished business from earlier. Tom hated it when the cracks in his parents' marriage showed. Had they never loved each other? He set the thought aside. It would only stir up memories of New Year's Eve, 1966, when he went to the kitchen for lemonade only to discover Dad with his hand up Elsie Sullivan's blouse – "Elsie's had a funny turn" being the explanation for Dad "loosening her clothes".

Ted took his other sock off then set about rolling a cigarette.

'You know what I reckon, Tom? If they close the docks, they might as well bulldoze the Island.'

'They won't,' said Tom. 'It'll just be smaller ships up this end, bigger ships down at Tilbury.' A snippet from his economics O-level came back to him. 'Economies of Scale,' he said. Although, now he thought about it, wasn't that an argument in favour of closing the local docks?

Ted lit his ciggie, took a drag, sucked it deep into his lungs, and then casually propelled smog into the room.

'Your grandad was in the docks, you know. And your great grandad. If they close it all down, there'll be nothing for you young 'uns. Nothing.'

'I wasn't planning to work in the docks. You know that.'

'Do I? What exactly do you plan to do for a living?'

'Not sure.'

'Not sure? You go to a bloody grammar school! You're supposed to be clever!'

'Don't take it out on him, Ted,' said Rose, reappearing at the door. 'You were young once.'

'Don't I know it! I had to work on a bloody farm during the War! Five, I was!'

Tom winced. Not only did Dad have a booming voice, he also had plenty of form for expanding anything to do with his childhood into a speech entitled: "How I saved the Gloucestershire farming operation as an evacuee."

'For two years, rain or shine, I was milking goats, cleaning coops, running errands! I couldn't sit around idle!'

'Idle?' For Tom, this was a wilful disregard of a young man's right to exist on his own terms. 'Look, can I have money for my birthday present. I'm saving up for a guitar.'

'What for?' said Ted. 'You've got one upstairs.'

'I'm talking about an electric one. And I'll need an amp. I thought ten quid for my birthday and twenty for Christmas.'

'Thirty quid? I don't believe what I'm hearing.'

'It's my future we're talking about.'

'Not at thirty quid, it's not.'

Tom gave up. Clearly, his dad struggled with grasping important issues.

In the snug front room of the Sullivans' cottage in Macquarie Way, sitting on a new pink floral settee, Tom and Neil were munching bacon sandwiches in front of the large colour TV set. With the irritant known as Micky out somewhere, they were looking forward to having *Dr Who* materialise on BBC1.

Alongside the two boys, Neil's mum, Elsie, was studying the *Radio Times*. She never bought the *TV Times* and wasn't averse to lamenting its lack of class. Tom liked Elsie. He just wished she wouldn't wear dresses with low necklines.

To their left, sat bald, irritable West India Dock stevedore George Sullivan – a man with less warmth than a January plunge in the Thames.

'Comfy?' George asked Tom.

'Yeah,' said Tom, admiring the new settee. 'It's nice.'

'Two hundred quid, but they threw in a free telly.'

'Twelve inch black and white,' said Elsie, not sounding

too impressed.

'Yeah, alright,' said George. 'Means you can watch something while you do the tea.'

Tom wondered – did Elsie still have funny turns? Judging by the books on the mahogany shelf – *Secret Love, Dare To Desire, Breathless Love* – she hadn't given up hope.

'Sorry about Dad,' said Neil. They were in the sanctuary of the Sullivan twins' cluttered bedroom.

Tom opened one of the four small tins of Heineken lager he and Neil would be sharing and idly flicked through the *Look-in* magazine on Neil's bed – which Neil thought interesting and Tom thought a waste of 7p, apart from Benny Hill's cartoon adventures, of course.

'If you mean him boring me about the future all through *Dr Who,* you should hear *my* old man.'

'I have,' said Neil, lifting the lid off a small aquatic tank.

'I'll tell you something, Neil. When I leave school, I'm doing something different. Something that reflects my… well, something that isn't the usual boring crap.'

'A prog rock guitarist?' said Neil, picking up a small tub.

'Yeah, well… funnily enough, I was thinking about how to get girls more interested in prog rock.'

'Yeah? You no doubt remember what Tony Cornish said about the audiences at ELP, Genesis and Camel.'

'Yeah – ten thousand blokes, four women.'

'Do you know what I think?' said Neil, turning to his terrapins. 'In my experience, girls find us serious music fans a bit too intellectual.'

'Yeah, although…'

'Ollie's done a two-inch poo!' cried Neil. He then

sprinkled smelly pellets onto a raised plastic platform and gave Ollie a shove in the right direction.

Tom hoped his friend was wrong.

'Neil... how do you fancy coming to a party?'

Neil looked wary. 'Where?'

'I'm having one for my birthday.'

'Really?'

'Yeah. Fancy it?'

'Will there be girls there?'

'No, just mates. Mind you, Dad'll be over the Nelson till three a.m. and Mum'll be pissed next door with Mrs Cryer, so I could sneak in half a dozen semi-naked babes.'

'Not Megan Vanderlin then?'

'Well... not sure about the situation there.'

'She's okay,' said Neil, brushing an errant pellet off his jumper. 'She's sensible and she works really hard. Any news on *Selling England*...?'

'No.'

'You must really like her. I mean to lend her a Genesis album.'

Neil's skinhead twin brother Micky barged into the shared bedroom.

'Alright girls?' he greeted in his usual boorish manner. 'What's that posh scrubber been saying?'

'Nothing,' said Tom. He slumped back on the bed while Neil extracted two brand new LPs from his collection. It was a long-standing regret of Tom's that both twins had survived birth. And why did the school have a siblings policy? Everyone knew it was bloody hard to get into All Saints, what with the Eleven Plus and the interview, but once Neil was in, so was his annoying brother.

'Speaking of parties,' said Micky, confirming Tom's suspicion that he'd been eavesdropping, 'you ought to invite Cheryl. I mean, seeing as you've already groped her tits.'

'Grow up, Mick,' said Neil, placing twelve unblemished inches of Hawkwind onto the turntable.

Tom watched Neil lower the stylus with a clunk onto the rim of the vinyl. There would be no girls at his party. Too much trouble. He'd have a less stressful time with the likes of Neil. Neil was reliable. Okay, so he was boring, but he liked good music.

'Lend us 30p,' said Micky.

'No,' said Neil. 'And don't you lend him anything, Tom. It only goes on cigarettes.'

'Go on,' said Micky. 'I'm seeing Carol from Upper North Street, If I buy her a Coke, she'll—'

'No!'

'Screw you then!' Micky grabbed a jacket and left.

'And the same to you!' said Neil as he and Tom began rhythmically nodding their heads to Dave "Spaceman" Brock, Nik "Madman" Turner and the mighty Lemmy.

While enjoying the music, it occurred to Tom that Megan Vanderlin and her secret boyfriend might also be in a bedroom listening to an LP. Although they would have more options. Not that Megan seemed the sort to…

Or was she *exactly* the sort to…?

He decided to persevere with finding a way to win her back. In seven days, he'd be sixteen. It was probably just a matter of acting like a man and fighting for his woman. Chivalry and honour. That kind of thing. Of course, it would mean making some actual musical progress so that he'd become the talented rock guitarist she thought he was.

8. HELLO CELLO GIRL

Crossing the busy East India Dock Road on Monday morning, Tom pretended he didn't know that Micky Sullivan was twenty yards behind him. Having successfully avoided him on a packed bus off the Island, he wanted to keep it up all the way into school.

Up ahead, by the main entrance, Darbs was loitering with an album under his arm.

'Darbs, I'm having a party for my birthday. Fourth of October at my place. Fancy it?'

'Music? Women? Party Sevens?' Then, as Tom and a hurrying Micky joined him… 'You *are* inviting Cheryl Allbright?'

'Course he is,' said Micky, breathlessly. 'He's got a job to finish.'

Tom noted Darbs' album. *The Man Who Sold The World*. Unknown territory.

'Where did you get it?'

Darbs threw a glance into the entrance hall to indicate the source. 'Barry Cohen.'

Big, chunky Barry was chatting with cello girl Claire Cross.

'You know Bowie wore a dress on the original cover,' said Tom, as they made their way inside.

'Yeah, RCA banned it.'

'Yeah,' said Micky, 'they thought he was one of them hermaphrodites.'

'Transvestites,' said Tom. 'Bowie's not a hermaphrodite. That's Greek mythology.'

'You almost sound knowledgeable, Alder,' said Mrs Dorset, approaching with the Late Book, 'which I find highly improbable.'

Tom took a breath. He'd show her…

'Hermaphroditus was the son of Hermes and Aphrodite,' said Tom. 'He was brought up by wood nymphs on Mount Ida, but he ran off and met the water nymph Salmacis. She wanted him as a lover, but he rejected her. She wasn't having that though, so she entwined herself around him and pulled him under the water where their bodies merged into a single mixed-sex being.'

There was a silence. Then applause. Tom wasn't used to it. He looked into their faces. Barry, laughing. Claire, with light from the window reflecting off her National Health specs. Darbs poking his tongue out.

'Okay, get moving,' barked a discomfited Mrs Dorset.

Tom didn't feel like mentioning "The Fountain of Salmacis" from Polly's Genesis album *Nursery Cryme* which he'd borrowed and taped onto one side of a C-90 cassette (other side, Mike Oldfield's *Hergest Ridge*). Perhaps, from now on, she wouldn't see him as stupid.

In the playground at mid-morning break, Tom spotted Claire Cross again.

Cello. Music. Maybe it would be worth a try.

'Claire, you can play, right?'

'Need a goalie, eh?'

'Not football, music.'

'Ah, you want me to play cello at your party. Okay.'

'How do you know about my party?'

'Neil was telling most of East London about it.'

'Bloody Neil…'

'What, I'm not invited?'

'Well, it was just going to be me, Darbs, Polly and Neil. And Micky.'

'Ooh, cosy. And there was me thinking you were chatting me up.'

Tom blushed. Since when did Claire Cross talk like this? In fairness, he'd never paid her much attention.

'Are you asking me to ask you out?'

'Are you asking me if I'm asking you to ask me out?'

'What?'

'What is it you want, Tom?'

'Would you show me a few bits and pieces?'

'You wanna see my bits and pieces? What, before a first date?'

Tom was flustered again. 'I'm talking about music. Nothing complicated. I mean, just—'

'Fry's Chocolate Cream. One bar. Lunchtime.'

'What?'

'Being deaf might slow your progress as a musician.'

'Oh… right. A bribe. Fair enough.'

'What stage are you at?'

'Well…' Sod it, this was no time for bullshit. 'I'm nowhere, Claire. Just picking out notes at random.'

'Yeah, I heard the tape.'

Tom tried to ignore that. 'I need to learn some chords – basic stuff, really.'

'That would make sense. Have you learned how to tune it yet?'

'Yeah— no. No, I haven't.'

'Elephants And Donkeys Got Big Ears.'

Tom frowned and Claire laughed, but not unkindly.

'EADGBE,' she said. 'Elephants And Donkeys Got

Big—'

'—Erections!' rasped Micky Sullivan. 'Elephants and donkeys get big erections.' He seemed pleased with that. 'Music, ennit.'

'I'll see you later, Claire,' said Tom.

'FCC, lunchtime,' she said, heading off to her mates.

'FCC?' said Micky. 'What's that – a band?'

'No, Mick.'

'Listen, about the party – you don't mind Carol from Upper North Street coming, do ya. Good man. Say no more.'

'We weren't going to have—'

'I mean you gotta have girls. Unless you fancy Neil.'

'What I'm saying is—'

'You rock band leaders. All the same. Girls, girls, girls.' Micky strolled off.

It was a fair point. He couldn't be a potential Rock God if he spent the whole party talking to Neil. Maybe Micky had done him a massive favour. Maybe a small mates-only party would be rubbish. After all, his mum wouldn't mind a few sensible girls there – if he asked nicely. And his dad... well, he'd be over the Nelson till three in the morning

He wondered about Claire. She did seem to be more interesting than he'd previously thought. Okay, so she was a bit quirky, but she was well-behaved. A few more like her and he'd have the perfect party.

He raced after her.

'Claire? The party – you're invited.'

At lunchtime, walking to the shops, Tom cheered himself with an idea for *Devil's Advocate*. A poem. *There was a young man named Danny, but we'll call him Bob, who desired a session of fanny, but had only a tiny knob…*

Up ahead, Barry Cohen and Brenda Brand were returning from the sweet shop eating Curly-Wurlies. Perhaps he'd invite them to the party. The son of a local councillor and the daughter of a primary school teacher – they were just the sort of tame kids he needed to beef up the numbers. And maybe Brenda would fancy Neil.

As he reached the shop, Megan came out opening a packet of Opal Mints. For a brief moment, their eyes met. And that was too much to allow a walk-by.

'Meg, alright?'

'Fine. You?'

'Yeah,' he said, enjoying her upmarket accent once again. 'Look, they set me up.'

'If you want to see Cheryl, it's okay.'

He thought about Megan's secret boyfriend. This is where the fightback would begin in earnest.

'I don't. I want to see you.'

There, he'd said it.

'Then maybe you should choose your friends more carefully. They don't respect you.'

'There are certain people I'm stuck with for a bit. We all are.'

'Tom, you're talented, you're musical, you work hard. You don't have to take any nonsense from them.'

'It's not forever, Meg. They're not exactly a big part of my future.'

'Shall I wait for you then?' she said.

'Wait for me?' Marriage flashed through his mind.

'While you're in the shop.'

'Oh… yeah.' Phew. Could have been embarrassing.

Inside, waiting to be served, Tom thought back to this time last year. To Terry Seers. Now a City trader, Terry had been the coolest kid in school. His hair was long and tremendous, his eyes piercing and intelligent, his voice commanding, yet understated. He'd stood in this very shop, *Selling England by the Pound* tucked under his arm, talking to Tom. Well, okay, Terry was speaking to some bloke called Dirko, but Tom had wandered between them at the magazine rack. "Dirko, man, if you want respect, you have to separate yourself from the sheep. You have to create your own territory by word and deed. Blokes respect that, and women's vaginas respond by readying themselves for sex. Start right now, man. Be your *self*." It blew Tom's mind. He rushed out the next day and bought *Selling England by the Pound,* and waited for men to respect him and for women's vaginas to ready themselves for sex. Except…

Leaving the shop with a packet of Opal Mints that he didn't really want – more than two gave him a guts ache – he smiled at Megan.

'So you definitely don't want to go out with Cheryl then?' she asked.

Tom popped a mint into his mouth and began to chew.

'I'm my own *self*, Meg. Some of the more stupid blokes might lust after Cheryl, but if you want respect, you have to separate yourself from the sheep. You have to create your own territory by word and deed. Blokes respect that, and women's… women do too.'

'I like that,' said Megan.

He was pleased. And curious. It was time to invite her to—

'Hard work!' said Megan. 'If anyone messes around and distracts you from your O-levels, cut them off. If they mock your band, cut them off.'

'Absolutely,' said Tom. *Must take some guitar lessons.*

'There's no room for losers in our lives, Tom.'

'Agreed.' He then spotted Neil approaching with the raised hand of peace.

'Alright Tom, Megan. Just going to the shop. You okay for six tonight?'

'Yeah,' said Tom.

'Up to no good?' asked Megan.

'We're recording a couple of songs,' said Tom. Once Neil was past them and out of earshot, he added. 'My own songs, as it happens.'

Megan nodded. 'I'm impressed. What sort of songs do you write?'

'Oh, you know…' Having not written any, he found it hard to describe them. 'Universal themes.'

'Love?'

He blushed. 'Er, yeah, sort of.'

'Fancy a bit?'

'What?' Tom's shock lasted until he saw that Megan had pulled out a bar of Fry's Chocolate Cream. 'Damn, I said I'd get one of those for Claire.'

Megan shot him a look.

Tom gulped. 'Claire Cross. I said I'd get her one from the shop. As that's where I was going.'

'Neil's telling everyone you're having a party.'

'Yeah! Absolutely! You're invited, obviously. First girl on my list.' *No - crap!* 'Apart from Claire.' Damn, he needed a fib to devalue Claire. 'I've only invited Claire to set her up with Darbs. He's nuts about her.'

Megan smiled a little and Tom considered the matter closed. He even thought about asking her out, but no – he was saving up for a party and an electric guitar. And besides, he'd have her all to himself on Saturday night.

Yes, Saturday night. Everything was shaping up very nicely.

9. G-G-GIRLFRIEND

Tom left home early on Tuesday morning. Seeing Neil at the bus stop was a measure of just how early.

'See *The Sweeney*?' said Neil.

Tom didn't like answering obvious questions first thing in the morning. Of course he'd seen *The Sweeney*.

'Good guitar session,' said Neil, switching to the time they had spent together before going their separate ways to specifically watch *The Sweeney*.

Tom said nothing. It had been a terrible session, full of messing about with the tape recorders and achieving almost nothing. And besides, he didn't want to talk about the band. In fact, since yesterday's chat with a certain female sixth-former and his mum's subsequent agreement to a few sensible girls attending his party, he'd been desperate to use the words "Megan" and "girlfriend" in the same sentence. It was surprisingly difficult though – even with just Neil present.

'My… my…' *Girlfriend! The word is girlfriend!* 'My… g…'

'You okay?'

'…guitar needs replacing.'

'You're not kidding.'

'And we need a new name for the band. Golden Pyramid isn't right.'

'Black Mass,' said Neil.

'What?'

'I've been thinking the same thing.'

Tom baulked. 'Sounds a bit like Black Sabbath.'

'True. What about White Mass.'

'Sounds like a puddle of vomit.'

'Oh.'

An old Thames sailing barge floated through Tom's thoughts. Brown sails.

'Brown…'

'Brown Mass?'

'Don't be disgusting, Neil.' Brown sails. With a reddish tinge. 'What about Red Sails?'

Neil turned his nose up. 'Nah.'

'Think about it, Neil. It's the colour, almost, of the sails on the Thames barges.'

'But it's like that song, "Red Sails in the Sunset".'

'So? It's better than sticking a colour in front of Mass.'

'True, but how about something more ambitious than boats.'

They came up with some options but all of them were rubbish.

As they crossed the Blue Bridge, Tom eyed a Fred Olsen ship on the river, waiting to come into the docks. Was that the Black Watch? Or the Black Prince? Would one of those make a good name?

'How about Universal Explorer,' said Neil.

'Universal Explorer?' Tom had to admit it was a good name for a band. He wondered if it might even attract a better singer than Neil.

For Tom, arriving at school ages before the bell always had a weird vibe. It was free time, yes, but only in the way that sitting in a dentist's waiting room is free time.

'You're in early,' called Megan from up the playground.

'Yeah,' he said, fleeing Neil to join her.

Although the party situation had been dealt with, he still needed to learn more about her secret boyfriend. Obviously, if he came straight out with it, he'd have to admit to spying on her. It was just as well he had a Trojan horse Genesis LP in place.

'How are you getting on with *Selling England*?'

'It's good. I was going to have another listen tonight.'

'There's no better thing, Meg. Sitting alone in your bedroom with just Peter Gabriel and the boys for company.' He looked into her face for any giveaway signs.

'Yes,' she said. 'Should I bring it back?'

'No rush,' he said, feeling that he'd need a little longer to solve the St Paul's Way mystery.

Claire Cross came over.

'I'm still waiting, Tom.'

'Just a second, Claire.' Tom turned to Megan. 'I just need to sort something out with Claire.'

He felt ridiculous leading Claire away. What would this look like to Megan? Not good, that was for sure.

'Listen, Claire. Could you do me a big favour and not mention to Megan that I'm crap at guitar.'

'Doesn't she know?'

'Just promise you won't mention my name and "guitar lessons" in the same sentence to anyone.'

'Okay, but that kind of complication pushes the price up.'

'Eh?'

'I'll keep it a secret if you help me with English Lit.'

'English Lit? Me?'

'Yeah, for the mocks.'

'I think you've got the wrong man.'

'Come off it, Tom. I heard you reeling off the Greek classics. Hermaphroditus and all that. I mean if you know all that stuff, English Lit must be a doddle.'

'You've got the wrong end of the stick, Claire.'

'You help me with *The Chrysalids* and *Nightrunners of Bengal,* I'll teach you to play guitar and read music. Deal?'

'*The Chrysalids?*'

'And *Nightrunners of Bengal.* Deal?'

He sighed. Now he'd have to read two entire O-level novels before Christmas. This made his mind up. No way was he ever coming into school early again.

'Okay, deal.'

She scribbled something on a piece of paper and handed it to him.

'My address. Pop round tomorrow after tea.'

He looked back to check on Megan, but there were just some boys kicking a tennis ball about.

'It can't be tonight,' said Claire. 'Mum and Dad have friends coming over and I'm cooking them *Spaghetti Bolognese.*'

'Right,' said Tom, wondering what *Spaghetti Bolognese* tasted like. 'Tomorrow then, after tea.'

He headed off towards the fire gate, where he hoped to find a mate or two, but he was waylaid.

'You're having a party then,' said Cheryl Allbright from the entrance to the science block.

'Oh…'

She came over and smiled, all warm and friendly.

'Sorry about what happened. I mean it. I like you.'

'I don't think you do.'

'I do. Why don't you invite me to the party? I'd be your friend.'

'Er, well…'

'I bet you've got quite a few girls going, haven't you. I know Megan and Claire are going.'

'Yeah, well…'

'What time then?'

'Er…'

'About eight?'

'Um…'

She licked her lips in a suggestive way.

Tom gulped. And what if Megan caught the flu and couldn't come? Or worse, brought her secret boyfriend? After all, it wasn't like he fancied ponytail Claire Cross.

'Yeah, okay.'

Cheryl smiled.

The following day, after mince and mash for tea, Tom walked up to Claire's with his guitar slung over his shoulder. He reckoned any onlookers would see a young Bob Dylan: a street-wise troubadour roaming the highways and by-ways. Okay, so he didn't have a proper guitar strap, just a bit of washing line, and the three-string side was pressed to his back to avoid giving said onlookers the opportunity of pointing out the bloody obvious. Overall though, he felt quite musical.

Strolling up Farm Road – a name on no map, but one used by locals to define the middle part of East Ferry Road – he began to think up a song lyric.

You are the water

Stormy

I am the boat

Locked in

By dock gates.

Maybe there would be a ten-minute guitar and keyboard interlude at this point, and then a reprise of the lyric. A bit like Pink Floyd's "Echoes" on Polly's *Meddle* album.

He paused at the Blue Bridge to take in the view of the

Thames to the east and the docks to the west. Then onward. Claire's street was just up on the right.

Arriving at her door meant making instant friends with a black cat, who circled his feet with a definite view to gaining entry to the house. He rang the bell and was soon facing a secret service grilling from special agent Mrs Cross.

'You must be Tom.'

No, I'm Jack the Ripper. 'Yes, that's right.'

'I see you've met Archie.'

'Oh, er…' Tom stooped to scratch Archie's head.

'Helping Claire with English Lit then, eh?'

'Yes, that's right.'

'She says she's going to teach you guitar in return.'

'Yes, that's right, Mrs Cross.'

'Call me Francine.'

'Okay.'

'Up you go then. Not too much noise though.'

Tom headed up the stairs. Archie started to follow… until Francine took hold of him and carted him away to the kitchen.

Claire shared the rear bedroom with Tracey, her nineteen-year-old sister who was out with boyfriends most of the time. When Tracey was there, Claire had to use their parents' bedroom for music practise.

The room itself had yellow walls and grey woodwork, a combination that suggested a willingness to break with tradition. Better still, the back of the house looked out over the Thames and the entrance to the West India Docks.

'It must be nice to live by the river,' said Tom.

'Mmm,' Claire concurred.

Tom glanced at the posters over the twin beds – Rod Stewart and David Essex over Tracey's; a print of an oil painting over Claire's.

'His last major work,' she said.

'Whose?'

'Manet.'

'Oh. She looks a bit like you. Without the glasses, I mean.'

'Thanks. That's Manet's *Bar At The Folies-Bergère* and she's a prostitute.'

'Oh. Sorry.'

'Right, English Lit first.'

'No, guitar first, Claire.' He stared her out. It wasn't hard, although he had a sneaking feeling that, behind those glasses, she might have allowed him to win. 'And we're still agreed about keeping this quiet, right?'

'I said so, didn't I?'

He tried to ignore her glasses. She wasn't bad looking in a way. Better looking than the girl in the painting, anyway. No, he had to stop that. He had come to learn.

'So, how long have you been playing the cello?' he asked, eyeing the instrument in the corner.

'Since eleven. I started piano at seven, flute at nine.'

'You're joking.'

'Mum took me to music lessons at the Dockland Settlement. Shame your parents didn't send you over there when you were little.'

'They tried to. I didn't fancy it.'

'Shame – it's only a hundred yards from where you live.'

'Cost much, do they? Cellos?'

'That one would set you back around fifty. So, not great news that I could do with the next size up.'

'Expensive business.'

'It will be this time. That one came from a friend of the family. Mum and Dad know a few of the well-to-do people who come down.'

Tom knew that the rich with a conscience occasionally got involved at the Dockland Settlement. Some of the local big-mouths called them interfering, patronising tossers, but Tom thought it okay that people cared enough to get involved, whoever they were.

'Anyone famous?' he asked.

'An uncle,' said Claire. 'Not a real uncle. It's what I've always called him. He's one of the Lyle family.'

'Lyle?'

'Tate and Lyle. The sugar people. We go over to his flat near Harrods for lunch once a year. He's got a full length oil painting of Lady Lyle hanging up.'

'Classy.' Tom knew the huge Silvertown refinery, but hadn't considered the owners might be upper class.

'Right, guitar,' said Claire. 'Strum for me.'

Tom did so. The sound from his cheap battered instrument was unearthly.

Claire leaned close to his ear.

'What we have there,' she whispered, 'is a fucking mess.'

Tom was shocked. He'd never heard her swear before. He quite liked it.

She pulled away and played an imaginary guitar chord.

'You do know you're missing some strings,' she said.

'Very funny. I thought we still might be able to do a bit. Besides, I've come to a decision. I'm having money instead of birthday and Christmas presents this year. With a bit of pocket money and doing odd jobs I should be able to buy an electric guitar next year.'

'Yeah, well, let's stick with the acoustic for now. Tracey's got a nice one.'

While she got the guitar from beside the wardrobe, Tom glanced at the spines of the albums by Claire's bed:

Chopin, Dvorak, Maria Callas, Frank Sinatra, Miles Davis. All quite dull, really, compared with Yes and Genesis.

A moment later, he was holding, for the first time in two years, a guitar with six strings. It was a Fender and it felt like genuine progress.

Claire pressed a string down onto a fret.

'See how the strings are nearer to the fretboard than on your guitar. That's called a low action. Actually, it's not that low, but it's a lot lower than yours.'

'Right, so mine's got a high action then?'

'Too high. It makes it harder to play because you have to push the strings down further.'

Claire knelt before him and detuned the instrument.

'Now let's learn how to tune it,' she said. 'Elephants And Donkeys—'

'Get Big—'

'*Got Big Ears!*' she said, cutting him off. She then whispered. 'Mum's got big ears too.'

'Ah. Understood.'

With the rules of communication established, the lesson began.

'Now, if you hit the bottom E.'

'Er…?'

'You might know it as the Big Fat String.'

'I think I do, Claire.'

'Well, not anymore you don't.'

Tom plucked the open sixth string and let its unknown bass note vibrate freely. Claire gave the relevant tuning peg a turn. And another. And then one more. Tom considered the weird upward woy—oy—oing sound as somewhat representative of the shift he was currently feeling – that of getting in tune.

'So that's an E,' he said, plucking it.

'Yes, there's your Elephant right there.'

Claire then showed him how to hold the sixth string down at the fifth fret to get an A.

'Now match the next string's open sound to that.'

Tom plucked the fifth string, but the sound wasn't anywhere near the held-down note.

'Grab your peg and twiddle it,' said Claire, curling her ponytail around her finger.

Ignoring her unintentional innuendo, he did so. Again, the upward woy—oing sounded like progress, although minus the warm glow he'd felt when Claire did it for him. He then wondered if the innuendo *had* been unintentional.

Once the instrument was properly tuned, Tom ran his right index finger down all six strings. It was a revelation.

'That's brilliant, Claire.'

'Stand aside, Jimmy Page, eh?'

'Absolutely.' He knew she was joking. But *he* wasn't.

'Maybe next year you'll be good enough to play something at your birthday party.'

'Yeah…'

'All the girls at your feet.'

'Yeah…'

'This year you'll just have to settle for a dance and a snog with me.'

'Ye—what?'

'Now,' she said. 'I need your fingers to do something…'

Later, in Neil's bedroom, between trying to record a few things onto his and Neil's cassette recorders – there was a ban on using Micky's – Tom thought about the party females. There would be sophisticated, mature Megan, jokey Claire, sexy Cheryl, Carol from Upper North Street and Brenda, who was coming with Barry Cohen.

Of course, Tom knew he was now well overdue in publically airing the words Megan and girlfriend in the same sentence.

'Looking forward to the party, Neil?'

'Yeah.'

'So's… yeah. Yeah. So's. Yeah.'

'You okay?'

'So's my girlfriend. Megan.'

Flushed with heart-thumping, blood-rushing elation, he pounded the E major and A minor chords Claire had taught him, albeit now with fewer strings.

After a session in which – despite Tom breaking his skinniest string – they recorded a few bits and pieces, they began to pack up. That's when Micky came in, pulled the curtain aside and retrieved his cassette recorder, no doubt with a C-120 tape running.

'Give me that,' said Neil, far too late to stop his brother getting away.

10. LOVE, WAR

It was Thursday morning in assembly. Amid boys excitedly discussing last night's BBC1 showing of the Ali-Frazier *Thrilla in Manilla*, Darbs nudged Tom.

'I'm looking forward to your latest work, Mr Shakespeare.'

Tom said nothing. He hadn't come to school to suffer mockery.

Darbs nudged him again.

'Well?'

Tom thought of the song-sonnet he'd come up with. Would it do?

I am a boat
Behind dock gates.
But this dock has three gates
One leads to the flowing River
Another to the deep still Lake
And a third to the Torrid Sea
Which gate shall I choose?
Or is it true that
All water is One
And that you
Are all water?

Sitting with Neil in English Lit, Tom felt less confident. What if the class heckled?

No. He was a potential talent. He would prevail.

'You've definitely done it then?' asked Neil.

'Yes, Neil. Stop worrying.'

'And you didn't have any trouble with the iambic pentameter?'

'What?'

'Shakespeare's sonnets are all in iambic pentameter. You knew that, didn't you?'

'Right,' said Mr Reid, 'we have about ten minutes left. Alder, what do you have for us?'

Tom rose. There was an air of expectancy.

'I bet it's rubbish,' said Micky.

Tom clutched his scribbled poem of unknown pentameter and cleared his throat.

'In your own time,' said Mr Reid.

Tom looked around. Were they ready for this? Was *he* ready for this? He cleared his throat again.

'I am a boat...'

'Not the Titanic?' said Danny Collins.

The class erupted.

'Get on with it, Alder,' said Mr Reid.

He had to do it. He had to share his powerful elegy to love.

'I... I...'

'Aye-aye, captain?' said Danny.

The class erupted once more. Tom gave up.

'Can I have a detention instead?'

There was much jeering and mockery. Mr Reid shook his head.

'Alder, you are pathetic and you will undoubtedly throw away your future. Now sit down, shut up and try to absorb something useful.'

*

After school, heading for the bus stop with Neil, Tom wanted to discuss his girlfriend Megan, the party, the band, and possibly his girlfriend Megan again… but Darbs gate-crashed the moment. He was meeting his mum at his nan's on the Island.

'The old girl had a fall,' he explained. 'We thought she was a goner. First time I've ever thought about her not being around. Weird, eh?'

Tom thought of his grandad, largely unvisited apart from special occasions. It wasn't lost on him that Grandad's street was practically across the road from school.

'I'll see you tomorrow,' he said, suddenly leaving them.

He was soon outside a row of tired-looking Georgian houses that the local authority kept threatening to pull down. Opposite was St Matthias Church, which had been facing closure for years. If the area could have spoken, it would have shouted for help.

At one of the houses that had been split into flats, he rang the ground floor bell. Almost instantly, he was greeted by a wheezing man of sixty-three who, thanks to emphysema brought on by smoking eighty cigarettes a day, looked much older.

'Alright, son?' said George Alder. He had his coat in his hand.

'Alright, Grandad? Thought I'd pop in to see you.'

'I was just about to pop out. Still, they can wait. How's tricks?'

'Not too bad,' said Tom, following his Grandad inside. 'I've been wondering if to leave school next year or stay on.'

'I had to leave at fourteen. Had they given me the chance, I'd have stayed on till I was thirty!'

He cackled and fell into a coughing fit.

'Cup of tea, Grandad?'

George gave a red-faced, watery-eyed nod and took to his armchair to light a cigarette.

'How many girlfriends you got?' he called to Tom, now in the pre-War kitchen.

'One's enough trouble,' Tom called back.

This triggered more laughter and more coughing.

A few minutes later, sipping tea in the sparse front room, George touched on an important subject.

'Birthday soon then.'

'Saturday.'

'Sixteen, eh? I posted you a card this morning.'

'Thanks.'

'Shame you didn't come earlier. Could have saved me the postage.'

'Sorry about that.'

'So how's Mum and Dad?'

'Same as always.'

'Oh well.'

George indicated one of the numerous photos on the mantelpiece.

'Remember that?'

'A bit,' said Tom. It was of himself aged seven in the churchyard across the road at a fete. He remembered it mainly as being his first trip anywhere without Danny.

'Happy days,' said George with a wistful look. 'Of course, the sixties was a good time for the docks. Work? They didn't want you to go home. Overtime? We could have worked ten days a week if we'd wanted. It's all changed now. Bloody recessions and cutbacks and gawd knows what else.'

'Dad says they might be opening a new deep water dock at Tilbury.'

'Tilbury – I wouldn't give you tuppence for it. This is

the heart of the docks. All through the Blitz we worked. We took a terrific bashing, but we never lost a single day's work.'

Alarm bells rang in Tom's head. This had the hallmark of a Grandad Alder lecture, minimum duration: twenty minutes. He needed a diversion, and fast.

'Did I tell you I've started playing guitar?'

'Yeah? Your dad played guitar.'

'Dad?'

'Eh? No, I meant… no, not your dad. Someone else. Ignore me.'

But Tom couldn't ignore him. Grandad had a look that suggested something terrible.

'Who played guitar then?'

'Listen Tom, you'll be sixteen. A man. Why don't I introduce you to the gang?'

Grandad was already up and grabbing his coat.

'What, right now?'

'It's only over the road.'

They were soon in Poplar Rec. It gave Tom a bad feeling because this daytime oasis of open green space was a well-known evening haunt for homeless alcoholics. Surely, Grandad's mates weren't cider guzzlers?

'Funny how time flies,' said Grandad. 'I remember being a boy just after the Great War. The summer of 1919 it was. We lived in the same terrace where you are now. Course it wasn't old then. I used to run out to help bring the cows down to the dairy for milking. Can you imagine that down your street? A herd of Jerseys?'

Tom tried to picture it.

'So where's the gang?'

'Oh, they're all here.'

Tom worked out that Grandad was staring at the monument.

'My little mates from school,' he said.

Tom was surprised.

'You went to Upper North Street School?'

'Yeah, me and my brother, Len.'

Tom had a feeling of dread. He knew that Grandad had lost a brother when he was young, but no one had ever bothered to tell him the details.

'Thirteenth of June, 1917,' said Grandad. 'The first daylight bombing raid on London. None of yer Zeppelins. It was Gothas. Airplanes. Heading for the docks, by all accounts. Except one of their bombs fell on the school. It went right through the roof, through the girls' class, through the boys' class and into the infants' class where it exploded. Can you imagine that? A shrapnel bomb going off?'

Tom didn't wish to try. He looked up at the eighteen names. Obviously, he'd been saddened the first time he'd read them, especially as so many of the dead were five-year-olds, but after that, it was just a war memorial.

'So your brother was inside?'

'We both were. He was my twin. Lost part of his brain. We had to feed him like a baby. For Mum, it was all about dignity, so we never mentioned it outside of home. He died five years later. That's why his name's not on the memorial. It's not easy losing a brother. You never ever forget.'

Tom understood all too well. He'd lost Danny.

'I respected my mum's wishes,' said Grandad. 'When I met your Gran, I told her Lenny died young – illness. So your Dad grew up never knowing the real story.'

'Why are you telling me then?'

'Right time, right person.'

Tom nodded and squeezed his grandad's hand.

*

Although Friday at school felt like a stint in Wormwood Scrubs, Tom consoled himself that he was an inmate due for a weekend parole and a *bloody brilliant party!*

During the morning break, he spied his girlfriend in the playground with Sangheeta Sharma. A wave of warmth got to him. Yes, impressive, mature, womanly, grown-up Megan was the one. All he had to do was find a way to challenge her about St Paul's Way without admitting he'd followed her there on his bike.

Yes, Megan… but not now with Sangheeta.

Cello…?

It was coming from the ground floor music room's open window. Cello and piano. Although he had always thought this type of music to be twee piffle, this bit seemed okay. The window was a little too high to see over the books piled on the sill. But how many people in school played cello?

He entered the corridor and stopped at the closed music room door. Peering through the glass panel, he watched Claire playing. His secret guitar tutor. So talented. He had an urge to hear more clearly. But would she want him watching her? After all, he had never expressed any interest in classical music, or particularly defended it as a valid choice for others.

That now bothered him. Many viewed progressive rock as a disease. As a fan, he defended it with heart and soul. After all, he had to fight musical fascism, didn't he? But if he was against musical fascism, why did he stop fighting the bullies once they switched from sneering at prog to sneering at classical?

Opening the door a crack, he tried to imagine it as a new piece penned by Rick Wakeman of Yes for the next album. The cello's rich tones, he decided, were expressive, the piano alive. In fact, now he was listening more attentively, it was like the instruments were two blokes in a pub telling a third bloke a dramatic story of love and murder.

An urge came over him. Listening to Claire and future keyboardist in Danny's band, Craig Lycett, he wanted to declare his musical solidarity. He wanted them to know that their music was okay.

He eased into the room, studying their labours, their intense concentration, their presence in a world of their own. And then it hit him. They were amazing.

And as the piece ended...

'That was great!' he said. 'Absolutely great!'

Craig Lycett didn't look too impressed.

'When you say great, don't you mean boring?'

'No, I like classical music. What were you playing?'

Claire chuckled. Maybe she didn't believe him.

'Brahms,' she said. 'Cello Sonata No. 1, the *allegretto quasi menuetto*. You'd probably like it more if you heard it by someone who can play the cello.'

Tom was shocked.

'What are you on about? You are brilliant.'

Claire drew her bow across the cello. It took a moment for Tom to recognise the tune. And as he did so, Claire sang Art Garfunkel's "I Only Have Eyes For You" directly to him. Tom's spine tingled. It was an emotional overload. He was on the verge of blowing a fuse.

The bell sounded. The music room would soon start filling up. Tom hoped he wasn't glowing red.

'She never sings to me,' Craig complained.

Claire smirked. 'How about getting those strings tomorrow, Tom? We could go Up West.'

'Tomorrow's my birthday.'

'So?'

'Oh. Okay.'

On the coach after lunch with Neil, waiting to be whisked away to games at Goresbrook, Tom willed the hands on his watch to speed up. Actually, forget the clock; he wanted a calendar to flip over like in an H. G. Wells fantasy. This was his last day as a fifteen-year-old. Tomorrow, he would be sixteen. Mature. A man.

Some stapled papers landed in his lap.

'Page four,' said Micky, moving along the aisle dishing out more copies.

Tom groaned. 'Is there any point to this?'

He turned to page four of the second edition of *Devil's Advocate*. It featured a concert review.

> Universal Explorer, Millwall
> Review by Seymour Dross
> In one of the year's most anticipated events, Alder and Sullivan, under the Universal Explorer banner, kicked off with an ambitious acoustic offering entitled "Pling-Pling-Whine". Unfortunately, an early bum note by Alder did little to lift Sullivan's despondent gorilla vocal styling...

Tom tossed the magazine in the air. It landed a-flutter on Barry Cohen in the seat in front of him.

He hoped that would be it, but no. Danny came over from his seat proffering a cassette.

'Universal Explorer, *Live in Millwall*,' he said. 'Only 50p, Tom. You could play it at your shitty party.'

Tom launched himself at his former brother, throwing

punches. They grappled and clung on, each trying to floor the other, until Micky and Polly began to pull them apart.

'Save it for football,' said Mr Garner from his seat up the front.

The fight broke up.

'I enjoyed that,' said Micky.

Tom sat down, flustered and furious.

'You might have to get used to that kind of thing,' said Barry Cohen, turning round from the seat in front. Tom didn't get it. 'Fighting. Punch-ups.'

'What are you on about?'

'I shouldn't say but... I heard we'll be merging with Broadlands.'

'What?' Broadlands was a rough and tumble Secondary Modern school.

'Yeah, they're going to demolish All Saints.'

'*What?*'

'I overheard my dad on the phone at lunchtime.'

Tom was aware that Barry occasionally popped home for lunch and that his dad was a local councillor, but...

'Broadlands?' The rumour was already rippling through the coach.

'We'll become a four forms per year school called Blackwall Comprehensive,' said Barry.

Neil looked ill. Tom felt weird too. It was like being told your mum was running off with the milkman.

11. GUITAR GIRL

Standing outside a music shop in Charing Cross Road, a mere seven hours away from being with his refined adult girlfriend Megan at the party, SIXTEEN-YEAR-OLD Tom studied his reflection in the window. The hair and jeans looked spot on, but the grey Harrington jacket over a wrinkled cheesecloth shirt let the side down a bit.

He lowered the zip a little. And a little more. It was better, but probably not cool enough for an LP cover.

'Don't you have mirrors at home?'

His eyes shifted to Claire's reflection. With her hair hanging free over a baggy red jumper, she looked different. Like a young woman.

It was always good to be out of school uniform.

School…

He was glad the changes wouldn't affect him. He didn't really have an opinion on whether comprehensive schools were a better idea, but he did think having bigger schools was pretty stupid. Anyone could see that they would never be better, whatever system—

BANG! Loud, shocking… the IRA seized control of Tom's thoughts.

He turned.

Blue-black smoke.

It was billowing from the exhaust of a rusty Austin 1100. It wasn't death, just a dodgy carburettor.

Claire looked shaken too.

'Thought it was you-know-who for a minute,' she said.

'Don't be daft,' said Tom, patting her reassuringly on the arm.

They didn't need any reminders that terrorists were dealing death in London. They had recently bombed the Hilton Hotel in Park Lane and some shops in Oxford Street.

'I was imagining my first album cover,' said Tom, turning back to the window.

Claire laughed in a friendly, kindly way.

'That's great,' she said. 'It's worth thinking big. Too many people think small.' She turned, searching out something. 'I think Bowie did the *Ziggy Stardust* cover round here somewhere. Or was it off Regent Street?'

Tom didn't care where Bowie did the *Ziggy Stardust* cover. He was getting a warm glow. Maybe it was to do with him being honest with Claire. She knew his musical shortcomings, yet it didn't seem to matter. It was like having a second Neil in his life. Only she was funnier. And more talented.

'What sort of guitar would suit me best?' he asked.

Claire peered through her glasses at the Gibsons on display.

'The Les Paul's good. You'd look alright holding one of those.'

He stared at the gleaming white electric guitar and had to agree. *Anyone* would look good holding one of those.

'Come on,' she said, going inside.

They headed past the sales desk to the impressive display of acoustic guitars. A handwritten sign advised: "Patrons playing Stairway To Heaven will be asked to leave." Tom wondered why.

Claire smirked. 'Do you dare me to play it?'

'Wow. Can you really play "Stairway to Heaven"?'

'Yeah, pretty much.'

Tom was impressed. 'I wonder why it's banned?'

'Wake up, Tom. The opening is the first thing anyone learns.' She inclined her head towards the bloke behind the counter. 'Can you imagine hearing the start of the same song played badly twenty times a day?'

'Ahh, fair enough.'

Claire picked up a Gibson acoustic and showed Tom the height of the strings above the fretboard.

'Yep,' said Tom. 'Nice low action for...' He checked the ticket. 'Fifty-nine quid.'

'Try it,' said Claire, handing him the guitar.

Tom looked across to the man at the counter. Judging by his lack of reaction, it clearly wasn't necessary to ask permission first.

Raising his right knee to support the instrument, he held down E major. Despite sounding a little out of tune, it was amazingly easy to hold down the three necessary strings.

'I have to have this guitar, Claire.'

Claire laughed. 'There are loads of others to try first.'

'No, it's either this or one like your sister's.'

'Try a Strat,' she said, starkly, firmly.

Tom let his knee drop. With great care he returned the acoustic to its berth. She was suggesting he picked up a Fender Stratocaster electric guitar.

'You're kidding, right?'

'I wanna see you hold a Strat. A white one.'

He felt almost giddy.

Over by the electric guitars, Tom made a thing of studying lots of other guitars first. Claire tutted though and grabbed a white Fender Stratocaster. She all but thrust it at him.

'The Strat,' she said.

'I was just getting round to it.'

He placed his foot on a raised platform and rested the guitar on his thigh.

'This next song's for the lady in the front row…' He pinged a few strings. 'Sounds tinny.'

'It wouldn't with a Marshall 50 and four-by-twelve stack. Believe me, that would sound amazing.'

Tom did believe her, even though he hadn't fully understood her.

'It's an amplifier and speaker cabinet,' she added.

'Oh.'

'Okay, let's try some major chords,' she said. 'Show me your dicky D.'

As far as Tom could tell, she had said it in a suggestive way. A notion supported by her raising an eyebrow. Tom blamed the *Carry On* films. When it came to innuendo, everyone was a comedian. *Carry On Plucking.*

'My dicky D then…'

He arranged his fingers into an almost impossible position, and then Claire improved the situation by moving one of them along to the next fret. He strummed the chord, but one of his fingers was deadening one of the strings.

'Impressed?' he asked.

'Not half. How long can you keep your D up?'

'Not long. It makes my fingers ache.'

Claire picked up a copy Telecaster.

'Yes, I do like a man who can handle his D.'

'Do you?'

'Yes, I do. Now, while you hold that, I'll show you my open C.'

Tom looked around, relieved that the shop assistant was on the phone.

'Nice open C,' he said, while Claire strummed gently.

'Okay,' she said, 'now give me an F.'

He stared at her, searching for the line between jest and request, and noticed that a reddishness had spread across her cheeks and neck.

'F…' he said, trying in vain. 'No, I don't know how to do it.'

He carefully put the Strat back.

'Archie likes you,' said Claire.

'He told you, did he?'

Claire laughed. 'Mum likes you too.'

'Well, that's good. I like Archie. And your mum, of course.'

'It's important,' said Claire.

'That your mum likes me?'

'No, that my cat likes you.'

Claire picked out another guitar.

'This is a good one,' she said. 'A CSL Strat.'

It looked the same as the Fender, but was about half the price.

'Looks alright,' said Tom, casting an eye over it.

'It's a Japanese copy. A decent one.'

'It's still forty-nine quid,' said Tom, studying the label.

'You'll have to get a Saturday job then.'

'I've got one.'

'Not your mum's Freeman's round. A proper one. The butcher's pays a fiver for a Saturday.'

'I'm not working in a butcher's.'

'Woolworth's then.'

'That's easy for you to say. I notice you're not working on a Saturday.'

'Yeah, well, I phoned in sick.'

'Oh. Right. So, where do you work then?'

'Woolworth's.'

An hour later, having bought strings and a plectrum,

Tom wasn't in any hurry to return to the East End. Luckily, Claire suggested further exploration. He enjoyed her company – even though she seemed to always be one step ahead of him.

In that spirit, she suggested they find out where Bowie did the *Ziggy* photos, and while he wondered if that was a good idea, she was already asking a cab driver stuck in the traffic if it was far.

They had a laugh walking down to Cambridge Circus and a minor thrill when they spotted a bloke who they thought might be Bryan Ferry and a woman who they were even more certain was Joan Collins.

In Heddon Street, off Regent Street, they had great fun pretending to be David Bowie as they posed outside K. West, the defunct furriers at No. 23. A French couple asked if K. West was famous and Claire told them *in French* about Tom being David Bowie's brother. Then they did the Bowie pose in the phone box nearby. Tom had never imagined that the simple combination of a boy, a girl and a phone box could be so wildly hysterical.

Afterwards, they went to a Wimpy Bar for cheeseburgers and chips with ice cold Cokes. And all the time, they just talked and laughed. And then she told him that he should let the whole world know he was learning to play guitar from scratch, and not care what anyone thought. And Tom just marvelled at her carefree attitude and laughed some more. At one point it even occurred to him that anyone looking at them would think they were out on a date.

12. THE PARTY

Mum coming into the front room with two cups of tea was Tom's cue to switch the vacuum cleaner off. It was 5.25 p.m. and preparations for the party were going well. In a few hours' time he and Megan would be dancing to "You're The Best Thing That Ever Happened To Me" by Gladys Knight and the Pips. Snogging too, probably…

'Don't leave that in here,' said Rose, indicating a big brown vase standing guard by the fire place.

Tom took the tea and sat down. He had no interest in vases.

'You wouldn't believe how many guitars I saw today, Mum.'

'I wish you wouldn't waste your money. You've never been musical.'

'Of course I'm musical. It's just I've never had the right instrument. I mean that guitar upstairs… the action's too high.'

'Your nan bought you that.'

Tom recalled his mum's mum winning at bingo just before Christmas, 1973 and splashing out on presents for everyone.

'No, I'm grateful. I'm just saying – it's not a professional instrument.'

'Don't let your nan hear you say that.'

'Of course I won't.'

Just then, sipping his tea, something came to mind.

'Did Dad ever play guitar?'

Rose's face drained a little.

'No.'

'Only Grandad thought he was a guitarist then changed his mind. I'll ask him. Find out what's what.'

'No, don't do that.'

'Why not?'

'Ted's done a lot of things, but he never played guitar.'

'Even so, I'm curious to find out who did.'

Rose took a sip of tea. Her expression suggested she was wrestling with something.

'It was Ted's brother, Harry. He was the guitar player. Played in a band. Pubs and clubs. That's who he meant. The less said, the better, I reckon.'

Dad's brother. A man rarely mentioned.

'How come we never see Uncle Harry? I mean I don't even get a birthday card.'

Rose took another sip of tea before she answered.

'They fell out.'

'I know that, Mum, but why? What happened?'

'Brothers fall out sometimes.'

The front door opened. Ted was back from fishing.

'Now,' said Rose, 'how about we move the armchairs together to give you a bit more room?'

It was 7.30 p.m. and Ted had gone to the pub. Tom, by now wearing "the look" and several glugs of Brut 33, was fretting over the fact that Rose was still loitering.

'Mum, what time are you going into Mrs Cryer's?'

'I'm not. She's coming in here.'

'What? You said you were going in there!'

'That was before you asked to have girls round.'

'You're joking.'

'Just be glad your dad doesn't know.'

'But Mum!'

'Oh don't make a fuss. We won't be in your way.'

'You're going to make me look like a little kid.'

Tom plonked himself down on the settee and stared at the coffee table. It looked good hosting two Watney's Party Sevens, a dozen various shaped glasses and a bowl of Twiglets.

'Shall I light the fire?' said Rose.

'No, we'd melt!'

Rose huffed and went out to the kitchen.

Ten minutes later, Tom answered the door to Neil, who was wearing a girl-repelling white roll-neck baggy jumper and purple velvet super-wide flared trousers. Had a gust of wind caught him, he might have ended up across the river in Greenwich. Just as well he was weighed down by half a dozen albums, a box of singles and eight small cans of Mackeson.

'Neil – that's the same bloody booze my mum drinks!'

Before Tom could close the door, Mrs Cryer appeared.

'Do we sing Happy Birthday now or later?' she said.

Tom gave her his best instant chuckle.

In the front room, he put *Ziggy Stardust* on the record player and regretted not taking his Kodak Instamatic up the West End earlier. He and Claire could have mocked up their own *Ziggy* cover.

7.50 p.m. came and went.

7.55 p.m. It became apparent that Neil wasn't speaking.

'Well, say something,' said Tom.

'Not yet,' said Neil. 'I'm saving it for the party.'

7.58 p.m.

'No-one's coming,' said Tom. 'It's a disaster.'

7.59 p.m. Micky and fellow skinhead Carol from

Upper North Street arrived; him in a white Fred Perry top, bleached jeans and brown bovver boots by Dr Martens, her in a black Fred Perry top, black Levi's and black army boots. Tom wasn't sure if their presence made the party better or worse.

'S'gonna be a fucking wild night, right!' said Carol.

On the plus side, they had brought eight Neil-funded cans of lager, which Micky placed alongside the unopened Party Sevens and Mackesons.

8.04 p.m.

'Where's Megan?' said Neil. 'You don't think she's busy?'

'Shut up, Neil,' said Tom.

Barry Cohen arrived wearing a green suit with a red shirt and blue tie – but he wasn't with Brenda Brand.

'Hi,' said sari-clad Sangheeta Sharma.

'Brenda couldn't make it,' said Barry. 'So…'

'Great! Come in.'

Tom realised that the car outside was full of Sangheeta's family. Her mum was shooting x-ray laser eyes at him. He turned and grabbed his own mum, to show her off at the door. Satisfied, the Sharma family drove off.

In the front room, Barry and Sangheeta duly put their lagers and large cola on the table then moved to claim the little area by the bay window.

8.07 p.m.

'Still no sign of Megan,' said Neil. 'You don't think she's ill?'

Tom sighed. 'I said shut up, Neil.'

The doorbell rang. Tom raced to answer.

Claire! … and rugby-shirted Polly with West Ham-shirted Darbs. They had brought with them more lager, bitter, some Hirondelle red wine and cries of Happy

Birthday.

Resplendent in a tight-fitting woollen rainbow dress, Claire had ditched her glasses and was wearing make-up. It wasn't one of those movie moments, where the woman's specs come off and, *voila*, instant goddess. Claire looked the same, but with smaller eyes. Even so, Tom found her fascinating and enjoyed opening a Party Seven and pouring some for her.

Micky nudged him.

'Why did Barry bring the tinted one?'

Tom quickly turned the hi-fi up.

'Leave it out, Mick. Sangheeta's okay.'

'Send 'em back to India, that's the answer, mate.'

'Sangheeta's not from India,' said Claire. 'She's from Uganda.'

'Yeah,' said Tom.

'Good ol' Idi Amin,' said Micky. 'Chucked 'em all out, didn't he.'

'That's enough, Mick,' said Tom, grateful that Barry was engaging Sangheeta in a boring but loud debate on the pros and cons of All Saints turning comprehensive.

'Sangheeta's dad was a millionaire,' said Claire. Tom had heard the story before but never believed it. Somehow, now, he did. 'They only allowed him to take fifty quid out of the country.'

'Fifty quid?' He felt sorry for them. 'It must have been hard.'

'Shouldn't have come then,' rasped Micky.

'Oh shut up, Mick,' said Tom.

Micky looked ready for violence. Then he softened.

'Only mucking about. What's the Watney's like? Any good?'

8.12 p.m. Tom and Neil were by the door as the bell rang. It was Megan with a bottle of cider and a birthday card.

'Thank God,' said Neil. 'Tom was getting worried.'

Before Tom could tell him to bog off, Neil was helping her peel off her anorak to reveal an old but nice blue dress. Tom thought she looked amazing, but he would have thought that had she been wearing a sack.

'Fancy a dance?' said Tom, nervously.

'No thanks,' said Neil.

'I was asking Megan.'

'Oh.'

'Not yet,' said Megan. 'I want to mingle.'

As Neil headed for the record player, the doorbell sounded again. Tom answered it to find Cheryl bursting out of a skinny pink top alongside someone quite unexpected.

'I hope you don't mind me bringing my new boyfriend. You know Tony, don't you.'

'Alright, Tom?' said Tony Cornish.

With tan Oxford brogues, comfy old grey jeans, the smartest white silk shirt ever under an unzipped brown leather jacket, karate king Tony looked cool. He was also fully armed with a case of 45s and a carrier bag of booze.

He didn't hang around, either. Swiftly denying Neil's Cozy Powell instrumental drumming single access to the turntable, Tony got things going with the first of his 45s: Van McCoy's "The Hustle". Within seconds, feet were moving towards the middle of the room and Tom was wondering how he and Tony might become mates.

Polly came over. 'You and Megan okay?'

'Yeah, I'm just waiting for the right moment.'

'What for?'

'She has to mingle first.' Tom wouldn't make a second move just yet. He'd hover.

Meanwhile, Tony produced a bottle of vodka. Tom's

pondering on how it might be shared out was cut short by Tony splashing some into everyone's existing drinks. Tom was pleased. It was turning into a real party.

13. THE SLOW SLIDE INTO HELL

For the next forty-five minutes, the party continued to liven up with more laughter and louder voices. While Tom waited for "the moment", he listened in on the conversations of the dancers: Polly lecturing Cheryl on politics, Neil telling Tony Cornish about Tangerine Dream's *Rubycon*, Carol from Upper North Street educating Claire and Megan on boys. And when Tony put on "Sailing" by Rod Stewart, they all started singing along. Except for Barry and Sangheeta by the window, who didn't seem to notice that there was a party happening around them.

Tom smiled at Tony.

'So how long have you been seeing Cheryl?'

'I haven't. She heard I'd split with Suzy and asked if I fancied going to a party.'

'Oh, so you're not going out with her?'

'Not my type, mate. I prefer girls who look like they've got a bit of a future. Know what I mean? I do like a good party though.'

Tom comprehended that Cheryl was thereby still unattached. Only, now he saw that she wasn't chatting with Polly, she was seducing him.

Two beers later, Tom was beginning to feel bolder than usual. It also occurred to him that he was about to overtake his record alcohol intake of Christmas 1974.

There was something strange about the music, too.

"Hey Fatty Bum Bum", "Black Pudding Bertha", "The Funky Gibbon" – all songs he had previously disliked, but that now appeared to be drenched in tremendous fun-time glory.

'Take over, Neil,' said Tony, by the record player. 'Just need to see a man about a dog.'

Neil nodded self-importantly. Then, as "Delilah" came to an end, he dipped into the red leatherette box he'd brought and extricated "Autobahn" by Kraftwerk. Ten seconds into it, all the dancers sat down.

Tom wondered if to join them, but Darbs came over, leaving Claire free to talk to Megan.

He patted Tom's arm. 'Good party, mate.'

'Cheers, Darbs.'

'Er... what's the story with Claire?'

'Story?'

'She's under the impression I'm nuts about her... well, it was Megan who told her. And Megan said it came from you.'

'Claire's... very interesting.'

'Nice one, Tom. I owe you.'

Darbs moved in on Claire, leaving Tom annoyed that his mate had construed a neutral comment as permission to go ahead. Still, it wasn't technically any of his business. And besides, hadn't "the moment" arrived?

Tony came back from the toilet.

'Neil, you Womble! It's supposed to be a party!'

Tony remedied the situation with the Bee Gees' "Jive Talkin'". Within ten seconds, the girls were dancing again.

Tom decided this was it. He danced over to Megan. He smiled. She glowered.

'Claire said you went up the West End.'

'Yeah, to buy some guitar strings.'

'She said you went for a Wimpy.'

'We were hungry. '

'I didn't know you were dating other girls.'

Tom blanched. It felt silly to still be dancing but he didn't know how to stop. Thank God the music was drowning their voices.

'It wasn't a date, Meg.'

'I wouldn't have minded going Up West.'

'But Claire knows all about strings.'

'So do you. Surely.'

Tom stopped dancing. 'Yeah, look. About me and guitar playing.' He thought back to Claire's advice. 'Thing is, I can't play.'

'What?'

'Claire's teaching me.'

'Oh.'

'From scratch.'

'So why did you tell me all those lies?'

'I didn't mean to.'

'You let me say all that stuff to Danny about you starting a band. That makes me look pretty stupid, wouldn't you say?'

'You're exaggerating, Meg.'

'Me? Did you say I'm exaggerating?'

'Look…'

'I mean if you lie about the little things…'

'Come off it, Meg. What about your secret boyfriend?'

'What secret boyfriend?'

'The one who lives up… it doesn't matter.'

'Tom, you're a bloody dreamer!'

Tom was mortified. Everyone was watching. Then Rose came in drunk and tearful.

'Oh, for God's sake,' said Tom, steering her back out and down to the kitchen.

'She wanted to say Happy Birthday,' said Mrs Cryer.

'Couldn't you take her next door?'

'Yeah, alright. Come on, Rose. Let's a have a cuppa.'

By the time he'd seen them out and returned to the front room, Megan was chatting to Tony Cornish. Tom let a couple of songs go by, but they continued talking. Unhappy about it, he decided it was time to unleash some targeted love songs. First up, Art Garfunkel's "I Only Have Eyes For You".

Megan and Tony started dancing to it.

Tom was aghast.

Just then, Claire staggered back from the loo, commendably drunk.

'I fancy a snog,' she announced.

Tom was ready to accept, just to show Megan he couldn't be hurt. Only Darbs beat him to it. Meanwhile, Neil held up a single by The Sweet.

'Tom, "Teenage Rampage". Your old favourite.'

'Don't be stupid, Neil. I'm not a kid anymore.'

While he grabbed the record off Neil with one eye on the bin, Polly put "Rock Around the Clock" on.

Claire threw her arms up. 'You can dance the foxtrot to this!' Next thing, she was showing Darbs the moves, while wittering on about the timing being 4/4 and not 3/4 like a waltz.

Tom began to crumble. It was his birthday and he didn't have a girlfriend.

No. He was sixteen. And Megan wasn't lost to him yet. He sorted out some singles and thrust them at Neil.

'Put these on.'

First up was Tammy Wynette, "Stand By Your Man".

He danced alone, but stared at Megan.

Tony broke off and sorted out some singles. He gave them to Neil.

'Put these on.'

Neil put on "That's The Way I Like It" by K. C. and the Sunshine Band.

While Tony started dancing with Megan again, Tom pushed Neil aside and put on Gloria Gaynor's "Never Can Say Goodbye".

Tony also pushed Neil aside, even though he wasn't in the way, and put on David Essex, "Hold Me Close".

Tom gave up. He couldn't win. Not against a black belt with a silk shirt. Defeated, he put on 10cc, "I'm Not In Love".

Tony removed it and put on Fox, "Only You Can". He danced close with Megan and, God, it was like they were having sex.

Tom turned to Neil. 'Can you believe that?'

'Yeah. Megan wants to be an accountant and Tony's doing business studies after his A-levels. They make a good pair.'

'Neil?'

'Yeah?'

'Shut up.'

Tom went to the back door for some air. This was all wrong. Looking out over the darkened garden, he tried to retrace events, but a record-breaking amount of alcohol was clouding matters.

Heading back, he saw Megan and Tony coming out of the noisy front room. He ducked into the middle room. They stopped just outside, with Tom behind the half-open door, in the semi-dark, spying through the crack.

'Who do you like then, Meg?'

'All kinds of bands.'

'You say that, but every girl has someone they secretly fancy... oops, I mean whose music they love.'

Megan laughed. 'Like Freddie Mercury, you mean?'

'Queen? No way! They're playing Hammersmith next

month!'

'Are they?'

'Yeah, I've got tickets! I was going with my brother, but his girlfriend's sister's getting engaged, and he's been told his presence is definitely required. D'you fancy it?'

'What me?'

'Yeah you.'

'I've never been to a concert before.'

'Then I'll take that as a yes.'

In the other room, Johnny Nash's "Tears on my Pillow" was coming to an end.

'How much were the tickets?' said Megan.

'Two-fifty each. Bang in the middle of the stalls.'

'Oh… I can't afford it. My dad won't let me get a Saturday job, even though we're always short of—'

'Hey, it's my treat. I thought I was going on my own.'

'Are you sure?'

'Hundred percent.'

'Thanks, Tony.' She leaned up and pecked him on the cheek. 'You're a really nice bloke.'

In the other room, someone put the Bay City Rollers on: "Bye Bye Baby".

'Got any Queen at home?' said Tony.

'No.'

'I'll lend you *Sheer Heart Attack*. It's brilliant.'

'Confession time,' said Megan. 'I made this mistake before. Thing is, our record player's really old; likely to carve up an LP. I have to go to my cousin's up St Paul's Way to listen to anything.'

Tom felt his soul shrivel.

'No, you don't, Meg. You only have to come round to Narrow Street.'

'Are you sure?'

'Absolutely. As long as you don't mind my mum

fussing over you with cups of tea and biscuits.'

'Sounds great,' said Megan.

'And Queen have got a new album coming out next month. I'll get it and we can have our very first shared intense experience of… listening to it together.'

They giggled.

Tom was mortified, but to step out from behind the door would be truly appalling. They would think him a peeping Tom. He would have to repair the damage later. Yes, he'd get Megan away from Tony and put her straight. No need to make a complete arse of himself right now.

'Why don't you come back to my place now, Meg,' said Tony. 'Listen to some Queen.'

Tom was alarmed.

'I'd like that.'

What? No! Tom's foot unhelpfully clunked the big brown vase he'd put there during preparations. There was a silence. Then a hand pushed the door open.

Tom emerged with a pasted-on smile, unable to speak.

'Jesus!' said Tony. 'Were you spying on us?'

Megan sighed. 'You're meant to be sixteen, not ten.'

Neil came out of the front room grinning drunkenly.

'Everyone having a good time?'

Megan pulled Tony away.

'Come on, let's leave the kids to it.'

Tom half-followed, helpless as Megan and Tony retrieved their coats from the same coat hook. What act of a spiteful God had made them choose the same bloody hook when there were four on offer?

'Hold the door,' said Barry Cohen, emerging from the front room with Sangheeta Sharma.

'Great party,' said Sangheeta.

'Yeah, thanks for the invite,' said Barry. 'Neil says you

want to play the summer dance next year. I'll sort it out with the committee.'

Then he and Sangheeta were outside, the door left wide open, and a drunk Micky was staggering out of the front room and into Tom's face.

'Should've invited Danny.'

'Oh shut up, Mick.'

'Should've. He's yer brother.'

'No, he's not.'

'Course he is. I heard me mum talking about it.'

'No, Danny was adopted.'

Micky shrugged. 'Both were, s'what I heard. Still brothers, though…'

Tom's heart raced. This was rubbish. Danny had been adopted then reclaimed. Full stop. End of story. There was no mystery around the birth of Tom Alder.

Micky trudged up the stairs, loo bound.

Megan looked back briefly from the path, but Tom's eyes were misting up. This wasn't how his sixteenth birthday party was meant to be. Blinking away excess moisture, he looked to stupid Neil and then back to the departing Megan and then to Cheryl, Polly and Darbs doing a conga out of the front room and past him towards the kitchen singing a falsetto "I Can't Give You Anything But My Love".

Surely even this blackest, bleakest of clouds had to have a silver lining?

Drunk Claire wobbled out of the front room, leaned against the wall by Tom and gave him a wan smile.

Claire… With her messed-up hair and smudged lipstick, she was a law unto herself. Why hadn't he noticed her years ago? She was funny, she was warm, she played cello, piano, flute and guitar, she could play "Stairway to Heaven", she cooked *Bolognese* and danced the foxtrot, spoke French, drank beer and whispered swear words in his ear!

It occurred to him that a man could fall in love with someone like Claire. Well, good! He was sixteen now. A man. He'd bloody well ask her out!

'Claire…?'

'Darbs has asked me out,' she said before sliding down the wall and vomiting over his red Puma trainers.

'Darbs? But…' He felt like screaming. Instead he went to the kitchen. Mum's stout was the answer. Several cans of it would do the trick. Watching the conga going round the garden, he decided that he'd gone right off parties. And life in general. Like the Blues guitarists of the Mississippi delta, he'd suffered enough pain in his pursuit of love. Come the morning, he'd start writing songs about it.

It was either that or go back and tell Claire he'd love to go out with her.

He went into the hall and kneeled by Claire's prone frame. Her head looked uncomfortable squashed against the skirting board.

'Claire? Don't go out with Darbs. I'd love to be your boyfriend. I really would.'

Claire looked at him through drunken eyes.

'Claire? Can you hear me? We could combine guitar lessons with going to see films and… well, classical concerts. You can join my band, too. We've already got a gig lined up for next summer. Claire? What do you think? Me or Darbs?'

Claire's drunken eyes closed for the night. He wouldn't be getting a reply until Sunday at the earliest.

1976

14. FOREVER AND EVER

It was the first day of July and the afternoon heat was slowly turning Tom Alder into a human casserole. Ninety degrees Fahrenheit. The sweet life if you're wallowing in the Mediterranean; the sweaty life if you're working on an old house in Millwall.

God, what he would have given to be swimming in the sea. Thin Lizzy were on the radio. "The Boys are Back in Town". This boy had never left.

His boss Nat Hiscock had just got back from the builders' merchant and was assessing Tom's attempt to pull out an old sash window frame in the rear half of the through-lounge.

'That, son, is a right mess. You've done more damage than the Luftwaffe.'

'It doesn't want to come out, Nat.' While heavily-sweating Tom's hair, arms, vest, shorts and Doc Martens were covered in old plaster dust that was turning molten and would likely set later to encase him in solid gypsum, 40-year-old Nat looked fresh in his open-neck "Man At

C&A" shirt and summer slacks.

'Where's Mrs Dale?'

'Dunno,' said Tom. 'Upstairs, I think.'

'One simple job…'

'It's *almost* out, Nat.'

'Yeah, so's half the bloody wall.'

Tom was annoyed. While Nat had been to Turner's for a bag of cement, a cup of tea and a chinwag, he'd left Tom – only four days into his working life – to spend the whole time yanking, sawing, hammering, crowbarring and kicking the bloody thing. But the sound of someone coming downstairs dispelled the discord.

'Mrs Dale!' cooed Nat as their elderly customer appeared.

'Is everything alright?' she asked, suspiciously.

'How sensible of you to ask,' said Nat with enough charm to woo a coachload of Women's Institute pensioners. 'You wouldn't believe some of the ignorant people I have to deal with. Now, how about we have one of your lovely cups of tea?'

'Is that wall meant to look like that?'

'As you can see, we've almost removed the old frame, but, sadly, my apprentice uncovered some unsafe brickwork, which he has, of course, removed.'

Tom looked at Nat with some uncertainty, although not as much uncertainty as Mrs Dale.

'Yeah,' laughed Nat, 'only sixteen, but a demon for doing the job properly.'

Mrs Dale stared at the seasoned builder… and at the holes around the twisted frame.

'Come on, Mrs Dale,' said Nat, taking her by the elbow and leading her out. 'You look all in. Must be the weather. Let's get that kettle on, eh?'

Nat wasn't kidding about the weather. According to

the bloke on telly, the extreme heat was set to continue indefinitely. The past week's temperatures had already been unbearable and the Government's latest message was to conserve water as supplies were almost exhausted. Tom was almost exhausted too.

With Nat and the customer gone, he got back to enjoying the Thin Lizzy chords resonating around the room. He could have played like that had he kept up the guitar lessons with Claire Cross. Now he was wielding a sledgehammer and felt a million miles away from performing in a band.

'Fancy a Coke?' he asked Chris Lowe, a lanky, nineteen-year-old nutter from Poplar who had been with Nat's building operation for two years.

'Nice one,' said Chris, currently dealing with his guttering repair job by sitting in the alley outside the back of the through-lounge studying *Playboy*. 'What do you reckon of her though?' He held up a double page spread of a woman in a state of undoubted readiness.

'Nice face,' said Tom.

Chris laughed and Tom made his escape.

Outside, the air shimmered above the oven-hot pavement in a way that he half-expected Lawrence of Arabia to materialise. As it was, the figure seemingly hovering towards him was that of retired stevedore Bill Bryant in his bowls club blazer and tie.

'Alright, Bill,' said Tom. 'You wanna watch you don't melt in that lot.'

Bill ignored the comment and reported that "they" were thinking of turning the docks into a giant housing estate. Bill often reported what "they" were up to.

'You've seen that Quarterdeck Estate,' he said. 'Imagine fifty of 'em all stuck up together, side by side like a bloody Lego set!'

'Yeah,' said Tom, 'I know what you mean, Bill.'

'It's all backhanders, you know.'

'Yeah, more than likely.'

'I dunno why they have council meetings in the town hall. Might as well have 'em in the pub. Know what I mean?'

'Yeah.'

'Anyway, I'm off up the club,' said Bill.

'Hi Tom.'

Tom turned to see Claire Cross approaching. A joyous feeling lifted him but he opted to play it cool. He'd fancied her ever since the fiasco known as his sixteenth birthday party but they had hardly spoken beyond Hello's and See You Tomorrows during the intervening nine months. The severe mockery he got at school regarding the party and the ensuing Mile End Odeon Embarrassment made it very much a defining case of twice bitten, twice shy.

Instead of dwelling on what might have been with Claire, he spent the weeks following his birthday revising for his January mock O-levels – in which he scraped together four passes. After that, he stuck his head into his books and ignored Jim Callaghan becoming Prime Minister, rising unemployment, the IRA blowing up bits of London, factory closures on the Isle of Dogs and the Brotherhood of Man winning the Eurovision Song Contest with a silly song and even sillier dance. There were some things that couldn't be ignored though, like the *Rock Follies* TV drama, Cheryl Allbright's ever-expanding frontage and Genesis appointing Phil Collins as their singer.

'Claire, hi. I'll catch you later, Bill.'

'How's the job?' she asked.

She had a boyfriend, of course. He knew that. An

eighteen-year-old bassoon player called Steve, who she met through some inter-schools classical music thing.

'It's alright,' he said nonchalantly, while far more interested in the way the sunlight played on her long flowing hair. 'We're working on a house round the corner.'

'No point,' said Bill Bryant – having stalled two yards away. 'No point building a giant council estate if there's no jobs. Not unless someone's taken a bung.'

'Yeah, Bill,' said Tom, 'Take care, eh?'

'Righto, son, see you later.'

As they watched him trundle off, Tom thought back to the date he set up with Claire the Friday after his sixteenth birthday. How he'd felt smug at defeating his mate Darbs in gaining her affections, and how happy he'd been while waiting for her outside Mile End Odeon. And how confused he was when Darbs turned up. When Claire arrived, she made it clear that they could all be friends but having Darbs tell her at the party that Tom was a tosser made Darbs the boy least likely to go out with her. For a fleeting moment, Tom had felt like bursting into applause, but then Claire turned on him. Apparently, being placed on his subs' bench at the party in case Megan Vanderlin didn't work out wasn't the way to impress her either. Tom didn't fancy seeing a film with Darbs so he went home. After that, the guitar lessons he'd been having under cello-playing Claire's tutelage came to a crashing halt and his self-taught efforts eventually fizzled out. Getting it wrong with Claire the previous October still ranked as the single most stupid error he'd ever made. But right now, on a hot July afternoon, he felt the optimism rising.

'Yeah, we're doing a bit of renovation work,' he said. 'Handy too – I can fall out of bed at eight and be at work by two minutes past. I expect I'll have a few more muscles before long.'

She didn't react so he made himself busy by brushing some genuine workman's dust from his short-cropped hair.

'How are things with you?' he asked.

'Oh, you know, enjoying the start of the holidays. Not that they're meant to start this early.'

Those who had finished their exams were meant to continue on until the end of term but, in practice, never did – himself among them.

'You'll miss sports day,' he said.

She smiled. And so did he. He'd only left school the week before. A long Friday of celebrating and then a strange weekend knowing that on the Monday he'd be working for a mate of his dad's. School, having dominated his life for so long, was now a thing of the past. That giant presence, those laughs amid the boredom, all reduced to memories.

'Just been up Brenda Brand's,' said Claire. 'Listening to Demis Roussos.'

'Rather you than me,' said Tom, pulling a face.

A silence descended on them. Tom tried to think of something to break it but couldn't.

'Well, I'll be off then,' said Claire. 'Just popping round my aunt's.'

'What A-levels are you going for?' he asked with some urgency. He didn't want her to leave.

'Music, French and History,' she said. 'Why didn't you stay on, Tom?'

He searched for an answer. As a grammar school fifth-former, he'd faced a deadly choice of staying on for two more years of schoolwork in the sixth-form or leaving and getting a white-collar job. He thought he'd been quite smart in finding a third option.

'I'm earning a few quid and I've got plans,' he said. 'Doing building work with Nat's just the start.'

'Well, good. I'm glad you're happy.'

A ship's horn rumbled down the road from the nearby Thames.

'So… how's the boyfriend?'

'Lucky swine's in Devon for the next week and a half.'

'Nice.' Or was Tom the lucky one? The Docklands Summer Dance was only two days away.

'Yeah, Brixham,' she said.

'Brixham, nice. Er, I don't suppose you're going to the dance on Saturday?'

'I hadn't planned to.'

'No, well, I was just thinking we could go together. As mates, I mean.' What if his working-man-manliness won her over? Would she dump Bassoon Boy? Or was that unethical thinking? 'I'm still practising those chords you taught me,' he lied.

'If you're serious, you should think about starting a band. I don't mean like before, acting like you'd play the summer dance, I mean for real. You should be getting out there and showing the world what you're capable of.'

'Yeah…' God, Claire was so focussed. Why had it gone so wrong with her? 'So, Claire? How about meeting in the Waterman's then? Before the dance? About half-seven?'

15. SECOND THOUGHTS

It was Friday, the second day of July and, if anything, it was hotter than the previous day, which had sautéed Tom's head.

After lunch, hot and tired, he popped into Mrs Dale's kitchen, where he expected to find Nat drinking tea with their customer. Instead, he found her alone, outside the back door, sipping a glass of orange squash.

'He's spending a penny,' she said.

'Oh.'

'This lot certainly needs a bit of work,' she said, indicating shin-high grass that had turned to hay beneath the relentless sun.

'Yeah,' he agreed, examining the fingertips of his left hand. They were red from a three-hour session with his crappy acoustic guitar the previous evening – his first in months. He'd developed a personal dislike for the substandard instrument and it was only the fact that it had been a present from his nan that he'd kept it. That said, she did live in Southend, so she probably wouldn't know if he threw it on a skip. Then again, he didn't want to buy a replacement acoustic guitar. He wanted an electric one.

'Actually, you might be able to help me,' said Mrs Dale. 'How much d'you reckon a new patio should cost?'

'You should ask Nat.'

'I'd rather not. I thought you might know. Only I've

got a landscape bloke from Barking coming round tomorrow to give me a quote.'

'I'm no patio expert.'

'Mrs Dale!' roared Nat. He had appeared almost magically behind Tom. 'What's all this about a landscaper coming round? *I* do patios! I'm a landscape specialist.'

'I thought you were a renovation specialist.'

'Mrs Dale, I'm a *general* specialist!'

'A general specialist?'

While Nat revisited Turner's to arrange for a delivery of patio slabs and sand, Tom set about cutting the bone-dry weed-strewn grass in the scorching heat. Seeing as Nathaniel Hiscock and Co. (Landscape Division) didn't possess any gardening equipment, Tom had to make do with the caked-up electric mower he found in Mrs Dale's shed.

Workmate Chris wasn't laughing.

'Extra skills? That's extra money.'

'Yeah?'

'Yeah! When he comes back, tell him. Extra skills is extra money.'

Tom didn't feel happy about asking Nat for a pay rise, but he didn't want to look like a kid who was too scared to talk wages with the boss.

While he struggled with the mower in the long grass, he thought it over. He was on twenty quid a week. Chris was on twenty-five plus the £7.70 unemployment benefit he claimed. Tom had been advised to do likewise. He'd even gone up the dole office in Dod Street and was halfway through filling out a UB40 claim form when he realised his conscience would never allow him a full night's sleep again. Nat muttered something about bleeding hearts when he told him he'd torn the form up.

Nat was well into a conversation with Mrs Dale in the through-lounge when Tom went to see him. Short of bashing him with a shovel, Tom couldn't quite work out how to attract his attention.

'My Stan was seeing less and less ships,' Mrs Dale was saying. 'Nothing like the sixties.'

'Same in the building game,' said Nat. 'Landlords stopped improving their properties.'

'I mean the Government stuck big money into Tilbury and we got sod all.'

'Then the councils put up huge housing estates only the big firms could handle.'

'I mean I know the big container ships couldn't get this far up river, but even so…'

'I mean how was I supposed to build a tower block?'

'Last thing my Stan said before his coronary was it would all be down at Tilbury by 1980.'

'I mean I only had a Bedford van and a cement mixer.'

'Unless they dug the Thames a bit deeper.'

'And both of them were knackered.'

Mrs Dale left to put the kettle on leaving Tom free to mention the extra skills money he'd be requiring.

'Ha-ha,' said Nat. 'Ha ha ha ha ha.'

'I'm serious, Nat. Twenty's not enough.'

'It'd be £27.70 if you had any brain cells. That's, what, fourteen, fifteen hundred a year? Not bad for a boy.'

Returning to the garden, he found Chris waiting to mock.

'Doubled your money, have you?'

Tom set about clearing the patio area a bit more. He was having second thoughts about working for Nat Hiscock. Claire had a point. Why did he leave school?

'Shagged some right ugly bird last night,' said Chris.

'Oh yeah?' said Tom, not wanting to listen. In truth, he hated Chris. He was a busy-body, always trying to be helpful to other people by effectively taking over their lives.

'I'm generous though,' said Chris. 'Gave her the goods on her mum's sofa to the satisfaction of all parties.'

Tom hoped that didn't include the mum, but chose not to ask.

'The sand and slabs should be here soon, Chris.'

'You know the best way, don't you?'

'Yeah, you stamp down the sand then level it off with a bit of wood.'

Chris laughed. 'I meant the best way to do the business to the lady's satisfaction.'

Tom answered this challenge in the only way possible.

'Of course, I do,' he lied.

Chris laughed. 'Yeah, sorry. There's me trying to tell you how to guarantee she hits the jackpot every time when you probably know more about it than I do.'

Tom wanted to cry out: *please reveal unto me the secret!* But he couldn't. Because if he did, then Chris would have something over him. He would have to report his progress to Chris. Chris would appear in the pub and test him or appear in a restaurant when Tom was out with a girl. *Remember what I taught you, Tom.*

Hearing a lorry pulling up, he headed off to the front of the house.

Yes, why had he left school?

No, it was fine. He'd made the right decision. Okay, so he did miss certain aspects of life at All Saints Grammar, but he was happy being a working man. Out the front, reaching to lift the first of the sandbags, he knew his worth.

'Oi you!' A red open top sports car had pulled up. The

driver, a girl of around eighteen was staring at him. 'Me dad about?' she asked.

It was clearly Nat's daughter, Natalie. He'd heard plenty about her from Nat, and now here she was, in the flesh. His initial reaction was that she fell short of her dad's description of "a smashing girl."

'He's around somewhere.'

'Go and get him then. And tell him to hurry. I ain't got all day.'

Tom stared at her for a defiant few seconds. Then he buckled under her intense stare. As he went inside to find his boss, he understood perfectly that she saw him as insignificant. The kind of bloke she would only consider as a potential boyfriend if every other man on the planet was dead. Even then he was probably flattering himself.

Later, at home, Tom learned that Grandad Alder had been struggling with the high temperatures. Heat exhaustion, according to the doctor. Tom was worried. Grandad was a heavy smoker with emphysema. He didn't need this ridiculously hot weather.

Up in his bedroom, listening to Tangerine Dream's *Rubycon*, he thought a little more of his grandad. He lost his twin brother when he was five. A bomb dropped from a German plane on a Poplar school during the First World War. Then he lost a son. Not dead, but banished and never talked about. Then he lost his wife, his health and his job.

Hardly one of life's winners.

Tom wondered if that kind of bad luck was catching. He lost his brother Danny back in 1967, when Danny's real mum turned up to reclaim him. What kind of adoption was it where Danny could be reclaimed like a suitcase left at the King's Cross railway lost property office?

Then there was the Micky Sullivan revelation of the previous October; that Tom himself had been adopted. He'd been wrestling with that one for nine months.

He'd have to ask Grandad about it at some point. He was the man responsible for co-producing Harry Alder – currently the main suspect in the "Tom's Real Dad" investigation. Of course, that still left the question of his real mum's identity.

Not that Tom was actively investigating. He was too scared. He wished he could be a bit more like Nat Hiscock. Certain of everything. Always on *terra firma.* Seriously, how exactly did people get to be on such solid ground?

He eyed the aquatic blue cover of *Rubycon,* propped against the wall beside the record player. Back in November, having listened to its otherworldly ambient electronic music for the first time, he'd disliked it. Now it was one of his favourite albums. With judgment like that, how could he ever be certain about anything?

He looked to his cheap guitar in the corner. Surely, he had to start a band. Surely he had to push it all the way to see where it might take him.

He went downstairs. He'd phone Neil to ask if he fancied a spot of practice.

As he reached the phone, it rang.

Tom picked it up hoping it wasn't anyone he didn't want to speak to.

'Hello?'

'Is that you, Tom? It's Claire.'

'Claire?'

'It's about the dance. Steve's holiday's been cut short. His mum broke her leg. Anyway, he's okay about the three of us going together. Seeing as I'd said I'd go with you, kind of thing. Anyway, I won't take no for an answer and you'll love Steve. He's a great bloke.'

'Right,' said Tom, knowing he would hate each and every atom of the thing known as Steve.

16. HEAT OF THE DAY

Tom was disappointed. What a great feeling it had been the previous evening, to give Rose a fiver out of his first week's wages towards his keep. How sour that little victory had turned, with Ted now complaining that it ought to be ten.

The words "wasting it up the market" and "bloody-well grow up" had already featured, so it wasn't likely to be an argument that would end with them all shaking hands and agreeing to respect each other's point of view. In the end, Tom handed Rose the extra fiver.

Ted took it off her.

'Sorry, Rose. I owe Nat Hiscock a fiver.'

That wounded Tom. A fiver that Nat had paid him would soon be back in his boss's pocket.

'No, I'm popping up to Norman's,' said Rose, taking it back. 'I might get something for the boys.'

Norman was the widower of Rose's dear-departed sister, Victoria, who had succumbed to cervical cancer early in 1975. Norman was doing a brilliant job of raising Tom's younger cousins, Terry and Jack, but was always grateful for any financial help.

Ted shrugged but Tom was annoyed.

'I don't see why you won't let Mum get a job.'

'Don't start, Tom,' said Rose.

'I'm the man of the house,' said Ted. 'Not you. When I married your mum, I promised her dad I'd look after her. They were a proud family. Had a big reputation round Wapping. He'd be spinning in his grave if I sent his daughter out to work.'

'She does a Freeman's round.'

'That's different. That's just knocking out a bit of gear. Everyone does that. Even if it's not always official.'

Tom sighed and Ted turned the subject to fishing. Nat was picking him up for a day of rods and reels somewhere in Essex.

'A good spot, under the trees for shade,' he said.

Tom hoped they both fell in.

Up at Chrisp Street Market, Tom hit a clothes stall. Unable to decide whether Claire would be more impressed by a blue Carlsberg lager vest or a green Guinness T-shirt, he ended up with the half-price navy blue Fred Perry tennis top the stall-holder pulled from under the counter and threw at him – which Tom suspected to be linked to a load of similar items going missing from the docks.

Next was the shoe shop. He didn't desperately need a new pair but, with his wages, some savings and ten quid from Rose specifically to put towards buying shoes, he entered the shop.

The first surprise was the mess. There were boxes everywhere, as if the place had been turned over.

The second surprise was the girl serving. It was Carol from Upper North Street. Okay, she had more hair than last time he saw her. That had been at Christmas, when she was a confirmed skinhead who was seeing Neil's caveman twin brother, Micky.

'Carol, alright?'

'It's you. Thingy. How's it going?'

Thingy? Was that the mark he had made on the world thus far?

'Yeah, alright. You?'

'Yeah, not bad.' She looked around the shop, as if that backed up her statement.

'I'm after size eights,' he said. 'Something to go with jeans.' Rose had bought him a pair of flared Wranglers that his only shoes – black brogues – failed to match up with.

Carol looked around for a moment then plucked a box from the mess.

'We're stock-taking,' she explained.

'Oh, right,' said Tom, taking the box.

He opened it to find round-toe brown shoes with yellow, red and green inset panels where they laced up.

'I'll take them,' he said.

Outside, he headed for the record shop, but froze. Ten yards away, Megan Vanderlin was peering into a shop window. If the Human Race ever appointed someone to sit in judgement on the worth of Tom Alder, it would be a toss-up between Mr Reid at All Saints and next year's Head Girl there, Megan Vanderlin. The fact that she had almost become his girlfriend was a dull, distant nightmare of a memory. If she saw him now, she would weigh him up. She wouldn't say anything out loud but her demeanour would scream that leaving grammar school to take a building job was a form of madness.

Well, Megan, you snob...

She turned. He ducked behind some bins.

'Hello Tom. Are you okay?'

'Megan, hi! Just dropped two pence. Must've rolled away. Hot weather we're having.'

'Yes, very hot.'

'Yeah, the bloke on the radio reckons it could get up

to ninety-six Fahrenheit.'

'Yes, that's certainly hot.'

'Thirty-five in centigrade, apparently.'

'Yes, very hot indeed.'

'Well, nice to see you, Meg. Must be going.'

Escaping to the record shop, Tom felt the usual religious experience on entering. It was a feeling so deeply satisfying that not even Our Kid singing "You Just Might See Me Cry" could dispel it.

With great relish he thumbed through every album in the shop. They were all there: Pink Floyd, Genesis, The Stones... okay, so Cliff Richard and the Wurzels were given house room too, but this temple was open to all. No fear or favour.

In the end, he settled for a long overdue purchase of Camel's *Moonmadness*.

Rather than head straight home, he popped round to Grandad's – something he did once or twice a month these days. As it was, ringing the bell failed to elicit an answer. Luckily, Tom's mum had given him a key, in case Grandad was resting in bed.

Just as he was about to use it, a neighbour's head popped out of an upstairs window.

'An ambulance took him away about ten minutes ago. To the London.'

Fear gripped him.

'Was he alright?'

'It's the heat. He couldn't breathe. I tried phoning your mum but there was no answer.'

'She's probably up my uncle's but I don't know the number.'

With that, he was away to the bus stop.

Waiting for a bus – the phantom 15 – to Whitechapel, he couldn't stop his mind racing to conclusions. Would he get there too late? Or worse, just at the moment Grandad breathed his last? Two Asian men were eyeing him. Yes, he probably looked a little too animated for comfort. It was likely they would let him on first to see where he sat. Then they would sit as far away as possible. That was how he always handled the weirdo-at-the-bus-stop scenario.

As it was, the bus came along with the blond-bearded conductor raising a hand.

'Room for one only,' he said, indicating that Tom should board. The Asian men stepped back.

Passing into the body of the moving bus, Tom was surprised to see half a dozen empty seats. The conductor smiled at him in a conspiratorial way, as if to indicate that they were on the same side. Tom found it petty and pathetic. He said nothing though.

At the hospital, he eventually found Grandad in a ward at the back. He'd been rehydrated and cleaned up but looked grey and small sitting up in bed. The nurse advised Tom to apply some pressure on the matter of smoking.

'They're saying you need to give the ciggies the elbow, Grandad.'

'Yes, well, I was thinking about taking a break.'

'They don't mean until you feel better. They mean permanently.'

'Permanently?'

Tom smiled. Grandad Alder was a predictable old so-and-so.

'Is it the heat, Grandad?'

'Tell me about it. Worse than the Sahara in that flat.'

'It'll pass. It can't last forever.'

Grandad had a good cough then took a sip of water.

'How's the job going?' he asked.

'Not too bad. We're renovating a house round the corner from home.'

'That's handy. Nat Hiscock behaving himself?'

'Oh, you know Nat.'

'Yeah… anyway, it's Saturday. A working man like you has the world at his feet. Going anywhere tonight?'

'The Dockland Settlement. There's a dance on.'

'Cor, that takes me back. Used to have dances there before the War. Arthur Crane and his Black Dominoes Orchestra. Some of the blokes met their wives there, or if they were lucky, someone else's wife.' He cackled at that and descended into another coughing fit.

In truth, George Alder looked knackered. Tom could only hope the heatwave would end sooner than the forecasters were saying.

As he waited while Grandad recovered his breath, Tom wondered if to talk about the family. It felt terrible to ponder it, but how long did Grandad have to live? Not that he considered him a candidate for a coffin right away, but there were things he needed to know. Things he'd regret not asking.

'I was thinking about Uncle Harry,' he said.

'Oh yeah?'

'I mean what with him being a guitarist in a band.'

'That was years ago. Probably takes no interest in it now.'

'You wouldn't advise I go and see him then.'

'Eh? What's brought this on? Pumping me for information in case I peg out?'

'Of course not! I was just thinking, that's all.'

'I shouldn't bother, Tom. You've got your own life to live.'

'Why doesn't anyone keep in touch with him?'

'Ancient history, boy.'

'Where does he live?'

'I don't know. West London, somewhere. Hardly matters really. You got a girlfriend?'

'A girlfriend? Ohh, I'm working on it, but—'

'That's the way, Tom. Look to the future. That's what it's all about. Now let yer old grandad get some rest.'

Two hours later, Tom was in his bedroom eating a cheese and onion roll while listening to the Camel album. He wished he had the guts to ask Rose for his birth certificate but he was scared it might confirm his fear that he was adopted. If only Micky Sullivan hadn't got drunk that time. If only the stupid idiot had kept his thoughts to himself.

Luckily, Neil called round. With the temperature in the mid-nineties Fahrenheit, did Tom fancy going to the Lido?

Yes, he did. It was a bloody brilliant idea.

Annoyingly, half an hour later, getting off a 277 outside Victoria Park, they spotted a long queue. On the plus side, at the back of the queue were four teenage girls.

'Alright?' said Tom to the girls.

'Hello, it's the Tarzan twins,' said one of them, setting the tone for the sweltering wait.

For Tom, the Lido usually promised more than it delivered. Today though, with the sun beating down from an azure sky to bake the heads of everyone in Britain, it was the obvious choice. Except there was a commotion brewing up ahead.

'They've shut the door!' came a cry.

'Fuck that!' said someone. 'Kick the fucker down.'

There was a bigger commotion and a lot of movement. Then a cheer went up and everyone roared in.

'You're exceeding the limit!' cried a wizened old bloke as Tom and Neil hurried past without paying.

Getting changed, Tom wondered if Neil was maybe holding him back in the girl stakes. In truth, most of the girls he knew viewed puny boys like Neil as just that – boys. Neil was brave, of course. Entering the lions' den of the Lido where dozens of older blokes would poke fun never fazed him. Shouts of "I've seen more meat on a butcher's pencil" and "if he turns sideways, he disappears" were the norm.

Passing through the men's arch to the sun-baked poolside, Tom picked a spot between the bobbing bodies and plunged straight into the inviting water.

'Argghhhh! Jeeeeezus! It's bloody freezing!'

Hauling himself out, he almost bumped into a familiar figure.

'Claire?'

'Made the fatal error, I see.'

'Yeah, what with the earth crashing into the sun, I thought the water might be a bit warmer than the Arctic Sea.'

'This is Steve,' she said, indicating the blond bloke appearing at her side.

Once again, Tom had an icy feeling, but this time it was in his veins.

'Alright, Steve?' he said, noting that Steve was at least two inches taller than him and had chest muscles.

'This is Tom,' said Claire.

'Ah, the boy who offered to stand in for me.'

'I've known Claire since she was eleven,' Tom pointed out.

'Now, now,' said Claire, 'let's not get over-excited. Is that Neil on the diving board?'

It was. And his massive belly flop gave them a tension-busting laugh.

'Maybe Neil should provide the entertainment at the dance,' said Steve.

'He will,' said Tom. Then he jumped back into the water because freezing to death was preferable to seeing Claire's precious bikini-clad body two inches from a bloke he despised.

17. THE GATHERING

Having got ready listening to Mike Oldfield's *Ommadawn,* Tom came downstairs in his new Fred Perry top and denim cut-downs to find *The Music Man* on TV and Rose singing along to "76 Trombones". He waved and departed.

Outside, even though it was seven p.m., the temperature would have given the Gobi Desert a run for its money. Luckily, the local oasis was only a five-minute walk away.

At the bar of the Waterman's Arms, taking a first sip of his lager while waiting for the others, he enjoyed the relative calm. Of course, by half-eight this place would be packed and pungent. But, by then, he'd be at the dance with his mates plus Claire and the mistake known as Steve.

He wasn't looking forward to it.

He wasn't looking forward to Monday either. After one week of working for Nat Hiscock, he was fed up. He thought about school. So many memories…

Mr Grimshaw welcoming them on their first day, the stunned silence when Grimmo announced Keith Byers' death from leukaemia in the second year, the visit of Princess Anne in the third, his fight with Micky Sullivan in the fourth, Dawn Taylor leaving at fifteen with a bun in the oven, Mr Reid ignoring Tom's claim of mistaken identity over a broken window and stating that the cane he was about to lash across Tom's arse would "hurt me more than it hurts you, Alder", Neil Sullivan losing his eyebrows in a Bunsen burner prank, the dissected frog Danny Collins put in Brenda Brand's lunch box, trying to peek at Miss Norris undressing on a school trip to Wales…

'Alright, Tom?' It was Neil entering in a dark brown T-shirt and purple corduroy shorts.

'Neil, what do you fancy?'

'Lemonade, please.'

'Not drinking?'

'Trying to avoid falling into a pattern.'

'But you only drink two small cans of lager once a week.'

'Yeah, well…'

'Go on, it's a million degrees and I've been paid. My treat.'

'Maybe one lager then. Just for refreshment.'

'Right then. One refreshing pint.'

'You getting one for Micky, too? He was just coming along with Jackie.'

'Who's Jackie? And no, I'm not. He can buy his own.'

Skinhead Micky came in with a girl in a red Fred Perry top. For some reason, she reminded Tom of Carol from Upper North Street.

'Drink?' said Micky.

'No, we're fine,' said Tom.

'This is Jackie. You remember Carol from Upper North Street?'

'Yeah.'

'She's my sister,' said Jackie.

Tom struggled to make sense of it then gave up.

'Does the bloke behind the bar mind you being underage?' Jackie asked Micky.

'Nah – he's underage too.'

Once they had been served, Micky clinked glasses with Tom.

'Up the workers, eh?'

Tom smiled. He found Micky a bone-headed caveman but here they had something in common.

'Yeah, the workers,' he said.

'I'm working too,' said Neil. 'School isn't a holiday camp.'

'So, how's the building game?' asked Micky, ignoring his brother.

'It's great, Mick. Couldn't be going better.' There was no way he was giving Micky an opportunity to take the piss.

'Working with that Nat Hiscock, I hear,' said Micky. 'He rewired the Brewer's place a few months back and blew the main board!' Micky roared with laughter at the thought.

Neil's brow furrowed. 'Yeah, well, now he's got Tom helping him.'

'What, to blow up people's houses?' Micky laughed some more.

'You sound tough, Tom,' said Jackie, practically licking her lips.

'What him?' scoffed Micky. 'We all went to see the Who at Charlton and they had these laser lights. When they came near us, Tom ducked.'

Micky gurgled with laughter at the memory. Tom, less so.

'Big firm, is it?' asked Jackie.

'No, Nat's a one-man band,' said Tom. 'Self-employed.'

'Self-employed,' said Micky, 'because he's the only bloke who'll employ him.'

'He did a bit of time,' said Tom. 'He's alright though.'

'A two-stretch, wasn't it?' said Micky.

'Pentonville,' said Neil. 'For receiving.'

'Blimey, half the Island could go down for that,' said Micky, laughing.

Tom couldn't argue with that. Buying knocked-off goods was a part of life. Even the local police did it. He brushed a speck off his new top.

'So, how's things with you?' he asked out of politeness rather than any interest in Micky's new job as a van driver for a paper warehouse.

Micky's laughter died away. 'Yeah, going well. Twenty-four quid a week.'

'He has to work forty hours for that,' said Neil.

'Better than being at school. Especially that chemistry lab. You know the one, Tom – where you used to take girls for a quick grope. I wouldn't fancy putting my head in there anytime soon.'

Jackie laughed. 'He told me he stuffed a fish behind a cupboard.'

Neil frowned. 'What, a dead one?'

'Nah, it was one of them air-breathing fish, you doughnut,' said Micky.

'It's a shame about the school,' said Neil.

The rumour that All Saints Grammar would be demolished had proved false. However, the rumour that its pupils would join forces with secondary school Broadlands to form the new, bigger, Blackwall Comprehensive in a brand new building had been correct. In short, the new building wouldn't be fully ready in time for September, so the All Saints and Broadlands sixth-forms would be merging at the All Saints site while the rest of both schools would take up occupancy at Blackwall. In a further twelve months, all remaining sixth-formers would switch to the new building.

'No uniform for sixth-formers,' said Neil. 'They've decided to treat us like grown-ups.'

'It's a shame they had to merge the schools,' said Tom. 'Can you imagine having four forms in each year?'

'Don't start painting a rosy picture of All Saints,' said Micky. He turned to Jackie. 'I was only there because of Neil.'

'Siblings policy,' said Neil.

'He was academic so we both had to go,' said Micky. 'No-one said because I'm good with my hands, we should both go to Broadlands.'

Tom nodded. It was a fair point.

'Hello,' said Micky, 'it's gone dark all of a sudden.'

Framed in the pub doorway was Sangheeta Sharma in a sari, jeans and trainers combo. She was followed inside by Barry Cohen looking a bit naff in white shorts and black T-shirt.

While Barry hit the bar, Tom nodded at Sangheeta.

'You must be used to the heat more than us,' said Micky.

'Uganda's a lifetime ago,' said Sangheeta.

Sangheeta had been in the year above Tom at school, and he'd never actually spoken to her about Uganda before. It seemed a good time to start acting like a grown-up.

'Was it as hot as this?' he asked.

'Yeah.'

Suddenly, possibly to stop Micky from butting in, he felt like knowing more than just the weather.

'What was it like? You know, to be booted out?'

Sangheeta seemed surprised.

'It wasn't nice, Tom.'

Barry turned round. 'Oi, Alder, stop chatting up my

girlfriend and explain why you're not playing tonight.'

'Oh… well… you know.'

'Hello, look who it is,' said Micky.

Tom turned to see Claire entering with her boyfriend.

'Great,' he sighed. He'd been hoping Steve would go down with dysentery but he looked super-healthy in a white T-shirt and bleached Levis while Claire looked cool in a pale yellow cotton dress and sandals.

While Neil was talking to Jackie, Micky pulled Tom aside.

'She's well up for it, this one,' he said.

Tom stole a glance at Jackie. 'Yeah?'

'Yeah, her dad's got a garage round Teviot Street. There's a light in there and a bit of old carpet.'

'Jeez,' said Tom. 'And to think there are mugs out there paying for a room at the Dorchester.'

'I'm just getting a bit of experience, that's all.'

Tom found Micky disgusting. Yes, he was jealous of him, but surely a man had to have standards.

'Forty-five pence, please,' the barman said to Barry. Tom imagined Jackie saying the same to Micky before a romantic encounter.

'That went down quick,' said Neil, studying his empty pint glass.

'Let me get you another,' said Tom, keen to escape Micky for the rest of the evening and possibly the rest of his life.

No sooner he hit the bar, Steve was nudging him.

'I'll get these,' he said. Annoyingly, his white T-shirt and tan made him look like a Californian lifeguard.

'Cheers,' said Tom, hating him and his Hai Karate aftershave and his haircut too.

'Don't mention it.'

Tom smiled at Claire in a way he hoped conveyed

what any easy-going mature adult he was these days. This was particularly important, what with the Docklands Summer Dance just over an hour away and a plan forming in his head of how to steal her away from Steve.

18. HEAT OF THE NIGHT

It was the third All Saints summer dance at the Dockland Settlement in East Ferry Road. Inaugurated by a bunch of sixth-formers back in 1974 who wanted a booze-up with a couple of bands drawn from their own ranks, it offered a good night out for any students who looked old enough to drink.

If the heat on the street was oven-like, the atmosphere inside, with sweaty sunburnt bodies covered in gallons of after-sun and cheap fragrance, was hellish. Hopes of keeping cool were vested in tins of beer kept in a couple of metal bathtubs. Unfortunately, the ice blocks vital to the success of the operation had melted away faster than a bunch of locals being asked to assist the police.

Tom arrived with Micky and Jackie, Claire and Steve, Barry and Sangheeta, and Neil. The first people he was hoping to see on entering were his former schoolmates Polly and Darbs. As it was, he found himself nodding to Danny, who was sporting a suitably short haircut for the weather.

'Alright, Dan?'

'Not too bad.'

It was weird to think that after tonight he might never speak to Danny again. It prompted questions about the family to bubble up. Not wanting to go there, Tom took in the opening band sorting out their equipment and DJ Terry Farmer, late of the Upper Sixth, cross-fading "Silly

Love Songs" by Wings into Abba's "Fernando". When he turned to Danny again, his one-time brother had gone to join a couple of blokes from the Upper Sixth.

Tom sighed and sought out his own crowd. There he found Steve regaling Claire with a story.

'…his C string snapped and nearly took his nose off!'

Steve laughed. So Tom *faux*-laughed along with him.

'Well, I did say cello can be dangerous,' said Claire.

Tom laughed again but this time on his own.

'Neil!' he said, stepping swiftly away.

Neil was discussing the drought with Barry and Sangheeta. While Tom thought what he might add to such a boring conversation, Polly entered wearing a black string vest and denim cut-downs.

'Hey!' Tom called. 'Che Guevara!'

Polly grabbed a beer and joined them.

'How's the working man?' he asked. 'Joined a union yet?'

'Not much chance of that. Where's Darbs?'

'Not coming. He and Cheryl Allbright went to Bethnal Green. The Dover Castle.'

Tom shrugged. He wasn't too bothered. Darbs had left school but wouldn't be starting his investment banking job in Moorgate for a few weeks yet. Cheryl had an upcoming interview with a foreign bank in Bishopsgate. The chances were that he'd never see either of them again.

'So, Poll, a nice big summer of loafing around then, eh?'

'Yeah, and why not. I worked bloody hard enough on my O-levels. Should be interesting when we get the results.'

'Yeah, although I'm not sure I'll need them in the building game.'

'Yeah, strange you going through five years at grammar school to end up renovating houses. A good thing though. Building's an honest enterprise.'

'Yeah? You obviously haven't met Nat Hiscock.'

'I mean it's honest, as opposed to banking or insurance – which is where the likes of us usually end up. Supporting the status quo for the rich.'

'I'm assuming you're not too bothered about the school turning comprehensive.'

'All Saints turned grammar after the War, right? Well, that created something new in Poplar. An institution that turned young cockneys into outsiders. We're not the same as other locals. We're different. That's the system for you. Turning us into some weird hybrid. I mean don't try joining the ranks of the middle classes. We don't belong there either.'

A sixth-former on stage addressed the microphone.

'We're The Atom Heart Mothers and this is "Roll Over, Lay Down".'

The band launched into the Status Quo song. It didn't sound too bad.

Tom nodded occasionally at Polly, who was talking politics, but he was bored with the conversation and wondered how he might get a crack at Claire. It occurred to him that no sooner Steve went to the loo, he'd have, what, two minutes? Maybe three? He needed to work out what to say. No point in turning up at Claire's side then talking about the bloody weather.

'...pat us on the head, right?'

'Right, Poll, right.' For all he knew, Polly was advocating they burn down Parliament. 'You put it well.'

What if he waded in with something about music? What if he told Claire he was taking her advice and starting a real band? What if he invited her to join?

Oh Tom, you clever little bastard…

He made a note to not call himself that. It might end up being closer to the truth than he'd like.

'…just ask yourself *cui bono*? For whose benefit?'

'Yeah.'

'Mind you, it should be public schools, too. Why stop at bringing the working classes together through comprehensive schools? Why not bring the whole country together?'

'Yeah.'

'Chop out the fee-paying schools, the church schools, grammar schools… just have one kind of school so that everyone gets the same education.'

'Yeah.'

Neil drifted into their orbit.

'Anyway, on other matters,' said Tom, more to Neil than Polly, 'Claire was saying I should start a band. A real one. We can still call it Universal Explorer though.'

'Right. Is that a good idea?'

'Political music's the way forward,' said Polly.

'Yeah, possibly,' said Tom, feeling a need to write love songs that would make the girls blow a fuse. He could write the odd political song too. After all, he'd soon be seventeen. It was important to have depth.

He looked over to Steve.

Go to the bloody loo!

Steve smiled back at him.

Bollocks.

But – good news. Tom needed the loo. He'd go straight away and then when he returned he'd be in a perfect position to wait for Steve to go. Judging by the amount of Long Life he was knocking back, it wouldn't be long.

In the gents, Tom was disappointed to find Micky

Sullivan unzipping in preparation. Standing alongside him, Tom let loose.

'Not a bad do,' said Micky.

'No, not bad.'

'Don't know if to ease off the beer so I can slip inside Carol later, or just get hammered.'

'Jackie. You're with Jackie.'

'Yeah, but I'm still seeing Carol on the side.'

Tom's mind was too boggled to comprehend what hellish arrangement Micky had plunged into, but it sounded horrible. He finished his business and gave his hands a quick flick under the cold tap, leaving Micky to no doubt continue pissing for another three or four minutes.

Outside, with The Atom Heart Mothers playing The Eagles' "Take it to the Limit", Barry Cohen passed Tom on the way to the gents.

'Neil says you're starting your band again.'

'Bloody Neil. Mouth the size of Blackwall Tunnel. Yeah – a bit late for tonight though.'

Tom resumed his place with Polly and willed Steve to go to the bloody loo.

But Steve kept drinking and talking to Claire.

The Atom Heart Mothers' set was short. The support band always did half an hour. The main band – Westferry – would do an hour. Amid the applause, Danny took to the stage and the mic.

'Let's hear it again for The Atom Heart Mothers!' He paused for the cheer. 'Okay, Westferry will be on in about forty-five minutes. We had been expecting the greatest band in Millwall to play tonight – Tom Alder and Neil Sullivan's Universal Explosion, but they're lost in space somewhere.'

Laughter went up, but not from Tom, who couldn't

understand why Danny had to poke fun at him.

'Okay,' said Danny, 'until Westferry, I leave you in the capable hands of our esteemed DJ – Poplar's answer to John Peel – Mr Terry Farmer!'

A cheer went up, Billy Ocean's "Love Really Hurts Without You" came on strong and people started dancing.

Danny came over to Tom.

'Sorry – couldn't resist.'

'Yeah, well, I will get a band up and running.'

'Sure you will.'

As Danny wandered off, Polly latched onto Tom again.

'Did I mention I'm joining the Young Socialists?'

'Directly in the pay of Moscow, eh?'

'There's no pay and we come under the Labour Party.'

'Same thing according to Nat Hiscock.'

'Yeah, well, I've been thinking about it for some time. I just wanted to get the exams out of the way first. I reckon this lot needs waking up. I mean it's time there was a fight back. I mean take the docks. Hundred and fifty years they've been open.'

'Hundred and seventy-four,' said Neil. 'Well, 174 since the West India opened, 128 the Millwall.'

'That's not actually the point…'

Steve was still drinking like a whale. He'd have to visit the toilet soon though. Then Tom would move in on Claire.

'It's a world in flux, Tom. We need to stake a claim for ordinary people before it's too late.'

'Come the Revolution, sort of thing?'

'Well, that's a sixties thing, but look at the problems we've got with Ireland. We can't trust politics in its present form to deal with that.'

'Can't we?'

'And take the National Front. They applaud the murder of Asians and get 15,000 votes in Leicester.'

'That many?'

'It's the papers that stir it up.'

Tom couldn't believe it. Steve was opening another beer. Had he paid in more than Tom? The idea was moderation, not drink as many as you can until you're pissed at everyone else's expense.

'Take *The Sun*. They reported "3,000 Asians Flood Britain" and twenty-four hours later that newsagents in East Ham gets daubed with racist graffiti. It's hardly a coincidence.'

Hollow legs. That's what Tom's grandad called it. A man who drinks without ever going to the khazi.

'...and shops stoned and set on fire in Southall.'

He had to go soon though. Otherwise he'd start to resemble a beach ball.

'... two Asian students stabbed to death in South Woodford... and that kid outside that cinema in West London. What did that Nazi bloke say? "One down, one million to go." I mean, seriously, the time has come to act.'

'Right, Poll.'

'I mean... have you ever, you know... thought of joining?'

'Eh?'

'The Young Socialists?'

'Er...' Tom wanted to see social justice too, but couldn't a guy do well for himself and buy a nice car without being called a class traitor? Did that make him a liberal? Or a conservative? He had absolutely no idea.

'Not sure at this stage, Poll, but good luck.'

Danny was dancing with three girls. It was clear that

they were each trying to dance themselves into his gaze. Neil Sullivan had started dancing too, just behind Danny, possibly hoping to claim a rejectee. However, with no control over his body, he was doomed to failure.

'I might have a dance,' said Tom.

Polly humphed. He wouldn't be dancing.

To the strains of Candi Staton's "Young Hearts Run Free", Tom started dancing on the edge of the group, but somehow contrived to manoeuvre himself between Barry and Sangheeta.

'I don't have any updates on my time in Uganda,' said Sangheeta. 'If you'd like to ask me about any other aspects of my life, feel free.'

Tom smiled and tried to think of something intelligent and interesting. He couldn't.

'I didn't know you liked disco,' said Barry.

'I don't,' said Tom.

'Maybe your band will play next year's dance,' said Sangheeta.

Tom smiled and walk-danced his way to Neil.

'Neil, you ought to get a job with the BBC.'

'Why?'

'Because you're already a bigger broadcaster than them.'

Three dances later, Tom needed the gents again. He looked over to Steve, drinking and chatting with Claire. Donna Summer's "Love To Love You, Baby" filled the air and Tom thought back to buying it in cold February, closing his eyes and pretending he was with Claire. Now it was hot July and he wanted more than ever to be with her. Claire, not Donna Summer.

As he reached the gents, someone raced up behind him and clapped him on the shoulder.

'Alright, Tim?' said Steve.

'It's Tom.'

Lining up together put Tom off. He simply couldn't go. He was sure this is how it was in the jungles of Africa, with lower primates giving way to their leaders. Worse still, Steve had half a brewery in his bladder waiting to hit the urinal.

'Claire's quite a girl,' he said.

'Yeah,' said Tom, trying to eke out his wee in order to not look inferior.

'Quite a girl,' Steve repeated as gallons flowed like the Thames into the sea.

'Yeah.'

'I'm almost in there, mate. Hope it's been worth the wait.'

Tom despised him. How could Claire get involved with dross like this? Why couldn't she see that someone like himself was her ideal man?

'She's only sixteen,' he said, pointedly. 'She might decide to wait till she's twenty. Engaged. Married, even.'

Steve, still pissing like an elephant, laughed. 'Nah, her resistance is almost gone. Give it a couple more weeks and I'll be well in place to bang it one.'

It? This was Claire Cross, the love of his... Well, this was Claire Cross and she was no "it".

'One thing I'll say about Claire,' said Tom, desperately trying to think of the words that would crap all over Steve's sordid plans, 'is she... well... you know.'

'Know what?'

Tom left. And hoped. And even prayed.

Claire was talking with Neil.

What would Tom open with? Cello? Prog rock? Politics? Steve and his sordid plan?

'Get us a beer, Neil.'

'Blimey,' protested Neil, before going off.

'Did I ever mention how much I hate working for Nat Hiscock?'

'No,' said Claire.

'I know I've only done a week, but I already know it's not for me.'

'You've been telling everyone it's great.'

'Yeah, well, it's not. He's a nightmare.'

'Get another job then.'

'I would but... well... I might have left school too early. I might have, you know, made a mistake in leaving.'

'Come back then.'

'I can't. Can I?'

Steve returned from the gents.

'I got the beers,' said the returning Neil.

'Cheers,' said Steve, taking the one meant for Tom.

'I'll get another one,' said Neil.

'Look, you're starting a band,' said Claire. 'How do you fancy starting lessons again? I mean you're probably a lot better than last time we practised together, but...'

'I'd love to, Claire.' God, he'd be back in her life, and back in her bedroom overlooking the river. He'd be able to conduct himself in a way that would make Steve look a wrong 'un. 'Claire, let's do it. Let's concentrate on music. Let's put aside the baser stuff of life.' He eyed Steve when he said it, but Steve was too busy drinking his beer to notice.

Westferry were good. Much better than in '75. They were tighter and had a funkier sound. Tom wished he could play like that.

Once the applause had died down, Danny got up on stage and took to the microphone.

'Another round of applause for Westferry!' Everyone

responded enthusiastically. 'Okay, good news. The committee has decided that, due to the success of the summer dances, this year we're going to have a Docklands Christmas Dance!'

A drunken roar went up.

'Who knows, perhaps we'll be dancing once again to Westferry! Better start learning those Christmas hits, fellas!'

Tom wondered… nah, stupid idea.

Neil nudged him. 'Hey Tom, we could play that! We could open for Westferry!'

'Neil, you're drunk.'

'Neil's right,' said Claire. 'There's your opportunity – go for it.'

Neil smiled, looking pleased with himself. Then he keeled over.

'What happened there?' said Steve.

'Well,' said Tom, 'after eight refreshing pints, he passed out.'

While Tom helped Neil to a quiet spot just outside the main room, Danny came out.

'Is he okay?'

'He'll live.'

Tom suddenly got a bee in his bonnet.

'Can we go outside?' he asked.

Tom propped Neil sitting against the wall and went out into the garden. Danny followed.

'Well?'

'Micky told me something. Last October, to be exact, and I was going to ask you about it a hundred times…'

'I know what you're going to say and I'd advise you to forget it.'

'Were we both adopted?'

'Okay, first of all, try to understand that I've been

protecting you.'

'You what?'

'It's okay. You're old enough to know what I know.'

'But I'm older than you. Seven months older.'

'Yeah, listen, we weren't both adopted, okay.'

'We weren't? Right. Phew.'

'Only one of us was adopted, Tom, and it wasn't me.'

'Wha…?' Tom caught his breath. Any remaining uncertainty had just taken flight like a flock of birds reacting to a gunshot.

'I was as good as adopted for seven years but it was actually long-term foster care.'

'But… but… how long have you known?'

'About me? Ever since my mum dragged me away. You though, I've only known a year or so. Micky heard his mum and your dad talking. I don't think he got all the facts but he's not wrong.'

Tom felt terrible. Not just this confirmation but the fact that Ted was still close enough to Elsie Sullivan to discuss stuff like that.

'For what it's worth,' said Danny. 'My mum didn't appear out of the blue, she appeared out of St Clements.'

'Oh…' So Danny's mum had been in a mental hospital up at Mile End. Not information anyone would share easily. 'I didn't know.'

'And now you do.'

'You don't think I was a foster-care case too?'

'Ted said you were adopted. If it helps you to see that as foster-care then go with it.'

Tom sighed and wondered about his real mum, miles away somewhere, a ghost to him. Or was she local? Had he seen her? A face on a passing bus or in the market.

'Do we know who my mum is?'

'No, we don't, Tom.'

'Who's our dad then?'

'You think we have the same dad?'

'I don't know. Have we? I mean if we have then we'd still be...'

'Brothers?'

'Ted's brother, Harry, played guitar.'

'What are you on about?'

'My grandad mentioned him. More to the point, he slipped up. As if he didn't mean to say it.'

'Say what?'

'Something doesn't add up. I had this feeling he was talking about my dad. And the way he brushed it away. I mean we're both handed to Rose and there's this bloke, Ted's brother, gone to West London under a cloud... Do you think that's why we both took up the guitar? Harry Alder?'

'It's a musical instrument, Tom. That's all. Look, I was with Ted and Rose while Mum was ill. It was foster-care. That's all I know. And frankly, that's all I want to know. My dad is as good as dead. If you want to find out who your real parents are, ask Ted and Rose.'

'I can't just ask them. *Oh, by the way, who are my real parents?*'

'Then don't. Seriously. And don't ask me again either.'

He watched Danny go back inside. Then he followed, to check on Neil.

It was midnight and Tom's back was beginning to ache. He'd been leaning against the railings in Island Gardens, overlooking the Thames and the Old Royal Naval College in Greenwich on the opposite bank for an hour or so.

What would be his ideal moment, he wondered. What set of circumstances would have to exist for him to be content? Well, standing in Island Gardens on a hot summer night was a good start. The view of Greenwich was frankly second to none. So far, so good. Having Claire Cross at his side. Playing the guitar in a band. Not working for Nat Hiscock. That would be a major improvement. Finding out the truth about his real parents?

He decided he would talk to Rose. Not tonight, not tomorrow, maybe not next week – but at some point. It was childish not to know. He would go to Rose and insist on hearing the truth, however bad. Then, if it was relevant to Danny, he'd share it with him.

He would also accept that Claire had a boyfriend, and that Slippery Steve would work his oily charm on her over the next couple of weeks before sliding his manhood into her. It sickened him, but he would accept it. It wasn't like Steve was a Satanic High Priest corrupting an innocent girl. If Claire removed her underwear it would be because she wanted to, not because Steve told her to.

He then decided Universal Explorer would play the Christmas Dance. Only with a new name.

The Thames swirled below him, its waters black and mysterious. He sometimes thought of hiring a boat and sailing past Southend to the sea, then turning south and west through the Channel to the Atlantic and letting the wind take him where it wanted.

Then he changed his mind about Slippery Steve. He would fight that arse-wipe all the way to Claire's undercarriage. Steve would not gain access. No sirree! He would find a defender standing at the gates of her womanhood, deflecting and blocking his every slippery move.

In fact, Tom felt sure he could do a fair impersonation of Steve's stupid voice. And didn't Claire's nosy mum always answer the phone first? *Hi, it's Steve. Thanks for agreeing to take your knickers off. That is you, Claire?*

Yes, that would set the oily toe-rag back a few months.

19. THIRD THOUGHTS

The long hot summer, much like the Bee Gees' "You Should Be Dancing", had looked set to last forever, but was now just a sweat-stained memory. It was a late September morning and Tom had been working for Nat Hiscock for almost three months. Having tackled three windows, a patio, two front doors, erected a shed, re-wired two houses, plumbed another, fitted a kitchen, attempted to fix a gas boiler, laid four carpets and set up a tank of tropical fish, he was now stripping a room in Nat's daughter's flat in Thermopylae Gate in readiness for decorating.

'This is the stuff,' said Nat, back from the builder's merchant with a couple of tins of cream emulsion. 'Lighten those walls up a treat.'

'Natalie wants the radiator painted red.'

'What? Where is she?'

'She's out. Had a hairdresser's appointment.'

'Ah fair enough. Classy girl, my Natalie.'

Tom kept his mouth shut.

'Talented too,' said Nat, taking out a pack of Senior Service.

'Could you give me a hand with the stripping, Nat? Chris said he'd help but that was half an hour ago.'

'Chris is grouting the bathroom and you should count yourself lucky. When they close the docks, I'll have me pick of workers.'

'Poor sods,' muttered Tom, possibly too loudly.

Nat lit a cigarette, sucked in and blew out a stream of smoke.

'This place'll become a desert. Thousands of acres of empty jetties and wharves.'

'Yeah...' Tom used a wet sponge and stripping knife to attack a stubborn patch of wallpaper that seemed to date back to the previous century.

'It ain't right, son. All those men working on all those ships. All thought they had a future.'

'You couldn't start on that other wall, could you, Nat?'

'I'll just see about a cup of tea.'

Nat slipped out. Tom stopped, fed up. Then he had a strange moment where something clicked in his head.

'I have to pop out, Nat,' he called to the kitchen.

'What for?'

'I won't be long.'

Tom went home, changed into some smarter clothes and headed for the bus stop.

Ten minutes later, aboard a bus heading north along Manchester Road, he felt nervous. Luckily, someone had left a local paper on the seat. It would help take his mind off the future.

CAN THE DOCKS BE SAVED?

The Surrey, East India, London and St Katherine's Docks have already closed. The West India, Millwall and Royal Docks are under threat. With container ships docking at Tilbury twenty miles downriver, the authorities appear to have no plans for the local workforce. The Government and Port of London Authority should not contemplate a complete closedown until...

He couldn't concentrate enough to read so he switched to thoughts of the band. He was seeing Neil later. They were learning some Thin Lizzy stuff. Difficult but fun. And they would – with a bit of luck – be performing it at the Docklands Christmas Dance. Okay, a lot of luck. And they still needed a drummer and bass player.

Crossing the Blue Bridge, he looked out over the Thames. Life was a bit like a river, he supposed.

Passing Claire's street on the right, he smiled. He even saw Archie the cat on the pavement and took it as a good omen. Yes, he was doing the right thing.

Entering school, he went straight to the office.

'Yes?' said the receptionist whose name he had never known.

'I've come to see Mr Grimshaw.'

'Mr Grimshaw's at the new school.'

'Oh. Who's in charge then?'

'Mr Reid.'

'Oh.' The last time Mr Reid had spoken to him was back in June. He was an acting deputy head and had seen fit to call Tom a gnome.

'He's teaching right now. I could fit you in at break?'

Tom thanked her and went off to see if any of his mates were in the lower sixth-form room. It was strange, making his way there. It was like a ghost school, with most of the rooms empty.

As it was, he found a dozen sixth-formers reading and chatting. A few of them were strangers – former Broadlands pupils. Among the others, none were his close mates but they exchanged hellos. It was odd too. Sixth-formers had always worn school uniform. This lot looked ready for a trip to the pub.

He kept the purpose of his visit to himself, citing something about seeing someone about something.

There was a *Devil's Advocate* open on the table.

EDITORIAL TEAM
MR G. T. GARNER, Executive Editor
Margaret SLATER, UppVI, Editor
Daniel COLLINS, LowVI, Asst. Ed.
David POLLARD, LowVI
Claire CROSS, LowVI

Margaret Slater. Excellent. Danny hated her. And, if he recalled correctly, she hated him.

Polly came in simmering about something.

'Garner's backing out,' he said. He spotted Tom. 'Hello, stranger.'

'What's poor old Garner done now?'

'You know the Clapton rant?'

'Er...' Tom didn't.

'Eric Clapton. Birmingham Odeon. Going on about Enoch Powell being right?'

'Yeah, now you mention it.'

'We've been trying to cover it in *Devil's Advocate*.'

'And Garner won't have it?'

'He objects to the political aspects. I mean, seriously, it's not a poxy concert review!'

'Right.' Tom recalled something about Eric Clapton going on about Britain becoming a black colony and how we should keep Britain white. By all accounts, he was pissed.

'We're thinking of backing the Rock Against Racism thing. Did you see it in the *NME*?'

'Er...?'

'Some guy called Red Saunders wrote to the *NME*.

Anyway, he's calling on us to back a new movement.'

'Right.'

'As he says – "who shot the sheriff, Eric? It sure as hell wasn't you."'

'Bob Marley song?'

'They're calling Clapton rock music's biggest colonist. Seriously, where would he be without the blues and R&B? You fancy joining?'

'Me?'

'Yeah. I mean it's early days and we haven't organised anything yet…'

'Let me get back to you, Poll.'

'Yeah, okay. Actually… why are you here?'

'Hopefully, I'll have an answer to that question quite soon.'

Tom headed off to see Mr Reid.

It felt like a long wait outside his room, although it was no more than ten minutes. Then the door opened and he was beckoned within.

'Mr Alder, having Her Majesty the Queen pop in would have been more of a thrill, but no less surprising. How may I help you?'

'I'd like to come back, Mr Reid.'

Reid eyed him more attentively. 'Would you now? Would you indeed?'

'Yes, sir. I've made a mistake.'

'You are aware that, academically, I consider you a lost cause.'

'I know I didn't pull my weight for most of my time here, but I did turn it around in the last six months. I mean I got six O-levels, sir, and I'm prepared to do re-sits if needed.'

'Sixth-form is for dedicated students, not for those who demotivate others by snoozing ninety percent of the time. You might think it clever to remedy your own shortcomings with a late burst of activity, but it is unacceptable to the school. Go home, Mr Alder. And when you get there, telephone me.'

'Go home and phone you?'

'Yes, that way, should you be displeased with what I have to say, you won't be able to throw any punches.'

'Punches? But…'

'Alder, you are a heel-dragger. Personally, I never liked your casual attitude to the first class education offered to you here at All Saints. Now please leave.'

Tom felt like shit. He sloped out disheartened. Annoyed too. And frustrated. He felt bitter towards Reid. The sanctimonious old bastard.

He returned home to change back into his working clothes. There was a flat in Thermopylae Gate waiting to be painted and that cream emulsion would certainly brighten those walls up a treat. Leaving home, he pulled the front door shut behind him. Except the mat had travelled and stopped it closing. He pushed the damned thing open and kicked the bloody mat back into the hall. And he eyed the phone.

The sanctimonious old bastard.

He stood there, motionless. His eyes became moist. It wasn't fair. He was sixteen and he'd screwed everything up. He was going to do so much. Achieve so much. Gain respect. Be acknowledged as someone doing something. He was going to start his own band. Play the Christmas Dance. He was going to have a girlfriend. The bald fact was he had nothing but a job he didn't care about, working for a bloke who didn't care about him. And the acting head at his old school thought he was a piece of dirt.

Well, screw you, Mr Reid.

Tom picked up the phone and dialled directory enquiries.

'All Saints School, Poplar, please.'

A minute later, the line to Poplar was ringing.

'All Saints School. How may I help?' It was the receptionist with no name.

'Mr Reid, please.'

There was a click, then a silence. Then: 'Hello?'

'Mr Reid? It's Tom Alder…'

20. SOMETHING BEGINNING WITH S

The wind carried a hint of rain. Just the odd spit, so that Tom couldn't be sure if he'd soon be in for a soaking or not. He looked up. The clouds were shifting at a fair rate. Coming up from the south-west. The tiniest droplets of water from the Atlantic, coming in high over Cornwall, Devon… Somerset? Then what? Wiltshire or Hampshire? Or both? Then most definitely across West London, Central London, The Tower, The Highway, Commercial Road, the East India Dock Road and into his face.

It was strange getting in early. He used to see it as a small defeat for freedom. Not now. He was too full of relief to see it as anything other than a bloody good result.

He thought back to the phone call.

'I just want you to know—'

'Ah, Alder – decided to show a bit of spine, eh? Good man. Come and see me on Monday morning and we'll work out what to do with you.'

'You mean…?'

'It's a second chance, Alder. Grab it with both hands and hang on like merry hell.'

'Yes, Mr Reid, I will.' He wanted to express his thanks but Reid hung up.

'Ha!' is all he could say. ''Ha!'

He'd raced round to see Nat and could still see his former boss rocking back on his heels, feigning shock. 'You're giving me the elbow? After all I've done for you?'

Today wasn't just Monday the twenty-seventh of September. It was the start – or restart – of his life. And it felt bloody great. He'd see the secretary, learn her name and sort out which three A-levels he'd be taking. Based on his O-level results, English Language, English Lit and History seemed favourite, assuming no timetable clashes. His soul felt more in tune with Music, French and History, but one out of three matches with Claire Cross wasn't bad. The main thing would be going into a lesson and sitting down and opening his text book and reading the first few words and thinking of Nat Hiscock as a dream. Well, a recurring sodding nightmare but…

Megan Vanderlin. By the school entrance. She waved.

'How are you?' she called.

'I'm fine. Head Girl, I hear.'

'You're doing the right thing,' she said as he neared. 'Work hard.' She sounded like a teacher.

'I will.'

Inside the main entrance, he watched her go off. Such certainty. He'd heard she was no longer going out with Tony Cornish, the son of a scrap metal dealer who left in the summer. Apparently, they had been quite a team for a while. There had even been rumours of sex in the gym, although there were always rumours of sex in the gym. By all accounts, Tony was now going out with the daughter of another scrap yard owner. Maybe they'd form a conglomerate.

Of course, his own income had vanished and resuming his mum's Freeman's round wouldn't make up the shortfall. Still, that was a sacrifice he was willing to make. The best thing was knowing he'd squirreled away enough cash to buy an electric guitar.

The school office was empty so he headed for the lower sixth-form room. Claire was loitering by the door with Polly. She seemed genuinely pleased to see him.

'Learnt any good chords lately?'

This was a new start. Having thought he would practice with her back in July, his prolonged loyalty to Nat and hatred of Steve, along with Claire's busy social life, had seen their intended joint sessions amount to a single bout of ninety minutes, in which it became clear he hadn't practised much during the previous nine months.

'See that about Rhodesia,' said Polly. 'White rule to end. It's progress, Tom. The world's starting to move in the right direction. We just need to keep applying the pressure.'

We?

'Yeah, good news, Poll. As you say, things are moving in the right direction.'

Inside, Danny was doing a crossword. He barely looked up.

'Alright, Dan?' said Tom, taking a seat.

'Something beginning with S,' said Danny. 'Simpleton? No, too long. Sap? Nope – too short.'

'Sensible?' said Tom. But he didn't want a fight. He wanted to fit in. 'How's Framework going?' he asked, referring to Danny's band.

'Framework is no more,' said Danny, sounding like John Cleese. 'It is an ex-band.'

'Oh. Why?'

'Not good enough.'

'Yeah, but with practise…'

'With practise, I would've become good, not inspirational or amazing. Seriously, never waste time doing something that only offers a chance to be average.'

'So, that's it? You just walked away?'

'Time to set my sights on Modern History at Oxford.'

Tom could see the ambition in his eyes. Nothing was

going to stop Danny.

Tom's first lesson was English Lit. They were a couple of weeks into *Coriolanus*. Within ten minutes, he knew he would never love the play, but it didn't matter. He would study it and understand it enough to tackle the A-level exam paper. School life, he felt, was ultimately far simpler than he'd previously believed. Why struggle with Shakespeare? When they did *Macbeth* for O-level, he struggled because he never read it cover to cover. That simple act – of reading the bloody thing – could have saved him two years of moaning and groaning about it. So, *Coriolanus* would be read with academic gusto. Not with love or passion, but to make life simple.

That said, it did seem a bloody long play.

Afterwards, during the mid-morning break, he sought out Claire. Unfortunately she was with Polly and half a dozen others. It was hard swinging the conversation around to playing in a band, especially with Claire seemingly more interested in politics than usual. He blamed Polly, who was on a mission to force innocent people into grasping political fundamentals, whether they wanted to or not. Although, in Claire's case, it seemed she wanted to.

He did manage to get her alone for a few minutes though. A few precious minutes to lay out his vision for their future.

'So… how's Steve?'

'We're still together, but…'

But? Hooray for "but"!

'So, Steve isn't quite…?'

'We were going at different speeds. Thanks for phoning my mum, by the way.'

Tom blanched. His heart raced. He reached for the nearest lie.

'Phone? I don't…'

'We're going at the same speed now – my speed.'

'I hope it works out for you,' said Tom, hoping that Steve would fall in the Thames and be swept out to sea. 'Speaking as friends, though, how about getting together for guitar? I'm definitely putting a band together for the Christmas Dance.'

'As long as you're serious. I mean it's only two and a half months away.'

'I mean what I say. Guaranteed. I've even saved enough for an electric guitar.'

'Right, I'm going to take you at your word, Tom Alder. I'm going to teach you to be a better guitarist who plays in a band that will perform at the Christmas Dance. If you back out of any of that I'll bash you over the head with my cello.'

After school, Tom had Claire Cross in mind, but it was Sangheeta Sharma who joined him at the bus stop.

'Going to the Island?' he asked.

'Yeah, a friend's in Saundersness Road.'

A group of boys came running across the road. At first, Tom thought they were hurrying for a bus, but there was no bus. One of them punched him in the side of the head. As he turned away, he glimpsed two of them kicking Sangheeta to the ground. Tom lashed out blindly, in anger and confusion. Nothing made sense and then they were quickly gone, running away, their voices leaving a trail of racist expletives. "Fucking Paki-lover" stood out.

He helped Sangheeta up, but she pushed him away and dusted herself down.

'Are you okay?' he asked.

'Do I look okay?' she said, moving from anger to tears within those four words.

'All part of the fun of living round here, I suppose,' he said. He wanted to put an arm round her but decided not to.

Sangheeta reeled the tears in.

'This is my home,' she said.

'Exactly right.'

'I'm not going anywhere.'

'Why should you? Everyone round here's family came from somewhere else originally.'

A silence fell on them. But Tom didn't want any silence making things worse.

'I mean two hundred years ago there was sod all here,' he said. 'Even the oldest Islanders have their roots elsewhere. The North of England, Wales, Scotland, Ireland, Holland, the West Indies, China, India... and you go over to Bethnal Green and the so-called originals are French Huguenots, Russian Jews, Irish Catholics... I mean having the daughter of a Ugandan millionaire is a step up for the area.'

Sangheeta allowed herself a smile.

'I might have exaggerated that bit.'

'Well, why not.'

'Dad owned part of a shoe business though, so we were never short of money... or shoes.'

Tom smiled. Up ahead, a 277 came into view.

They were soon aboard, downstairs, up the front.

'I was twelve. We were in Mbale, not far from where they grow coffee on the mountain slopes. I remember the African and Asian boys playing cricket. And I remember crowding around a newspaper. Amin had given all Asians ninety days to leave the country. He called us parasites.

We thought it was just another of his mad moments but we lost the lot, Tom. I don't even have any photos of me as a kid.'

'You don't have to talk about it.'

'We would've gone to India but we didn't have Indian passports. Luckily, because Britain used to own half the world, we had British passports. When we drove to Kampala...' Sangheeta's jaw tightened, 'we were stopped at every checkpoint. They just threw our stuff around, nicking...' She trailed off.

'Tough time,' said Tom.

'At one checkpoint, a guard took my suitcase.'

'Seriously, Sangheeta, you don't have to...'

'It had all my clothes in it. Everything. Dad tried to stop him, but three of them attacked him. I've never been as scared as at that moment.'

Tom sighed. Why couldn't people just get on with life? Why did someone have to cop the blame?

'We kept thinking we weren't going to make it. We kept thinking we would be killed. I can't tell you how amazing it was when we made it to the airport. Then they put us on a British Caledonian flight to Stansted and when that plane took off we went nuts. It was like a party. We were so happy to be together even though our whole lives fitted into a carrier bag.'

They passed Claire's turning then reached the Blue Bridge. To their left, an anchored ship waited on the river for high tide in order to enter the West India Docks.

'We were taken to a camp in Devon. Bed at six because there was no heating. It felt like another planet. The Women's Voluntary Service were good though... made us feel really welcome... in their green uniforms, handing out blankets and cups of tea. Gave us a sense of dignity. And a meal with potatoes, carrots and braised beef.' Sangheeta chuckled. 'I couldn't believe they just dropped the potatoes and carrots into hot water and called it cooking! I refused to eat it but dad made us. Hindus can't eat beef but he said we're in England now – eat up!'

Tom wanted to hug her. 'So how come you ended up on the Island?'

'Dad had a friend in London, so we ended up in Tower Hamlets.'

'Well, I'm glad you came,' said Tom. 'Just thought I'd mention it – you know, a sort of belated welcome.'

Sangheeta smiled. 'Dad was funny. He dragged us around every London landmark. We had to make this our town. We had to fit in. We could hardly keep up with him! The Tower of London, the Science Museum, the Changing of the Guard, Speakers' Corner, Madame Tussaud's... I was twelve, I was being sent to a new school, and I was looking out over this lot – factories and docks, grimy chimneys belching smoke, great big cranes unloading ships... I must admit I cried. Silly eh?'

'Not silly,' said Tom.

21. WHAT'S PAST IS PROLOGUE

At home, after tea, Tom sat opposite Rose, who was half watching the television news, half reading *Woman's Own*. Ted was still out, not back from a union meeting. Tom guessed they were in the pub by now.

'I don't suppose it'll solve much,' said Rose. 'They complain about only having two or three days' work a week, but the Board pays them when they're idle. They still get their book stamped.'

'Yeah,' said Tom. He knew the National Dock Labour Board paid the men to hang around if there were no ships to load or unload. He also knew the situation was getting worse year on year. The problem for him, as a young man, was it all felt so stale. The same old thing, over and over.

'There's a lot of history, of course,' said Rose.

'Yeah,' said Tom, wary of running over old ground for the millionth time.

Unexpectedly, it occurred to him that this was an opportunity to discuss their own history. But as soon as he realised it, fear bubbled up. It was like that first time on the high board at the swimming baths. It was a long way down. But now, as on that occasion, he decided he couldn't keep putting off taking the plunge.

'Mum?'

'Hmm?'

'Who are my real parents?'

Rose looked up from her magazine. Dread filled her rapidly draining face. Her hands began to shake. Tom felt guilty.

Even so...

'Is Uncle Harry my dad?'

Rose took an age to gather herself. Even then, her voice was shaky.

'No. Ted's your dad.'

'I mean my real dad. Biologically speaking.'

'Ted is your dad.'

'Yeah? Then why did he tell Elsie Sullivan I was adopted.'

Rose swallowed. 'Did Elsie tell you that?'

'No, she's never said a word. Micky overheard them.'

Rose looked wounded.

'Harry was no good. He liked to put it about. Thought he was bloody Elvis.'

'Is he Danny's dad, too?'

'Ted's got a cheek discussing that with Elsie.'

Tom had no idea if Ted had discussed Danny's dad with Elsie, but Rose appeared to have just confirmed it.

'What about my mum?'

Rose's eyes moistened. 'She was eighteen when she had you. Me and Ted couldn't have children of our own, so... I mean it's hardly *Coronation Street*. Just ordinary people trying to do their best. You have to remember it was different then. No birth control pill, no NHS abortions – you'd go to some local woman in a back room with knitting needles and God-knows-what. Girls died but nobody spoke. It was illegal, see. I mean you're right to ask. You're nearly seventeen. You get a legal right at eighteen, but it's all forms to fill in and long waits. It's only right I save you the bother.'

Rose disappeared into the kitchen to make them a cup

of tea and possibly pull herself together.

Tom stewed, waiting. He thought of Ted groping Elsie. Were all the Alder men afflicted by strong urges? Did it run in this particular family? Having men who were obsessed by you-know-what?

Returning with steaming mugs, Rose detailed briskly how she lost her own chance of having children when she suffered a disastrous miscarriage. Then, a few frustrating years later, Ted's brother Harry reached seventeen and stopped being a boy.

'Quite a talent, Harry was,' she said. 'Like I told you before, he played guitar in a band. Always seemed to have three girlfriends on the go. It all went bad, of course. One of them, the poor girl we took you from, was so desperate to start again, she moved to family in Essex. The whole business with Harry didn't seem so glamourous then.'

'Where in Essex?'

'I don't know. *I didn't want to know.* And we never kept the birth certificate or anything, so I haven't got her name. Thing is, me and Ted had been thinking about adopting so it all fitted together. The only worry was that the authorities might not have allowed it, so Nat Hiscock got us a fake birth certificate for you as that seemed for the best.'

Tom was stunned. It took a moment to gather himself.

'Why wouldn't the authorities allow it?'

Rose looked down. 'I was on medication… for my nerves. Had been since the miscarriage and the operation I had to have after it.'

Tom felt a pang of guilt at asking.

'What about Danny? He said it was foster care.'

'Danny was different. I mean his mum was only sixteen when she had him. Of course, they left the father's name off the birth certificate, but… I mean… well, everyone involved tried to force her to give up the baby, see. Almost went mad, she did, demanding the baby back. I was just acting as a sort of foster-mum, unofficially like. You know, trying to help out.'

Tom felt terrible. In a way he wished he could un-know the whole damn business.

'Didn't the neighbours think it all a bit strange?'

'Too true. We were all living in Wapping, see. By the river, where I grew up. Ted said it was all getting a bit of a fuss and we should move down to where he came from.'

'The Island?'

'Yeah, Ted's family's been on the Island going back generations. I was worried that someone might have asked questions, but it turned out the council had hundreds and hundreds of children in care – more than enough to keep them busy.'

Tom shuddered. What a thought. All those kids in big old children's homes. He'd avoided that, thank God. And Danny had too.

'Danny said his mum was in St Clements.'

'Yes, she was. After she came out and took Danny back, she met some bloke and moved to Bethnal Green. Never kept in touch. The last thing she said to me was she didn't want to be reminded of the past.'

'She came back though.'

'Yeah, broke up with the fella. Got a flat in Poplar. I certainly never thought you two would end up at school together. You took long enough to tell me.'

'I didn't know what to say.'

'No, well, it was a surprise when I bumped into his mum up the market and she said Danny had seen you at school. I suppose I was thinking you hadn't recognised him.'

'Oh, I recognised him. But what about Harry? What do you know about him? Nowadays, I mean.'

'Not much. There's no contact or anything.'

'Did he settle down?'

Rose hesitated. 'I think he did, yeah.'

'Did he have any kids?'

Rose clearly didn't want to answer. 'I'm not too sure, Tom. Ted phoned him once, back in the sixties. There was talk of a daughter.'

Tom was stunned.

'I have a sister?'

Rose fought back tears. 'A half-sister. Lynn. Must be thirteen by now. I'm sorry I never told you. Ted wanted to. He's always wanted you to know the truth but I was scared you might choose Harry over us. Silly, I know.'

Tom felt a rising anger, but he tried to stay above it, like a not-very-good surfer on one of those monster waves at the start of *Hawaii-Five-O*.

'I'd love to meet her,' he said. It would be amazing. Life-changing, even.

'You can't,' said Rose. 'They don't want anything to do with you.'

Tom felt a black hole opening up to swallow him.

'But… how can they think that? They don't know me.'

Later, in bed, unable to sleep, Tom stared at the ceiling. Lynn wasn't fully formed. What did she look like?

It bothered him. To have a sister… *a sister!* … and for her family to reject him. It hurt. If they met him they would find someone warm and willing to embrace them. Lynn would meet a brother who was a serious student, a musician, a passionate young man on the brink of a meaningful life. How could they reject all that?

He smiled. His little sister. He'd be able to put her on the right track regarding life. Well, once he'd worked out his own life first.

He wondered how he might yet get an address or a phone number. What if Rose had the details written down somewhere? Or Grandad?

But no – not if this other family didn't want to know him. To push himself at them would be truly horrible.

The following morning was all about doing things the right way. He got up early, caught an early bus and smiled at the Blenheim on the river, waiting for the Blue Bridge to rise and let her into the docks. He arrived at school early, chit-chatted with friends and made plans for the day. Then he saw Danny.

After a lifetime of never feeling his equal, he had news that would shake his now confirmed half-brother's world. Annoyingly, Danny was pre-occupied with a different disaster – the termination of *Devil's Advocate*. Having a magazine run from All Saints when eighty-five percent of the readership was at Blackwall had been deemed unworkable.

'I spoke to Rose,' said Tom.

'Oh?'

'Harry *is* our dad.'

'I see.'

'And we have a sister.'

'What?'

'A half-sister called Lynn. Her family don't want to know us though.'

'Then why have you told me, you stupid, immature, fucking little baby.'

22. GUITAR BOY

It was the Saturday after Tom's seventeenth birthday. After all the fuss he'd made over his sixteenth, this one, on the Monday, had been low-key. He'd listened to a couple of Mike Oldfield albums with Neil while they shared a few tins of Heineken, and you couldn't get any lower-key than that.

He was pretty excited now though – he was on a Central Line train heading west. He wasn't exactly sure where. He was using a sixth sense in the hope that the right stop would reveal itself to him. He was now at Lancaster Gate and so far nothing had flared up in his inner mind, soul or third eye. By Holland Park he was getting bored. At Shepherd's Bush he got off.

He was disappointed. Shepherd's Bush was a dull place.

He yawned. He'd been awake since six thinking about this. Now, four hours later, he wished he'd stayed in bed.

But no – he was on a mission. Okay, so it was a long shot, but what the hell. He eyed a girl. She looked about fifteen. Too old.

Then he saw a bloke.

It was completely and utterly ridiculous, of course. Insane, no less.

Even so…

'Any idea where the BBC is?' he asked the man, knowing that the BBC was somewhere in this neck of the woods.

'White City or Lime Grove?' said the potential Harry in a thick Scottish accent. Tom didn't expect his real dad had turned into a Scot.

'Don't worry,' he said, turning away.

He wandered over to the taxi rank.

'Yes, guv?'

'Have you seen anyone who looks a bit like me?'

The cabbie frowned.

'Like you…?'

'Yeah, a bloke in his thirties. Maybe the eyes? If you look at my eyes?'

'Are you trying to hypnotise me to get a free ride?'

'Or it could be a girl of thirteen who looks a bit like me.'

'Piss off, mate. I'm trying to earn a living!'

The other cabbies wandered over in support, so Tom walked off. Nearby were two girls. Thirteen or so.

'Excuse me, do you know Lynn Alder?'

They shook their heads.

'Or a bloke called Harry?'

They looked uncomfortable.

'It's okay, I'm not a weirdo. This Harry and Lynn. They're my family.'

The girls moved smartly off. Towards a police officer.

Tom turned and headed the other way. He soon found himself in Uxbridge Road where he tried a newsagent's.

'Hello, I'm looking for a man named Harry Alder. Has a daughter of thirteen called Lynn. Might look a bit like me.'

The newsagent shrugged.

Tom sighed and travelled three miles down the seemingly never-ending road, looking into hundreds of faces. Then he crossed over and headed back to

Shepherd's Bush accepting that a) West London was a big place and b) he was an idiot.

He got back on the Central Line. He was due to meet Neil and Polly at Tottenham Court Road Station in half an hour. He'd forget this escapade had ever happened. Yes, he could go to Somerset House and look up birth and marriage certificates, yes he could badger Rose or Grandad into giving him Harry and Lynn's details. But, at the end of it all, he couldn't help thinking Danny was right. He had Ted and Rose, a home and prospects. What was the point in disturbing ghosts?

Tom, Neil and Polly were excited looking in a Charing Cross Road shop window. It was the same one Tom and Claire had looked in the year before. Annoyingly, she was at some classical schools thing at the Royal College of Music. She'd suggested he put it off till the following Saturday but she'd already put him off the previous weekend due to some long-standing cobblers with Steve and an exhibition.

'Come on,' said Tom. 'Inside.'

'I've never seen so many guitars,' said Neil in hushed tones, as if he were entering a church.

'Shame I can only afford the one,' said Tom.

'What's that about?' said Neil, spotting the sign that asked patrons to refrain from murdering "Stairway to Heaven".

'It's to protect staff sanity,' said Tom. He wouldn't be troubling them on that account. He didn't know how to play it.

'You do realise you're more solvent than the government,' said Polly, referring to Britain having to be bailed out by the International Monetary Fund.

'Not for long, Poll,' said Tom, eyeing a copy Stratocaster.

First though, he wanted to handle a real one. So he reached for a red Fender.

'Oi! What's your game?' It was a long-haired hippy behind the counter. He was so serious about something he even put his roll-up ciggie down.

'We're just trying them out,' said Tom. It occurred to him now that being there with Claire had a different look to being there with two teenage boys.

'Unless you're buying a Fender, stick to the copies.'

'Righto.'

Tom sheepishly did as instructed and picked out a copy Strat.

'Now you're going electric, you should pick a new name for the band,' said Neil.

'You reckon?'

'Pity all the colours have been used up,' said Polly, seemingly not interested in such matters.

'Pink Floyd, Black Sabbath, Blue Mink...' said Neil. 'What about Sky? Black Sky.'

'No,' said Tom. 'Too depressing.'

'Moon then. Black Moon.'

'Neil, you are obsessed with calling the band Black something. What about Blue Moon?'

'Dark Moon.'

'Half Moon?'

'Half Moon... maybe.'

'It's not the name,' said Polly. 'It's the songs.'

Tom guessed Polly, champion of *The Ragged Trousered Philanthropists*, was about to urge him to write political songs.

'Enoch Powell's saying we should give a million settled immigrants a grand each to piss off out of Britain.

Someone needs to be writing songs of protest about that kind of bollocks. Sod it, I'm going to see if they've got a Bob Dylan songbook.'

Polly wandered off and Tom strummed some chords.

'Sounds tinny,' said Neil.

'Yeah, but with a Marshall fifty-watt amp and four twelve-inch speakers in a cabinet...'

'Is that what you're going for?'

'Er, no, probably just a little combo.'

'Still, it's the start of an important journey,' said Neil.

'Yeah, maybe I should write about it.'

'A rock diary?'

'Yeah! No... not a diary. There's no way I'd write it up every day. A journal though. The key moments. The first recording session...' He thought back to him and Neil in his bedroom with a cassette tape running. 'I mean a *real* recording session, then the recording contract is signed, then it's the first single, then the album and the tour.'

'Yeah, we'll play Hammersmith.'

'Yeah, a journal. Something for the grandkids to read.'

He played E major and A minor a few times and truly wished he could afford a Marshall stack that would pin listeners to the wall.

A tired Tom spent the afternoon overcoming a lack of sleep with the excitement of playing his CSL red and white copy-Stratocaster in his bedroom. It was just a shame his new Columbus combined amp and speaker didn't create the classic rock sound; just a loud ringing noise. He'd need a fuzz box to remedy that.

After an hour or so, it was time to show it off to Claire. She would be at home, possibly thinking about getting ready for her date with Steve. What if he got in there first and they played guitar for a couple of hours?

Tough luck, Steve.

He didn't suppose Claire would be impressed with his amp, so he just took the guitar. Twenty minutes later, as he approached Claire's house, Archie came hurrying along from down by the pub to say hello.

'Look what I've got, Arch. A copy Strat.'

Archie meowed.

'That's right, Archie, it *is* Japanese.'

He knocked on the Cross' door. Claire's twenty-year-old sister, Tracey answered.

'She's not in. They're round Grandad's new place, helping him settle in.'

'Oh.' Tom had been told a few days earlier that Claire's grandad was moving back to the Island from Bow.

'You can wait if you want.'

'Oh. Thanks.'

He would wait all week to see Claire. Archie wasn't so bothered. He sauntered off back towards the pub.

Tracey showed him to an armchair then she flopped onto the sofa. Her breasts almost didn't fit into her green army camouflage vest, and as for her jungle shorts, they had ridden up so high that they were revealing some seriously soft-looking inner thigh. Funny how you could dress for summer in October if you had central heating.

Tom looked around for something else to stare at. Ah, a row of black and white photographs lining the mantelpiece.

'She's a cheeky cow, sometimes,' said Tracey.

'Is she?'

Tom's eyes flicked past her body to the window. It felt stuffy indoors.

'She gets away with it though. Being younger. And

more talented. And more dedicated.'

Tom yawned. In comparison to his own home, the Cross family had so much *stuff*. Books galore, a big colour telly, hi-fi separates, leather three-piece, new carpets. They even had a six-berth caravan at Point Clear. Claire liked to put it about that her dad did armed robberies rather than the more prosaic explanation that both her parents were lecturers at North-East London Polytechnic.

'So,' said Tracey, 'what have you two got planned for tonight then?'

'Nothing. I think Claire's going out with her boyfriend.'

'Oh, so you're trying to break it up. Well, why not. If you want something, go for it. That's my motto.'

'Well…'

'Ever heard of the Hole in the Wall?'

'No.'

'It's a rock music pub near London Bridge. They play all that progressive, heavy crap.'

'Oh.' Maybe he would take Claire sometime.

'I'm only going 'cos a guy I'm shagging is into it.'

Shagging. What a great word.

'Sounds interesting,' said Tom, battling to keep his cool.

'What, the music or the sex?'

'Well…' Jeez, time to be a man of the world. 'Both.'

Annoyingly, he felt his cheeks beginning to burn.

'Cup of tea?'

'Er… thanks.'

Tracey…

She eventually returned without the tea.

'Let me show you something.'

She beckoned him to follow.

In the bedroom she shared with Claire, her underarm

deodorant reached his nostrils. Mixed with a hint of stale sweat, it smelled womanly. His eyes wandered to the poster of Manet's *Bar At The Folies-Bergère*. Then Tracey started snogging him.

Was this it? Was he to lose his L-plates here? If so, would he be able to meet Tracey's standards? Or didn't it matter? As schoolmate Barry Cohen (virgin) once said, you've either been to Cornwall or you haven't. It doesn't matter if you went by helicopter or clapped-out Cortina. Looking at Tracey, he felt he'd soon be able to report that he had indeed been to Cornwall, and that he'd travelled at ninety miles an hour in an E-Type Jag with the roof down.

'Hey, Sleeping Beauty?'

'Uh?' Tom opened his eyes. He was on the sofa, fully-dressed, half-asleep, cuddling his guitar. Tracey was standing in front of him proffering the promised cup of tea.

'I said do you want a biscuit with it?'

'Oh, sorry, must've fallen asleep.'

'Any good dreams?'

'Er... no.'

Claire returned just as he was finishing his tea. She loved the guitar and they were soon up in her room, taking turns to play it. Then Tracey called up that she was going out.

'We're all alone, Claire.'

'Good job there's a sturdy guitar between us then.'

'Nothing but a copy of the best will do, Claire.'

'It's also a good job you're a gentleman who respects that I have a boyfriend.'

'Yeah. Otherwise...' Tom laughed. But the laugh died

young. He wasn't happy.

'What's up, Mr Virgin? Do tell?'

Tom pulled a face. 'Shut up, you loony. Anyway, you're a pathetic virgin too.'

There was a pause in which a great chasm opened up before him.

'Guilty as charged, m'lud,' said Claire. 'Only don't go telling everyone, eh? It's so uncool.'

'Really? I never knew. Remind me – why aren't we in love? I mean what are we waiting for?'

'The Russians to invade? The Beatles to reform? Women to get equal rights?'

'You know what I mean.'

'Well, we're mates, aren't we?'

Tom sighed. 'Yeah… I just sometimes think… you know… that we're…'

'Destined to be lovers?'

'Do you always have to take the piss?'

Claire kissed him on the cheek.

'Another tea?' she asked.

He followed her down to the kitchen wishing he was older.

'Do you reckon I'm really good enough to form a band?'

'Yeah,' said Claire, filling the kettle. 'I've seen those old blokes with the big drum on their back, little cymbals on their ankles, a banjo…'

'A proper band.'

'What, like an actual proper band?'

'Yeah, like an actual proper band.'

Claire plugged the kettle in. 'They said it couldn't be done… but he would show them. He would form an actual proper band.'

'I'm serious. I want to play at the Christmas Dance.'

'Um, haven't we had this conversation a million times before? Yes, form a bloody band, Tom Alder. Form an actual proper band.'

'Would you join it?'

'Me? No. I can help you though. I mean isn't it time you did some auditions, proper rehearsals – you know...' she leaned into his ear and whispered, 'like an actual proper band would?'

Tom brightened at the thought.

'Yeah.'

'Remember though, the Christmas Dance means no Pink Floyd. It's all Showaddywaddy and Abba.'

She started singing and moving to "Dancing Queen".

'No, it's not. We can do Thin Lizzy and stuff.'

'Hey, now you're talking.' Claire played some imaginary guitar chords before switching to getting the tea cups out. 'Shame your beloved Genesis don't write pop songs.'

'Don't be ridiculous, Claire. That will never happen.'

She laughed and started singing the chorus of "I Know What I Like" in his ear. He almost melted.

Then she stopped suddenly. 'Actually, we need to get a move on. Steve's calling round in twenty minutes.'

23. AUDITIONS

Tom ran through the tunnel at Tottenham Court Road tube clutching his new electric guitar. Whoever was chasing him had fallen too far behind to matter now. He was free to start busking again. Where was he though? He climbed a flight of stairs and came to a bright light. He was standing at the back of a stage. A band was out front playing to a big audience.

Surprisingly, Peter Gabriel came to stand beside him. Was this a Genesis gig? It was! But didn't Peter quit the band last year? Yes, but he was now overseeing their progress – and they were lacking "something". He knew Tom couldn't play, but his advice was to sit with Steve Hackett and follow his guitar work. That way, no one would know the truth and Tom's "something" might emerge to save Genesis from oblivion.

Peter pushed him forward. Amazingly, it worked and the fans were having a great time admiring this new guitar god. But then catastrophe struck. Hackett started adding classical bits. Tom was worried he'd be unmasked as a fake. He looked to Tony Banks for support, but, behind his forty-seven keyboards, Tony was laughing. He could play classical too! Ha-ha! To avoid embarrassment, Tom attempted to sing – but Phil Collins beat him to the microphone. Tom tried to shove him off the stage, but Mike Rutherford swung his bass at Tom, who dived aside and… fell out of bed.

Tom got up and dressed in thirty seconds. A quick go on the electric guitar he'd owned for a week, a splash of water on the face and he flew downstairs for a speedy cup of tea and slice of toast. It was Saturday morning, 8.35 a.m., and he was due in a rehearsal studio at ten. Not his or Neil Sullivan's bedroom, but an actual, professional rehearsal studio in Furze Street, Bow.

Okay, so it didn't sound like a glamourous address. Hardly Soho or some converted country house in Buckinghamshire. That said, it had been booked by a contact of Claire's, so it was bound to be okay.

The minicab dropped Tom and Neil off at the address in Furze Street at ten-to-ten. It would have been earlier, but they couldn't find it. Eventually it became apparent that the crumbling Victorian pile just off Devons Road was actually the studio. It wasn't the slick glass-fronted complex Tom had in mind; more something they forgot to clear away after the Nazis bombed it during the War.

Going up to the first floor felt amazing. This was exactly how Pink Floyd and the Rolling Stones would have started their careers. Okay, so there was a sense that heavy metal music should be banned in case the building fell down, but it was still chest-puffingly brilliant to be arriving with a guitar case.

Tom wondered if any great musicians had ever played at Furze Street. A young Jimmy Page, maybe? Some blokes eyed him. He was being assessed. They were wondering who this new guy was. And, until he played his first chord, they had no idea if he was a Clapton or a Crapton.

It occurred to him to not play.

'This is cool,' said Neil, entering their booked room.

'This is the first step,' said Tom, looking around what was in essence a dilapidated windowless whitewashed space. 'I'll write it up in the journal later. Get all our victories down on paper, eh?'

'So, fame here we come.'

'Yeah. Here, you set up my guitar. I want to check on the opposition.'

Tom wandered out to the next studio. As he neared it, the door swung open and he got a blast of pungent smoke and reggae.

A dreadlocked guitarist in a Spurs T-shirt stopped playing and eyed him. 'Yeah?'

'Sounds good,' said Tom.

'Well, come in and listen proper.'

'Oh… er… okay.'

He ventured in. A band of five players kicked off again. They were tight and pumped out a really good tune.

'You like Bob Marley?' said the guitarist over the sound.

'Yeah.' In truth, he'd never heard any Bob Marley. 'What's the song?'

'It's "Concrete Jungle", and ain't that so?'

Tom nodded. 'Yeah.'

He gave it a moment then made his excuses. Back in his own space, Neil was twanging the Strat.

'Tom Adler?'

It was a bloke at the door carrying a long guitar case.

'Alder, yeah. You must be Jerry.'

'Tom and Jerry,' said Neil.

'Shut up, Neil.'

'My mates call me Jez.'

Phew.

'Is Den with you?'

'Yeah, can you give us a hand?'

They all went down to help with the drums.

Within fifteen minutes they were ready to start with the audition. Only, Tom didn't want to call it that as it was more a case of whoever walked in would be better than him. If anything it was him being auditioned by them. He just hoped they would give him a chance.

At least they looked the part – if it was a quick look: Nervous Neil on vocals, Terrified Tom on guitar, Jez on bass and Den on drums.

'So… "The Boys Are Back In Town" then,' said Tom.

There were two false starts and then a third start that was good but took a wrong turn when the vocals kicked in. Finally, at the fourth attempt, they got clean through to the other side of the first chorus.

Tom's exhilaration was tempered by the fact that they were rubbish.

'Let me and Jez have a go,' said Den.

Tom and Neil stood back and let them play.

This time, it was tighter. And Jez singing the vocals not only looked a bit like Lizzy bass player and vocalist Phil Lynott, but he shared Lynott's ability to sing in tune.

Then they invited Neil to sing and it all sounded a lot worse. Then Tom joined in to complete the terrible sound they offered as a unit.

'Not too bad,' said Den. 'I reckon we're all a bit rusty.'

'Yeah,' said Tom. 'It's a new guitar too. A bit different to what I'm used to.'

'Let's have a look,' said Den, coming off the drums to take the Strat. He bashed out a few chords and a mini solo, and sounded better than Tom by a million miles.

'Not bad, these Jap copies. Solid.'

'Well,' said Tom, 'shall we try it again?'

'Who's the second guitarist?' asked Jez.

'Oh I'm seeing him tomorrow. At the Bridge House.'

'Right. Just us then.'

They played "Boys Are Back" until they were bored, then Tom drew their attention to the second song he'd chosen. Peter Frampton's "Show Me The Way". He'd been rehearsing this one for twice as long.

It was better. Jez even nodded at him halfway through.

They were on their way. Universal Explorer, or Half Moon, or whatever the hell they were going to call themselves, were actually on their way. Now all Tom needed to do was practice till his arms fell off. And possibly find another singer to replace Neil.

The following morning, before opening time in a pub under the A13 flyover in Canning Town, a number of musicians milled around waiting to take to the stage for their auditions. If Terry the guv'nor at the Bridge House liked them, they would be booked for gigs over the coming weeks. It was an exciting place to be, as a few Bridge House bands had already shown signs of making progress in the world of music.

Tom waited by the bar with Neil while the guitarist they had come to see chatted with his mates by the stage. Sitting at the bar by Tom, a guy in a T-shirt and dungarees looked like he'd come to do some decorating. He was enjoying a cup of tea he'd cadged off the landlord. To Tom, seeing people drink tea in a pub looked weird. Like seeing Morris dancing at a Hell's Angels rally.

'Is he playing?' Tom asked the landlord.

'Yeah, once they get everything worked out. How about you?'

'Not today. Spent yesterday in the studio. I'm here to

check up on a guitarist.'

'Right. I hope it works out.'

Tom couldn't help himself. A stream of bullshit was lining itself up and he was powerless to prevent it spurting out.

'What's his band called?'

'Café Racers. What's yours?'

'Universal... Universal. Although we might change it.'

'What about Black Horizon?' said Neil.

Tom ignored him.

'I play a Strat,' said Tom. 'A new one. Good body. Solid. It's got a good tone too.'

'Yeah, a Strat won't let you down.'

'Yeah, I'm kind of exploring new ways to put guitar music on the map. For me it's all about crossing Hendrix with Hackett; Gilmour with ... and standing back to hear the points of, like, accord, and finding something in there. Something new.'

'Oi Knopfler.' It was someone calling to the dungaree guy from the other side of the pub. 'Mark, we're on.'

The dungaree guy got up on stage. Tom noted the really old Gibson Les Paul. Weirdly, it had two cutaways. Beside it, on the chair sat a small amp.

Poor bloke.

Tom was soon watching him play. It was a sort of bluesy style. Terry the landlord seemed to like it. Tom almost wondered if to offer this guy a role in Universal thingy, but no — they were there to hear someone called Roy, who Claire knew from her classical circles. Roy wasn't classical himself but had a younger sister who was.

As it was, when Roy's band took to the stage, he wasn't bad. His big chords sounded good and his solos were okay. Unexpectedly, he sang too. And what's more, he was up for playing in more than one band.

On the bus home, Tom stared out of the window at the run down area around the docks. There was a kind of listlessness in the air. On one side, the long high dock wall hid the waterside inactivity, on the other old buildings slowly crumbled. It felt like a decay that couldn't be halted, so why bother to try. But he wanted to break out of the malaise and do something, anything, to get things going.

Passing Claire's turning, he looked out for her or even Archie but all was quiet. Crossing the Blue Bridge, he spied a Thames sailing barge on the river. Its reddish-brown sails fired up a memory of a conversation he and Neil had a long time ago.

'Red Sails,' he said.

'What?'

'The name of the band. Red Sails.'

'What about Black Sails?'

'*Red* Sails.'

He felt like telling Neil to stop interfering. Of course, that would mean telling his best friend he was no longer required. Although Neil had probably already worked out that Roy was a better singer.

He closed his eyes. The thrumming of the bus engine blended with his thoughts. Music press journalists ushered him into a room. They wanted to know how he was effectively changing the face of music. The secret, he revealed, was a brilliant formula he'd invented. It essentially guaranteed an endless stream of new material, and its name... Every Good Boy Deserves Favour. Everyone applauded. It was a revelation.

'You alright?' said Neil.

'Yes, of course I'm alright.'

'You look a bit down.'

'Of course I'm not a bit down.'

But Neil must have used second sight or something because Tom had the feeling it wasn't only Neil who didn't have enough to offer the world of music. Sooner or later, Tom would also be found out and most likely chucked out of his own band. Maybe he needed a simpler kind of music. A type even *he* could play effectively. But who would listen to that? Who would come to see a band thrashing out simple chords? It didn't seem much of a prospect.

24. DOOPS

With the autumnal weather getting ever colder, Polly suggested they cheer themselves up with some live music. Tom was okay with that, but couldn't understand why they had to go up to the Princess Alice pub in Forest Gate.

'Seems a long way,' he said, disgruntled at having agreed on the understanding that Claire would be going too. How he hated slippery Steve for producing last-minute surprise classical concert tickets. Even Neil had cried off, citing a sprained ankle suffered at the hands of a disobliging door step. Of course, Tom telling him he was no longer needed by Red Sails might have been closer to the truth.

'It's not that far,' said Polly. 'A bus ride to Mile End and one stop on the Central Line.'

'Yeah, and a walk from Stratford.'

'Blimey, it's Columbus discovering the New World all over again.'

Tom didn't like going to Stratford. It reminded him of his ill-fated attempt to become a karate expert at Stratford Kyokushinkai.

As they approached the pub, something seemed odd.

'Looks like they've got bouncers.'

'Yeah,' said Polly.

'I've seen him before. I'm sure he works in Millwall Dock.'

'Yeah, I did hear something about the dockers supporting the event.'

'How do you mean, event?'

'You know I was telling you about the Eric Clapton thing…?'

'Yeah?'

'And the letter to the *NME*?'

'Yeah?'

'And how they got a lot of people writing in wanting to do something about the fascists?'

'Yeah…?'

'This is that thing. Rock Against Racism's inaugural gig.'

'Sounds a bit political.'

'It is, but in a good way. It's people power.'

'I don't think this is such a great idea, Poll. You should have told me.'

'You might not have come.'

'*Might* not?'

'Come on, we'll have a beer and listen to a few songs. If it's crap, we'll get a cab back to the Island. Have a drink in the Waterman's.'

'Yeah, well…'

'Good man.'

It was busy inside. There was a big banner declaring "Black and White Unite". Some band members were setting up and there was a queue at the bar.

While Tom joined those waiting to be served, Polly started talking to two women who Tom didn't like the look of. Not that they weren't attractive, they just looked a bit political and possibly three or four years older than him. That said, Polly was connecting with one of them. Tom could see that. It was different though. Whenever he saw blokes connecting with girls, it was always laughter that did it. The bloke says something, the girl says something, they laugh. He'd seen it dozens of times. This wasn't like that. Here, Polly was saying something that, judging by the intense look on his face, must have been earnest. The girl, judging by the intense look on her face, said something equally earnest back. The next thing – they're both nodding in earnest. No laughter, but a connection nonetheless.

'Tom, could you get Janine and Ann-Marie a drink while you're there? They're both on vodka and orange.'

Great, thought Tom, two expensive drinks for two political types he didn't know.

'Need a hand?' said the girl not connecting with Polly. She had a posh voice. Not like Megan Vanderlin. This was genuine. She also looked deeply attractive in a fluffy grey jumper; a bit like a cuddly kitten.

'Thanks,' said Tom. 'You must be…?'

'Ann-Marie.'

'I'm Tom.'

'I know. David just called you it.'

David? No one called Polly "David". Not even Polly… until now, obviously.

'So what brings you to Forest Gate?' he asked.

'Are you a cockney?'

'Er, yeah.'

'I love cockneys. You're so real.'

'Am I?' Tom pinched his arm to check. 'You're right.'

'I'm from Petit bourgeois-ville. You might know it as Moreton-in-Marsh.'

Tom didn't know it as either.

'We're from the Island,' he said. 'The Isle of Dogs.'

'Cool. We're squatting in Cassland Road.'

Squatting? He'd never met a squatter before.

'Can't you afford the rent?'

She laughed. 'Rent…' And she laughed some more.

'Cassland Road,' mused Tom. 'I think we're linked by the 277.'

Her brow furrowed.

'The bus that goes from the Island to Hackney,' he explained.

'Oh. So… do you think Rock Against Racism can provoke change?'

Tom had absolutely no idea if Rock Against Racism could provoke anything, apart from himself into leaving if their music was no good. But he did think Ann-Marie had a great smile.

'Yeah, I think Rock Against Racism can provoke change,' he said.

'Of course you do. You wouldn't be here otherwise.'

'It won't be easy,' said Tom. 'I mean there'll be hurdles to overcome, people to persuade, the focus to be fine-tuned.'

'I'm glad you get it, Tom. I think some people are just coming for the music.'

'You have to expect that, Ann-Marie.'

'Call me Doops.'

'What?'

'Ann-Marie du Pont. My friends call me Doops.'

'Doops,' he said, preferring Ann-Marie by some considerable distance. 'I like it.'

'Of course, what's needed are more bands,' said Doops. 'Bands with commitment.'

Tom was frustrated. He'd planned to get her all excited with talk of his own band. But now, knowing she'd have him up on the stage singing "We Shall Not Be Moved", he decided to leave that bit out.

'There are loads of bands out there, Doops,' he said. 'The right ones will come forward.'

'I think I fancy you,' said Doops.

Tom steadied himself.

Face, do not flush.

'That's the nicest thing anyone's said to me today. Apart from Polly... David calling me his comrade.'

'Gosh, I can't compete with that,' said Doops.

Tom got the drinks and the four of them moved to a relatively less busy spot. Although even that became crowded as the pub continued to fill up with hundreds of punters.

'This connects me to reality,' said Doops. 'Where I come from it's all so fake. My parents have absolutely no interest in South Africa or Ireland.'

Tom nodded. Nor did his.

'Still,' he said, 'the IRA are a nuisance, aren't they.'

'True, but they have a just cause.'

Tom was taken aback. 'Yeah, but murdering that bloke who ran the Guinness Book of Records. What did he do?'

'He shouldn't have got involved. You start putting up rewards for info and you're in trouble.'

Tom really didn't understand whether Britain should be in or out of Ireland. Despite the steady stream of depressing news reports on the shootings and bombings, it simply felt like none of his business.

'Good atmosphere,' he said, looking around.

The atmosphere was in fact great – smoky and ebullient. Tom liked singer Carol Grimes' gutsy delivery, too. Her version of "A Change Is Gonna Come" really hit the spot. If Rock Against Racism fizzled out in Forest Gate it still would have been worth it – because Doops was a definite possible.

'What are you doing after, Tom?' she asked towards the end of the evening.

'Not sure. Going home, I expect.'

'Why don't you come back to Cassland?'

'Er… alright.'

'Good.'

'See,' said Polly, 'politics and music go together like wotsname.' He was clearly half-cut. Tom not so – he didn't like getting drunk too far from home.

'What we need are more bands,' said Janine – seemingly her first non-political words of the night.

'Tom's in a band,' said Polly.

'Tom?' quizzed Doops. 'Was that going to remain a secret?'

'No, it was just a matter of timing.' Tom didn't want to make too much of the fact that he felt zero commitment to the cause.

'Red Sails!' said Polly. 'Tom's band.'

Doops laughed. 'Of course! What else!'

Tom didn't get it. It was a hybrid between the reddy-brown sails on the Thames barges and the old song, "Red Sails in the Sunset".

'Red Sails…' mused Doops, 'the good ship Socialism voyaging into a bright future somewhere just over the horizon. It's so evocative, Tom. Christ, I want you to fuck me right now.'

Tom gulped. He had no idea where the socialism thing came from but the Dweller in the Pants was well up for breaking its duck with a posh bird from Moreton-in Bourgeois at a squat round the back of Victoria Park.

25. CASSLAND ROAD

As they flagged down a taxi, Doops smiled at Tom in what he assumed to be a *knowing* way. Janine had smiled at Polly in a likewise fashion but Tom's political friend had a sickly look about him.

'Actually, I won't come,' said Polly. 'I think a walk to the station will do me good.'

'Come on,' said Doops, pulling Tom into the cab. Janine called see-ya to Polly as she joined them.

Tom was nervous. How exactly was this going to work?

'Whoa! Hold the door!'

Janine, on the point of closing it, looked out into the night and laughed. A few seconds later, a bloke in his early twenties with a stupid Catweazle beard jumped in with them.

Tom was aghast. Who the hell was this?

'Tom, meet Oz,' said Janine.

Not the Wizard of Oz?

'Hi,' said Oz. Like Janine and Doops, he looked four or five years older than Tom. 'That was a blast, yeah?'

'Yeah,' agreed Doops and Janine.

'Yeah,' Tom echoed weakly.

'Tom's a local,' said Doops. 'Isle of Dogs.'

'Oh wow,' said Oz with what Tom could only construe as reverence.

'Millwall,' said Tom.

It felt weird. He and Doops were supposedly going back to Cassland Road with a strong possibility of doing the deed, except he had a feeling that now they weren't. If anything, the next few hours, he was guessing, would be the four of them talking politics. Except, it wouldn't be a few hours. He'd make his excuses and get to the bus stop in time for the last 277.

'We're in on something big,' said weirdy-beardy Oz. 'I mean it was bound to happen, but it's good to be there at the start.'

'You seen any beatings, Tom?' asked Janine.

'Beatings?'

'NF attacking minorities.'

'Oh. Right. Yeah, I got beat up myself a while back. I was with a friend. She was thrown out of Uganda by Amin, now she's getting it from the NF in Poplar.'

'Your friend's a Ugandan Asian? They had it tough.'

Janine patted Tom's hand, as if he'd achieved something worthwhile in being at the bus stop with Sangheeta Sharma when a bunch of Nazis showed up.

'We've had reports of loads of beatings in the East End,' said Oz. 'Mile End, Stepney, Whitechapel...'

Tom didn't like to hear of people getting kicked around just because of their skin colour, but he always felt it was up to the police to sort it out. Not himself, and certainly not Home Counties types squatting in Hackney.

'Did you know the NF recruits outside football grounds? West Ham, Millwall... You're Millwall, right?'

'No, I'm West Ham. Millwall is where I live.'

'Right, so south of the river.'

'No, Millwall's north. On the Isle of Dogs.'

'Are you sure?'

Tom felt his hackles rise.

'I'm quite sure, Oz. We had a local football team

before the First World War – Millwall – only they moved south of the river to New Cross to get a bigger ground.'

'Oh, right. Unusual.'

'Not really. Arsenal started in Woolwich, not Highbury, and West Ham don't play in West Ham.'

'Yeah, well, football's not my thing,' said Oz. 'What we need are more people like you, Tom. Do you remember that thing on TV – a reporter interviewing an NF recruiter who said he got people outside West Ham, bought them drinks and wound them up about immigration to the point where they smashed up a Pakistani shop. We need people in place to give the other side of the story. To show that violence isn't an answer.'

'Yeah,' said Doops, 'did you see that story about that Indian woman in Leamington Spa? Fascists dragged her from her home and set her alight.'

'Yeah,' said Janine, 'and the newspaper reports about the "4-star Malawi Asians" started plenty of trouble.'

Tom did recall stories of racial tension in other parts over the summer, but he felt he was being ambushed.

'The Race Relations Bill going through the Commons got a lot of coverage,' said Oz. 'Stoked it up nicely.'

'Yeah,' said Doops, 'lots of nice juicy stories about illegal immigrants.'

'Time to fight back,' said Janine.

'Right,' said Oz and Doops.

'I love the way music and politics combine as one,' said Janine. 'That's one way to fight back.'

'Yeah,' said Tom, feeling that, in England, music and politics didn't go together. Well, okay, the Strawbs had sung "Part of the Union", but that was just a novelty record. The Americans had people like Bob Dylan. The times were a-changing there.

'Tom's in a band,' Janine told Oz.

'Red Sails,' Doops added.

'Man, you are just what Rock Against Racism needs. You symbolise us, Tom. A working class activist, growing up among the fascists and standing firm.'

'A local hero,' said Doops.

Tom nodded emptily. 'Yeah...'

For some reason, he'd gone right off the idea of getting naked at Cassland Road.

The squat was a tall Victorian house with neglected rooms lit by bare lightbulbs. Accessed by a broken back door, there was running water and, thanks to someone by-passing the meter, electricity for a few small one-bar heaters. Janine made some undrinkable coffee and the four of them sat on brown corduroy beanbags and deckchairs to put the world straight.

Tom felt a fraud. He didn't know anything about politics. He didn't even care about politics. With that in mind, he decided to give it twenty minutes then leave.

Doops smiled at him.

'Stay the night?'

He gulped. He didn't know what to say. Doops was wrong for him. Why was she bothering?

'Yeah, okay,' he heard himself say. It was as he'd suspected – his hormones would have the biggest say in how the rest of the night unfolded.

'I was talking to a couple of Islington faces at the pub,' said Oz, but, for Tom, his voice trailed off into the background because a dilemma had just arisen. Doops had asked if he wanted to stay the night. What she specifically had not said was did he fancy spending it with her. It dawned on him that the invitation could easily have meant him curling up on a beanbag, alone, in

Cassland bloody Road. Yes, she'd said in the pub that she wanted him to fuck her but now he wondered if that was just posh-speak for "I quite like you."

But how could he address the issue? What if weirdy-beardy Oz burbled on till four a.m.?

As it was, weirdy-beardy Oz burbled on for ten more minutes then made his excuses and went up to bed. Tom was relieved. What would happen next?

'I'm calling it a night, too,' said Janine. And off she went.

This was scary. His fate was approaching fast. His heart and brain wanted to share this moment with Claire Cross but his hormones pointed out, with some glee, that Claire was probably underneath Steve's big chest at this very moment.

'Come on,' said Doops.

She took his hand. His heart raced and there was a definite stirring in his underwear. It was strange because had Claire come along to the pub none of this would have happened. He felt bad though. There was no denying he still thought an awful lot of Claire. And surely Steve's tenure as boyfriend would end soon…

Doops led him upstairs to a small bare room with a mattress on the floor and some clothes in a couple of carrier bags. It was so horrible, even the pants-stirrings ceased. Still, he needed to act in a mature way.

'What music do you like?' he asked.

Doops lay on the mattress and removed her underwear. No ceremony, no chit-chat. Tom didn't know where to look. Well, he did but he didn't like to, in case she didn't like him looking – even though that seemed unlikely.

'I used to like David Essex. Then I grew up.'

Tom's stomach began to feel tight. He also felt a bit

hot. Maybe the one-bar heater was a superior model to those downstairs.

'A few of the girls at school like him,' said Tom. 'They reckon he's got nice eyes.'

'Yeah,' she said, getting under the covers, 'that's true.'

'Some of his early stuff was good. I liked "Rock On" and "Lamplight".'

'Boys take music too seriously. It's just meant to be fun. Save your serious side for grown-up activities.'

'Yeah, I suppose…'

'Actually, how old are you?'

'Seventeen.'

She laughed a little.

'What's wrong?' he asked.

'Nothing at all. Seventeen's a great age to be.'

He stopped himself asking exactly how old she was. It felt intrusive. And besides, he was about to sleep with her so right now had she said she was thirty it wouldn't have made any difference. Although, he hoped she wasn't thirty.

'Twenty-three,' she said.

'Eh?'

'Your eyes were asking.'

'No, seriously, age is nothing to me. I wouldn't care if you were thirty.'

But something was wrong. He didn't want this to happen with someone he'd only just met. He wanted it to be with someone special. Someone who meant something to him. Someone he could build a future with…

'Come here.'

'Right.'

He sat beside her. She was amazing. So confident and generous. He'd always thought he'd meet the right girl, fall in love with her and then fall into bed with her. Well, he'd met her and fallen in love with her – but fate had stitched him up by introducing an irritating pillock called Steve.

'Tom? Do you know what really flips my switch?'

'No?'

'Shall I show you?'

Tom couldn't believe it. Was she going to teach him?

She took his hand and licked his fingers. His cannon almost fired.

There was a noise downstairs.

'Hang on...' Doops got up and went to the landing.

Tom's manhood shrank back to boyhood. They were in a squat in Hackney. The only thing rising now was fear.

'Hello?' Doops called into the dark.

'Only me,' said a voice from the depths.

Doops came back in. Tom, still sitting on the floor-level mattress, found her pubic region staring him directly in the face.

'It's Phil.'

Tom rose quickly to his feet.

'Who's Phil?'

'My boyfriend.'

Tom felt the whole world being sucked away from him.

'You have a boyfriend?' he asked uselessly.

'He said he was staying over at friends in Oxford. Do you mind sleeping in the lounge? Only Phil will want to... you know.'

Tom was appalled. How could people live like this? How could Doops not care who she shagged?

He passed Phil, a guy of around twenty, on the stairs.

'That's Tom,' Doops called down.

'Hi Tom,' said Phil.

They exchanged brief pleasantries then Tom found

himself in the hall by the lounge.

Now that his hormones were calming down, he was glad that Phil had turned up. It meant he still had hopes of a special moment with someone else. Breathing in a final draught of the rebel atmosphere, he left by the back door. He'd soon be crossing Victoria Park as part of the four-mile walk to the Millwall end of East Ferry Road because he'd missed the last bus – although, happily, that meant an hour in which he could think about Claire and the band.

Well, Claire mainly.

26. OH CLAIRE

The following Saturday evening, Tom was in the Waterman's Arms waiting for his mates to join him. While he waited, he had the privilege of standing ten feet away from Nat Hiscock, who was lecturing some poor bloke.

'Ten years old, we were, sneaking over the Mudchute to see the anti-aircraft guns. Then, next thing you know, we're running back to Saundersness Road School, just a few yards up the road, where they're using it as a Home Guard post and my mate's older brother's a medic, and boom! …and, well, even now the school's still in two halves.'

Tom willed one of his friends to appear.

'My daughter went there,' said Nat. 'Lovely girl. All the top firms are after her. She could work in any business, any industry.'

Neil came in. Tom sighed and ordered him a lager.

'Four weeks then,' said Neil, clearly referring to Tom's band playing at the Christmas Dance.

'Yeah, four weeks,' said Tom. 'Hopefully, no disasters are lying in wait.'

'Why do you say that?'

'Something usually goes wrong. It'd be nice for life to turn out good for once. Even if it's just for one night.'

Polly arrived.

'Heard the news, Tom? The news you've been waiting

all year to hear?'

'West Ham have signed Pat Jennings?'

'Claire Cross has split up with her boyfriend.'

Tom felt the earth move beneath his feet.

'Who told you that?' He needed more than second-hand gossip.

'Brenda Brand.'

That made sense. Claire saw Brenda occasionally to play records.

'So Steve's gone,' said Tom, trying to stay calm. 'Shame. I liked him. Lovely guy. Bassoon player, by all accounts.'

'Well, we all know that,' said Neil. 'It wasn't a secret.'

'I'm just saying,' said Tom, struggling to contain his joy, 'it's a shame because he and Claire made a nice couple and… well, I was hoping it would work out for them.'

'What a load of bollocks,' said Polly. 'You've had your eye on Claire for a whole year. Ever since she got drunk at your party.'

'We're mates,' Tom insisted. 'I mean, obviously, if we…'

'She'll be down later.'

'What?' Tom couldn't believe it. He checked his attire. Damn, had he known he would have gone with the Ben Sherman shirt instead of the rugby top. He'd have splashed on some Denim aftershave too.

'Brenda said they were coming for a commiseration drink.'

Tom took a sip of lager. 'Well, obviously, we won't invade their… oh shit, it's Darbs. Oi, haven't seen you in yonks!'

Darbs joined them and flashed some cash.

'Drinks, boys? On me, natch. Barings Bank pays its

rising stars very well.'

He got the pints in and seemed very much the young man about town. Leaving school made him look at least two years older.

'You still seeing Cheryl Allbright?' asked Neil.

'Enough to make you blush, son.'

Darbs nudged Tom, slopping half an inch of lager out of his full glass.

'What's all this I hear about you and some posh sort?'

Tom flashed a look at Polly.

'I heard from Janine,' said Polly.

Tom didn't see what that had to do with Darbs having all the details.

'Doops,' said Darbs, 'what a dopey moniker.'

'It was nothing. Just someone I met in a pub.'

'Leave off, Tom,' said Darbs. 'You were in bed with her and had to do a runner when her boyfriend turned up. Oh, alright, Claire?'

Tom's blood froze.

Even as he turned, Claire and Brenda were heading straight back for the door they had just come in by.

'Oh no...'

'Well, don't just stand there,' said Neil. 'Go after her. Tell her you're nuts about her.'

Tom hurried out into the street. Claire and Brenda were walking quite fast towards the main road.

'Claire!' He caught up with them. 'Nothing happened. I'm not interested in bloody Doops.'

Claire stopped. She had moist eyes. 'Doops?' She headed off again.

Brenda shrugged. 'She packed Steve up for you, Tom.'

As Brenda hurried off after Claire, Tom got the idea that he wasn't welcome to accompany them any further.

*

A week or two passed, or maybe it was longer or shorter. Tom was too deep in a vortex of schoolwork, band practise, song-writing and moping over Claire to notice. Yes, he saw her regularly in school but no, they didn't speak. On a particularly bleak Wednesday, he was lying on his bed, thinking about her and listening to Pink Floyd when his mum called him down for his tea.

Fishfingers and chips didn't seem a fitting meal for a man nearing his first gig while suffering the loss of Claire Cross for the second time in his life.

Eating off a tray in the front room, half-watching *Today,* he wondered if to include one of his own songs in the set list for the Docklands Christmas Dance. Not that he had a long list to choose from. He'd only written two songs, and they weren't actually finished. Besides, "I Miss You" and "You Are My World" might not work. Maybe it was better to stick to the planned setlist:

1) Thin Lizzy's "The Boys Are Back in Town"
2) The Eagles' "Lyin' Eyes"
3) Pussycat's "Mississippi"
4) The Real Thing's "You To Me Are Everything"
5) Peter Frampton's "Show Me The Way"
6) Slade's "Merry Christmas Everybody"

They weren't all Tom's choices, but Jez and Den said it was one song to grab attention, four for the girls to sing along to, and one for all to join in with. That way, the band would be part of someone's great night out and they would be in with a shout of paid bookings via word of mouth.

Just then, quite unexpectedly, the telly caught his eye. It was footage a band playing a live concert. It was heavy, noisy rock music. Not in the usual sense, it was more…

simplistic. But, and this was quite the thing, the punters were going mental. They were absolutely into the singer's staring-eyed, inarticulate cavemen delivery in a way he knew the docklands crowd would not be when he served up "Lyin' Eyes" and "Mississippi".

Who the hell were these geezers? Because, frankly, Neil could sing better and he, Tom Alder, could play as well as the guy on stage any day of the week.

The next thing he heard was even more astonishing. Presenter Bill Grundy said the band had received FORTY THOUSAND POUNDS FROM A RECORD COMPANY!

What? The world seemed to lose its bearings over the next couple of minutes as the interview descended into swearing. Tom found himself whooping in a mix of awe and shock. This was impossible.

Rose popped her head round the door.

'What's going on?'

'There's a band swearing on telly.'

'Don't be silly,' she said before disappearing again.

Just then, Tom put a whole fishfinger in his mouth. Big mistake. One of the band members called Bill Grundy a "dirty fucker" and the fishfinger flew out into the fireplace.

A couple of minutes later, the phone rang. It was Neil.

'Were you watching *Today*?'

'Yeah, who the f... who were they?'

'The Sex Pistols. Unbelievable, eh?'

'Absolutely.' There was still a residue of glee in Tom's voice at the memory of swearing on tea-time television.

'I might get the single,' said Neil. '"Anarchy in the UK". What do you reckon?'

'I reckon they sounded rubbish for forty grand.'

'Yeah, I reckon the single should sound better than

that live clip. Don't you?'

'Well, yeah, obviously, but…'

'Punk rock they're calling it. Could catch on. I mean the crowd looked like they were into it.'

That was the bit that fascinated Tom the most. Punk rock hadn't so much introduced itself to the music world as kicked the door down and lobbed a grenade.

Later, in his room, Tom studied a lyric he'd been writing.

You are a bird on the water
I am a boat on an inland sea.
When you fly away, I must await the tide to be free
But when the tide is high will I follow you?
Or will I venture into a wider world across the deep blue.
Or perhaps you are the world and all journeys lead to you.

Would the Sex Pistols want to perform that?

He doubted it. He didn't want to perform it either.

The following Saturday at ten a.m., Tom was first at the rehearsal studio. It was the final run-through as next Saturday was the Big Day – the Docklands Christmas Dance. Full of excitement, he'd invited Claire to come and take a look. Yes, he knew she wouldn't be his girlfriend anytime soon, but he still wanted to be friends. She said she couldn't promise. This wasn't so much to do with any busy schedule, more that their status even just as mates had taken such a nosedive that the repair process was still in the very early stages.

Jez arrived. Tom was pleased. They would spend the first half of the two-hour session fine-tuning the guitar solos and big finishes. Only Jez was saying something about a mix-up, and that he and Den couldn't do next Saturday.

Life itself came to a halt.

'You promised,' said Tom, pretty much shaken to the core.

'Thing is, the other gig's a posh wedding in Hertfordshire. Twenty nicker apiece.'

Tom understood that his offer of a couple of cans of Long Life at the dance didn't exactly match the wedding money – by about nineteen and a half quid – but surely it was the principle of the thing?

Jez didn't see it like that and departed. With the door left half-open, the sounds of the normal world drifted in. People coming and going. Gear being lugged up the stairs. An innocent curse as something fell to the ground.

Tom was in a state of shock. This was a snub of life-altering proportions. His reputation would be crushed like an ant under the giant boot of expectation. Now everyone would see the real Tom Alder – a complete and utter hopeless, useless, pointless failure.

But...

This was no time to panic. Panic wouldn't achieve anything. He'd get his head clear and think up a Plan B.

Then it occurred to him that, any minute now, Claire might turn up.

He took a breath.

He wouldn't lie. She would be okay about him amounting to nothing. It was par for the course really. This was why she would never be his girlfriend. She could see through his fakery and bluff.

It felt like an opportunity to grow up a little. To take it on the chin.

Or would Claire take pity on him and join the band?

Tom, guitar; Roy, guitar; Claire, guitar.

No, that wouldn't work.

Maybe Claire could play bass? Or drums?

He sighed. Then he sat with his back to the wall and studied the set list.

"The Boys Are Back In Town"…? Not for long, mate. They were about to piss off to a wedding in Hertfordshire.

He felt like laughing. And crying. Both really. He began to hum, quite absently, the chorus of "You To Me Are Everything" over and over. Then he began to sing it.

From the doorway, a voice joined in. He didn't look up. He just kept singing. And so did Claire. It was an amazing feeling, although, after thirty seconds, he felt like stopping. Only he didn't want to leave her high and dry because…

He wondered if she knew he loved her.

Eventually, she stopped, and so did he.

Then, as Roy arrived, Tom thanked him for coming and revealed the dilemma.

There was a pregnant silence.

'See the Sex Pistols?' said Roy, changing the subject.

'See the girl Bill Grundy tried to chat up?' said Claire. 'Now *that's* a look.'

Tom vaguely recalled a girl but he was unable to focus on anything that didn't revolve around his doom.

'I could borrow a bass,' said Claire.

Tom gazed up from the depths of self-pity.

'You play bass?'

'I'll muddle through. And we'll get Dave from Westferry to play drums. I mean he'll be there anyway.'

'How will we persuade him to do that?'

'*We* won't have to,' said Claire. 'I know he fancies me so I'll take him out for a drink.'

Tom felt an excruciating pain in his heart. Claire, his

beloved Claire, would go on a date with an ugly, sweaty drummer to save the band.

'I can't ask you to do that, Claire.'

'Look, you need this to happen. I know you – it'll set you back half a lifetime if it falls apart. Just leave it to me.'

'Sounds like a plan,' said Roy.

'Do you really think we can do it?' said Tom, still ready to stop Claire going out with a drummer, even if it meant total humiliation.

'Of course we can,' said Claire. 'This is your band. Stand up and fight for it.'

Maybe she was right. Maybe next Saturday didn't need to be a cataclysmic disaster after all. Filled with hope, they took the gear home then Tom and Neil went to see their beloved West Ham play at home to Middlesbrough.

West Ham lost 1-0.

27. IF THE SEX PISTOLS CAN DO IT…

Tom re-entered the Dockland Settlement in a state of euphoric near-panic. He was on a knife edge of joyous hope and near-suicidal despair. What if tonight went brilliantly? What if it was a pile of shite? Who could tell what the Fates had in store for him.

He had already been in once, to set up his guitar and amp. Dave from Westferry had been full of calming words and Claire seemed to think it would be fun. How weird that she had dyed her hair jet black with pink strands. How could Claire Cross be a punk? She wasn't from Chelsea, or wherever they were based. She reckoned it should have been white like the girl on the telly, but school might have objected. The pink strands could be washed out, apparently.

Not that he'd paid attention. His head had been, and still was, full of thoughts regarding Claire and Dave having been down the pub the night before. What happened in the pub, or directly afterwards, he had no idea. It wasn't like he could ask her. What if she said Dave was now her boyfriend? Tom would have run right out of the building and kept on running till he reached Southend. Then he might have thrown himself in the sea. Or worse, spent a couple of weeks there.

Confidence. That was the key. Even if he didn't have any it was important to look as if he did.

He smiled at a few people but he felt sick. This was no

knife edge. He couldn't perform here tonight.

He smiled at Claire.

'Let's form a punk band,' she joked. Or was she serious? Annoyingly, she went off to talk to Dave.

Tom needed a beer.

Didn't he?

Or would it come straight back up?

Micky Sullivan came over and nudged him.

'Doing any Zeppelin?'

'Alright, Mick? Surprised to see you here. How's work?'

'Driving for a new firm. Bloody Indian sweets. I pick 'em up from Southall and bring 'em back to East Ham. I won't touch 'em, mind. I mean you don't know what's in 'em, do ya!'

Micky laughed in a conspiratorial manner that Tom disliked.

'Tom!' It was Polly. 'First Rock Against Racism gig, eh?'

Micky snorted.

'No, Poll,' said Tom, wishing he could call the whole thing off.

'I'm pulling your leg, mate. I know you're not into it. But never say never, eh?'

'No, of course not.'

'Good man.'

Micky frowned and departed.

'So what songs are you playing?'

'Thin Lizzy, then the Eagles...' said Tom, feeling queasy.

'Not exactly the Sex Pistols,' said Polly.

'Good luck, Tom,' said Brenda Brand. She planted a kiss on his cheek.

'Thanks Brenda.'

Neil came over. 'All set?'

'Neil…' Tom motioned him aside.

'You don't have to apologise again, Tom. You were right to move me out of the band.'

'No, I just wanted to say… well… lucky you, mate, because I'm shitting myself.'

'First night nerves. It's a well-known phenomenon.'

'No, you don't understand, Neil. I can't do it.'

It was a relief to admit it. In truth, he'd known it for ages. But now, twenty minutes before Red Sails were due on stage, he knew it all the way down to his bone marrow.

'Are you sure, Tom?'

'I'm… actually…'

Tom hurried off to throw up in the gents.

When he returned, Danny was waiting for him. Well, Danny could have his little victory. Tom had no way to defend himself.

'Neil said you're struggling.'

'Bloody Neil…'

'Look, you're a stupid sack of shit, but don't let it beat you. It's just a gig. Think of it like going to the dentist. Once it's over you'll wonder what all the fuss was about.'

Tom was in a dream. Danny was being nice to him. Perhaps he'd died and gone to Heaven. No, it would be closed for lunch when he got there and he'd have to go the other way.

'Thanks, Dan.' It was all he could say.

'Seriously, Tom. Go for it. You'll never regret it.'

He eyed Danny. How ridiculous was this thing called life. Just an endless series of mishaps and wrong-turns.

'I wish we could see our sister, Dan.'

Danny nodded. 'Me too.'

It was weird. As if something needed putting right.

Tom hurried off to throw up in the gents again. He felt like a bag of wet cement. He stayed in there for ten minutes trying to think of other things. Like a country walk with Claire. And a swim in the sea with Claire. And at the end of the day they would kiss...

He emerged to a fuller room and a few ironic cheers as he was summoned to the stage. He was no performer. He recalled last year in Mr Reid's class, bottling out of a poetry reading. Well, that failure would be overshadowed in the way that losing a game of football over the park is overshadowed by the Battle of the Somme.

Neil appeared looking as worried as Tom had done in the gents' toilets mirror.

'You okay, Neil?'

'Don't worry about me. You just get up there and show everyone you're not scared.'

'I don't think I... shit, this is going to be the worst day of my life.'

'No, it's not. Just get up there and don't you worry about a thing. We haven't been best mates for our entire lives for me not to support you.'

Tom smiled a little. 'Thanks Neil.' Good old dependable Neil. What a pity he was a useless twit.

Claire called him over.

'It's time.'

Tom swallowed drily. He looked to Neil for support but he couldn't see him. There was no way out.

'Come on, playmates,' said drummer Dave. His voice seemed to slow down. In fact, the whole world seemed to be slowing down. Maybe it was a quirk of Nature, so that your worst ever moment on Earth would last longer.

'Are you okay?' asked Roy.

Tom didn't answer.

'Look,' said Claire, 'if this is about Dave. He doesn't

know it yet, but I won't be seeing him again. Okay?'

Tom looked into her eyes. Such lovely eyes. And such a stunningly brilliant girl who he had failed to spot existed until last October. After which he had come up with umpteen ways to screw things up. Now, just as she was opening the door to a relationship, he feared he might vomit over her breasts. She probably wouldn't like that. Dave would no doubt hurry over with a cloth and wipe said breasts. And suggest she remove her top…

'Grab this,' said Claire.

'Eh?' It was his guitar. 'Oh. Right.'

He took his place in the line-up, over to the right of the stage. In fact he was so far to the right that another step and he would have fallen off – which held a certain fascination for him.

Claire smiled at him.

Claire Cross.

Smiled.

At him.

What was the matter with him? This was his chance to show the world, to show Claire, to show Danny, to show himself, that he could do it. Yes, he was scared, but to hell with it all – he would give it a go.

Danny hopped up to the mic.

Was this Big Joke time?

'Ladies and gents of All Saints past and present, I give you our very own… Red Sails!'

No it wasn't Big Joke time. Danny hopped straight off the stage and people were applauding. For the first time, Tom began to feel that everything might be alright. They had a proper drummer, Roy could sing and play, and Claire…

Claire is going to be my girlfriend. She would be seventeen in a week's time and he knew, by then, they would be madly in love with each other.

Dave counted them in. 'One-two-three-four!'

They began to play. It was okay. The Boys Really Were Back In Town! For Tom, life was finally falling into place. He looked out across the intrigued, interested faces... and to Neil by the fire alarm.

There was smoke coming through the door. And a thumbs-up from Neil.

What? No!!!

The building was on fire. And stupid grinning Neil was smashing the glass and setting off the fire alarm. It was pandemonium. People fled screaming. The gig was over before it had begun. His best mate, Neil Sullivan, had saved him – the stupid fucking incompetent dipstick!

1977

28. NEW HORIZONS

New Year came in cold and turned snowy – the kind of weather Tom usually hated – but he barely noticed. He was too busy walking around humming 10cc's "The Things We Do For Love", even occasionally breaking into actual song, which was embarrassing in public.

Of course, Claire had been furious about Neil's stupid answer to Tom's stage fright, and furious about Tom having such a numbskull mate. Apparently, setting fire to a building had no place in sensible problem-solving. But she mellowed by the seventeenth of December – her seventeenth birthday, which twelve of them celebrated in the Waterman's Arms.

And now, hanging around in the playground before the start of the new term, Tom was happy because Claire was his mate again. On the down side, she'd told him she was holding off on boyfriends for a while. She was worried that next time she'd fall in so deep it might affect her schoolwork. Tom was okay with that. After all, she was in his band and that meant endless opportunities for her to fall for him. And he knew that when she did, it would be forever.

Claire swept aside her jet black fringe. The pink streaks had gone – thanks to the school being anti anything that even hinted at rebellion. Even the jet black was under review.

'Maybe we really should be a punk band,' she said. The cold air turned her breath into little puffs of fog.

'Yeah…' Tom laughed because he wasn't sure if she was being serious. They had yet to plot their next move regarding Red Sails. Of course, Polly was urging them to do a Rock Against Racism gig, but Tom didn't think they had practised enough for that. After all, they hadn't technically played a gig yet. And seriously – would a Rock Against Racism crowd want to hear them play Pussycat and the Eagles?

'I wouldn't mind a crack at singing,' said Claire.

The idea excited Tom.

'Good thinking,' he said. He was freezing but he didn't want to go into their form room where they would have no privacy.

'I could share with Roy,' said Claire.

'Yeah… although there's still the drummer problem.'

'You mean not having one?'

'Trust me, Claire. I know about music and not having a drummer is a problem.'

'Amazing. It's like you're some kind of expert.'

'Punk rock then. We'd need a new name.'

'No, I like Red Sails. That's your name for your band. No need to change it.'

'Red Sails then. Okay.'

'Maybe the first album could have a punk title. *Nuclear Beach.*'

'Maybe,' said Tom. He'd been thinking it would be

called ...*in the Sunset.*

'Well, something explosive anyway.'

'You really think punk will take off?' The doubt he had was that the punk revolution might fizzle out before it got started. After all, David Soul headed a singles chart that included Johnny Mathis, Abba, Showaddywaddy, Tina Charles, Smokie, Paul Nicholas, Dana and Mud. It was a lot to overcome.

Still, on the other hand, playing punk made sense. Keeping it simple, he'd flourish with Claire alongside him.

'Are you cold, Tom?'

'F-f-f-freezing,' he exaggerated.

As they headed inside, he dismissed any lingering doubts about the potential longevity of punk. EMI had signed the Sex Pistols, hadn't they? They would probably sign loads more bands over the coming months to really get things going.

Yes, punk would thrive and he'd be able to rock on with Claire forever.

Eating cornflakes in the front room on the Saturday morning, Tom was disappointed. It wasn't just the wind blowing smoke back down the chimney and filling the room with airborne soot – EMI had sacked the Sex Pistols. Rose was reading an article about it in the newspaper.

'Good riddance to rotten rubbish,' she said. 'Disgusting bunch of layabouts.'

That was easy for her to say. Mums generally didn't like young people who lacked respect for everything they, themselves, held dear. Rose almost spat when she read about the "disgusting amount of money" they had received for being "rude and untalented."

Dad Ted was no different. 'Bring back National Service. That'd sort 'em out.'

Ted and Rose had been struggling. The overtime that used to bump up Ted's wages was no more than a distant memory. With the Port of London Authority closing the West India Import Dock, he was now scratching around on the South Quay minus a few of his mates who had been reassigned to the Royal Docks and Tilbury. Rose had enquired about a part-time job in the baker's but Ted had blocked it. To Tom, it simply couldn't go on. He explained to Ted that it was okay for women to go to work, and that it didn't reflect badly on the man of the house. Ted said if things turned really bad he could always accept the PLA's voluntary redundancy package – currently worth a few grand – and find another job. But what other job? There was rising unemployment and Ted was likely to burn through any severance pay and end up skint. And anyway, Tom didn't believe him. Ted would never voluntarily leave the docks.

'I hope you're working hard at school,' said Rose, eyeing a picture of Johnny Rotten as if he might gob at her.

'Of course I am.' Okay, so it was hardly a rebel punk answer, but having fought to get back into All Saints, he tended not to muck about.

That evening, Tom was meeting Neil, Brenda and Claire in the Waterman's for a drink. Not that he wanted to see Neil or Brenda. It was just that Claire had laid down some rules to prevent her and Tom accidentally getting "too serious".

Tom and Neil were the first to arrive.

'Funny how boys don't show their emotions,' said

Tom, while waiting for the barman to notice them. 'When they talk, I mean. You know, like girls do.'

'You got emotional that time Tony Cornish said Genesis were crap.'

'Music's our way in,' said Tom, ignoring Neil's stupidity.

'Yeah, *Wings Over America*,' said Neil while Tom ordered two halves of lager. 'I wouldn't mind getting that. It's got some Beatles tracks on it too.'

Tom nodded. The new one from Paul McCartney and co. sounded like a reasonable choice – assuming you had the bucket-load of cash required to buy a triple album. Luckily, the latest Genesis offering was a normal, one disc LP.

'*Wind and Wuthering* for me,' he said. 'I've heard good things.'

Claire and Brenda came in. Tom felt a little cushion of air form beneath his feet.

'Claire, alright?' he said coolly. 'Brenda, good to see you.'

'Hi,' said Neil. 'You two look nice. Going anywhere later?'

While signalling the barman for two more halves of lager, Tom shot Neil a "you useless pinhead" look. Claire and Brenda had obviously made the effort for meeting up with him and Neil. Hadn't they?

'Er… are you?' he said, specifically to Claire.

'Yeah, I've got a date,' she said.

Tom gulped.

'Who with?' said Neil. 'Only Tom's often singing your praises, Claire.'

Tom baulked. 'Do me a favour, Neil – go and set your head on fire.'

Claire laughed. 'I meant I've got a date with you, my

mates.'

It was a good evening. And Tom felt he learned a bit more about Claire – particularly from Brenda. He was getting the idea that Claire was worried about s-e-x, mainly because she felt she wasn't ready. It wasn't stated outright but that's how it came across. That's why, he believed, Claire was holding him at bay for as long as possible, because when she gave in she would devour him in bed.

He could hardly wait.

A few days later, Tom bought *Wind and Wuthering*. It was the second track on side two that nailed him to the spot. "Blood on the Rooftops" written by Steve Hackett and Phil Collins. Hackett's acoustic intro mesmerised him. It seemed that he and Hackett were fellow guitarists in the same way that he and George Best could both kick a ball. What was it Danny said? About not wasting time being mediocre?

Listening to it in his bedroom with Neil, he voiced his dissatisfaction.

'I couldn't play like that in a million years.'

'You'll get there.'

'Are you listening to this?'

Tom turned up the stereo. It was delicate, intricate, and achingly beautiful. And Neil didn't argue.

'Still,' said Neil, 'you're going to play punk. That'll be your passion from now on.'

'Yeah…' said Tom, not feeling much punk passion. Even the cheap fuzz box he'd bought, though it distorted the sound beautifully, couldn't hide the fact that he wasn't a particularly inventive guitarist. Fine for punk, but what if you wanted to be a creative musical force?

Before they could discuss it further, Tom was called to the phone.

Downstairs, he put the receiver to his ear.

'Hello?'

'Tom?' said a breathy female voice. 'It's Doops.'

That was the last thing he'd been expecting – a call from Ann-Marie du Pont, the girl from the squat in Cassland Road.

'Where did you get my number?'

'From Polly. He's a good friend, isn't he?'

'Yeah, look…' he checked that his mum couldn't hear. 'What is it, Doops?'

'Phil's going to Australia for six months, so I'm going to be on my own.'

Tom tried to process the information but all he could see were thighs opening.

'Um, what about Oz and Janine?'

'I mean I'll be all on my own, bed-wise.'

'I see.' And he could see. Definitely.

'Who's going to share my hot little bed?'

'Um, well, I might soon have a girlfriend.'

Idiot! Idiot! Idiot!

'Tom, take my number.'

He was shaken. And tempted. But he wouldn't. It was like that song, "The Things We Do For Love". 10cc had released it for Tom and Claire, not for Tom and Doops. It was just a matter of asking Claire out. Yes, that was the answer. He'd ask her out. Okay, so last time he tried that, at his sixteenth birthday party, it backfired. This time, though, it would be different. Hopefully.

29. OPERATION GIRLFRIEND

On the bus to school, Tom was pondering life and its complexities. As they crossed the Blue Bridge he looked out over the Thames and wondered about Lynn. It was an emotional tug that flared up every so often. He'd set it aside though. He couldn't get involved with people on the other side of London who didn't want to know him. And really, what right did he have to disrupt the life of a young teenage girl?

At the next stop, Claire got on. Tom had to switch seats to get to her. Straightaway she was going on about putting politics into music. That was Polly getting into her head. Tom was getting a little bored with it but Polly was a mate and you couldn't just tell him to shut up about something that was taking over his entire life. It didn't leave any room for him to turn to the subject to dating though.

'You should get a bit more into it,' said Claire.

'I went to that Rock Against Racism gig, didn't I?'

'Ah yeah, the one where you met Whoops.'

'Doops.'

'I hear she's been in touch.'

'What?'

'Hang on, I've got a megaphone here somewhere…'

'I can hear you perfectly well, Claire. When did you start spying on me?'

'Doops told Janine, she told Polly, he told me. Not

that it's any of my business.'

'You and Polly talk a lot, don't you.'

'You're not jealous, are you?'

'Don't be daft.'

'So, you and Doops aren't actually…?'

'No. She's like Polly – into politics.'

It had been bothering him, of course. Why had Polly given Doops his number? Surely not to clear a path to Claire? Maybe his thing with Janine was over…

'So when do I get to meet her?'

'Who?'

'Doops.'

Tom wondered – was Claire after weighing up a potential rival?

'I expect we could team up with Polly and Janine at some point. Then we could get Doops and Oz involved.'

'Oz?'

'Doops is nuts about him. Only she doesn't like to show it publically, because Oz is such a serious political type.'

'Right, gotcha. Only Polly said her boyfriend's called Phil and he's about to fly off to Australia. He's got family there or something.'

'Phil… yeah, now you mention it, I do recall a Phil. Maybe you're right. Maybe Phil's the boyfriend. To be honest, I have so little to do with them I hardly know who's who.'

A vision of Doops' thighs opening came to him. This annoyed him because he was meant to be asking Claire out.

'Um, Claire…?'

'I know exactly what you're thinking.'

'Really?'

'You're thinking if we get to know Oz and Doops

better, we'll get to know their mates who organise Rock Against Racism gigs. I like it.'

'Yeah. That's exactly… yeah.'

The following Friday night, they met up at the Alexandra pub by Victoria Park. There was Tom, Claire, Polly, Janine, Doops, Oz and four anarchists in their late teens and early twenties who were squatting in nearby Victoria Park Road.

Tom felt as proud as a peacock until he began to suspect that Oz fancied Claire. It was a worry – Oz was intelligent, had a good degree and had travelled around Europe. From what he was able to overhear, Claire was going on about certain classical music haters at school who weren't just ignorant about it but *proud* to be ignorant. Oz was being sympathetic. Tom wanted to be sympathetic too but Doops was in his face and, on one occasion, patting his bum.

At around ten, ditching Oz's anarchist friends, they got some cans from the off license and went back to the squat in Cassland Road. Tom, with Doops continually smiling at him, was keen to get away but Claire couldn't stop talking with Oz.

'A strange month, January,' said Oz. 'I see Jim Callaghan came down to Millwall Dock.'

'Yeah,' said Polly, sounding unimpressed by the Prime Minister's visit. 'He appeared to say a lot about the area's future, but never actually made a commitment.'

Tom wanted to talk about music or football or careers. Polly switched to talking about the International Socialists becoming the Socialist Workers' Party.

'I might join,' he said.

'Makes sense,' said Oz.

As an hour lumbered by, Tom began to wonder.

Would Claire want to stay overnight? If so, would she share a beanbag with him? But no, he didn't want them to sleep together with Doops upstairs. What if she came down at a vital moment?

Then Oz dropped a bombshell. 'One of you might be able to help me out. I'm after somewhere to live in Tower Hamlets.'

Tom didn't want Oz living with him.

'They'll give me a hard-to-let council flat,' Oz went on, 'but I need to be living legitimately in the borough and be on the point of becoming homeless. Anyone fancy vouching for me?'

Tom absolutely did not. 'Cassland Road is Hackney,' he said. 'Can't you apply to *them*?'

'Not from a squat.'

'You can use my address,' said Polly. 'Just say you're a cousin and we're chucking you out. My dad won't mind.'

Oz nodded. That appeared to be just the ticket.

'Well, we'd better be going,' said Tom.

'You sure you won't have another coffee?' said Oz to Claire.

'We don't want to miss the last bus to the Island,' said Tom.

'Tom's right,' said Claire.

As everyone exchanged farewells, Doops gave Tom a hug and whispered in his ear. 'Think of me.'

Tom tried his best to keep from blushing.

Then, as they left via the back door, it became apparent that Polly, hand in hand with Janine, wouldn't be leaving with them.

On the way to the bus stop, Tom broached it.

'I wonder what Polly and Janine might be getting up to about now-ish.'

'Probably discussing post-colonialism or the

redistribution of wealth,' said Claire.

Tom smirked. 'Yeah, right.'

'It's Janine's period and she won't be removing her underwear.'

'She told you that?'

'Yeah, and about now she'll be telling Polly.'

'Poor old Polly,' he said, sharing the frustration his mate would be struggling with. 'Mind you, she could… I mean… well… so what did you make of Oz and his gang?'

'Interesting.'

'Yeah…'

Tom decided to ask her out. Right now. No messing about.

'Claire?'

'When I say interesting, I don't just mean the politics.'

'No, well…'

'I mean Oz has done so much. Did you know he's been to Italy, Greece… he just *loves* the classical world. I love meeting really interesting, experienced people like that. Don't you?'

'Oh yeah, definitely.' Suddenly the idea of asking her out seemed a duff one.

'Sorry, you were going to ask me something.'

'Yeah, I was wondering… you know… about the band. I was wondering what kind of music we should be concentrating on.'

'I thought we agreed on punk?'

'Yeah. I'm more just… well, confirming it's what you want.'

'It's up to you, Tom. You can work really hard to push into more challenging areas or just enjoy yourself playing three chord punk. You just need to decide.'

But he couldn't decide. Musically, his tastes and ability

simply didn't match up. And he tried to explain that to Claire – at length. And then the bus deposited him on the pavement by Millwall Fire Station. And all he could do was wave to Claire and think about Doops.

30. ENERGY

Late in wet February, Tom was practising hard. He'd changed his mind about playing punk. He'd decided it was more important to become a better musician, to be able to play at the top end of the rock spectrum – the more complex chords, the extra-twiddly solos, the different time signatures.

He wrote up his and Claire's progress – and disagreements – in his journal, *A Journey Into Music,* in which he was recording his road to potential stardom. Unfortunately, the perfect moment to ask her out had yet to present itself. Or if it had, she was giving off a vibe that didn't encourage him.

They continued going out as part of a group of mates, of course. A Wimpy in Bethnal Green Road with Polly and Janine, a trip to Upton Park with Neil and Brenda to see West Ham beat Stoke 1-0... but Claire seemed restless. She didn't laugh when he joked that if she gave him a couple of years, he'd blow her away with his ability to play like Pink Floyd's David Gilmour. And when he joked about them having three musical kids and forming a heavy metal family band, it went down like a lead balloon tied to a crashing plane.

And then there was Doops.

He wasn't sure what he was doing in Victoria Park on a Saturday morning. Yes, taking a stroll by the duck pond was a nice way to pass the time, but...

Okay, he was up there to walk straight through the park to visit Cassland Road, to try to catch a glimpse of her. When she actually came along the street, as bold as brass, walking towards him, he hid behind a tree. Good job it was the trunk of a mature plane tree. He was able to move around it unseen as she passed within a yard of him.

This was a moment that could alter his life. She was older than Claire. And she wanted him. So would he go the distance and chase after her?

He stepped out from behind the tree and followed her. He was five yards behind guaranteed sex.

At the next plane tree, he hid again.

He sighed. What was he doing? Watching Doops make her way to the shops, he couldn't locate that same, more profound feeling he had for Claire.

He turned and headed back through the park. On the bus home, he accepted that he'd gone there for one reason only. With Claire not yet ready for that kind of thing, it had seemed a reasonable solution to his hormone problem.

Oh yes, his hormone problem. It wouldn't give him any peace. Of course, regular encounters in Doops' bed would resolve that. Her thighs would open for him to reveal her moist...

Hormones. They could strike at any moment.

Rather than go home and play some records, he went to Island Gardens and wondered about his place in the world.

The Poplar, Blackwall and District Rowing Club were busy on the river, with half a dozen boats in action. Beyond them, on the Greenwich side, the Old Royal Naval College stared back at him. Did the navy still use it? He wasn't sure. And wasn't it once a hospital? He'd seen that on a sign somewhere. Just along from the old college, *Cutty Sark* looked impressively lost. Her tall, ageing masts supported a spider's web of rigging but she would forever lack the sails to take her on any more adventures.

He headed to the foot tunnel and descended the stairs. He used to hate the old pedestrian route to Greenwich. When he was a kid, he always imagined it caving in and the whole of the Thames sweeping over him. He still did. Grandad said they closed it during the War and you had to get a rowing boat across. That was the old way. Before the foot tunnel existed, there had been a ferry service and a reason for Westferry and East Ferry Roads leading to Ferry Street. There was such a lot of the past hereabouts. He really needed to learn more about it.

Surfacing in Greenwich, he went to the riverside for the view of Island Gardens, the dockside cranes and factory chimneys. Far-off industrial sounds caught his ear. Clunking, clanking. Iron on iron. Iron against concrete. A heavy drill. A shout. The sounds of the present, all distant, carried on the wind over the water.

He thought of the future. What did Mr Reid say at school? By the Year 2000, we'll have flying cars and nuclear-powered electricity that will be too cheap to meter. On the downside, technology will cut the working week in half, giving everyone more leisure time than is good for them. Tom thought the Year 2000 sounded great. The only downside was that he'd be forty.

He imagined seeing himself over in Island Gardens. A young man staring out across the water from his usual spot. But what kind of young man? A happy one? Well, potentially – if he put a few things right.

One evening, entering the Waterman's Arms, he found

Neil and Polly discussing music.

'I quite like Fleetwood Mac,' said Neil. 'I might get *Rumours.*'

'All I can say is thank God for Floyd's *Animals,*' said Polly.

'Yeah, it's about time Pink Floyd got political,' said Tom, not meaning it.

'There's a gig you should both come to,' said Polly. 'Up Islington.'

'Not sure,' said Tom.

'Doops and Oz are coming.'

Tom didn't want Doops. He wanted Claire. He wanted to commit himself to her, to love her. Maybe she would go too.

'What sort of music is it?' he said.

'Music we need to know about,' said Polly.

'I'll pass,' said Neil.

Tom was persuaded. The next day he mentioned it to Claire but it clashed with some classical thing she had already planned with a violin-playing friend. This annoyed him because Claire really wasn't helping him shake off the fact that he fancied Doops.

A couple of nights later, he met up with Polly. They, in turn, ended up in a North London pub with Oz, Janine and Doops.

'No Claire?' Doops asked Tom.

'She's busy.'

Doops raised an eyebrow and gave him a little grin. Tom felt no love. But he did feel lust. Enough to run a power station.

Oz got the drinks in and Tom tried to get into the high energy vibe. It felt odd though. At first, it seemed a little like the Princess Alice gig of a few months back. But it dawned on him that this was a Far Right version of that happy musical get-together. It was loud, noisy, shouty punk with lots of references to killing blacks and burning down the Parliament of Traitors to White Britain. He was there undercover. This was a recce into enemy territory. He even found himself talking to a nice bloke in a business suit who, unbelievably, attempted to recruit him into something.

This he reported to Oz.

'Some weird NF bloke in a pinstripe.'

Oz looked over. 'He's not NF. He's League of St. George. The intellectual Right. Probably trying to sign you up to one of their satellite organisations. The League is ultra-exclusive but they need intelligent idiots to do their dirty work.'

Tom felt out of his depth. He wanted nothing to do with politics, Left or Right. He wanted to play music and get a proper girlfriend. Not smash the state.

On the way home, he firmed up his view into a vow. All the faffing around was over. Politics and punk were out. He was going to be a serious musician. It would take months of practice – years even – but there was no other way forward.

'Coming back to Cassland?' asked Doops, brushing her hand against the front of his jeans.

A certain part of his anatomy screamed from his pants to get stuck in. He could be breaking his duck in half an hour. And he wanted to. He so desperately wanted to. But he loved Claire, and he loved music and he hated politics and he particularly hated political types pulling him this way and that as if he were a piece of Plasticine to be moulded and remoulded as others saw fit.

'Not tonight, Doops,' he said, turning down the absolute certainty of shedding his innocent status. He felt like weeping a little. Even so, he was going to stick to his vow.

'Are you sure?' she said, brushing her hand against the front of his jeans again.

'Well, maybe just for coffee,' he said.

Doops smiled.

Next day, in the lower sixth-form room with Claire, the punk thing flared up again.

'I think you're wrong,' she said.

'Punk doesn't work for me. It's too immediate.'

'That's the point of punk. It's all about the energy. You can't go back to being a bedroom guitarist.'

'Why not? I mean until I'm ready…'

He quite liked the fuzz pedal he'd bought and knew, if he practised hard with it, options would open up…

Claire grabbed his arm and ushered him outside, away from prying eyes and ears.

'You'll never be ready, Tom. Never. You will mull it over, you will tinker, you will faff around, you will—'

'Faff? Me?'

'Yes, you! You'll faff around and avoid getting to grips with what matters most in a band – playing to the public. That's people, by the way. They come and listen to bands playing music.'

'I won't be in my bedroom forever.'

'Yes, you will.'

'You don't know that.'

'I know you, Tom. I do pay attention to people I care about.'

His heart raced. She cared about him. He was so relieved. And he gave thanks to God as he thought back to the previous evening when, somewhere near Kingsland Road, on a bus with Doops' hand inside his jeans, he forced himself to change his mind and bail out.

'Well?' said Claire. 'Are you going to play or faff?'

'I think, Claire, on this occasion, you'll just have to accept it.'

'I think, Tom, on this occasion, I won't.'

'And what, exactly, does that mean?'

'It means I'm quitting the band. I trust that's exact enough for you.'

'What, just like that?'

'I don't know how else to quit a band. I mean I could try to disappear in a puff of smoke.'

'Be serious, Claire.'

'I am being serious.'

Tom was upset. How could she quit the band? They had yet to play a gig and he hadn't got around to asking her out.

A few weeks later, he wrote up his musical progress in the journal. He had yet to add Claire's departure, but now did so. Then he threw the journal in the bin and phoned Neil.

They went to the Bridge House to see a band, any band. Just some rock and roll normality. It turned out to be a very good new outfit called The Tom Robinson Band. They were quite political and when Neil joined in with the chorus of a song called "Glad To Be Gay", Tom did not. He was annoyed it wasn't ordinary pub rock, annoyed that he wasn't in the same league as the band's guitarist and annoyed that this Tom Robinson bloke was up there doing it exactly how he wanted to and bollocks to anyone who didn't like it.

'I threw my music journal in the bin, Neil,' yelled Tom over the music.

'What for?'

'Don't worry, I got it out again. Thing is, I can't see where the journey's heading next. Apart from into a brick wall, I mean.'

'Don't give up. Something good might happen.'

However far from his goals Tom had felt, at that moment, supping a third pint in the pub under the Canning Town flyover, he knew he was truly lost. He thought about giving up on Claire. He could do as Neil did and stick to fantasising about Felicity Kendal in *The Good Life*.

Later, leaving the pub in an unusually drunken state, Tom bemoaned his lot.

'It could have been worse,' said Neil. 'You could've had Micky for a brother.'

'Ha! I can top that!'

'You're drunk, Tom.'

'Too bloody right. I had Danny for a brother, mate. Dan-bloody-nee. How's that for a laugh?'

'I only know what Micky told me – about you both being adopted. And that was only what I heard him telling you at your sixteenth.'

'Yeah, well, I knew you heard. Poking your bloody nose in. I suppose between you and Micky half the world knows about it by now.'

'Micky wouldn't tell anyone. He looks up to Danny.'

'And you? Who've you told?'

'I wouldn't tell anyone, Tom. Not about something like that. You're my best mate.'

'Yeah, well, whatever…'

'I'm going to get the bus.'

'Yeah, you get the bus, Neil. Get the bloody bus… no, Neil, wait. Neil! Mate…'

Tom hurried after him.

'Forget the bus. Let's walk. I need to sober up and it's

a long story.'

Neil puffed out his cheeks. 'All families have things go wrong, Tom. Polly's mum and dad are divorcing, Tony Cornish's dad's got a bit on the side, Brenda's mum's on her second marriage...'

'I need to tell you everything, Neil. Only don't go telling everyone...'

As they crossed the Iron Bridge from Canning Town into Poplar, Tom began to tell Neil *almost* everything. The part about having a sister called Lynn, he would leave out. That was too personal and painful to share with anyone beyond Danny.

Later, reaching home feeling only slightly less drunk, Tom phoned Claire.

He got her mum first.

'Hi, it's Tom Alder. Sorry, it's so late. Can I speak to Claire, please?'

Claire had him down as someone who faffed around, did she? Well, he could be decisive. He'd show her. If she wanted to place obstacles in his way, he'd overcome them. If this phone call, this moment of truth, was Mount Everest, he'd climb it. If it was the Atlantic Ocean, he'd swim it. If he had to reach for—

'Tom?'

'Claire! Fancy coming out with me on a date?'

'Yeah, okay.'

31. AMOUR

In April, just after Easter, Tom and Claire finally went on their first date. For Tom, with Claire no longer in the band, it felt slightly less than perfect, but he was happy.

She hadn't snatched at his original suggestion to go out straight after the 11:30 p.m. phone call in which she agreed to his request. His follow-up suggestion that they go out the following evening was rejected too. It seemed Claire had a strange notion that Tom was obsessed with the idea and needed to calm down.

Arriving at Mile End Odeon, he smiled. He was finally out with *his girlfriend* and they were about to see *Jabberwocky*.

'Here we go then,' he said holding the door for her. He felt like adding "our first date" but didn't want to overplay the moment in case she repeated it loudly and someone overheard and then sat near them and watched their every move the whole way through the film.

'Our first date,' said Claire, loudly without a trace of concern that two girls nearby might hear.

The two girls turned away giggling, confirming Tom's worst fear. Still, by procrastinating at the sweet counter over whether to go for Fruit Pastilles or Refreshers, he was able to ensure that he and Claire went in after them in order to sit as far away as possible.

Taking their seats, he smiled at his girlfriend again and wondered if to hold hands. Maybe not straightaway. But when? Halfway? And what if their hands became clammy and sweaty? Would he pull away? Or would he wait for *her* to pull away? Or would they just sweat it out together?

As it was, he became absorbed enough in Michael Palin's misadventures to put off the decision until near the end of the film, by when it seemed an afterthought.

Outside the cinema, Claire nudged him.

'Mum and Dad are out and Tracey's round her boyfriend's. I reckon if we hurry we could have my place to ourselves for half an hour. If you fancy a snog?'

'Oh right.' It sounded like a bloody brilliant idea.

At the bus stop, Tom thought about his own sister. For some reason he wondered if Lynn had seen *Jabberwocky*.

'What are you thinking?' asked Claire.

'Oh nothing.' He wasn't ready to discuss his half-sister with Claire. Hell, she didn't even know he had a half-brother who Claire had been at school with for the past five and a half years.

'You're doing it again,' said Claire. 'Drifting off.'

'I was thinking about the band.'

Claire checked her watch. Tom checked his.

'Bloody buses,' they said in unison.

Tom wondered what else they might achieve in unison. As it was, they spent the next twenty minutes shivering at the bus stop in unison as the temperature plummeted.

'Must have got stuck in an avalanche,' said Claire, cursing the 277 service.

The bus finally arrived and they managed to claim a double seat.

Claire nudged him.

'You might as well get off at your stop. Mum and Dad are bound to be back by now and Tracey won't be far behind.'

Tom's heart started thumping.

'My bedroom's free.'

'Tom...' Claire leaned in close and lowered her voice. 'I really like you. I think you know that. But I'm not ready to hang around in your bedroom while you work out how to trick me into a massive snog-leading-to-the-inevitable with no possibility of escape.'

Tom laughed. '*No Possibility of Escape*. Good name for an album.'

Claire's mouth was close to his ear.

'I do like you.'

Tom was pretty hot under the collar. God, he loved her. Why wouldn't she snog in his bedroom? It didn't have to lead to the inevitable. And anyway, just because it was called "the inevitable" didn't mean they actually had to do it.

By the time they were approaching his stop, most of the passengers had already got off and there wouldn't be too many potential witnesses to their farewell.

'This is my stop,' he said.

'I know.'

'Better get going then or I'll have to walk back from the shops.'

'Thanks for asking me out, Tom. I really enjoyed it.'

'Right, well, I'll be getting off then.' He gulped because he had forgotten to breathe. Then, reminding himself that he was seventeen, he leaned over to kiss her. Their timing was once again in unison because she too leaned forward and, aided by the bus going over a pothole, their teeth banged together.

'Oww!' she protested.

'Erm... right, I'd better...'

For some reason, possibly temporary insanity, he

patted her thigh.

Holy shit.

He leapt off as the bus stopped by the fire station. A moment later, it roared away. He watched it pass out of view as the bend took it towards Christ Church.

Deeply in love, he turned the corner into East Ferry Road. All he needed now was to get Claire back in the band.

Over the next couple of weeks, they went out three more times. Each time, Claire made sure she was in a position to escape the inevitable, but Tom enjoyed what she did allow. Quite a bit of snogging and listening to music in her bedroom. She even bought him a present – a classical LP.

'Stretch those music muscles, Tom.'

When he suggested that she re-join the band, she seemed dubious.

'The Damned are worth a listen,' she said. But top of Tom's to-buy list was former Genesis singer Peter Gabriel's first solo album.

Then, a week later, with no progress on the band front, surprising news that promised to take their personal relationship to the next level came on the 277 bus to school.

'Do you know Point Clear?' said Claire.

'Er… Essex Riviera, right? And… don't you have a caravan there?'

'Mum and Dad are opening it next weekend.'

Tom was curious. Claire's cheeks looked very slightly flushed.

'A sort of spring clean, is it? For the new season?'

'Yeah. Fancy coming?'

Tom's heart began thumping while his brain boiled over with possibilities.

'Who's going?'

'Mum, Dad, you and me.'

'They don't mind me going?'

'They've known you eighteen months, Tom. They trust you.'

'Do they?' He was slightly disappointed. They obviously saw him as some inexperienced schoolboy who occasionally had guitar lessons with their daughter. Okay, so they were right, but it still annoyed him. 'So, would you and me…?'

'There's a sofa-bed for you.'

'Absolutely. I wasn't suggesting… I mean I'd love to come.'

Claire lowered her voice. 'If I let you go for it with me, you'd rock me and the bloody caravan over. That would take a bit of explaining.'

Tom felt faint. 'I'm guessing our "moment" will require distance from your parents.'

'Our moment is still a little way off, so be patient…' she leaned up to his ear and whispered, 'you sex-mad loony.'

He smiled and started humming "Somethin' Stupid". God, he loved Claire Cross. She was just the most amazing female on earth.

'He's number one, isn't he?' said Claire, referring to Frank Sinatra's compilation album at the top of the LP charts.

'No,' said Tom. He leaned close to her ear to whisper. 'You're number one.'

32. THE CARAVAN

After what seemed like the timespan of the Roman Empire, the long-awaited Saturday to Sunday stopover at the caravan was upon them. Tom was beside himself with all manner of positive vibes. Playing with a constantly meowing Archie in the Cross' kitchen while they got ready, he realised that his biggest challenge would be to appear unfazed by the prospect of sleeping under the same flimsy roof as his girlfriend.

He could see it now. Three a.m. Lying awake. The sound of Claire breathing a few yards away. It was hard to think of anything more romantic. Of course, it would be unwise to get too physically excited in case it was Mrs Cross he was hearing. Or worse, Mr Cross.

He casually eyed the calendar with "caravan + Tom" scrawled beside the date. Feeling curious, he flipped over from April to May. There were a couple of other caravan entries…

'You alright, Tom?'

He nonchalantly abandoned the calendar and smiled at Mrs Cross.

'Fine, thanks.'

Once Archie was placed in the care of a neighbour and the final checks had been made, they were ready.

'I hope Francine and I don't cramp your style,' said Mr Cross as they drove off. 'If you and Claire want to…. you know.'

Tom was aghast.

'…do any studying,' Francine added.

Tom sighed quietly.

'Brought any books?' said Mr Cross.

Claire had warned him to bring a book. Well, her parents were lecturers, after all. It was bound to be the first thing they would worry about. Their teenage daughter not studying.

'Shakespeare,' said Tom. It was a name capable of placating any parent – or lecturer.

'You can't beat the bard.'

'No, Mr Cross.'

'Roger, please. It's Roger.'

'Oh, right.' But Tom couldn't think of Claire's dad as Roger. It made him sound like a pirate.

The journey to Point Clear was uneventful. Dull, if anything. With Claire sitting in the front alongside her dad, leaving Tom in the back with Francine, the conversation lacked a certain zing. In fact, the only thing of interest had been Mr Cross enthusing about the Martello tower. Tom was intrigued and wondered if the Martello tower was anything like the Eiffel Tower.

On arrival, Tom was unimpressed by the vista. Point Clear consisted of a few residential streets, caravans and… more caravans.

'Clacton isn't far,' said Francine, invoking the ultimate insult to a dull place – its proximity to somewhere else.

For Tom, though, it didn't matter. He was with Claire.

After a reviving cuppa in the caravan, Francine got started on the cleaning. As Claire prepared to join her, Mr Cross shooed her away.

'Go and show Tom around.'

Tom was relieved. Cleaning caravans wasn't high on the list of things he wanted to do.

Outside, Claire took a lungful of fresh air then clapped her hands in a business-like manner.

'The Martello tower!'

'Great.'

On the short walk, Claire pointed out some of the different types of caravan. To Tom, they all looked capable of hosting a fun weekend for a bunch of blokes, or a bloke and his girlfriend. Then Point Clear ran out of caravans and they were looking at an old, dull, squat grey structure.

'Ta-da!' sang Claire.

'The Martello tower?' guessed Tom, a tad disappointed.

'Originally designed to ward off Napoleon, it now serves to ward off boredom.'

'Shame Napoleon didn't invade,' said Tom. 'He might have knocked it down.'

Next they looked at the sea.

'Glad you came?' Claire asked.

'Very glad.'

She smiled. Maybe she felt responsible for dragging him out of London to a place where it was likely that nothing interesting would happen. Well, how could it? Her mum and dad were there.

'Nice fresh air,' she said.

He couldn't argue with that. No industrial chimneys here.

'Come on,' she said, 'let's try the other way.'

She took his hand and off they went, walking into a kind of wilderness.

'Lots of birds here,' she said. 'Of the feathered kind.'

'Yeah, it's nice.'

'It's popular with the family. If it's not Mum and Dad coming down for the weekend, it's Tracey or my nan or Auntie Vi or Uncle Sid.'

'Do you ever come down? On your own, I mean.'

'There's no way Mum would let us have the caravan to ourselves, Tom. Besides, we've agreed that I'm not ready yet, haven't we.'

'Did Steve come down here?'

'No. No, he didn't.'

Despite what she had just said, Tom wondered if this was the moment to push his luck.

'I was just thinking. You know, you and me…'

'See, the thing with Steve was… he was always going on about it. That's why I like you, Tom. You're not pushy.'

'No, exactly.'

'That's why you might get a bit further than Steve. In time.'

'Right… well… fair enough.'

Something began to brew. If he *could* get Claire back to Point Clear *alone*…

What if there was a week where the caravan was free and Claire was away at, say, "her friend's house"? Janine's! Yes, what if Claire had "a friend" in Janine? Mr and Mrs Cross would swallow that on the basis that Janine came from Money-by-the-Water. Polly wouldn't object to confirming it: "Yes, Claire is spending the weekend with her friend Janine." Meanwhile, Claire would be in the caravan with Tom for a weekend of… well, not looking at the Martello tower.

'I wonder how Polly's getting on,' said Claire, staring out across the barren expanse.

'Polly?' Polly's parents seeking a divorce came to mind.

'I hope he doesn't get hurt.'

'Why would he get hurt?'

'He's going to a demo.'

'Is he?'

'He's your friend. Don't you listen to him?'

'Trust me, Claire. I've listened to plenty of Polly.'

'Yeah, well, the police are expecting a small number to shout down the National Front. But the SWP are organising something bigger.'

'You're well out of it.'

'I do want to do something. Maybe the SWP's a good way to get involved.'

Tom wasn't so sure. Actually, he *was* sure – that it was a stupid idea. But he wanted to be with Claire, and look out for her, and protect her if need be.

'I meant to tell you,' she said. 'I'd like to re-join the band.'

'Oh. Right. Brilliant.'

'But only on condition we get a focus on what we're trying to achieve.'

'Okay. We can discuss that. I'm sure we'll see eye to eye.'

He moved in close, eye to eye. They laughed. Then they tried lips to lips.

Later, after a walk of two miles, seven kisses and three hugs, they returned for the evening meal. Francine had put eggs, ham and mushrooms on the side.

'If you youngsters wouldn't mind cooking,' she said. 'It's omelettes.'

Claire eyed Tom. 'Do you cook?'

'Oh, a bit,' he said, unable to reveal his non-cooking status to someone he was keen to impress.

'We're just going for a quick walk,' said Francine.

'A bit of fresh air,' said Mr Cross. 'Might take a look at the Martello tower.'

'Right,' said Tom. *See you in three minutes then.*

Watching them go, something odd struck him. In all his years, he'd never seen Ted and Rose go out for a walk together.

'Right then…' said Claire.

'Yes, right then…'

'I don't think our "right thens" mean the same thing, Tom.'

'Eggs then…' His face felt hot enough to cook the omelette. He didn't like telling lies to Claire. He'd have to admit he wasn't a cook. Their love would survive it. And frankly, *how* did you get the ham and mushrooms inside the eggy bit?

She whispered in his ear. 'I love a man who can cook.'

Oh God, he couldn't disappoint the girl he hoped to marry one day.

'Okay, here we go then.'

He put the frying pan on the hob and lit the gas under it.

'Good,' said Claire. 'I'll set the table.'

Tom tapped the first egg with a knife. Nothing happened. What were they – bullet-proof? He rapped it harder. The knife went straight through, splurging slimy, gooey egg all over his hand and trouser leg. He tipped what remained into the pan. It sizzled but drily and stuck to the bottom. Something was wrong.

'You okay?' said Claire. She was sitting at the laid table.

'Fine.'

There was a smell coming up, but it wasn't a nice aroma of frying. Then he spotted half a pack of lard.

Shit.

He quickly unwrapped it and put the white half-block in the frying pan. It spat at him like the tongue of the Devil.

'You sure you're okay?' said Claire.

'I'm fine.'

He tried to lift the pan off the heat but the handle slid through his slimy egg-whitey and lardy hand, slopping some of the melted lard onto the hob, where it caught fire. He tried to dab it out with a tissue but that caught fire too, forcing him to drop it. It landed on his shoe, setting his laces on fire.

'Claire, I think I'm doing it wrong.'

Claire hurried over, turned off the gas, dampened a tea-towel and put it over the flames.

'Why don't you sit down?' she said.

Tom sheepishly took a seat and felt bad as Claire scrubbed everything, including the ceiling, back to normality. Then she whipped up a delicious-smelling ham and mushroom omelette.

Tom was disappointed. He still hadn't learned how to fit the ham and mushroom inside the eggy bit.

'Playing any concerts?' Francine asked Tom as they tucked in fifteen minutes later.

'Concerts? Not at the moment.'

'We're doing a gig for Rock Against Racism,' said Claire. 'In May.'

Tom gave her his politest "what are you talking about?" look.

Claire smiled. 'Polly had a word with a couple of his friends.'

Mr Cross then regaled them with stories about the area. One related to a flood in the 1950s that killed hundreds of people when low pressure pulled a lot of the North Sea over the defences and washed everything away. Tom was glad about that. Now he wouldn't be able to sleep. Not that he would have slept much anyway. Not with Claire six feet away behind a flimsy partition.

Later, on his back in his makeshift bed, he felt strange. It was as if he were now part of the Cross family. Then, as always happened these days when he thought of families, he thought about his sister. Where was she sleeping tonight? It was funny. Females had hardly figured in his life until recently. Now he had Claire and Lynn.

Around one a.m. he finally drifted off. His last thoughts concerned this very caravan and how he might get Claire back to it without her parents.

33. LET'S HEAR IT FOR...

Back at school on the Monday, during mid-morning break, Polly recounted his exciting weekend. While Tom was taking in the coastal treats of Essex, he'd been on the rampage with the SWP.

'There must have been a thousand National Front lined up behind the Old Bill. It was pretty scary. Anyway, while they marched through Wood Green, we made our way to some school where they were going to end up. So there they are coming towards us and there's, what, three thousand of us...'

'Sounds like an ambush,' said Tom.

'Too right. Eggs, rotten fruit, you name it. Anyway, next thing you know, we're chasing them. Do you know Turnpike Lane?'

'Get on with the story, Poll.'

'Well, a load of them are still marching up to the North Circular. Anyway, they've gone down Powys Lane and it's all ended up at Broomfield Park. You've seen the battle scenes in Lawrence of Arabia? Like that, it was. I ducked out after that. The police got well involved and I'm not as mad as some of our lot.'

'Oh yeah, the peaceable socialists. Standing up for liberty by punching people they don't like.'

'The people we don't like are called fascists, Tom. Had people punched a few of them in the thirties we wouldn't have got Hitler destroying half of Europe.'

'You're lucky you didn't get nicked.'

'Yeah, there were a few arrests on our side. And a few taken to hospital.'

'Sounds crazy,' said Tom, shaking his head. This wasn't the way forward. At least not for him, and certainly not for Claire.

'I'm looking forward to your gig,' said Polly.

Tom sighed. 'Rock Against Racism needs to focus on what matters. The minute they start rioting, I'm off. And so is Claire.'

'Fair enough, Tom, but you don't speak for Claire.'

'No, well, but I do care about her.'

'So do I, Tom. So do I.'

Tom didn't like the way he said it.

Claire brought Den the drummer back into the fold. His act of betrayal in the run-up to the Christmas Dance was forgiven – although a smiling Tom made a mental note to look out for another drummer.

Their rehearsals clicked into gear quite well. The band sounded okay. The line-up was Roy and Tom on guitars, Claire on bass and Den on drums, with vocals split equally between Roy and Claire.

The choice of songs for their upcoming forty-minute set proved less straightforward. Tom thought they should keep "The Boys Are Back" but Claire wanted to add a girl-related lyric and chorus, which Tom found disrespectful to the songwriter. In the end, with Roy and Den weighing in, they came up with a bunch of songs they all liked, even though it would mean Tom struggling in places.

Later, when he was alone with Claire, he had a bit of a moan about it.

'You just have to practice more,' said Claire. 'The only person holding you back is you.'

'You're very harsh sometimes, Claire.'

'It's because I care about you. I wonder why sometimes, but there it is. I care.'

The songs giving him most trouble were their arrangements of the Flamin' Groovies' "Shake Some Action", the Stranglers' "Get a Grip on Yourself", Heatwave's "Boogie Nights" and Stevie Wonder's "Sir Duke". As a struggling guitarist, Tom found them a bit like climbing Everest.

'Maybe we should try that punk idea again,' he suggested.

Claire appeared to be exasperated by that. But it didn't matter now. Things had moved on. Roy and Den weren't into punk.

Tom agreed to do his best but his shortcomings became all too apparent at their final rehearsal on a Thursday evening in a room above a Bethnal Green pub that Den got for free. Roy started to suggest that Tom might "just drop out a little" here and "fade back a little" there. Tom knew he would be okay if they rehearsed for a few more months, but, as it was, their gig at a pub in Hackney was the following Tuesday.

'Don't worry,' said Claire. 'The place will be noisy, they'll all be drunk.'

'And they won't hear me. Great. Remind me again why I'm on stage?'

'Honestly, you'll be fine,' said Claire. 'Just be more confident.'

'Like you, you mean?'

She kissed him even though Den and Roy were there.

He would write up her comments in *A Journey Into Music.* His journal needed to show the lives of those around him, especially Claire's positive influence.

In the Waterman's Arms on the Friday night, Polly was full of it.

'This is just the start. Soon you'll be writing your own stuff. Rebel music. Now music. It's what Britain is crying out for.' He was reacting mainly to the National Front gaining almost 120,000 votes in the Greater London Council election.

'Yeah, well, someone needs to do something,' Tom agreed.

'Not someone. *You*. Write the songs people need to hear.'

Maybe Polly had a point, but it wouldn't be easy. Judging by the album charts, people didn't like rebel music or now music. They preferred Abba, The Shadows, Frank Sinatra, The Hollies and Glenn Miller.

Claire suggested Tom go out and buy an album of raw power that he could learn and do justice to. A simple punk-style album that he could bring to the band *with passion* and get them to adopt. Apparently, there were albums out there right now by the Damned, the Clash and the Ramones.

On the Saturday, Tom dragged Neil over to the King's Road in Chelsea in a last-ditch attempt to embrace punk. If it worked, he would turn Red Sails into a punk band. His passion for the genre would win the day. Claire was right – you can't argue with passion.

On the District Line from Mile End, he wondered what kind of scene they would walk into.

'Do you think they're rough?' said Neil.

'Only in the way they look.'

'They're a bit smelly, aren't they?'

'We won't say that, eh?'

'Micky says they're not hard. More middle class rebels in tatty clothes.'

'I can't imagine Micky called them middle class rebels.'

'No, he didn't use the word "rebels".'

'Funny how there aren't any real punks on the Island or in Poplar.'

'There *are*,' said Neil. 'I saw a bloke with pink hair a few weeks back.'

'A bloke? One bloke?'

'And Claire's got black hair.'

'It hasn't really caught on though, has it.'

They left the Tube at Sloane Square and headed west along King's Road. There were punks dotted around in twos and threes.

'Well, we've come to the right place,' said Tom.

'Yeah,' said Neil, 'although now we're here, it feels like we've come to the wrong place.'

Tom agreed. For all the world it looked like bored middle-class kids had formed a club and created a shabby uniform.

They ventured further west and found more punks. What they failed to find was any kind of reason to join them.

'They say punk died the day The Clash signed with CBS,' said Neil.

'Yeah,' said Tom.

But for a musician that was part of the allure. The Sex Pistols got forty grand for signing with EMI. CBS Records gave The Clash a hundred grand. You couldn't overlook that kind of thing if you were wondering whether or not you should form a punk band.

They went into a record shop. Strapped for cash, Tom struggled for half an hour over which LP to buy. The

Clash? The Damned? The Ramones? In the end, he left with Genesis *Live*. Well, it was 50p off and he had long fancied owning a copy.

The gig at a pub in Hackney came around. A lot of the talk among the Rock Against Racism fraternity centred on the NF's GLC election performance. How could they get over five percent of the vote? And what could the Left do about it? Tom didn't think it appropriate to mention that the Tories had won the election by a mile and that the whole thing could be explained away in a single word: democracy. He was beginning to suspect that democracy wasn't good enough for some of his new friends.

'So,' he said to Claire, trying to embrace the moment, 'our first Rock Against Racism gig. Well, our first gig of any kind, really. I mean you can't count ten seconds on stage in Millwall.'

'Indeed not.'

Claire looked great, even with her freshly-spiked hairstyle. Tom had chosen to stay with his regular hairstyle, which hadn't changed since he was twelve – apart from the one time in 1975 when he grew it longer in pursuit of something he called "the look". As for the audience – they had a range of hairstyles, but "scruffy" would have covered about ninety percent of them.

'Best of luck,' said Neil.

Tom patted him on the arm. 'Whatever happens, Neil, do not burn the building down.'

Polly was there too, openly wielding a copy of punk magazine *Temporary Hoarding*, as were Janine, Oz, and Doops – and all wished Red Sails a fair wind. They were supporting a local reggae band called London Style Sound and Tom worried that Hackney's reggae regulars in the audience might not take to a bunch of outsiders. As it was, the first person to greet him was a face he recognized.

'Hey, the white Hendrix! Ha-ha!'

'Furze Street, right?' said Tom. 'Still playing "Concrete Jungle"?'

'Hey, we open with it!'

It turned out that this Jamaican-born musical warrior was called Trevor and, when not bestriding the stage, worked for Hackney Council as an admin assistant in technical services. Such mundanity helped Tom relax. He even had half a lager. Red Sails would be fine. As long as he didn't drag them down with his lack of rhythm or know-how. Or throw up on stage through nerves.

Either way, this would make a good entry in *A Journey Into Music.*

As it was, their opener, "Shake Some Action", struck exactly the right note with the reasonable-sized crowd. Tom concentrated on his timing, played in his big chords where required and let Roy do all the fancy stuff. Not that Roy thought it fancy – just regular playing. After that, Claire struck gold by singing "Get a Grip on Yourself" in a suggestive manner. It certainly got a laugh when she suggested it to Tom.

The rest of the gig flew by and Tom could finally begin to enjoy himself. By the time London Style Sound let rip with "Concrete Jungle", he was finishing his third lager, ridiculously pleased to have completed his first ever gig but now absolutely certain he wasn't in Claire's league. That said, nor was anyone else.

Outside at closing time, watching Den load his kit into his brother-in-law's Vauxhall Victor estate, there was a final round of congratulations.

'Brilliant,' said Polly.

'Definitely,' said Oz, patting Tom on the arm.

Doops winked at him.

As they broke up amid goodbyes and waves, Tom found himself with Neil.

'You'll be stars before you know it, Tom.'

Tom leaned in close.

'Claire's going places. Roy too, maybe, and Den. But Claire – it sticks out a hundred miles.'

'Yeah,' said Neil. 'Eighteen months ago, who would have known?'

Tom sighed. He had known since the week leading up to his sixteenth birthday, when it smashed into his brain that Claire Cross was amazing. He'd lost her and won her back a couple of times since then. But now he could see her moving onward and upward to a place he couldn't follow. If he lost her again, he knew it would be forever.

34. JUBILEE

To mark Queen Elizabeth the Second's Silver Jubilee, the BBC banned the Sex Pistols' single "God Save The Queen" and the Government declared an extended Bank Holiday from Saturday the fourth of June to Tuesday the seventh. Getting into the spirit of the thing, Tom rejected Option One, schoolwork, in favour of Option Two, which involved plenty of drinking and relaxing, although not quite enough of Claire. For part of the holiday, she would be away at Point Clear with Brenda and a girl violinist friend of theirs.

The festivities kicked off on the Friday night in the Waterman's Arms. There Tom met up with Claire, Brenda, Neil, Polly and Janine. Needless to say, Polly and Janine found the whole thing distasteful. How could the British public openly pledge themselves to an unelected Head of State? Tom, Neil, Claire and Brenda disagreed and didn't think the British public were likely to throw street parties in honour of Jim Callaghan, their elected leader.

Polly appeared to not like street parties at all. He seemed to feel that the streets had a more important role to play in British life, as a place for protest. According to Janine, Tom was still in the process of waking up. Although he was, apparently, ahead of many others. Tom politely deflected Janine's concerns. He didn't wish to see first-hand that the Metropolitan Police were targeting young black people in Lewisham and trade unionists at Grunwick's in Willesden. Janine and Polly had been to both and given him more than enough details.

While Tom kept his distance politically, Claire felt there was more she could, and possibly should, be doing to change society for the better.

'I'll tell you what I'd like to know,' said Tom. 'When am I going to see one of these Jubilee buses they've painted silver?' He swiftly moved to block Polly's scorn. 'Only joking, Poll.'

'Not funny, Tom. We're citizens not subjects. They want to take freedom away from us.'

'Yeah, fair enough – I heard about the Government blocking the Sex Pistols from getting to number one.'

Polly flared. 'Yeah, the bastards.'

'It's only a rumour,' said Neil.

To Tom, it seemed unlikely that the Government would fix the charts to stop "God Save the Queen" from reaching the top but he knew the story would get Polly going.

'Maybe we should have a protest march about it, Poll,' he said.

'Typical of the gutless BBC to ban it,' said Janine.

'They've banned the Stranglers too,' said Brenda, referring to "Peaches".

'There's a good rocking B-side to that,' said Janine. '"Go Buddy Go". You should learn to play it, Tom.'

But Tom didn't want to talk about the hard work of endlessly learning new songs in a band that was continually exposing his weaknesses. He wanted to have fun and enjoy himself. But that wasn't so easy when Claire agreed to go to an SWP meeting the following week with Polly.

'A date?' said Tom, when they had a moment alone.

'A political date,' said Claire.

'It's still got the word "date" in it.'

'Don't you trust me?'

'Of course I do.'

'And I trust you too – even at Doops' party tomorrow.'

'I'm going with Neil. The only more certain way to repel women would be to take my mum along with me.'

Yes, of course he trusted Claire. And Polly was seeing Janine, so yes, he trusted Polly too.

Most of Saturday came and went in the form of a morning hangover, an afternoon of watching the England versus Scotland football match on telly and a tea-time session of listening to Pink Floyd, Genesis and a snatch of the Schubert piano LP Claire had bought him.

Then Neil phoned – he didn't fancy going to Doops' and Oz's party.

For Tom, the conundrum loomed large. Would he still go? Polly would be there. Maybe it would be a good way for them to strengthen their friendship. Tom could use it to make it clear that Claire was his girlfriend. Janine would be there. Maybe he could subtly draw attention to what an amazing couple they made.

On the downside, Claire was at Point Clear and he still fancied Doops.

At six p.m., he decided that he wouldn't go. As a grown-up, he would not be led by his loins. Polly and Janine could bore each other to death and Doops could shag someone else.

By six-thirty, he was wondering if he might just pop along for a drink and a chat.

By seven, he'd decided to watch telly with his mum.

By eight, he'd decided to run a bath.

Mr Reid at school once said that great literature was the most important thing a student could fill their head with, and that all other thoughts and practices led to ignorance and misery, although blindness was just a myth. It got a titter but Tom knew the truth. Thoughts of literature never bombarded his brain. Thoughts of women did. And right now, he was thinking a hell of a lot about Ann-Marie du Pont. Okay, so she had probably slept with a bloke or two since she first came on to him. But so what? She was a great person. Friendly. Open. Caring and sharing. Maybe that was the plus side of socialism.

Rose came upstairs.

'What are you running a bath for?'

'So I can have a bath.'

'A bath?'

Tom frowned. 'That's why it's there.'

Rose looked puzzled. 'What time is it?'

'Bath time,' said Tom.

He gave himself the works: ears, neck... well, everything. Then he got dressed, combed his hair and splashed some *Hai Karate* around the gills.

By nine p.m., he was on a 277 heading north along Westferry Road. Even then, he kept wondering if to hop off at the next stop and walk back home. Passing a recently closed riverside factory with "No Future" sprayed next to the padlocked gates, he wondered about his own future.

Arriving at Cassland Road, he paused outside the house. Did it matter if he was unfaithful to Claire? Wasn't she starting to move away from him anyway? Not just in the direction the band was heading, but now with her deepening interest in politics. He wasn't stupid. He could see a time coming where they would have nothing in common. Yes, she kept confirming that they had something special and that he was the one, but they never seemed to get any closer to doing anything about it.

He chastised himself. It was his hormones again. They were shunting Claire aside. He slipped down the side of the house. He could fight stupid hormones.

He entered through the back into the kitchen where Oz and two other beardy blokes were smoking.

'Tom! You came!' Oz offered him the joint.

Tom declined. He placed his beers on the side, took one and headed into the front room in search of Doops, Polly and Janine. None of them were there.

Biding his time, he joined three women discussing abortion rights. He mainly sipped from his can while nodding at their earnest opinions.

Ten minutes later, with his beer can empty, he sighed. It was meant to be a party but there wasn't even any music. Just the drone of people going on about politics while puffing on shared skinny roll-ups. Where the hell was Polly?

'Anyone see the football?' he asked.

'Was there a match?' one of the women asked.

'England-Scotland. Scotland won two-one.' He decided not to mention how Gordon McQueen and Kenny Dalglish had given Scotland a deserved lead and how England could only reply with a pathetic late penalty by Mick Channon. He also decided not to mention how it was a great result for Ally MacLeod, the new Scotland manager, and surely the end for England's Don Revie. There was one aspect of the encounter possibly worth a mention in the present company though.

'It all went mad at the end,' he said. 'The Scotland fans stormed the pitch, ripped up the turf and tore down the goalposts.' He had their attention. Now to say something that would keep them. 'There's a lot of pent-up tension there, I reckon. They still see England as the old master.'

'Oh, so true,' said one of the women. 'Were there many arrests?'

Tom filled them in and then went on to talk about Rock Against Racism. The next ten minutes flew by as they got into an earnest chat about music. Then it switched back to politics and Tom was bored again. He didn't know anyone or why he'd come.

To avoid looking like a spare part, he went up to the loo, even though he didn't need to go. Then, on a gut feeling, he approached the only bedroom with a closed door. Doops' room. Just then, the door opened and a blond bloke came out.

'Tom!' It was Doops. By the door. Naked.

He felt like running.

'Come on, soldier,' she said, taking a step back into the room.

He moved to the door. She pulled him inside, pushed the door closed and flopped backwards onto the bed.

Tom was troubled. Hadn't she just finished shagging the blond bloke? What was he meant to do? Exactly how desperate was he? And would anyone find out?

'I was looking for Polly and Janine,' he said.

'They went to the off license. Probably popped in the pub for a couple. Cheeky so-and-so's.'

'Er, well, I'd better…'

'He got me close, Tom. Come and take me over the line.'

'Well…'

The door opened. It was some other bloke.

'Oh sorry,' said the other bloke.

Tom came to his senses. He was horrified. What

would Claire think?

'Sorry,' he said to neither of them.

He pushed past the other bloke, hit the stairs, escaped by the back door and hurried away from Cassland Road.

Jubilee Sunday was all about street parties. Neil called round for Tom in order to hang around one in Manchester Grove. Not that Tom was thinking about the Queen. He was thinking about himself. In essence, what did he actually want from his relationship with Claire? What did he want from the band? Basically, what did he want from life? He needed to place himself in the world. Work out who he was. Then people would see that he was on *terra firma*. They would see a solid person. A man of substance. A man at ease with himself. In short, a man.

'What did you get up to last night?' Neil asked as they slurped warm lager from small cans under a grey sky.

'Me? Nothing.'

The band was playing mainstream traditional jazz and Tom was sure if he stayed long enough they'd play "When the Saints Go Marching In" at least three more times.

'*Kojak* was good,' said Neil.

Tom assumed that Kojak had got the bad guy and looked cool, and all done without dropping his lollipop.

'What do you think of Doops?' he asked.

'I don't really know her.'

'You've met her though.'

'Yeah, but…'

'So, what do you think of her?'

'She's nice. A bit scary, but…'

'Scary?'

'You know, like a female version of the child-catcher

in *Chitty Chitty Bang Bang.*'
'Not your type then.'
Neil frowned. 'What are you on about?'
'I'm just saying, if she was stark naked…'
'What's happened, Tom?'
'Nothing. Forget it. So what happened in *Kojak*?'
Neil explained but Tom didn't hear.

Later, at bedtime, he listened intently to the LP Claire had given him. Laying on his bed in the dark, he took in Schubert's tinkling *allegro moderato* from the piano sonata D664. It felt like a story unfolding. It was the story of a hopeful young man strolling by the river. He sees a girl. They smile. A beautiful piece of music. A beautiful dream.

Jubilee Monday was all about Tom welcoming Claire back to civilisation but being unable to do so properly because they were never alone. This was mainly down to Claire suddenly deciding to go into Central London to see the Jubilee parade. With Neil and Brenda tagging along, there was no opportunity for privacy.

'So what sort of things did you get up to?' Neil asked as they boarded a 277 bound for Mile End tube station.

Claire feigned shock. 'Ooh Neil, you rascal. What a dirty mind you have.'

Neil turned red and tried to avoid the glances of the few other passengers.

'I simply meant did you explore or…'

'Neil, those kind of intimate details have to remain private.' But she ruffled his hair and relented. 'It was fun. All girls together.'

'I've never been to Point Clear,' said Neil.

Tom sniffed. 'Imagine the moon with a cold breeze.'

They watched the parade from St Paul's Cathedral. Annoyingly, Neil kept singing The Jam's "In The City". Tom suggested the Queen might not want to hear him singing punk rock, but Neil was adamant it wasn't punk, but something called New Wave. Luckily, the rain held off and they got to wave to the Queen. Well, Neil waved to the Queen; the rest of them just took in the impressive State spectacle.

Later, they returned to the Isle of Dogs and headed for the Waterman's, where Polly and Janine joined them.

'Didn't fancy the celebrations then?' asked Tom.

'Celebrations?' said Polly. 'To be honest, we were a bit busy.'

'*Very* busy,' said Janine, patting Polly's bum.

Tom hurt a little inside. Yes, he was glad that these two were mixing their molecules but when would it be his turn with Claire?

'So when are you playing next?' asked Polly.

'Next month,' said Claire. 'The Summer Dance.'

Tom shot her a look of complete surprise.

'I sorted it out on Friday,' she said. 'Before I went away. I was going to mention it to you.'

'What about Roy and Den?'

'They're okay.'

'You mean you asked them first? Priorities, eh?'

'Don't be silly. I had to make sure they weren't already booked.'

'No, well, fair enough…'

It didn't negate the feeling that he was the least important component of his own band.

'We'll look forward to it then,' said Janine.

'Anyone ever thought of going to India?' said Neil.

'What?' said Tom. He was furious now.

'I'd love to go to India,' said Neil.

'What for?'

'You know, to do the whole spiritual thing.'

'Right. So how does that work, exactly?'

'How do you mean?'

'I thought the whole spiritual thing was an inner journey.'

'It is.'

'Then why do you have to go to India?'

'Well, you stay in an ashram.'

'And what's an ashram?'

'I'm not sure, but the Beatles stayed in one.'

'The Beatles?'

'Yeah, I wouldn't mind finding illumination.'

'Go to Blackpool then. It's famous for it.'

'I'm just saying – there should be a spiritual element to life.'

'Opium for the masses,' said Polly. 'The only communal activity worth a light is the struggle against oppression.'

'I'm just saying,' said Neil. 'An ashram sounds nice.'

'Fair enough,' said Tom. 'When do you leave?'

Bank Holiday Tuesday held some much-needed promise. For starters, Tom went round Claire's straight after lunch for an all-afternoon guitar session. Outside, he was greeted by Archie.

Tom bent down to stroke his favourite feline's ears, neck and back. Archie purred his approval.

'Listen, Arch. I need you to work with me. We need to get Claire to fall in love with me. Got it? Can I trust you to work on that? There's a couple of kippers in it for you if you do.'

The session felt good. Not that he cared about playing.

He just loved being with Claire. It was as if she had enough energy for both of them.

Claire was keen for him to learn more chords, some of them quite complex. He just loved her voice, and her smile. Although she didn't actually smile much. But he did enjoy her earnest exhortations that he might yet make something of himself. With her support, he felt capable of achieving many things. He wasn't sure what things, but he knew that together they could achieve them, and celebrate those achievements by falling into each other's arms and…

'No, Tom, that is *not* a G sharp major seventh.'

Well, the alternative was to acknowledge the fact he wasn't in her league and that they might not have a shared future.

'Tea?' he suggested. 'Allow me.'

He went downstairs and filled the kettle. It all seemed very quiet. Where was Francine? While the water boiled, his eyes wandered to the calendar. Surely a little peek wouldn't hurt.

Returning to the bedroom with two mugs of tea, he mentioned how quiet it was downstairs.

'Yeah, Mum said she might pop round to Grandad's. How's yours, by the way?'

'Oh, the same. Not great. It's the anniversary of the Upper North Street School bomb next Monday, so I'll pop round. Sixtieth anniversary, as it happens.'

'Sixtieth? Maybe we should do something at school?'

'Yeah, maybe…' Tom always felt sad thinking of those German Gotha planes over the East End in 1917, of no-one on the ground understanding what they were seeing, of one of the bombs killing eighteen small children in Upper North Street School… but it was a private sadness. He didn't want to stand with loads of other people to "reflect" on it.

'You okay, Tom?'

'Yeah…' He was wondering. Shouldn't he share his secrets with Claire? Or did a man retain his secrets while the woman told all? 'I, er… I mean… well… there's something you should know about me.'

'You're an alien from Planet X? I bloody well knew it. It's the green scaly tongue. Dead giveaway.'

'I'm adopted.'

'Ohh.'

A huge, scary silence invaded the room. Claire looked tearful, which had not been Tom's intention at all. He needed to tell her then probably move on to brighter things.

'My dad was no good and legged in to West London. I don't know my real mum. Ted and Rose are good parents though. You won't tell anyone, will you?'

'Of course not!'

'Unless Neil's already told you?'

'Of course he hasn't. Neil's excitable and loves to tell everyone the latest news but he respects you.'

'Yeah, I suppose… and Micky wouldn't have told anyone. He respects Danny too much.'

'What's Danny got to do with it?'

'Yes, well… we were brothers for a while.'

Claire looked set to laugh but stopped herself. 'Go on.'

So Tom told her about Danny being his brother until they were seven, and of Danny becoming his brother again when he learned of Harry's one-man impregnation campaign. He stopped short of talking about Lynn though. That still felt too private to share with anyone apart from Danny.

Claire patted his arm.

'Do you hate him?'

'Harry? Yes. And no. He was our age, Claire. I just think he made some bad choices.'

'Dad's out till this evening,' she said.

'Is he?' Tom's hormones began pumping round his body. 'What about Tracey?'

'God knows. Might not see her till midnight.'

'Interesting.'

'Why, did you want to kiss your girlfriend?'

They plonked their teas down and kissed. They even lay on Claire's bed to get comfortable. Tom thought it was the most wonderful thing in the world – apart from them being fully clothed.

'Are you um…?' Tom wasn't sure how to phrase his thoughts. 'I mean…'

'What?'

'I was wondering. You know. If you were…' Tom gulped. He suddenly felt extremely hot. 'On the Pill, like.'

'Why do you want to know that?'

Tom gagged. 'Why? Did you say *why*? Why do I, *your boyfriend,* want to know the answer to the single most important question… no, one of the most… one of the more important questions… an important… a question of some interest… a degree of interest…'

They began to laugh.

'Of passing interest?' she offered.

'Of mild interest.'

'Of hardly any interest at all? Why do you want to know?'

'Because I'd love to… oh you know why, you nutter.'

Claire hit him with the pillow. 'Don't you call me a nutter!'

He grabbed the pillow off her and then he grabbed her and they kissed more passionately than they had ever done before. His hand even slipped into her undies.

'Well?' he eventually managed to gasp.

'I'm not ready yet.'

'My hand has evidence that says otherwise.'

'I'm not asking you to wait forever. You'll see.'

Tom huffed and withdrew. He was shot through with a disappointment so heavy it seemed to double his weight. They had known each other for ages and had been going out for two whole months. Surely that was long enough. Frankly, he'd soon have enough pent-up energy to power Concorde across the Atlantic.

'Don't be like that, Tom.'

He went to the window. The river was grey and static and seemed to offer little in the way of possibilities. Under the pretence of needing to scratch his nose, he took in her scent. It was so wonderful it almost made his nostrils explode. Such infinite complexity and promise.

Below, in the tiny garden, Archie was studiously grooming himself.

Claire appeared at Tom's side.

And she put her hand in his underwear. 'You got up too quick. Didn't give me a chance to ask my question.'

'What question?'

'If I rub this thing in here, what happens?'

'Oh… well, we could always find out.'

They lay back on the bed and she pulled his trousers down a little.

'He's a big fella,' she said, taking hold.

Tom's heart thumped and his world broadened. It wasn't actual sex but as compromises went it was brilliantly amazingly fantastically wonderful.

35. A SONG FOR YOU

The next few weeks flew by and Tom was very happy with his new arrangement with Claire. He was almost a man of the world. A half-virgin. A hirgin. But while things with Claire were going well, the band was a different matter.

The Docklands Summer Dance was approaching, but Tom didn't fancy it. It felt like the wrong get-together at the wrong time. Yes, they would play a set but anyone who knew anything about music would see he was a passenger in his own band.

Danny wouldn't take the piss, of course. He was getting too old for that. Well, that and him being appointed All Saints Head Boy for next year. No, he would just give a wry smile. All that stuff Danny said about not troubling himself with things he couldn't be brilliant at... it came back to Tom. He supposed the idea was that it didn't matter as long as you enjoyed yourself. But what if you didn't?

Back when he was fifteen, he'd craved the adulation of the crowd. Okay, so three months off his eighteenth birthday he still fancied being the next guitarist in Pink Floyd or Genesis, but he knew with absolute certainty that it wouldn't really happen. He wasn't going to be the next Gilmour or Hackett. Not by a million miles. He was only going to be the next Tom Alder and it all seemed pretty ordinary.

He thought back to the punk rock idea. Why hadn't he grasped that as a possibility? He could play as well as some of the people playing that kind of music. But they loved what they did. They thrived on its energy, its wild excesses. In a way, it was a true variant of rock and roll. He saw it for himself when Claire and Polly took him along to the Bridge House in Canning Town to see the Damned. But it left him feeling that something was missing. He preferred the new local band he'd seen there with Neil the week before; a heavy metal outfit with just as much energy called Iron Maiden. Not that he had the ability to play like them.

He was being harsh, of course. He didn't want to be a musical fascist. He was sure the Damned, the Clash and the others would make something of themselves with or without him boarding their ship. They had their fans. Passion would always come out of that relationship. He just didn't connect with it. That was the problem.

Neil handed Tom a can of beer.

'To calm the nerves.'

Tom looked around the large room filled with friends and schoolmates. Red Sails were due on stage in fifteen minutes.

He clunked Neil's can.

'Cheers, Neil. You're a good mate.'

'Are you alright? You look a bit down.'

'I'm fine. Thanks for asking.'

'It's purely selfish, Tom. I want you to relax so you can play and I don't have to…' he lowered his voice, 'burn the place down.'

Tom smiled. Apparently, the identity of the culprit was still unknown to the police. It was just like when Ronnie

Kray shot George Cornell in the Blind Beggar pub and no-one saw it.

As it was, the gig went well. Once the first song nerves were out of the way, Tom enjoyed himself standing alongside Claire, who was spellbinding. Of course, he had to hold back and fade away here and there but if they stuck with these songs for the next three months, he felt he'd come to the fore. Only, he knew they would ditch the songs in favour of others. And it was hard to keep up.

After the gig, he decided to get drunk. Polly latching on to him wasn't going to stop him. In fact, it was the perfect platform. Polly talking politics gave him plenty of glugging time. The alternative was to disagree with him, and that was hard work, and ultimately pointless.

Predictions about Grunwick's appeared to be on tonight's agenda. Polly was predicting that the violent industrial dispute at the photo-processing plant in Willesden would herald a renewal of union strength. Tom thought Polly should steer clear of predictions. Last time they had a drink together, Polly predicted that Rod Stewart, who had been at number one for four weeks with "I Don't Want To Talk About It", would give way to the Sex Pistols' "God Save The Queen". 'This will finally open up the singles chart to punk,' Polly had predicted. 'A landslide of new music will wipe away all the old crap at the top of the charts. Rod Stewart will not be number one next week. You'll see.'

It turned out that Polly was right. Rod Stewart wasn't number one the following week. It was country singer Kenny Rogers with "You Picked a Fine Time to Leave Me, Lucille".

Uninterested in an *entire* evening of hearing about Grunwick's, Tom reminded Polly about the Government stopping the Sex Pistols reaching the top when, despite being banned from airplay by the BBC, it had "obviously" been the best-selling single of Jubilee week.

Polly went for it. 'The Pistols can't get a gig in London these days. Or the Stranglers. Bloody blanket bans. I mean the GLC shouldn't have that kind of power.'

'Fair point,' said Tom. Then something occurred to him. 'How's things at home. With your mum and dad, I mean.'

Polly seemed surprised. 'What's that got to do with anything important?'

Tom shrugged.

Neil joined them. 'I was thinking of buying Donna Summer's "I Feel Love". I love that blend of disco and electronic music. It's like the Bee Gees teaming up with Kraftwerk.'

Polly waved such piffle away. 'We're talking about solidarity, Neil. Workers' rights. Jobs.'

'Jobs – yeah. Did I tell you my dad's starting—'

'Your dad, see,' said Polly. 'Good example. There's the Government and the PLA looking to close the Millwall and West India, *and* the Royals, and there's the likes of your dad standing up to them, saying no, you will not take away our right to work these waters.'

'What were you going to say about your dad, Neil?' said Tom.

'He's starting on the Knowledge.'

'What's that?' said Polly.

'The Knowledge,' said Neil. 'Learning the streets of London to become a cab driver.'

Polly looked crestfallen.

Tom nodded. 'Makes sense, Neil. Why wait till they boot you out? Why not have another job lined up.'

'Yeah,' said Neil, 'although I think part of it's down to the police investigating him for handling stolen goods on a massive scale from the docks. He says they'll drop it if he drops it. He reckons that's it – the game's over.'

Tom nodded but didn't say anything. He'd always known Neil and Micky's dad was a brazen crook. Especially in the run up to Christmas. Between him and Nat Hiscock – well, it explained why the Island didn't have a Woolworth's. It didn't bloody need one.

'Maybe you should mention it to Ted,' said Neil. 'Give him a shove, sort of thing.'

'What, the Knowledge? Yeah, I might.'

'Yeah, well,' said Polly. 'Don't forget about the struggle. It's all very well looking out for yourself, but we have to think of others too.'

'That's where he got the idea from,' said Neil. 'There are loads of other dockers thinking of starting it too.'

'It's not too late,' said Polly. 'With the right organizing...'

But Tom had endured enough politics for one night. He spotted Claire with Brenda and went over. Only he got waylaid.

'Tom, I'm very proud of you,' said a drunk Megan Vanderlin. Well, she *had* recently finished school for good.

'Thanks Megan. I know we got off on the wrong foot.'

'Never say never, Tom. You never know, one day we might, well, you never know, before I go to Warwick.'

He got the feeling he could chat her up there and then. But he smiled and pushed on to Claire and Brenda.

'Hey, how are you?' said Brenda. 'Great performance.'

'Thanks Bren, appreciate it. The real star's standing opposite me though.'

'Oh I know,' said Brenda. 'Anyone who can't see Claire's a star must be clinically dead.'

'I think we're getting a little carried away,' said Claire.

'We're not,' said Tom.

'Ooh, I can't wait for next weekend,' said Brenda.

Tom raised an eyebrow. 'Why, what are you up to?'

'Point Clear with Claire.'

'Again?' Tom realised that his exclamation might have sounded more like a protest. 'You two, eh? There's no stopping you.'

'And Michelle,' said Claire.

Michelle, he'd learned, was their violinist friend from Limehouse. It also explained "CBM caravan" on the Cross' kitchen calendar.

'She should be here soon,' said Brenda.

Tom took a swig of beer. His mind was racing. Claire, Brenda and Michelle would be at the caravan on the 16th to 17th of July He also knew that "ES" would be there 18th to 22nd, then Claire's parents at the end of term, 23rd to 7th of August, then "AV" 8th to 12th, then NOTHING for the 13th due to a family wedding in Peterborough. But, and it was an important point, he knew it was a family wedding CLAIRE WOULD NOT BE ATTENDING.

'Claire, do you think your mum and dad would let me and Neil go down there for a couple of days. Say, the thirteenth of August? I mean if it's available. We'd pay. And we wouldn't make a mess. Is it available? On the thirteenth of August?'

'Not sure, Tom,' said Claire. 'I mean yes, because Mum, Dad and most of the family are going to a dull wedding in Peterborough, and Tracey and me are staying at home.'

'So, it's definitely free then?'

'Thing is – Dad might worry about having young men on the loose at Point Clear.'

'Has he actually met Neil?'

'Tom, last time you were there you set the caravan on

fire. And Neil's hardly got a better track record, has he.'

'No, you're right. Anyway, what am I thinking? Neil's going to Pontin's in Somerset that day. Damn, I was really up for that. I wonder if I could persuade someone else…?'

Claire frowned but not too harshly.

The thing now, with that lovely little caravan available on the thirteenth of August, was to enact the master plan of getting Claire to tell her parents that she would be at a friend's for the weekend. He'd thought of Janine but was no longer sure Polly would play ball. But what about Brenda? Or this Michelle she was mates with? Maybe she would vouch for Claire staying at her place on the Saturday night, while Claire was with him on the Essex coast for a spot of the inevitable…

'Tom? Ha ha! Tom!'

Tom's brain took a moment to make sense of the signals it was receiving.

'Midge?'

'Tom! Ha ha!'

'Midge.' Tom's heart sank a little.

Claire looked surprised. 'You know Michelle?'

'Yeah, we um…'

'I was his first ever date,' said Michelle/Midge proudly.

'You kept that to yourself,' said Claire.

'I was twelve,' said Tom.

'Well, we were both fifteen, ha ha, but let's not split hairs. We went to see *The Golden Voyage of Sinbad*. Do you remember, Tom?'

'Yeah,' he said, 'one minute I was with Sandy Smith, the next minute I wasn't.'

'Good ol' Sandy,' said Claire. 'I liked her. Shame she moved to Tilbury.'

'Her dad got a good job down there,' Tom reminded

her.

'I knew her through music practice in Limehouse,' said Midge. But she didn't seem keen to dwell on the past. 'Let's dance,' she said, grabbing Tom's hand and pulling him to the designated dance area.

'Thanks for asking,' Tom joked.

'I've always liked you,' said Midge over the music. 'Ever since I first saw you. You handled it all ever so well.

'Handled what well?'

'I mean some people fall apart.'

'What, on meeting you?'

'Don't be horrible. I mean the occasion itself. Some people can't stop crying.'

'Leave off – *The Golden Voyage of Sinbad* wasn't that bad.'

'Tom, that's outrageous. I'm talking about the first time I saw you. Before *Sinbad.*'

'Before *Sinbad*? Where was that?'

He simply could not recall it.

'You know.'

'No, I don't.'

'Yes, you do – at your mum's funeral.'

The music seemed to slow down. As did Tom.

The following day, Tom and Claire took a picnic through the foot tunnel and up the hill in Greenwich Park. Tom had put all thoughts of his family out of mind, or at least he was trying to. He'd thought of arranging to meet Neil, to talk about it – not like boys, but like the girls did – only he couldn't. It was too much. There would have to be another chat with Rose, of course, the lying old cow. And what would he do about Terry and Jack? They were his half-brothers! But he couldn't just turn up at Uncle

Norman's. It would be horrible to invade their home and drag up all the pain of the past.

For now he decided to concentrate on the present and future with Claire. He'd even brought a little note book and pen in case they were inspired to write their first song together. In fact, he'd already jotted some lyrics on the first page and thought he might impress Claire with them if the moment was right.

Sitting on the grass by the Royal Observatory, they looked north over the Old Royal Naval College, the sweep of the river and the grey industry and crane-lined docks of the Island. By now, Tom was a studious journal writer – although that was mainly driven by the notion that if he stopped writing *A Journey Into Music* it would be another nail in his musical coffin. After all, he still held onto a slim hope that it might all turn out well.

The thing that gave him hope was his untapped potential as a songwriter. Or possibly, song co-writer. Alder and Cross. Or maybe Cross and Alder. Didn't Lennon and McCartney have issues like that? Anyway, he felt certain that writing together would bring them closer.

'Tell me something about you,' said Claire. 'Something I don't know.'

'Well…' *Tricky*. He didn't want to tell her about Lynn.

'I don't mean about being adopted. Tell me something funny.'

'Well… okay…' He took a sip of his Coke. 'I once got shut out of the Island.'

'What?'

'You know when you forget your key and you get shut out of your house? I once went round Grandad's on my bike and couldn't get back on the Island.'

'Seriously?'

'I was about ten and… well, it was when the Isle of

Dogs declared its independence from Britain. Remember?'

'Yeah, I do. Must have been, what, 1970?'

'Yeah, they took control of the bridges and I was on the wrong side. Loads of police there, as I recall. I had to go back to my grandad's. I stayed there two days because he said it would be morally wrong to cross the people's line.'

Claire laughed. 'A unilateral declaration of independence. I remember it well.'

But Tom didn't want to dwell on the past. He wanted to embrace the future.

'I reckon we should write song lyrics,' he said.

Claire stared ahead. '*On such a day,*
From blue to grey…'

She paused and Tom leapt in.

'*But when I'm with you*
The grey turns to blue.'

Claire smiled. 'You should send it to Black Sabbath.'

'I've written something else. I've been working on it for a few days.' He meant weeks. 'It's called "About You".'

'And is it?'

'What?'

'About me? Or is a general "you" you're referring to?'

'You sort of inspired it.'

'Go on then. I promise not to laugh.'

'You've spoilt it now.'

'Don't be such a little boy. Sing it to me.'

'I can't. Not here. Let me just…' He cleared his throat.

'Is coughing part of it?'

'Shut up.'

'I'll shut up then. As requested.'

He checked the little note book and gathered himself.

Then he spoke softly, not needing to look at the words.

'I see the world as Shakespeare saw it
Same eyes; just using different words here
I can't say it like he says it
Same passion; just maybe a little less clear

Claire stepped in.

'But if I could wake up one day
As a poet writing words as true
I'd gather up all my love
And put it in a song for you.'

Tom was overjoyed and immediately began jotting.

'It's amazing. Like we're meant to write together.'

Claire smiled but didn't commit. Something wasn't right.

There was a silence. A deep one.

'I don't think "About You" is right,' said Tom. 'I reckon we should call it "A Song For You". What do you think?'

'I don't know. When you look around… I mean even on our doorstep there are cuts in local services, the end of the docks, the rise of the National Front…'

Tom was still trying to see everything through Shakespeare's eyes.

'I want to take you to your caravan on the thirteenth of August,' he said.

'Is this another song lyric?'

'I'm serious.'

'We'll see.'

'Is that a yes?'

'It's an "I don't know."'

Tom sighed and Claire lay back on the grass.

'"A Song For You",' she said. 'You're right. It's a good title.'

36. INTO BATTLE

The following weeks saw many things: Tom's relationship with Claire going well, despite a lack of progress in one vital aspect; Tom struggling to keep Midge's words from haunting him; Polly among 10,000 pickets at a Grunwick's mass riot; the Opposition Leader Margaret Thatcher promising that she would stop mass pickets with a law change; unemployment rising; Ted rudely rejecting Tom's suggestion that he should do the Knowledge; Doops phoning Tom with a request for a get-together; Donna Summer topping the singles chart; Johnny Mathis topping the album chart; the new Yes album *Going For the One* entering at number three; Tom buying Hawkwind's *Quark, Strangeness and Charm*.

Polly was the only worry. While Tom became fascinated by the lyrics of Hawkwind's Robert Calvert, in particular the lyrical agility of the second verse of "Spirit of the Age", his friend obsessed about the National Front attacking a left-wing demo in Lewisham and vowed to be there when it all kicked off again in mid-August.

For Tom, mid-August would be about love not war. Particularly the thirteenth of August, when a certain caravan at Point Clear would be available. He and Claire would make love all evening, all night and in the morning too – all without getting out of a shared, warm bed. Ah, the Essex coast. No chance of Claire's sister coming home to spoil the fun! What really excited him was Claire having a dozen opportunities to tell him the caravan idea was off, and not taking any of them. He could feel the heat building.

With love in the air, he very politely told Polly to tell Doops to stop bothering him. It wasn't easy to say it but he felt liberated. Then something happened that helped salve Tom's guilty conscience at dropping Doops: her boyfriend Phil returned from Australia. It was a good omen. Now he would be utterly free of her as she and Phil bonked till Christmas, leaving him free to concentrate on persuading Brenda Brand to falsely vouch for Claire's whereabouts during the Point Clear Festival of Going-All-The-Way.

Typically, Polly had plans too. In the pub for a couple of halves on the Wednesday before Point Clear he begged them all to go to a mass rally in Lewisham on, yes, Point Clear Saturday. Claire would say no, of course. Only, she said nothing. It was then that her words on the hill at Greenwich came back to him: '…even on our doorstep there are cuts in local services, the end of the docks, the rise of the NF…'

She was very nice when she phoned him on the Thursday. She even invited him to come round after school on the Friday for an hour of the brilliantly amazingly fantastically wonderful thing she loved to do for him. Tom insisted that Polly's timetable still left them plenty of caravan time. As he understood it, they would shout at the NF until lunchtime and be back on the Island by two to collect their gear and catch a train. They could be at Point Clear by six.

Claire wasn't impressed. The whole thing sounded rushed. Tom asked if there were other dates – there weren't. Then Tom suggested spending the evening of the thirteenth making love at Claire's home – of course, he would leave if Tracey came home. Claire shook her head. Other matters seemed to be gathering greater importance.

Soaking up the enormity of the situation, Tom felt himself beginning to drift apart from Polly. Okay, so Polly and Janine were nice people, and yes, they were always inviting him to join them at the Roxy punk rock club in Convent Garden to see bands like the Adverts, X-Ray Spex and the Buzzcocks, but they were too dominant in his life. And while they thought the Sex Pistols represented something solid, Tom was struggling to get past the reason they sacked Glen Matlock – because he liked the Beatles. Wasn't that intolerance? Or was intolerance okay when it suited?

It was Saturday the thirteenth. While Neil and his parents headed for Pontin's Brean Sands holiday camp at Weston-Super-Mare, Tom's hopes of sniffing salty sea air had died. Instead, it was only danger he could smell as they headed for Goldsmith's College in south-east London. And not just from the upcoming demonstration. Polly seemed to be sniffing around Claire.

'Where's Janine?' asked Tom.

'We've split up. She's gone back home.'

'Oh.' Tom was surprised. He almost said "first your parents, now you" but stopped himself. 'Sorry to hear it. Still, a smart bloke like you…'

'It's not the end of the world,' said Polly, eyeing Claire.

Tom was incensed. If the NF didn't whack Polly over the head, he'd do it for them.

Over by Clifton Rise, they found a few hundred people milling around. The police had kept their distance initially but now denied them access to any point further east. As Tom understood it, the police were intending to escort a couple of thousand National Front supporters from New Cross railway station in an easterly direction, away from the SWP, and then turn south towards Lewisham Town Hall. Meanwhile, those around him were intending to charge after them and break up the march. Somewhat inconveniently, the police took the view that anyone now attempting to stop the march would incur their displeasure.

Tom was only there to protect Claire, although quite how he intended to do that wasn't clear to him. He wished people would be less confrontational, but Polly was in his element – a *de facto* Socialist Workers' Party sub-commander over Tom, Claire, Doops and the blond bloke who had emerged from her bedroom at the Cassland Road party. Leadership-wise, only Oz and Phil seemed to be above him.

While the more reasonable political and religious opponents of the NF were giving indignant speeches from the safe distance of a mile away in Lewisham town centre, the SWP believed in direct confrontation.

'It's not too late to hear the speeches in the town centre,' said Tom. 'We could get a bus. Might be some interesting viewpoints.'

Polly's jaw was set firm. Was this really the boy he used to swap prog rock LPs with?

'I feel so angry, Tom.'

Tom wondered if Polly's anger was purely political or if it had anything to do with Janine packing him in.

'Let's try to keep the anger to a minimum,' Tom suggested. Although, the mood was relatively light-hearted, as time passed something was undeniably brewing. There was a growing noise of unrest. It was an area of Afro-Caribbean, Mediterranean and white people that produced a high fascist vote. Sure, there had been problems with the police "attacking" peaceful anti-NF demonstrators in July, but Tom was worried the SWP would ramp things up this time.

'You sure you're okay, Claire?' he asked. 'You just say the word and we'll go.'

Claire shook her head. 'This is important, Tom.'

'Yeah, absolutely.' She forgot to mention that it was also terrifying.

With Clifton Rise now pretty full of protesters, and the NF yet to leave the railway station for fear of being chased, Polly was certainly getting excited about the power of protest. While Tom attempted to wallow in what might have been with Claire, persistent Polly turned to the familiar story of Cable Street – specifically how the East End stood up to Oswald Mosley's pro-Hitler fascists in 1936.

'Five thousand of Mosley's fascist Blackshirts demanded the right to march through the East End,' Polly said in a theatrically loud voice. 'And what did Parliament do about it? They gave Mosley's mob an escort of six thousand police!'

Tom was puzzled. It was like his schoolmate was making a speech to the crowd. And then he realised – he was!

'But ordinary East Enders – our grandparents – blocked their path. "They Shall Not Pass!" was the cry. "They Shall Not Pass!" And they did not pass. Despite the best and worst efforts of the police to break the line, the locals stood their ground and Mosley and his fascists were turned back. My grandfather was there! And I'll tell you what brought tears to his eyes. It wasn't the police baton breaking his arm; it was the sight of a bearded Jew and an Irish docker fighting side by side to stop the racists!'

A cheer went up. God, Polly was good at this stuff. Even Tom felt empowered, and he would have preferred to have been at home listening to Genesis.

Of course, it had been difficult at home. It was hard to be civil to Ted or Rose. He was still haunted by what Midge had told him at the dance. Not that he learned much beyond his real mum's identity. He was too shocked to pursue it. It was more a nod and a change of subject, followed by a change of partner and a complete avoidance of Midge for the rest of the evening. She had given him her number though. And she was a bright girl. Good-looking too. And her machine gun laugh was more down to nerves than any serious mental issues, and it wasn't so pronounced these days.

Plainly, Rose was the one he needed to talk to. Half a dozen times he'd tried to ask her about the funeral but he couldn't get the words out. In truth, he had taken to blanking out the whole business. The coward's way out, maybe, but it made life easier. At least for the time being.

'Fascists out! Fascists out!' went the cry.

Tom checked he hadn't lost any of his friends. It would be hard to stay close together amid three, four, five thousand anti-fascist protesters. With the NF yet to make their move, he got talking to some bloke who sounded a bit like Polly, and like Polly this bloke said the music scene was about to witness a sea change, a seismic shift away from all the old crap. Tom said he still had a soft spot for prog, but the bloke almost foamed at the mouth. Prog, it turned out, was posh, over-privileged Establishment bollocks and was already in its death throes. Tom couldn't bring himself to point out that the latest Yes album, *Going for the One,* was currently sitting on top of the UK album chart. The bloke went on about the validity of the punk revolution but Tom's ears were picking up on two women protesters complaining about some bloke's treatment of a friend of theirs.

'She's a sister, not a vagina on legs.'

Then the crowd around them began to move down towards the main road – despite the police trying to hold them back. There was pushing and shoving up ahead and Tom found himself being drawn into New Cross Road. They were moving east now, although again, the police tried to stop them. The two women protesters moved away. Tom wanted to move after them to hear more of this revolutionary talk, but Polly pulled him over.

'All stick together.'

'Okay.'

Tom found himself stuck moving alongside the blond bloke from the Cassland Road party. Worse still, the blond bloke recognised him and started talking about Doops, who was less than ten feet ahead of them with Claire. Tom wasn't overly worried that Claire might find out about him going to the party, but he was mortified by the prospect of any mention pertaining to Doops flashing her soggy business end at him from the doorway.

'Let's hope the Old Bill don't get too involved, eh?' said the blond bloke.

'Yeah.'

'Otherwise it's kick a couple of the bastards and run for it.'

'Right.' What bastards did he mean? The NF or the police? Tom didn't want to kick anyone. Especially not the police on the basis that had no problem with them. He just preferred to see them in ones and twos, not in hundreds. And being a lot further away from them was something else he preferred.

'Nigel,' said the blond bloke.

'Oh, right. Tom.'

'You were at the party.'

'Only briefly. A quick chat about abortion rights and I was out of there. Only had time to run upstairs to say bye to Doops and I was gone.'

'Yeah, Doops.'

'Yeah. She's nice.'

'Yeah… well, a bit cracked. She's in love with the scene, not the cause. A Che Guevara lover. Had, what, twenty lefty lovers, three doses of the clap, two abortions, and at least one mental breakdown. But who can resist her?'

Tom hated him. 'Well, some of us can keep it in our trousers, mate. Some of can see she's a sister, not a vagina on legs. Right?'

'Yeah, well… sorry, man. You're right. Thanks.'

Nigel evaporated into the crowd. Tom was glad to be shot of him but now he saw Doops in a whole new light. More pressingly though, voices were coming back at him. It seemed the police wanted to push them back into Clifton Rise.

'They're not going to,' seemed to be the general response.

Suddenly, worryingly, a gap opened ahead of him, forcing Claire and the others to one side. It was the police piling in and trying to force a wedge into the mass. Tom wanted to run but couldn't move.

Then the police withdrew and an ironic cheer went up.

Tom fought his way to Claire's side. He had to make sure she was okay.

'Claire?'

'We don't move from this spot, Tom. Okay?'

Why did she have to be like this? Of course, he knew the answer. Polly had lectured them all enough times on how this kind of response would have strangled the Nazis at birth. Hitler even admitted as much in *Mein Kampf,* stating how an early counter-attack on his organisation would have been the death of his ambitions. But this was New Cross not Nuremburg. It was different. Wasn't it?

The police pushed in again. Tom held firm, hoping he didn't panic.

Once again, the push was resisted and the crowd cheered.

Impossibly, this went on for an hour and a half. It was clear the police weren't keen on letting the NF march before they could be certain five thousand protesters wouldn't chase after them.

But then jeers went up. Were the NF finally on the move?

Someone addressed them through a megaphone. It was the police insisting they disperse. That wasn't very likely. From a window above them, loudspeakers suddenly pumped out Bob Marley's "Get Up, Stand Up". That seemed more of a message the crowd could get behind.

No-one moved. Tom jumped to get a glimpse. There were police on horses. This didn't look good. Emotions were running high. The cries of protest were jumbled. Snatches here and there. The ground felt hard underfoot. Tom didn't fancy it at all. He imagined a boot crushing his head against the road.

There was a big commotion. Horses were coming in. This was insane! He liked horses. He couldn't move. His heart was thumping like a drum.

'Claire!'

The space in front opened up, a chestnut horse barged him aside. It felt more like a tank. He couldn't escape. More horses were coming in. He was being pushed and pulled while scrambling to move away. He slipped. A horse stumbled and banged into people.

Shit! Let me out!

The noise was deafening. He couldn't protect Claire. He was mad to have come. This was New Cross but it was something else now. Unrecognisable. Hellish.

The police came in hard. Batons came down on them. More horses. More police. Screaming. Shouting. Then he was running. They had broken through. He was in a charge. NF flags ahead. Thousands of fascists. Hundreds of police. Five thousand anti-fascists chasing the tail of the NF dragon. He couldn't get away. To flee left or right would mean his head getting batoned.

'Claire! Polly! Claire!'

People were underfoot. He stumbled. He was up again. He was pushed on. Jesus, there was a horse struggling to turn. People were getting hurt. Why were there horses here? Why was anyone here?

'Oww!' a man in front of him was struck by a half-brick. Thrown from behind. More bricks came over. Wood, bits of rock, a bottle, more bottles. Smashing, clinking underfoot. He was on the verge of panic. Chaos. Screaming. Anger. Defiance. Pushing. Shoving. He had to get away. He had to escape.

His head.

He felt it.

Wet.

Red.

He tried to not pass out. Focus. Think. Run. Escape.

'We've split them in two!' It was Polly at his elbow.

But Tom had his eye on a way out. A side street. He ducked out. Breathing space. Some police.

'Help…'

The police officer eyed him with hatred. 'What d'you

want – a nicking or a kicking?'

'I can't get nicked,' said Tom. 'Owww!'

They were kicking at him. He fled back into the main road. Back into the mad throng. Where was Claire? Where were Doops and Phil and Oz? They could leave Polly to it. Seeing as he was clinically bonkers.

He pushed, he stumbled, and he pushed again. Which way was out? Which way was safety?

He brushed the red sweat from his forehead. He had to get away.

'Claire!' he couldn't see her. He couldn't see anything. He was close to tears. He wasn't a man and he didn't care.

Doops.

She was screaming.

'Doops!' He would bloody-well save her if it was the last thing he did. 'Doops!'

She saw him. She recoiled a little at his bloodied face but moved to him. He grabbed her outreached hand and pulled her to him.

'Let's get out of here,' he said.

The NF were just ahead. Someone let off red flares. Smoke filled the air. NF banners were captured and set alight. People were fighting, pushing, running. A police officer hurled Tom aside, his hand still linked to Doops'. They both fell but scrambled away. Someone spat at him. They ran. Fear had him but it had no more to offer. He was scared but he could still move. Away. Away.

The crowd began to thin. The march was heading down to the right. There was space off to the left. They hurried. They ran. They stumbled. Away! Away!

Twenty yards. Fifty. A hundred. They kept going.

They cut through the back streets to reach Creek Road. Then they found the north end of Deptford Church Street. This was Polly's regrouping point should they be split up. They collapsed to the pavement. Tom felt shaky, sick and weak. The adrenalin was leaving him and his senses were beginning to return to normal. He could smell the iron in the blood on his face.

'Come on,' said Doops. 'If we go through the foot tunnel we can get the 277 to my place. I'll clean you up.'

'If Claire and the others are heading back to the Island, this is the way they'll come.'

'Come back with me, Tom.'

'Doops… God, you are getting it so wrong. You need a partner. Phil, for God's sake.'

'Phil's not special, Tom. We're just old friends.'

'You need a bloody relationship. And not with me. I'm with Claire until the day she kicks me out. You have to stop snaring blokes. You've already proved you can get any of us.'

'I never got you, Tom. Never too late though…'

'Shut up, Doops. Ann-Marie. I'm not calling you Doops anymore. You need to meet someone who cares for you. Then you can shag their brains out – but guess what? It will mean something. Do you see? It will bloody well mean something.'

Doops looked upset.

'Why don't you go back to your parents for a bit?' he said. 'Have a breather.'

'You sound like Oz and Phil.'

'Hey!' It was Claire calling.

Tom was annoyed. Relieved too, but mainly annoyed. Claire was with Polly. He had no doubt heroically led her to safety. Or maybe Polly had fainted with fear and Claire had led him to safety. That would be better.

'What happened?' asked Claire.

'A glancing brick or something. I'm okay. How about you?'

'I'm okay but we should get you cleaned up, you poor thing. You need taking care of.'

'He won't listen,' said Doops. 'I offered to take care of him, but...'

'I mean he needs rest,' said Claire.

Tom felt his adrenalin returning. There appeared to be two women arguing over him. He quite liked it. Then it occurred to him that one was fighting to bed him while the other was fighting to send him to bed alone.

'Before you decide to go home,' said Polly, 'the plan is for a second protest at Lewisham Clock Tower. I'm just saying there's an opportunity to get back into it.'

Tom stared at him open-mouthed. 'What are you? Fucking insane?'

They waited another ten minutes, to see if Phil or Oz would show up. They didn't, so the four of them headed up towards Greenwich, the foot tunnel and the safety of the Island.

37. ANOTHER FINE MESS

A few days later, with his wound on the mend, Tom set off on foot for his grandad's. It was easier to go by bus or bike, but he wanted to feel the calm pavements under his feet and pause outside shops that weren't boarded up.

Passing the park, he tried to collect his thoughts. The news on Grandad wasn't good. All the reports were of a man in decline. Terminal decline, most likely.

On the plus side, Tom had received further sympathy from Claire, who brought round LPs by Miles Davis and Mozart for them to listen to. Sitting with Claire *in his bedroom*, they were among the best albums he'd ever heard.

He also saw Polly. Of course, Polly was awash with revolutionary talk. Unbelievably, he started banging on about music being at the forefront of change. Tom once again had to hold back from explaining that prog-rockers Yes were top of the bloody album chart while disco queen Donna Summer was top of the singles.

Polly was also full of comrades' reports from Saturday's front line; particularly the SWP being cavalry charged by the police up Belmont Hill. It left Tom cold. What got him heated was wondering what Polly was up to in getting himself ever closer to Claire.

Strolling up Farm Road, Tom tried to enjoy the peace of the Mudchute to his right and the Millwall Dock to his left. Reaching the Blue Bridge, he paused to take in the

West India Docks and the Thames. All was quiet at the back of Claire's terrace.

The bridge had just lowered having let the Blenheim out. The Fred Olsen ship was now turning downriver towards the sea, laden with passengers bound for the Canary Islands. There was no rush so he watched until it was gone from view. A sailing barge came round. And a tug. Birds swooped over the water. If it was ever possible to love a place, at that precise moment he truly loved the Island.

Crossing the bridge, he glanced down Claire's street. Archie was rolling on the pavement outside her house. Tom didn't stop though. He continued north to Poplar High Street.

Reaching Grandad's flat, he let himself in.

'Grandad? It's me. Brought you a paper.'

'Hello, boy.'

Grandad was in the front room reading a boating magazine.

'Planning on sailing round the world, eh?'

'I would if I could. Probably left it a bit late, eh?'

'Fancy a cuppa?'

'Thought you'd never ask.'

Grandad followed him into the kitchen where Tom filled the kettle.

'I was thinking about you recently. About your mates in the docks. Strong bonds. Indestructible bonds, really.'

'Yeah, good mates. Sometimes they meant more to me than family.'

'Really?'

Grandad reached down to the bowl of cold water by the back door in which he kept his bottle of milk.

'I never did enough to put things right, you know.'

'I found out I have a sister.'

'Oh.'

'Rose told me a while ago, but… well, how exactly do we discuss family in this family? It seems we don't.'

Grandad poured a little milk into the cups.

'We do talk, some of us.'

'Sorry, Grandad. I wasn't trying to stir things up. It's just that half the things I'm told are lies.'

'Well, sometimes, some secrets are best kept secret. People get hurt, see.'

'I didn't mean you. You told me about your brother.'

Grandad scratched his nose. Tom had been with him over at Poplar Rec for the sixtieth anniversary service back in June. Sixty years and the pain had yet to dissipate.

A few moments later, they were sitting in the front room with their cups of tea.

'Well then,' said Grandad. 'I suppose I ought to tell you about my brother.'

Tom was surprised. Was Grandad going gaga?

'You already did, Grandad.'

'Yeah, well, you're older now. Thing is, our Lenny didn't live at home. He was in a special hospital in Hampshire; a sort of home for the disabled. Mum was always ashamed that she couldn't look after him, but he was too ill for that.

'That's no-one's fault, Grandad.'

'Apart from the Kaiser, you mean.'

'Yeah, well… I meant…'

'Anyway, my dad thought it was for the best. He was very old fashioned. Proud, upright, loved his standing in the community. Born in the 1880s, see. They had funny ideas about handicapped people. It was a Victorian thing – hide them out of the way. Even the Royal Family did it. Horrible place it was. Green paint. That's my abiding memory. Green walls and disinfectant. We always left there feeling bad but what could we do?'

'Nothing, Grandad.'

'A change of subject, I reckon.'

'Right. Well. I was hoping to ask you about Harry. My dad.'

'Blimey, I meant a change of subject to West Ham or something.'

Tom bit his lip. Grandad sighed, took a sip of tea then settled himself.

'Harry was a jack-in-the-box, Tom. Never sat still. Good-looking too, which only made things worse.'

'So, Victoria fell for him.'

Grandad paused. 'Right, you know about Vicky then.'

'It's like I said. Everything I've been told is a lie. Even my birth certificate's a forgery.'

'Not a forgery, boy. That's 100% genuine that is. Nat Hiscock knew a bloke who knew a cleaner at the official printers. Bought a few blanks unofficially, like. Apparently, there was a steady trade in it – you know, to iron out the little wrinkles in some people's families. The only thing they don't tally with is the official record at Somerset House – but no one ever goes there.'

'But how did Vic's sister end up adopting me?'

'Well… Vicky thought she could tame Harry. Fat chance of that, eh? Anyway, once it became clear that you were on the horizon, so to speak, Harry did the decent thing and married her. Not that he had a choice – Rose and Vicky's dad promised to take him out on a boat, shoot his balls off and drop him in the Thames if he didn't willingly agree. He meant it too. He had that gun he kept from the War. An Enfield No. 2. Nicely looked after, it was.'

'So this was all before Norman.'

'Yeah, Norman was Vic's second husband.'

Tom wondered what he was meant to do about Norman. His instinct was that Terry and Jack should remain in blessed ignorance, but hadn't having top-secret siblings already contributed more than enough chaos in the family?

He also thought of Vicky and Rose's dad – his other grandad who died in 1973.

'He always seemed a big softie. With me, I mean.'

'You didn't mess around with him. Personally, I reckon my Harry had a screw loose. Brains in his jockstrap, see.'

'He's Danny's dad, isn't he.'

'Yeah, well... how on earth he got involved with that girl... Jean... young, she was. A bright girl, mind, but well...'

'Who was she? A friend of the family?'

'Yeah,' said Grandad with an almost unnoticeable waver in his voice. But Tom caught it and saw the look in his grandad's eyes and he knew there was more to it.

'What happened?'

'Well... Vicky being seven months' pregnant was no excuse. Anyway, you know how it turned out. I couldn't be prouder than I am of Ted. He's a real man. There's not one grain of doubt in him that he did the right thing in taking you and Danny on. Yes, he's a grumpy git sometimes, but so would you be if they kept threatening to take away your livelihood.'

Grandad had a good cough and Tom took a sip of tea. He owed Ted a lot. Certainly a lot more than he'd ever given his step-dad credit for.

'Harry did wrong, Grandad. Being a teenager's no excuse. I should know.'

'Why? What have you been up to?'

'Nothing! I meant age-wise. Speaking as a teenager.'

'Oh, well, yeah. Hopefully, you haven't inherited the Alder genes which have us Alder men losing our common sense around women.'

'Well, I'm okay on that score.' Tom took a quick slurp of tea. 'I wish I'd known Vicky was my mum.'

'Well, you got to know her as an aunt. I know it's second best, but at least you had that.'

'Thirty-two. Cervical cancer.' Tom felt emotional. 'It's not fair.'

Grandad sighed. 'I know, boy. Life can be like that sometimes.'

'Why has Rose hidden so much?'

'Fear, boy. Fear of the police taking you away, fear of the social services taking you away. I reckon she's survived the whole time on tablets from the doctor. Ted reckons even now she thinks you're going to run off to Harry. I told him – I doubt the boy's ever set foot in West London.'

Tom put his cup down. 'Do you think it was easy for Vic to give me away?'

'Not in a million years! You were precious to her. It's just… well, her dad said it brought shame on the family. It was him who told Harry to leave and never come back, and he told Vicky to give you over to Rose. He said it was just for a few weeks till everything settled down, but we all knew it was a one-way ticket. Vicky went mad, had a fight with both her parents. Punches were thrown. In the end though, she was still a teenager. Also she knew Rose couldn't have kids, so although she never agreed to it, weeks turned into months. Norman comforted her. Well, Harry might've been her first love, but Norman… well, she genuinely found real love there and, well, blow me down, next thing we know is Vic's bloomin' pregnant! Luckily, Harry had had already agreed to take the blame for his deeds so the divorce wasn't held up. Vicky got remarried and everyone was happy. Well, not happy, but they all got on with it.'

'I've always liked Norman,' said Tom.

'There's good as well as bad, Tom. Don't let that slip your mind. It's like when I'm over the Rec. Yes, I remember the terrible things that happened in our school, but did you know the same year they put up the memorial, there was also a big fair over there. They had this great big tall thing. Slipping The Slip, they called it. A great big helter-skelter thing. I mean I was only little…'

'Do you think it's worth you writing to him?'

'Who?'

'Harry. To let him know what's been happening? That I know about him? If you have his address, I mean.'

'He won't answer, Tom.'

'He might.'

38. PHIL POWER

The following Saturday, the plan was to see a Generation X and Cimarons Rock Against Racism gig at Hackney Town Hall. It was part of the re-alignment of British music. At least, that's how Polly described it. Of course, while the Stranglers had scraped into the Top Ten with their insistent "Something Better Change", the soppy Brotherhood of Man reigned at the top with the radio-friendly "Angelo".

Annoyingly for Tom, the first leg of the meeting-up process was Polly walking from his home in the old flats off Cotton Street to knock for Claire. They then caught a bus down to the bottom of the Island where Tom and Neil were waiting at the bus stop opposite the Lord Nelson pub.

Of course, Polly's interest in Claire wasn't all negative for Tom. It made him realise he needed to get his act together and show Claire which of them was the real deal. Instead of continually playing softly-softly, it was time to go on the front foot. Basically, he'd try his best to lead Claire to the inevitable before she packed him in for Polly.

Thankfully, he wouldn't have Doops all over him. Oz, Phil and Tom's advice had finally got through to her and she'd gone home to Moreton-in-somewhere.

On the bus, Claire nudged him. 'Michelle's coming. Watch out she doesn't leap on you.'

Tom sighed. What did the future hold? This occupied him as the bus took them off the Island, up through Mile End, across Victoria Park, round by Cassland Road and on to Hackney Town Hall.

Waiting for them at the bus stop was Michelle.

'Tom!'

'Hello Midge.'

Crossing the road were Oz and Phil, who would have cut through the back streets from the squat. While they all hooked up, Midge pulled Tom aside.

'I'm sorry if I upset you.'

'It's okay.'

'No, I hurt you and that wasn't the plan.'

'Seriously, Midge, it's okay. You haven't hurt me.'

'Vic and my mum were best friends. What my mum learned about Vic's past was in the strictest confidence. Okay, so my mum told me but I swear I've never said a word about it until I talked to you at the dance. I mean I just thought you would've known. I mean at the funeral, we stood away from you and Rose so I didn't realise you... I mean...'

'Slow down, it's okay'. Tom wasn't the slightest bit annoyed. In fact, he was intrigued. 'How well did you know Vic?'

'Oh Tom, you didn't know her as your mum. That's so sad.'

'I don't need sympathy, Midge. I'm just curious to know a bit more, that's all.'

'She used to look after me when my mum was at work. Mum had an evening cleaning job, see. Vicky, your mum, used to cook my tea and read me stories. I called her Auntie Vic.'

'So did I.'

'She was really special. Like a second mum. I'm sorry,

Tom.'

He felt empty. All that love going to Midge when it should have…

The others came over. They had been joined by a couple of blokes Oz vaguely knew. Tom didn't like the look of them.

'Real music tonight, people,' one of them said. 'None of that Elvis shit. The king is dead, right?'

'Hey,' said Phil. 'Elvis was cool. He broke boundaries. Have you listened to his Sun Records stuff?'

'No, but…'

'No, exactly. Go and listen to "That's All Right", my friend. Go and soak up the birth of rock and roll. And then tell me Elvis was shit.'

Tom liked that. And he liked Phil a little more now. Elvis Presley's recent death was no occasion for non-entities to spout garbage.

'Hey!'

Tom turned to find London Style Sound guitarist and Hackney Council admin assistant Trevor smiling at him. 'Welcome to my workplace.'

'Nice of you to have us, Trev.'

The two were soon discussing radical reggae, prog rock guitar stylings and whether local government administration offered a worthwhile career path. Tom was beginning to see that it might.

The gig was good. A snarly bloke called Billy Idol sang well as Generation X did their thing, and the Cimarons' lively brand of reggae hit the spot, especially a "black and white" chant-along. But Tom was annoyed when Midge herded him away from Claire again like a sheep dog rounding up a stray. While he was relieved when Polly failed to take advantage, thanks to a lengthy chat with Oz and Neil, he was slightly alarmed at Phil's move on Claire. They were laughing too much.

At the end of the night, he stayed on the 277 past his stop so he could walk Claire the fifty yards from her bus stop to her home.

'Stop worrying,' she said.

'I'm not worrying. I'm just wondering about you and me… you know, if we're heading in the right direction.'

'Of course we are. Another ten yards and we'll be at my front door.'

'Stop joking, Claire.'

'Why? You used to like me joking. Do I have to change now? Become someone different?'

'I didn't mean that.'

'Look, no-one's going all the way until I'm at least eighteen. I know it sounds silly, and made-up, and arbitrary, but that's the rule.'

'Eighteen? When did you decide that?'

'When I realised that at least three blokes are determined to get into my underwear.'

'I thought we had an understanding.'

'We do. You're my boyfriend and if you're patient, I'll be eighteen in December. That's not an actual appointment, by the way.'

'That's nearly Christmas, Claire.'

'I just want to wait, Tom. Why do boys think it's okay to keep going on about it.'

'I'm not Steve.'

'No, but sometimes you sound like him.'

Tom sighed. They had come to a halt outside her house.

'So, do you fancy Polly? Or Phil?'

Claire rolled her eyes and led him further along, until

they were by the pub.

'Polly's passionate. I like that. Phil's alright, too. He plays jazz. He's had a few paid gigs too.'

'Really? That's great.'

'Yeah, he plays guitar.'

'Guitar?'

'Yeah, you know – fat end, skinny end, strings attached.'

'Jazz guitar?'

'Yeah. Reach out and embrace, eh? It's the best way to learn new stuff.'

'I will. I promise.'

'Good, because I've invited him to jam with us.'

'What? Why?'

'So we can all embrace.'

Over the next couple of weeks, Elvis hit the number one spot with "Way On Down" and Phil started jamming with Red Sails. Annoyingly for Tom, Phil was a wonderful player.

'It's a good job we aren't interested in playing jazz,' Tom quipped to Claire, one afternoon at Furze Street.

'Do you like jazz?' asked Phil, having overheard.

'I saw Keith Emerson on Oscar Peterson's show. Last year, I think. That was good.'

'Emerson, Lake and Palmer… you a prog man?'

'Yeah. I suppose you're going to say prog bores you.'

'I don't think prog's big enough to bore anyone.'

'Oh. Fair enough.'

'You like Genesis?'

'Just a bit.'

'I saw their guy Phil Collins a while back. A band called Brand X. You seen them?'

'Er, no.'

'Serious jazz fusion outfit. Collins play drums like he invented the instrument. Very cool player.'

'Yeah, I heard he plays a bit of jazz on the side.'

'There's some great music out there, Tom, but what really gets me going is the thing you can't name, the thing you can't label. Elvis had it. Louis Armstrong had it. Claire has it.'

Claire blushed. Tom frowned.

'Are you saying Claire's...?'

'No, Claire's not suddenly up there with Elvis and Satchmo. I'm saying she...' He turned to face her. 'You, Claire, have it. Tons of it.'

'I think we're exaggerating,' said Claire.

Later, Phil got Tom alone.

'I just love to play with her,' he said.

'So do I,' said Tom.

'She's so cheeky and inventive. Do you reckon it's a music thing? Or is she like that all the way through?'

Tom didn't know whether to punch him or ban him from further sessions. Not that he could blame Phil. For all the world, it looked like Tom had been involved with Claire, Doops *and* Midge.

The simple fact hadn't changed though. Claire was still his girlfriend. It was just a case of fighting off not just Political Polly, but now Jazzy Phil too.

39. LOSING GROUND

September came around and with it the return to school for the start of the long haul towards the following summer's A-level exams. Except it wasn't All Saints Grammar that had them in its grip, but Blackwall Comprehensive. There was no big deal about it, though. The old place was to become a college.

That said, the new building was hardly inspiring – clearly the result of a transaction between the education authority and a breeze-block manufacturer. Still, it was a new era.

It would also be a new era for Island children too, as a new comprehensive was opening near Island Gardens. It made Tom smile. A generation of Island kids would be spared the race for the bus and catching a bridger. Any kids living near him would walk to school. Of course, for Tom at Blackwall, it would be a matter of continuing to catch bridgers for the next nine months.

As expected, Danny was appointed Head Boy and editor of a freshly-reinstated *Devil's Advocate*. A less expected, but sound appointment was that of Claire Cross as Head Girl – although it was a little awkward with a Head Boy and Head Girl also being appointed from the old Broadlands contingent to work alongside them in getting things underway at the new school.

Tom was proud of Claire. Well, he was proud of Danny too. No place for sibling rivalry when you're almost eighteen. The Head made a speech in assembly about them representing the best aspects of both the old schools and how pupils should seek their advice and follow their example. Tom was okay with that. What he wasn't okay with was the way Danny and Claire seemed to become closer after their appointment. At times, they came across as some kind of double act.

At the very end of September, Tom sat in on the first *Devil's Advocate* editorial meeting since the summer break. Well, he sat in the upper-sixth-form room while Danny conducted the meeting in a corner.

'Okay, welcome to our new members,' said Danny. Mr Garner couldn't be there due to other business, so Danny was free to flex his executive muscles. 'Just so we all know who's who...' Danny went round the table, 'Claire is my assistant editor, then, from Broadlands, we have John Gould, Lower Sixth and Keith Francis, 5-something.'

'5N.'

'Yes, well done, Keith. Never too young.'

Tom cringed.

'Some of us don't think of ourselves as Broadlands,' said Keith. 'Some of us have been at Blackwall for a year.'

'Those we have lost,' Danny continued, as if Keith hadn't spoken, 'including my predecessor, the supremely able Margaret Slater, now safely ensconced at Cambridge...' Tom guessed Danny had to be concerned at Margaret being the only one to make it to Oxbridge. '...and Sean Casey, who left at sixteen to join Tower Hamlets Council as a Junior Entrant.'

Tom eyed a copy of the sheet Danny was handing round. All it had was a list of names.

"DEVIL'S ADVOCATE"

D. COLLINS, UppVI, Editor
C. CROSS, UppVI, Asst. Editor
J. GOULD, LowVI
K. FRANCIS, 5N
MR GARNER B.A. Hons., M.A., Executive Editor

'Right, I've got some ideas for the first issue,' said the never-too-young Keith Francis, eyeing the sheet with disdain. 'Set the tone, kind of thing.'

'To business,' said Danny, ignoring him. 'I'd like to write an opening piece welcoming everyone back.'

'Why not write about the bread strikes?' said Tom, suddenly taken with the idea of knocking Danny off his perch.

'Sorry, Tom, you're not part of this committee.'

'It's not a bad idea though,' said Keith. 'My mum had to queue for an hour and a half for a loaf yesterday.'

'Yeah, actually, Keith, we conduct business through the chair, not through you and Tom Alder having a chat about domestic issues.'

'Through the chair,' said Claire, 'might I suggest we cover the bread strikes? I only ask because it's the same where I live. At least an hour queueing for four crusty rolls.'

'Okay, why don't you write that up then, Claire. Keep it short.'

'Now, how about this "Heroes" thing?' said Keith. 'I wouldn't mind writing an article about that.'

'What "Heroes" thing?' said Danny, clearly hating Keith's pushy persona.

'Well, Bowie's new single is "Heroes", the Stranglers' single is "No More Heroes"… It'll make an interesting piece about the nature of the heroes they're referring to. Plus, you've got old wave and new wave, and…'

'Yes, actually, I'm writing something along those very lines,' said Danny. 'So perhaps you could come up with something smaller.'

'Marc Bolan's death? I could do a nice piece about his influence on glam rock. I mean him and Bowie pretty much—'

'Yes, keep it short. And no gory car crash details, please.'

Tom winced. 'Am I the only one who finds having Marc Bolan's show still on TV a bit weird?'

'I could also write about Elvis,' said Keith. 'I mean he was the first rock and roll star. Been dead a month and he's still number one in the album and singles charts.'

'Keith, could we please leave room for others to speak?'

Claire cleared her throat. 'How about a piece on Maria Callas passing away?'

'No, Claire.'

'Is that a yes on the Elvis?' said Keith.

Tom was enjoying this. 'You remind me of Danny,' he told the junior member of the committee. 'I've got a fiver says you'll be the next editor.'

'How about a new name for the magazine?' said Keith. 'To reflect the fact that Blackwall is made up of two schools. I mean *Devil's Advocate* is a weak play on All Saints…'

'Not necessary.'

'Something like *The Wall*.'

'*The Wall?*'

'Looks like the writing's on the wall,' said Tom.

'And I propose a joint editor,' said Keith.

'Like you, you mean?'

'No, of course not. My vote goes to John Gould.'

'Oh,' said Gould. 'Thanks. Whatever you think's best.'

Tom smirked.

After the meeting, he pulled Danny aside.

'He's a sharp one, that Keith. He really does remind me of you.'

'Yeah, if you've finished?'

'Yeah, look… you ought to know Grandad wrote to Harry. It was over a month ago now and there's been no reply.'

'I see. Hardly surprising, I suppose.'

Tom felt bad. Danny had been very consistent about wanting all this family stuff firmly behind him. It was only Tom who kept dragging it all up.

'I just want you to know I'm putting it all behind me too,' said Tom. 'The whole family thing. I've got Ted and Rose and that's fine by me. Just thought I'd say.'

'Good. I say we forget the whole thing. To me, life's the thing in front of me, not all the crap behind.'

Tom felt he understood Danny a little more these days. The victim who overcame the odds to be the best. From now on, they could move forward as equals. As fellow grown-ups.

'Oh, there's just one other thing,' said Tom. 'Claire's *my* girlfriend. Okay?'

The following Sunday morning saw Tom, Claire and Den preparing for a session with Phil and his jazz skills. Roy wasn't invited on Claire's say-so. This partly annoyed Tom but there was no point in making a fuss. Had Roy been in, Tom would have been out.

Setting up, Phil asked Tom about the new school and sympathised about him having to make the change from grammar to comprehensive. Of course, Phil believed it would prove a wise move for Britain in the longer term.

'The thing with grammar schools is they drew a line at the age of eleven,' he said. 'Trust me, there are kids out there who are nowhere at eleven, but give them a couple of years…'

Tom thought of Keith Francis giving Danny a run for his money. Keith had been rejected by All Saints at precisely that age.

'Fair enough,' said Tom. 'If the rumour's right that all the rich, fee-paying schools are to be phased out too then you won't get an argument from me. Can't just have the working class stitched up, eh?'

The first thing they played was a simple E, A, B twelve bar blues. While Tom stuck to it with the occasional solo notes that conformed in text book fashion, Phil tackled the structure like a chimpanzee in a tree. He was anywhere and everywhere, but each flourish was sure-footed, or like a chimp, sure-handed.

When they grew tired of that, Tom raced into the opening of "Motorhead" by Motorhead, treating it like a fun throwaway that he hadn't spent endless hours getting right. Phil didn't join in but smoked a cigarette instead. He offered the pack round. Den took one. Tom and Claire declined, but then Claire wavered and took one.

It wasn't lost on Tom that this was the first time she'd smoked.

'Claire?'

'Stop fussing.'

'Your first time, eh?' said Phil. 'I love someone's first time. It's like a short story and you never quite know how it's going to turn out.'

Tom felt a nagging irritation, and not because Blackwall Comprehensive's joint Head Girl was meant to set an example.

'Follow me,' said Phil.

Tom thought he was about to go somewhere, but he started playing a complex repeating motif. Claire cottoned on and so did Den. Tom couldn't get the hang of it so he quietly picked out a few notes. It was about a minute into it that he realised they were playing a midnight jazz version of the old Frank and Nancy Sinatra song, "Something Stupid".

When Phil began to sing it to Claire, Tom hated him with all his being.

'What about Eddie and the Hot Rods?' he said. 'I've worked out the chords to "Do Anything You Wanna Do".'

Phil nodded.

'Good call,' he said. 'Or does anyone fancy a bit of floating?'

Without checking, he played a noodling style and encouraged Tom, Claire and Den to join him. Then he started singing the chorus to the Floaters' "Float On" and it all made sense.

'Why don't you shout out the chords?' asked Tom.

'Where would be the fun in that?' said Phil.

Claire said nothing, which Tom found disappointing.

Later, when they were leaving, and Phil was out of earshot, he pulled Claire aside.

'I'm not playing with him again.'

'I know, I know. It's okay.'

He wasn't sure what that meant.

The fourth of October came round fast. It was Tom's eighteenth birthday and the plan was for everyone to meet in the pub. But it was a Tuesday and people were either short of money or asking him to postpone it till Friday or Saturday so that they could enjoy it properly. In the end it was just Tom, Claire, Neil and Brenda.

Tom enjoyed it enormously. It was like the old days without having any of the blokes who fancied Claire around.

Claire was on good form too, although she kept telling Neil and Brenda how amazing Phil's jazz guitar playing was and how that might offer a new direction for the band. Tom thought of reminding her that Red Sails was *his* band but opted to leave it. Thankfully, the talk moved on from Phil to more regular fare, including how Neil had set up his hi-fi in the front room on Saturday evening so that he and Tom could watch Camel's *Sight and Sound in Concert* appearance on BBC TV while listening to a stereo "simulcast" on Radio One. Neil could have talked about that for three hours but they managed to divert matters onto the new school, A-levels, acne, Britain's undertakers going on strike, winter fashions, films, West Ham, holidays, part-time jobs, and university: yes or no?

In fact, it was only as they were leaving that Claire told him there would be another jam in a few weeks.

'I'll give you the songs in advance,' she said.

Tom nodded. He understood that she had held back in order not to spoil his birthday. She'd obviously spoken with Phil and they were no doubt in agreement that Tom wasn't good enough.

Any suggestions for further birthday celebrations that weekend were swatted away. Tom settled for a trip to Upton Park to see West Ham play Nottingham Forest. The fact that it ended in a dull nil-nil draw felt appropriate. Tom was trapped in an unresolved musical limbo. Only, he knew it wouldn't remain unresolved for very much longer.

40. I KNOW A GUY IN SOHO

It was a Saturday morning in early November and Tom was idly watching *Noel Edmonds' Multi-Coloured Swap Shop*. Outside the window, Ted was mounting his second-hand Honda moped with the runs of the Knowledge of London secured to a clipboard mounted over the handlebars. Seemingly, for Ted, Tom's "bloody interfering" was long forgotten and some kind of post-docks future was now on the horizon.

Rose was cleaning and polishing in the front room. She mentioned something about popping up the market later and perhaps having pie and mash.

'Fancy coming?' she asked.

'I can't, Mum. I've got a rehearsal.' He also had a hangover. He had spent the evening in the pub with Neil and Polly. It was meant to be fun but Tom found himself drinking, not talking as Polly tackled Friday's big newspaper stories: "Callaghan Warns of Winter Strikes; Labour Ready to Fight Unions on Pay", "I'll Stand Up to the Miners, Says Jim", "Lights Stay Off; Blackout Threat to Kidney Patients", "We'll Fight the Strikes"…

Rose started wiping the mantelpiece. 'I thought you had rehearsals on Sundays.'

'There's a new bloke in the band. Well, half in the band. I haven't actually accepted him as a member yet.'

'You must all be getting good by now. Think you'll turn professional?'

'You don't turn professional, Mum. It's not like footballers. But, to be honest, I'm not sure I want to play for money. Half the time it's just an endless round of pubs, clubs and weddings. Not everyone's fashionable enough to land a recording contract.'

Rose picked up her brown vase for a quick polish. 'No, I suppose not.'

Uncle Harry came to mind. They hadn't discussed him in ages but he was always there, on the edge of any conversation about the family.

'He's good,' said Rose, indicating Noel Edmonds on the telly. 'I like him.'

'Mum, I'm eighteen. Could we have a talk about our family? You know, where you tell me everything, then we forget about it and get on with the rest of our lives.'

'Tom…'

'I'm an adult.'

'There's nothing more to tell.'

'Yes, there is.'

'Tom…'

'What's the story with Jean?'

Rose sighed and gave up on the polishing. She took a seat but looked far from comfortable.

'Jean was like a little sister. Her mum died when she was ten and her dad didn't want her going into a children's home. Because he worked long hours as a long-distance lorry driver, she practically lived with us. I swore on her mother's grave I'd look after her and protect her, see. Then, on her sixteenth birthday…'

'Harry wrecked everything?'

'You could say that, yeah.'

'It's not your fault though.'

'No. No, it's not. Ted thinks it's his fault.'

'Ted's not responsible for his brother.'

'No, but best not mention it to Ted is my advice.'

The rehearsal space was at the back of a clothing factory on Commercial Road. Phil got it for free via some bloke he'd made friends with. The workforce finished at one p.m. on Saturdays and wouldn't be back till eight a.m. on Monday.

'I thought we might play an Ian Dury song at the Docklands Dance,' said Phil.

This was news to Tom. He couldn't recall stamping Phil's membership card.

'We did discuss it,' said Claire, possibly catching the look on Tom's face.

That was true. A couple of weeks earlier, Phil, Claire and Den were getting excited about an album called *New Boots and Panties*. According to Claire, it was possibly the direction Red Sails had been looking for.

'What about Roy?' Tom asked Claire.

'Roy plays in two other bands, Tom. He's not bothered.'

'No, well... I suppose that's okay.'

'Have you heard "Sex and Drugs and Rock and Roll"?' said Phil. 'It's got a lot going on in it.'

'Is that allowed?' said Tom. 'The sex part, I mean. Well, and the drugs part. I mean at the dance.'

Claire laughed, but not harshly. 'No-one's going to die of shock.'

'I've written a couple of songs too,' said Phil. 'I wouldn't mind working through them.'

'Yeah, well... me and Claire have written a song. Haven't we, Claire.'

'Er...?'

'You remember. "A Song For You". We worked it out

in Greenwich Park.'

'Only the lyrics.'

'Yeah, well, I've jotted down some chords since.'

'Cool,' said Phil. 'We'll give that a go, too.'

The session went well. Tom struggled in places but Phil was very helpful with tips and suggestions. The Ian Dury song was the least successful, but Tom's part in one of Phil's compositions, "The Girl", wasn't too difficult to master and the song itself seemed quite catchy. His own song, "A Song For You" also fared well once Phil had tweaked some of the chords and Claire had ramped up the rhythm parts.

They rehearsed the following weekend too. Then Phil brought in a four-track recording machine so that they could "get a more objective idea of what was working best." Tom felt strange. Happy and worried. Joyous and fearful. There was something right and something wrong. He didn't like to ask though.

Claire questioned Tom's commitment. *New Boots and Panties* was out there, so why hadn't he bought it?

Tom duly went up to the market. Only, *Seconds Out* had just been released – the new Genesis live double album. While he was deliberating, someone asked if they had the new Sex Pistols album, *Never Mind the Bollocks*. The bloke behind the counter said he didn't sell filth.

Tom bought Ian Dury's album but he felt like a traitor to Phil Collins and the boys. Worse still, playing it back at home, Rose walked in just as "Plaistow Patricia" came on. She didn't say anything, but even Tom winced at the unfettered tirade of expletives.

Then it was back to rehearsals with Phil, Claire and Den. And it was good. And, what's more, after this session, Phil announced that he'd arranged for them to go to a friend's small recording studio in Islington.

Tom felt like a whirlwind had swept him up. This kind of major development simply didn't happen to him. Phil seemed to take it in his stride.

'Claire's got the lot, Tom. We could do well.'

Well? What did he mean?

At the recording studio, Tom found the setting up unsettling. He just wasn't used to having a scruffy bloke watch them from behind a sheet of glass. While this guy twiddled a million knobs, Tom's heart raced. This was it.

Get this right and the sky's the limit.

Only, he couldn't get it right. His hands were made of wood. He had no rhythm. Claire smiled between doing her thing, which very simply comprised strong bass playing with a vocal delivery that could stop clocks. Phil, of course, was in his element playing twiddly bits and jazz funk chords. Tom tried to keep it simple and refused the opportunity to try a few solos. In the end, Claire played two guitar solos and then added some electric piano and ARP synthesiser that had been set up for another band.

They recorded six tracks in all. Phil thought maybe four were good enough.

Good enough for what?

'I know a guy in Soho,' Phil pronounced. 'It might be worth sending him a tape.'

Tom gulped.

'A record company?' asked Claire, also looking fairly anxious.

'Not exactly. He's a kind of middle man. If he likes it, he'll know who to try. Fingers in pies. That's the name of the game.'

They tried to act naturally as they left the studio.

'I really love Ian Dury,' said Claire. 'The Blockheads are incredible.'

'We've come a long way from thinking of doing punk,

eh?' said Tom.

'I love the Sex Pistols' energy,' said Claire, 'but you have to admit – that 4/4 time signature gets a bit samey.'

Outside, the sound of Tom Robinson's "2-4-6-8 Motorway" was coming from an open window.

'I've seen them play,' said Tom, desperately trying to look and sound like part of the music business. 'At the Bridge House. Nice bloke, Tom Robinson. Definitely got what it takes.'

Over the next couple of days, Tom let slip to Neil, Danny, Brenda, Polly, Rose, Ted, the lady in the newsagent's and the milkman that he was being considered by a couple of record labels.

A couple of days after that, he was waiting for Claire in the Waterman's Arms.

Nat Hiscock's daughter Natalie was in there. He smiled at her. She completely ignored him. Is that what he was? Invisible? Well, that was about to change.

Claire came in. He smiled at her too. She didn't smile back. Instead, her face suggested she had something to say but wasn't quite sure how to say it.

'Everything alright, Claire?'

'Yes and no.'

'What is it? The bloke in Soho get back?'

'No, not yet.'

'Still, he's only had the tape since Monday.'

'Er, since Wednesday. Not Monday.'

'Oh, a bit of a delay, was there?'

'Yeah, Phil... Phil...'

'Phil?'

'Phil went back in.'

'Back in where?'

'Into the recording studio.'

'Oh. Any particular reason? Like, maybe, to re-record

all my parts?'

'Something like that, yeah.'

'So, basically, I'm not on any of the recordings?'

'Er, no. And he pared it down to two songs.'

'*His* two songs?'

'Yeah.'

'So no room for "A Song For You" then.'

'No – although I really like it.'

'And how do you feel about that, Claire?'

Claire took a breath. 'I feel bad, I feel terrible, and I feel he's made all the right decisions.'

'I see.'

'I'm really sorry, Tom.'

41. GERMANY CALLING

November came to an end. There had been releases by AC/DC, Rush, Status Quo, The Jam, Bread, Cliff Richard, Diana Ross, and Queen, while the firefighters went on strike and Concorde started regular flights from London to New York.

On the political front, between stints on the picket line at the local fire station, Polly joined the newly-formed Anti-Nazi League. He urged Tom to join too, especially as the National Front were expected to be a force at the next general election. Tom declined but was happy to wear a small ANL lapel badge occasionally – i.e. when Polly was around.

Claire, meanwhile, had started making music in Berlin – *yes, Ber-bloody-lin* – with Phil and Den as they teetered on the edge of a deal. Of course, she had phoned to reassure family, friends and boyfriend that she hadn't forgotten them.

There was one event Tom, Neil and Brenda went to with Polly – a gig at the Roxy in Covent Garden, the home, heart and soul of punk rock. Tom had been before, of course, but yet again he couldn't get into it. He didn't like everyone pogo-dancing violently into each other, the constant spitting at strangers and, most of all, he missed Claire.

It ended it a fight, too. The pogo-dancing and spitting became competitive. Crazily, there was a Pistols vs Clash tribalism in evidence and someone punched Tom thinking he was a Clash man. Was that how punk was aiming to survive? He'd never seen Genesis and Pink Floyd fans fighting. Maybe the punks were misunderstanding the "Anarchy" Johnny Rotten had referred to.

It was strange at school, too, not having Claire around. Yes, she'd phoned him from Berlin but it wasn't the same. He'd been out with Neil the last time she phoned and now all the talk was about whether or not she had signed a deal.

In the playground, Neil came up to him looking excited.

'What's up, Neil?'

'News about Claire.'

'Don't tell me – Polly heard from Oz, who heard from Phil, who's with Claire.'

'No, Polly heard from Craig Lycett.'

Tom didn't get it. 'And so the news is…?'

'She's signed a recording deal. One of the independent labels. Stripeless, I think. See, that's the great thing about the whole punk explosion. Lots of independent labels getting in on the act. Now New Wave's taking over, it gets the benefit. They can move fast, make quick decisions.'

Tom felt cold. Maybe his heart wasn't working properly.

'How does Craig know?'

'Craig's joined the band.'

'Craig?'

'Yeah, they used to play cello and piano together.'

'I bloody know that, Neil.'

'Sorry.'

'Yeah, well, good for Claire. And Craig. I wondered where he'd disappeared to.'

Tom skulked away, into the upper-sixth-form room. Danny was doing something weird on several sheets of paper.

'Plans for an atom bomb?'

'I'm compiling a cryptic crossword.'

Tom assumed it was for the renamed and now sole school magazine, *Blackwall School News*.

Keith Francis came in. Danny kept his eyes on Tom.

'In the lower sense, take the 'p' out of this place and it'll turn very frosty. Six letters.'

With Danny repeating it a couple of times, Tom stared at the wall, ceiling and his shoes for inspiration, then shrugged.

'Poplar,' said Keith.

'Lucky guess,' said Danny.

Tom struggled to see it.

'Poplar, polar,' said Keith, for Tom's benefit.

'Oh yeah. Clever.'

Keith turned to Danny. 'It won't be popular though.'

'Too difficult?'

'Too boring. How about one crossword grid, two ways to complete it? One set of cryptic clues, one set of easy fun questions. You know, acknowledge the school's range.'

Danny sighed and looked out of the window.

Tom sympathised but there was no point in looking out of that window for salvation. The power station blocked the view.

But then something strange happened. Danny turned and nodded.

'Good idea, Keith. We'll do it your way.'

*

Just as Tom was beginning to hate himself for constantly humming the Bee Gees' "How Deep Is Your Love", he received good news. Claire was coming to England. The bad news was there wouldn't be time for her to visit the Island.

He still needed to see her though.

As he understood it, she would stay overnight at a hotel somewhere in London prior to spending the morning at the record company office. After that, she would be heading north for gigs in Liverpool, Manchester and Glasgow.

He got the address of Stripeless Records from directory enquiries and used a Tube map and his dad's A to Z London Atlas to plot a route there. Taking the day off school on the pretext of a heavy cold, he set off.

In essence, it would just be a plain ol' boyfriend meets up with girlfriend situation. Yes, she had expressly told him she would be incredibly busy, but once he was there, she wouldn't refuse a coffee with him. It would just be a half-hour for a chat, a bit of hand-holding, a quick snog and a general re-connecting.

Annoyingly, he found himself spending much of the journey pondering a criminal case that had captured the public's imagination. Having bought a newspaper to pass the time, he became familiar with a woman called Joyce McKinney, who had kidnapped her Mormon ex-boyfriend and kept him in a Devon cottage for three days as her sex slave. What Tom couldn't understand was why it was a court case. Weren't most men thinking the same thing – how do I get her phone number?

By ten a.m., he was in the reception area at Stripeless

in Soho. Unfortunately, Claire had been taken to a meeting elsewhere and wouldn't be back for an hour or so. Tom opted to wait by a coffee table covered with newspapers, all of which afforded a take on the Joyce McKinney sensation.

Two hours later, he saw her through the window. Claire! He had to play it cool. She was with someone. An oily-looking bloke old enough to be her dad. Worse still, judging by Mr Oily's demeanour, he bloody-well fancied her.

Mr Oily came in and nodded to the receptionist on his way to an inner door.

'We're going straight to Euston. Can you re-arrange my twelve o'clock for next week?'

He disappeared into a back room. Tom went outside.

'Tom?' Claire looked surprised.

'I thought I'd grab you for a coffee.'

'I can't. We're going to Liverpool.'

'I thought that was tonight.'

'Yeah, we're playing tonight but we're meeting a promoter there at six.'

Mr Oily came out with a folder stuffed full of papers under his arm. He walked straight past Tom to the edge of the pavement where he raised a hand.

'Taxi!'

The taxi didn't stop as it already had a passenger.

Tom introduced himself. 'Tom Alder, occasional guitarist in Red Sails.'

'Who?'

'We've changed the name, Tom,' said Claire, a little sheepishly.

Tom was shocked. 'Without telling me?'

'How can we help you, young man?' said Mr Oily, his eyes fixed on the street.

'I thought Claire might—'

'Taxi!'

A cab pulled up. Mr Oily got in.

'Sorry, Tom. I have to go.'

'When might you be back?'

'Claire,' said Mr Oily, 'let's not keep the driver waiting.'

'We've got these dates up north, then some TV and radio in Belgium, then we're back in Berlin for a bit. We're still trying to find our first single.'

'I'm glad it's going well.'

'Tom…'

'I'm worried about you, Claire.' He leaned in close. 'I'm worried you'll need someone and no one will notice.'

'Tom, you're very sweet.'

Inside the taxi, Mr Oily wasn't impressed. 'Claire, can we please get going. I don't want to miss this train.'

'One minute, Dustin. Tom, I really do have to go.'

'Best of luck then. You deserve everything because you really are the most amazing…'

'Don't exaggerate.'

'I'm not just saying it because we had an agreement to, you know, at some point soon-ish.'

'Now you're being silly. Just keep practising. You're a decent guitarist. You could still become the next David Gilmour.'

Tom sighed. Claire Cross, the love of his life, simply did not get it.

'Mike Yarwood, Claire.'

'Pardon?'

'The impressionist.'

'I know who he is, Tom.'

'Ever seen one of his shows on telly? Where he rounds it all off with a song?'

'What are you on about?'

'Mike Yarwood sings his big finale as Frank Sinatra, and then Dean Martin, and then Tom Jones… and it's great. You're totally drawn in. And then, right at the end, he says "and this is me" and he rounds off the song in his own voice. And it's shit.'

There was a silence.

Then Claire broke it. 'I see.'

'Claire, I could practice for the next ten years and become a copy of David Gilmour or Jimi bloody Hendrix, but the minute I say "and this is me"… there's nothing. There is no "me". Phil worked that out pretty quick and he was right.'

'Look, I really do have to go. Keep well, okay?'

He wanted to tell her he loved her, but he knew she wouldn't be able to return it. It was like those films his mum liked: *Brief Encounter* and *Casablanca*. He'd never liked those endings.

As she got in the cab, he called after her.

'Have a good meeting!'

And with that, Claire's cab was pulling away.

Watching her leave, he knew he didn't care about becoming a pop star. He simply wanted to be with her as she rose to the top – not just hear her on the radio and watch her on the telly. Worst of all, the great romantic lyricist in him was furious at the final words of farewell he had chosen for his tragic split from the love of his life.

1978

42. SURPRISE, SURPRISE

Ensconced in the Alders' smoke-filled front room on the first Saturday of the New Year, Rose was checking her charity bingo cards while humming "Mull of Kintyre", which had been at number one since November. Sitting opposite, Tom was finishing off a plate of Smash, peas and boil-in-the-bag cod in cheese sauce while wondering if each New Year was actually coming around faster. Certainly, old people always went on about time speeding up. Would 1978 be a good year? That was probably the greater question. Yes, he had his West End *Star Wars* ticket and looked forward to sharing the experience with Neil, and yes, he had put questions about his family out of mind in order to move on, but there were still aspects of his life that needed fixing.

That said, no matter what was on his mind, having someone sitting six feet away humming "Mull of Kintyre" wasn't helpful.

He started to out-hum Rose with "Stairway to Heaven" while he thought of Claire. She was back in

England after a month's recording in Germany with her band, the Westferries. Well, with local band Westferry changing their name to Cobalt Blue, Claire had wanted a name that would remind her of home.

She'd phoned a couple of times and, despite the seeming cancellation of their expected sex life together, Tom told her he understood how busy she was, and that there was no need to worry about making snatched phone calls to him. Indeed, when she phoned on her eighteenth birthday, much to his regret, he insisted on it. As soon as he put the phone down, he knew he'd made the biggest, most stupid mistake of his life. Three weeks later, he was still wondering – when was he going to learn?

Ted came in from the hall; his face red with the cold. He'd just got back from an outing on his moped.

'What the hell are you two humming? I thought we'd been invaded by wasps!'

'Cold out there, Ted?' asked Rose.

'Cold? Bloody North Pole, it is.'

Tom had come in just as frozen from his Freeman's round earlier, so could sympathize.

'I'll get you a cuppa,' said Rose, getting up and scuttling off to the kitchen.

'It's a joke out there,' grumbled Ted, clearly irked. 'Whoever's in charge ought to be sacked.'

Tom put his empty plate down by his feet. He knew not to make eye contact. The Knowledge was a two-year slog through London's streets in pursuit of a taxi driver's license. Moaning about it was to be expected.

'Roadworks on the Embankment, jams in Trafalgar Square, road closures on Shaftesbury Avenue *and* High Holborn,' ranted Ted. He was pulling down his yellow oilskin over-trousers. 'I mean until these stupid bloody councils develop some sort of strategy, I can't see any way it's ever going to improve. Am I right, Tom?'

'You're not wrong, Dad.'

Ted plonked himself down in an armchair and reached for his fags.

'Do you know where Billingsgate Fish Market is?' he asked.

'Isn't it in your map book?'

'I mean do *you* know where it is?'

'Me?' On the moon for all Tom cared. 'No Dad, no idea. No, hang on, it's in the City. Somewhere.'

Ted lit a cigarette, took a drag and sucked it down. Then, with utter contentment, he propelled smog into the room.

'Lower Thames Street,' he said. 'Leave East Ferry Road by a right into Westferry Road, left Limehouse Causeway, forward Narrow Street, left The Highway, forward East Smithfield, forward Tower Hill junction, bear left Byward Street, forward Lower Thames Street, set down on left.'

'Or,' said Tom, 'get to The Highway and follow the smell of fish.'

Ted ignored the joke, which didn't surprise Tom, as Ted only laughed a couple of times a year. Although, in fairness, since he'd started on the Knowledge, he had upped his quota a tad.

'It's an uncertain world, Tom. I don't mind you joking but remember – I'm out there in the cold doing my best.'

'I know you are. Mum and me are right behind you. A hundred percent.'

Tom headed up to his room. He still had over two hours to kill before he was due to team up with Neil for a drink in the Waterman's Arms. He played *New Boots and Panties,* carefully turning the sound down at the start of "Plaistow Patricia". Then he played *Seconds Out* by

Genesis. Finally, he went with side one of the Schubert piano sonatas LP Claire had bought him when she first became his girlfriend.

Later, coming downstairs, he met Ted in the hall.

'Any idea where the Stock Exchange is?'

Good God, not more cabbie talk.

'Isn't a little Knowledge a dangerous thing, Dad?'

'Tom, sometimes you can be a real smart-arse, do you know that? What exactly do you plan to do when you leave school?'

'Not sure. I mean I don't want to be a cabbie. I can't even drive.'

'I was only trying to get you interested in London, then... well, once you're twenty-one you could apply, if you were still interested.'

'That's years away, Dad.'

Ted huffed. 'It's your funeral.'

Tom winced. That word always dragged him back to Aunt Vic's funeral, and the fact that she was his real mum... which, in turn fanned the feelings he had about his broken family; especially Lynn, the sister who knew nothing of his existence. What kind of New Year was she having? What was she looking forward to?

He wondered. What would he do about it? He was eighteen, for God's sake. But how exactly do you justify barging in on someone else's life without an invitation? And hadn't he told Danny he'd given up on the mystery half of the family? Hadn't he vowed to stick with Ted and Rose?

'I'm going out,' he said.

Five minutes later, he was sitting in the Sullivans' front room.

'How's your dad getting on with his runs?' asked George, referring to the routes Knowledge of London students had to learn.

'He was out earlier,' said Tom.

'A few months now, ennit?' George pondered this like a soothsayer. 'That's when it starts to get hard.'

'Yeah…'

George had been on the Knowledge a bit longer, so was further through the *Blue Book* containing the four hundred or so routes the prospective cabbie was expected to learn by heart.

'Tell him he'll be fine once he's past Easter. He'll be into his stride by then.'

'Yeah,' said Tom, praying for a change of subject or, better still, Neil to bloody-well hurry up and come down.

'You sure you don't want a cuppa?' called Elsie from the kitchen.

'I'm fine, thanks.'

'Not that he has much choice,' said George, 'what with the state of the docks. Death throes it is now.'

'Tom doesn't want to hear all that, George,' said Elsie from the kitchen.

'Death throes it is,' insisted George. 'When I was a kid those docks were working all day, every day, even during the War. Do you know they never lost a day's work, despite the bombs?'

The rumble of Neil's feet coming down the stairs was all Tom needed to spring to life.

'We'll be off then. Bye.'

Outside, he chided his best friend. 'What took you so long?'

'You were early. Anyway, I thought I was supposed to be knocking for you.'

'Never mind.'

On the way to the Waterman's Arms, Neil asked the inevitable question.

'See *The Professionals* last night?'

'Yeah, not bad,' said Tom, referring to the new show's second outing.

Then Neil asked the other inevitable question.

'Heard from Claire?'

'No, Neil. Why would I have heard from Claire?'

'Well, she's back in the country. I thought... you know.'

'No, I haven't heard from her.'

'Fancy going to the Ferry House for a change?'

Tom was surprised. Neil never suggested where they might go. *Ever.*

'Okay.'

The Ferry House was fairly quiet. At the bar, they got the beers in and chatted about Genesis and the merits of their live albums compared to their studio albums. And then Claire Cross walked in.

Tom froze. Brenda was with her. He turned to Neil, who was trying to look smug but lacked the practice.

'You bloody little secret agent.'

'Why don't you and Claire have a seat over there? I'll see about debriefing my fellow agent at the bar.'

'Yeah, well, make sure you send a couple of drinks our way, you little...'

Neil chuckled and swapped a few words with Claire about the conspiracy. Then Tom and Claire took their seats at a little table.

'I think we've been set up, Claire.'

'Shocking, isn't it.'

'So how are you?'

'I'm alright. You?'

'Yeah, all good.'

'So...' she said.

'So... there are some good new shows on telly and

Polly still fancies you.'

'I know. Shame about his mum moving out.'

'Yeah… He bought you a ticket for the Clash at the Rainbow. Their show before Christmas, I mean.'

'Oh, I didn't know.'

'No, well, you were busy so he took Neil instead.'

Claire laughed. 'Good ol' Neil.'

'Phil might get jealous though.'

'Don't start.'

'And that record company bloke. He had his eye on you.'

'Dustin's the business manager. He's turned on by pound notes.'

'Only kidding. You'll be happy to know I've been practising my Ian Dury songs. Not to get into your band or anything; just to make me a bit better.'

'I'm glad.'

'Those Blockheads know what they're doing, don't they. I must've listened to *New Boots and Panties* twenty times. And I saw them on *Sight and Sound in Concert* before Christmas. "Sex and Drugs and Rock and Roll" was great. Funky, cool, almost jazzy. I can play a bit like that now. Not the jazzy bits but a solid rhythm. Solid-ish anyway. Sort of. Well, heading towards being able to be solid. So you and Phil will have… I mean… not that it's any of my business.'

Claire laughed a little.

'You're right, it's none of your business. But…'

'But?'

'But nothing's happened, so can we change the subject? I'm just trying to focus on the music. This is my big chance. People seem to think because I've signed a deal and I've been recording, everything is done and dusted. It's just the start though. We've recorded eighteen songs and we're still not sure about the single yet. We've got a bossy producer doing some remixing, Phil's going back to add some new bits, and it's possible we'll get absolutely nowhere.'

'So the rest of your life's on hold, is it?'

'Pretty much. I can't actually think about relationships because I don't know where I'll be next week or what I'll be doing. I've missed certain people though.'

'Really? People such as…?'

'Mum and Dad.'

'Absolutely. Of Course. Good ol' Mum and Dad. Anyone else?'

'Of course there is, silly… my sister.'

'Big Sis, right. Anyone else.'

'Obviously Brenda.'

'Yeah, and…?'

'Some of the teachers at school, that nice man who drives the half-eight 277, the lady in the baker's…'

'You are one horrible annoying friend.'

'Horrible annoying *girl*friend, surely?'

His heart thumped so hard he worried it might smash through his rib cage and smack her in the face.

'You really mean that?' he said as coolly as possible.

'Nothing's changed, Tom. Well, okay, everything's changed. I thought about you a lot over Christmas. I realised here was a nice guy who's been chucked out of his own band, his girlfriend's gone abroad and—'

'—his promised sex life's been cancelled?'

'Yeah, look, circumstances got in the way. No-one's to blame. The question is can we move forward with a new understanding?'

'A new understanding?' He didn't understand. 'You still fancy me then?'

'Yeah, must have bumped my head or something. I

felt really lonely in Germany.'

Tom reached out and squeezed her hand.

'Come on,' she said, 'we'd better join Brenda and Neil before we do anything embarrassing.'

At the bar, Brenda was explaining Polly's ongoing interest in the censorship debate. Apparently, the BBC had banned the new XTC single, "Statue of Liberty" and Polly had blown a fuse. Enough BBC record bans, enough GLC gig bans. Tom felt Polly had a point.

Afterwards, despite a harsh chill in the air, Tom walked Claire home. It felt reassuring to do something so fundamentally simple with his girlfriend, but as they stopped on the Blue Bridge to watch the cold, dark river roll by, he wondered if they really had a future. What if the Westferries were a big success? What if she toured America? What if the new understanding wasn't as good as the old understanding?

'You know what I missed?' she said.

'I know exactly what you missed – *Blake's 7*. It's a new sci-fi series.'

'Tom, we're supposed to be eighteen, not twelve.'

'Hey, you haven't seen it yet.'

'Shut up and come here.'

They kissed. He felt whole.

'When are you disappearing again?' he asked.

'I'm around tomorrow.'

'Yeah?' Tom's brain was racing. 'Fancy doing something? Together?'

'Actually, there *is* something we could do together. Come back in the morning. About ten. It'll make you think you're in Heaven.'

Tom's blood fizzed. This was it. They were going to do the business. There was a God!

43. THIS IS IT

The morning sun shone through Claire's bedroom window. Its reflection off her pure white dressing gown was dazzling. Tom blinked and felt awkward being fully dressed.

He smiled at her. She smiled back, but it was like she had something on her mind.

They moved together and kissed but she seemed cold and distant.

'What's wrong, Claire?'

The door opened and a teenage boy strolled in. He looked ridiculously unfussed about it all.

'This is Harry,' said Claire. 'He plays guitar in a local band. He's *very* talented.'

Tom screamed and woke up. It was dark. The luminous green hands on the clock indicated just after four a.m. He calmed down. It was probably a bit early to start getting ready for his visit to Claire's.

It was seven a.m. Still too early. Tom tried to go back to sleep but his head swirled with images of a picnic with Claire in Greenwich Park, of them on a Spanish beach, of the two of them harmonising on *Top of the Pops*.

After what seemed like several hours, but was in fact twenty minutes, he got up. This was it. The time had come. He was going to become a man. It occurred to him that maybe he should stop wearing winceyette pyjamas.

He went downstairs and made a cup of tea. The house was quiet. Ted and Rose rarely got up before nine on a Sunday. Right now it was half-seven. Ages before he could realistically leave for Claire's. He stared at the clock, willing it to hurry up. The clock, though, seemed determined to follow the tradition of sixty long, slow seconds to each aeon-lasting minute.

He finished his tea, went upstairs, got out his best Fred Perry T-shirt, his Levis and his newest pair of Y-fronts and laid them on the bed. Then he ran a shallow bath. He was washed and dressed and ready for love by eight.

At five past, feeling like a caged animal, he donned his Parka and went out. With almost two hours to make the twenty-minute walk to Claire's, his first priority was to avoid tiring himself out. That said, he definitely needed to burn off a little excess energy. Under a dismal, grey sky, he walked for a bit then checked his watch. An hour and fifty minutes to spare. Plenty of time to get himself into the correct mental state.

Which was…?

Cool would be the way. Or would Claire dislike that approach?

Scared was a good alternative. Or would she think him a child and send him away?

Business-like? Nope.

Resolute? What did that even mean?

He strolled over to Island Gardens. Ignoring the chill wind coming over the water, he beheld his favourite view – the grand Old Royal Naval College on the opposite bank. A man with an impressive camera was taking pictures of it. He nodded to Tom.

'Best view in London,' said Tom.

'I have a print of the Canaletto painting,' said the man, an American by the sound of it. 'Just had to take the opportunity to see it for real.'

Tom felt like awarding him a certificate: the Isle of Dogs' first ever tourist.

'Wasn't it Henry the Eighth who had it built?' said the American.

'Not quite,' said Tom. 'The original palace was built there over five hundred years ago. It was Henry the Seventh who had it rebuilt between 1498 and 1504. Henry the Eighth was born there. So were Mary the First and Elizabeth the First. What you're looking at now is the third go at it – Sir Christopher's Wren's Royal Hospital and the smaller house in the middle by Inigo Jones. That's Britain's first ever classical building.'

'You sure know your history.'

Tom was pleased. He'd been over there a few times recently to soak up the facts relating to his favourite view. He could have gone on about how the Royal Navy took it over in 1873 but the American looked busy setting up his next shot.

Meanwhile, a Thames sailing barge had come along. A rare sight these days. There were teenagers aboard on some kind of adventure thing. It looked fun. The distinct reddish-brown sails would soon fade into history, to be forgotten. That was the thing with life. You had to get on with it while you could. They *were* reddish-brown, weren't they? He supposed it depended on the light. Under a dull sky, they looked plain brown. It must have been under better skies that he named his band Red Sails. Under *much* better skies.

He left Island Gardens and headed for Manchester Road. Passing the Waterman's Arms he paused at the spot he almost lost Claire. Stupid Darbs had gone on about Doops just as Claire entered the pub. Poor Claire. Having just packed in Steve she found herself thinking Tom was just the same. It seemed a lifetime ago.

Crossing the main road by Christ Church, he popped into the newsagents for a Sunday paper. Not that he could muster the concentration to read it. He left the shop wondering if now would be a good time to take up smoking.

'Alright, Tom?'

Oh God. 'Neil? What are you doing out?'

'Just took some bits up to my nan.'

'Oh right.'

'What about you?'

'Headache. Just needed a walk.'

'I'll come with you.'

'A *quiet* walk.'

'Okay. I'll phone you later, if you like.'

'Yeah. Here, have a paper.' He gave Neil his unread *News of the World* and turned on his heels towards Claire's waiting embrace.

Except...

He caught his reflection in a shop window. He looked all wrong.

No, sod it, he was fine. He walked on again, faster.

But where? He could hardly head straight over the Blue Bridge. He'd be there far too early.

The Muddy.

Since some local action groups had taken a lease from the council and begun the process of turning the Mudchute into an urban farm, Tom had taken a liking to the place. Walking around the bridle path it was possible to imagine being in the countryside. Indeed, there was one part, on the southern perimeter, where 150 yards of bushy embankment hid all signs of urban life to the point that it really could have been Norfolk or Devon. It was a place a man could think.

And he was thinking in overdrive.

What if the occasion got to him and he underperformed? Or non-performed? After all, his equipment hadn't been fully road-tested and there were no reliable accounts of how the joint process worked. Micky Sullivan's "I banged it one" certainly lacked detail.

But maybe Micky's uncomplicated approach was right. Maybe you could sweat too much over it. Maybe it was really was a case of "Yes, Claire here I come." Maybe he should just get straight up there and make her eyeballs spin. Although – how exactly did a man make a woman's eyeballs spin? That bloke he used to work with – Chris Lowe. He knew. Or at least he said he knew. He could hardly phone him though.

He left by Farm Road where a couple of blokes were nicking the tall wooden planking that made up the fence. It was still too early for Claire so he headed back to Chapel House Street, past the 1920s council houses, and past the brand new houses that had risen from the rubble of the century-old homes so fondly remembered by the locals.

From there it was north up Westferry Road to Tiller Road and along to the Glass Bridge over the Millwall Dock. There he spent twenty minutes watching the still waters below. On the quayside by one of the big sheds, a security guard smoked a cigarette and stamped his feet to keep out the cold. Conversely, Tom felt hot. He was about to cross not just the Glass Bridge from Millwall to Cubitt Town, but the bridge between boyhood and manhood.

He checked his watch. Manhood was still an hour and five minutes away.

Down on the other side, he walked up to Manchester Road, where he turned south, away from Claire's, and back to the newsagent's where he bought another *News of the World*. He stood outside, freezing as he read a few pages. Then he gave it to a retired docker he knew and headed back to Island Gardens. It was cold and deserted. So was the river. He watched for a while then tried to write a song.

Slow moving water
Depths beyond unseen
Slow moving life
Depths beyond unknown
Love
Unseen, unknown…

He checked his watch, forgot the lyric, and headed slowly north towards the Blue Bridge. Twenty minutes later, he was studying the Thames sweeping round from Blackwall Reach. Half the world had rounded that stretch on its way to and from London. What stories this river could tell.

He turned to the West India Docks; once proud and busy but now doomed to a bleak, barren future.

'Alright Tom?'

Arghh! Polly!

'Polly, hi.'

'Lost?' said Polly, aboard a bicycle.

'No, I was just… you know… walking.'

'Fancy popping round for a cup of tea?'

'No! I mean no thanks. I'm… seeing Claire.'

'Lucky boy.'

'Yeah, we're just…'

'See you around.'

Polly rode south onto the Island. Tom was relieved. Love was calling and there was no place for chit-chatting with mates – especially those who fancied your girlfriend.

He reached Claire's house. This was it. Archie was in the window. He jumped down. A moment later, Tom could hear him meowing behind the door.

Yes, Archie. Our little plan has worked.

He wondered if he was supposed to bring Claire a box of chocolates or some flowers. Was it too late to get some? No, he was only delaying his arrival. Despite feeling sweaty and sick, he rang the bell.

There was no answer.

Good. He could go home and listen to an album. He'd prefer that. But, as he took a step away, the door opened.

'Goodness me, you look cold, Tom,' said Francine. 'Come in. The cab's due in ten minutes.'

'Oh, right. Thanks.'

Good. Mr and Mrs Cross would soon be gone.

'Hello, Tom,' called Mr Cross from the kitchen.

'Hi,' said Tom, wiping his feet on the mat. He closed the door behind him.

'Tea? Toast?' called Mr Cross.

'They haven't got time,' said Francine. She turned to Tom. 'I did tell him you wouldn't have time for a cuppa but he doesn't always listen.'

Tom was confused. Why wouldn't he have time for tea and toast before he and Claire… commenced revising for their A-levels?

'Tom, alright?' said Claire, beaming as she came down the stairs. 'Looking forward to my little surprise?'

He gulped. 'Er, yeah.'

Why was she mentioning it in front of her mum? Surely that took things far beyond a healthy mother-daughter relationship. No, Francine couldn't possibly know what they were about to get up to. Not in a million years.

'Do you know something, Tom,' said Francine. 'It makes the little hairs stand up on the back of my neck.'

Tom was mortified. Obviously, full credit to Mr Cross for being able to transport Mrs Cross to such heights, but he didn't wish to hear about it.

'I'm very jealous of you two,' said Francine, heading into the kitchen.

Tom was spooked but as Claire led him into the front room he forced himself to reconnect with reality. There was no way on earth that Francine was referring to hanky-panky, otherwise whatever next? Mr Cross slapping him on the back and wishing him good luck?

They sat down opposite each other and Claire checked her watch.

A cab was coming to pick someone up. Obviously not Claire's parents.

'Is Tracey going out?'

'She's already out. Stayed round her boyfriend's last night. Why, what's up?'

'Nothing.'

The only logical explanation was that he and Claire were going somewhere. In a cab.

But where?

44. IN HARMONY

Tom was with Claire in the back of a minicab heading west on The Highway. At any point, he could have asked what was going on but he'd opted to play it cool. There had been mention of her staying in a hotel. Maybe that's where they were headed. He was fine with that. Perhaps it was a posh hotel with a view of Hyde Park. They'd make love then stroll onto her balcony to watch the traffic pootling happily along Park Lane.

He smiled at her. 'Money must be alright.'

'How do you mean?'

'Taking cabs. The money must be alright.'

'Honestly, I've hardly had a penny. It's all expenses. They'll pay any cab receipts I give them but if I ask for a bit of spending money, they turn a bit funny.'

'Still, I bet the hotels are good.'

'You must be joking. Cheap and nasty. Designed to get musicians out fast so they spend more time in the studio.'

'Right.' That ruled out the potential hotel destination. 'They'll be choosing your clothes next, Claire.'

'They already are.'

Tom felt a rumble of discontent. If Mr Oily was involved in seeing Claire in various stages of undress, in the fake name of fashion choices, Mr Oily would find himself receiving a knee in the groin.

'So…' said Claire. 'Not curious where I'm taking you?'

'No, I trust you.'

'It's not a church, if that's what you're thinking.'

'A church?'

'No, it's not a church.'

Thank God for that.

'It's a cathedral.'

'A what?'

'A cathedral. You know, like a church, but bigger.'

'I know what a bloody cathedral is. But…'

'Don't knock it till you've tried it.'

'Tried what?' Surely they weren't going to do it in a cathedral!

The roads were quiet and the cab moved unhindered along Lower Thames Street past the fish market. Even with his limited knowledge, Tom knew they were in the City of London and that St Paul's Cathedral was nearby. They'd no doubt soon be stopping outside it.

They continued along by the river, out of the City of London into the City of Westminster, towards Big Ben. Tom guessed they must be heading for Westminster Abbey instead of St Paul's, but when they drove past it, he frowned.

'Um… Claire?'

'Patience.'

They were soon getting out by a grand old building halfway up Victoria Street. The sign informed him that it was Westminster Cathedral.

'Well, I never knew that,' he said, taking in the striped brickwork and tower.

'It's been here seventy-odd years,' said Claire.

'I never knew.'

'No, well, it's Catholic. Even the Queen only realised it was here last year, and she lives just around the corner.'

'Catholic?'

'She visited as part of the Jubilee.'

'Hang on, so you're a Catholic then.'

'And?'

'No, I... no. No problem.'

'It's never been something to shout about at school. People assume you're sending money to the IRA.'

Tom felt she was exaggerating but there were undeniably a small number who saw the armed struggle in Northern Ireland as a fight between Catholics and Protestants, rather than just their extreme fringes – especially every time a bomb went off on the streets of London.

'Dad's not religious,' said Claire, 'so mum held sway. She's half-Spanish, half-French. Francine Luisa Navarra. Her family came to England when she was a baby, during the Spanish Civil War. She was coming with me this morning but I managed to persuade her to step down.'

'I see. So your Sunday surprise isn't you and me... you know.'

'Oh, stop it, you nutter.'

They laughed but Tom quickly frowned.

'You're forgetting something. I'm Church of England.'

'So's the Queen.'

'Yeah, but... am I allowed inside then?'

'I got you a special dispensation from the Pope.'

'Yeah, right – but, seriously, what do we do inside? Pray?'

'If you like. We've actually come to hear the choir.'

'The choir?' Tom's heart sank.

'It's Renaissance choral music. All I ask is you leave your prejudice at the door and pin back your ears. This isn't some high school outfit. This lot will blow your socks off.'

'The best ever version of "All Things Bright and Beautiful", you mean?'

'It's Victoria, Tom. Vic-bloody-toria.'

'I know where we are, Claire.'

'No, you berk, Tomas Luis de Victoria. That's the music we'll be hearing.'

'Never heard of him.'

'Tom, there was a day not so long ago when you had never heard of your precious Genesis.'

'Yeah… well…'

'Now come on, and no swearing.'

They went inside. It was a lot bigger than Tom had imagined. Then he corrected himself. He'd never actually imagined the inside of Westminster Cathedral.

'I'm not saying I won't give it a fair hearing.'

'I know that. Anything else would be revealing a fascist tendency.'

'A what?'

'A tendency to take extreme pride in your own choices, leaving no room for a fair hearing of anything else.'

'I see. Is that a jazz reference?'

Claire reddened a little.

Once they were settled, Tom took in the architectural splendour of the interior. It really was impressive. Probably as impressive as St. Paul's or Westminster Abbey. Time he visited them too, he realised.

Claire nudged him.

'I listened to your *Selling England By The Pound* three times before I got into it. Same with *Kind of Blue*. Same with Beethoven's *Archduke* piano trio. Same with Shubert's piano sonatas and Van Morrison's *Astral Weeks*.'

'No worries on that score, Claire. I'll give Thomas Lewis Victoria a good listen.'

'Tomas Luis de Victoria.'

'Him too.'

It wasn't long before everyone was in place. Then the public murmur faded to nought and the singers rose.

Polyphonic tones came out of the body of the choir to fill the air. There was a lightness to the sound and yet a gravity too. Strikingly, the music appeared to be at home here, as if it were a thing in itself, a resident of the fabric coming to mingle with the visitors. Tom's mouth even opened a little to let out an almost silent 'Wow.'

Long before they left, he was a fan of Tomas Luis de Victoria. Quite a big fan.

Outside, he shared his new love.

'There's so much depth. I can't believe I've never heard it before.'

'I'm glad you liked it.'

Something occurred to him. Something quite important, given the circumstances.

'Claire, do you believe in God?'

'Yep. Maybe that's why I get myself tied up in knots over stuff. You know, what I should and shouldn't want… or do. How about you?'

'I don't know.' He tried to stop thinking about Claire's wanting… and doing. 'I mean if there's a God, how come it took him so long to break up the Sex Pistols?'

'You think God hates punk?'

'Maybe – and that's why he created New Wave.'

'Well, he certainly moves in mysterious ways, because I'm not even sure what New Wave is.'

Tom was sure. 'Elvis Costello, Talking Heads, Dr Feelgood, The Jam, The Stranglers, Ian Dury…'

'I mean I'm not sure they're linked by anything more than being around at the same time.'

'Yeah, I suppose. Do you think Tomas Luis de Victoria was New Wave in his day?'

'Yeah, him and Palestrina – once they'd seen off that punk Josquin des Prez.'

They strolled down Victoria Street to Parliament Square, Westminster Abbey, the Houses of Parliament, Big Ben and the river. On the Embankment, just east of Westminster Bridge, the water below them was murky and alive; the bridge itself causing distortions in the natural flow.

'Our river,' said Claire.

'Seems like another river when you see it here.'

'Yeah, I prefer it round the Island too.'

'It belongs to us down there. Up here, it belongs to London.'

'That's why I like taking cabs and buses. You see how you're connected to where you're going. You see the changes. The Tube swallows you up and spits you out. It's like you're in one reality then there's a bit of nothing then you're in another reality. Planes are like that too.'

'What will you do if the single does well?'

'I haven't thought that far ahead.'

'Liar. In your place, I'd go to bed dreaming about it.'

'Damn, you caught me out.'

They squeezed hands.

Of course, Tom knew if she did badly, she'd come back to the Island and lead a normal life with her boyfriend. So, in essence, their current bedtime dreams about her music career couldn't match up, which made Tom feel mean and small. The only comfort he took was knowing he'd never do anything to harm her career. That would be up to the public. Would they buy Claire's records? That was the big question. The public – they wouldn't just decide Claire's future. They would decide Tom's too.

45. CELEBRATION

The beginning of February saw the Alders move. The rent on the big house by the fire station was proving too costly. While Ted had happily paid up to enhance his standing in the community, times were much tougher now. Luckily, their landlord had a cheaper property just up the road. Not so luckily, Tom found it small and depressing. He also found the ceiling in his bedroom had damp of a worrying nature. Of course, the landlord promised to fix it.

Tom, meanwhile, knuckled down at school by doing old exam papers to get match fit for the A-level exams that were now just four months away. One of the main reasons for this laser-like focus on schoolwork was to keep his mind off the Westferries' first single, "Roll Me, Baby", which was about to be released.

Regarding the official launch party in Soho, which Tom wasn't invited to, news came back via Polly. From what Phil had told Oz, Polly was able to reveal that Claire had got severely drunk, snogged some bass player from another band and thrown up in Berwick Street. Unlike most people, Tom couldn't see the funny side. No wonder she hadn't phoned him. Even so, he felt as if he'd let her down by not being there for her.

A few days on, it was time for the Isle of Dogs version of the launch party.

Since Christmas, Tom had been saving his part-time

earnings. Now he was able to splash out on *Exodus* by Bob Marley and something for Claire. A little Valentine's Day gift: *Variations* by Andrew Lloyd Webber – an album of cello music played by Lloyd Webber's brother, Julian. He left it with Claire's mum, in case he wasn't able to see her on the day.

Approaching the Waterman's, an odd feeling crept up on him. A sense of dread. This wasn't just a celebration of the Westferries' first single; it was Claire's potential farewell party. If "Roll Me, Baby" did well, she might never return to the Island.

A car horn blasted him.

It was Tony Cornish in a red MG sports car.

'Alright, Tim!'

'Hello, Tone. How's it going? Still seeing that girl from the other scrap yard?'

'Nah. Ditched her before Christmas. Seriously – two years taking her to pubs, discos, restaurants, Benidorm… we just ran out of things to do.'

'Oh well.'

'Not easy finding the real thing, is it.'

'No.'

'I mean we shag loads of women then ask ourselves if we shouldn't be trying to build something more solid. Know what I mean?'

'Yeah…'

'That's my next move. Finding a decent girl. No more pissing about.'

'Well, good luck.'

Reaching the pub, Tom paused. How was he going to handle this? Was it a case of pasting on a smile and leading the "hip-hip-hoorays"? Or a more measured nod and "well done"? He pushed the door open a little. There they were, by the bar. The laughter, the happiness. Claire was with Phil. Why did she have to bring him here? And there was Drummer Den. God, the thought of having Den feel sorry for him. Even Craig Lycett was there.

Jeez…

He couldn't do it. He simply couldn't go in there and laugh and drink.

As he turned away, he caught her eye. Just a flash and the door was closing and he was away.

Someone came out of the pub. Footsteps. Coming after him.

'Where are you going?'

He stopped. The self-pity and sense of worthlessness were embarrassing.

She was at his side.

'Hey…'

He turned to her, to apologise, to seek permission to get away. But she leaned up and they kissed.

For a mad, crazy moment, his brain flooded with strange thoughts. Was this it? Was Claire giving up her future for love?

No, stupid. A-levels, music college, *love* – all were being side-lined for a chance to make something amazing of her life.

'Best of luck, Claire. Storm those charts, mate. Numero Uno.'

'Avoiding total failure would be a start,' she said.

He tried to smile. 'You've got a shot at the big time. Don't be embarrassed by it.'

'I'm not.'

'Well, don't feel sorry about leaving me behind then. I mean isn't that the whole thing about being young and aspiring? To go out there and give life a go with everything you've got?'

He felt this wasn't the time to mention the local council's junior clerk scheme booklet on his bed. No place for that in a Seize the Day conversation.

'I thought we had a new understanding?' she said.

'I don't want to hold you back.'

'You're not. Now come into the pub.'

'I feel awkward.'

'Don't be silly. Without you, I wouldn't have explored a side of music I considered inferior. You opened my eyes. Well, ears. Now will you please come inside. It's bloody freezing out here.'

He wasn't sure.

'Please, Tom. I want you to be there.'

He gave in and followed her.

No sooner he was inside, a familiar face popped up.

'Hello, stranger.'

Natalie Hiscock… crap.

'Natalie, hi.'

'I heard on the grapevine there might be a do.'

'I didn't think you knew Claire.'

'No, but I know the bloke who put her where she is today.'

'Phil?'

'No, *you*, silly.'

'Look, I played guitar with her for a bit, that's all.'

'It's all about women, ain't it. Maggie Thatcher, whatsername on the news, the first woman…'

'Anna Ford.'

'Yeah, and Claire making a single. And that new one who was in the paper. Blondie…'

'Yeah, all talented women.'

'Then little ol' me trying to squeeze in too.'

'Squeeze in where?'

'The music business. I told you I was a singer, didn't I?'

'I don't think so. In fact I don't remember us ever having any conversations at all.'

Natalie laughed it off. Then, as he tried to reach Neil, she blocked him.

'I've always found you interesting, Tom. You know – my kind of bloke. The kind of bloke I can get excited about. Know what I mean?'

Tom took a breath. Nat Hiscock's daughter was propositioning him. He couldn't get involved. Aside from the fact that Nat would cut his balls off, Natalie was a horrible spoilt woman who probably had a singing voice like an old Ford's screeching fan belt.

'Natalie, I need to see someone about something.'

He reached Neil.

'So, Neil. Abba number one in the album charts, eh?'

'Oh, I didn't know you were a fan.'

'I'm just making conversation to throw off the Princess of Darkness – no don't bloody look!'

'Right, well, a new number one in the singles too.'

'Yeah, thank God. How long was "Mull of Kintyre" there? Four years, wasn't it?'

'Two and a half months, I think.'

'Yeah, "Uptown Top Ranking". I really like it,' said Tom, referring to Althea and Donna's hit single.

'Bob Marley's in there too,' said Neil referring to "Jammin'" at number nine. 'Sort of a Jamaican thing going on, maybe.'

'Yeah, good. I like it.' He thought of Trevor, ensconced at Hackney Town Hall and his own plan to try Tower Hamlets. As jobs went, town hall admin wouldn't be the end of the world. Then he noticed Natalie edging closer. 'Yeah, interesting times, Neil. Interesting times, mate. Lots of new stuff. Keep talking.'

'Eh?'

'Keep talking. Lots of new stuff out.'

'Yeah, Tom Robinson's got an EP out.'

'Tom Robinson, eh?'

'Yeah, *Rising Free*. Four tracks. It's got "Glad to be Gay" on it. Remember singing along at the Bridge House?'

'I remember you singing along, Neil.'

'Must be a year ago now.'

'Yeah, well, good for Tom Robinson. Freedom and all that. Glad it's getting some exposure.'

'It's not. The BBC have banned it.'

'Oh. Oh look – Polly! Poll, just saying about the BBC banning stuff.'

Polly came over and effectively blocked the gap Natalie might have moved into.

'A government tool, that's what they are.'

'Still,' said Tom, 'Maggie Thatcher's getting popular. We might have a change of government before long.'

'I hardly think having the Tories back will improve the situation.'

'No, well, Labour are doing what they can, I suppose.'

'Yeah,' said Neil. 'Things are improving. Inflation under ten percent. First time in five years.'

Polly scoffed. 'That doesn't mean a thing, Neil. We've got a Labour government moving to the Right to head off Thatcher.'

'Well, it was up to 25% at one point…'

'Neil, the enemy isn't inflation. It's…'

Natalie squeezed between Polly and Neil.

'So,' she said, 'whose round is it?'

While Neil got the drinks in, Tom found himself being manoeuvred aside.

'So, you know the boss at Stripeless.'

'I met him once, but…'

'I reckon ordinary people like Claire, like you, like me – we deserve a chance. Don't we?'

'Claire's an amazing talent.'

'So am I, babes.'

'Yeah, look…' He looked around for help and found Roy smiling at him.

'Alright?' said Roy, coming over. 'And who's this?'

'We're in a meeting,' said Natalie.

'I'm Roy. I've played with Claire and Tom.'

'Really? What are you drinking?'

'Er, lager.'

Natalie aimed her tonsils at Neil.

'Oi, another pint of lager.'

Roy had a look in his eyes. It wasn't hard to read.

'Yeah, if it wasn't for us,' he said, 'Claire would be nowhere.'

'I know Tom got her out of all that classical crap and into proper music. What did you do?'

'I was in the band.'

Tom could see Natalie's brain cogs whirring.

'But Tom's the talent-spotter.'

'Er, well… yeah. If it wasn't for *my best mate, Tom,* Claire would be playing cello in a school assembly.'

'God, Tom, she owes you everything.'

'No, she's talented.'

'I'm talented too. I'll show you. You'll see.'

'Look, I have to be honest…'

'Yeah?' She fluttered her eyelids and suddenly looked close to tears.

'Look, I might be able to help a bit, but…'

'Thanks Tom. You're a lovely bloke. Reliable, like. Not like some of the shits I've been out with.'

'Yeah, well…'

'And I'll be *grateful*.'

'No, seriously. It's fine.'

'Excuse us,' said Roy, pulling Tom aside. 'What are you playing at? She's serving herself up on a plate.'

'I'm with Claire.' He looked over to Claire laughing with Phil, Craig, Den and Neil.

Roy sighed. 'This bird here might be another talent. I mean we need to get her into a studio and see if she's all talk, or if she's genuinely capable of *going all the way*.'

Tom sighed. 'I'm not sure, Roy.'

'That's your problem. You're never sure of anything. Apart from bloody Claire. Grow up, mate. Grow up and take control of your life.'

46. TOP OF THE POPS

Tom was burning up. He'd sat with Ted and Rose to watch *Top of the Pops* countless times over the years, sometimes excitedly, more often in semi-boredom waiting for the one or two performances that would lift the show out of the bland porridge of so-so chart music.

It had been an interesting start to March. Following a tip-off from Neil, whose mum bought *Radio Times*, he was able to catch the start of *The Hitch-Hikers Guide to the Galaxy,* a new sci-fi comedy on Radio 4. Meanwhile, on the music front, a young woman called Kate Bush had hit number one with "Wuthering Heights" while Debbie Harry turned out to be the most attractive female he had ever set eyes on.

Right now though, the big event was almost upon them. A first television appearance for the Westferries. He'd hardly seen Claire as she'd been rushing about promoting the single. She'd phoned a few times, of course, but it all sounded so alien to him. And now his stomach was churning. What if they were boring? What if they were brilliant? What if…? Suddenly, out of a blur of words coming from Tony Blackburn, Tom discerned, 'The Westferries with "Roll Me, Baby"…'

And there was Blackburn's smile, a burst of audience applause and Claire Cross on the telly. Claire bloody Cross on *Top of the* bloody *Pops*. With Phil, Craig and Den.

'*All I think of is you*

All I dream is a dream of two
I wanna rock you, lover
I wanna rock you only
And when I'm done rocking you
Baby, you can roll me…'

Okay, so the lyrics were trite, but it was fantastically funky, it was undeniably danceable, it was super-sing-a-long-able… it was a hit waiting to happen.

'Not bad,' said Ted.

'She's ever so good,' said Rose.

'Why didn't you stick with them?' said Ted.

Tom had to leave the room. It was all too much. Claire was going to be a star. Her singing was ace, Phil's funky guitar was spot on, Claire's bass melded with Den's drumming and Craig's synth strings gave the whole thing a light, breezy, chart-topping sound.

He paused on the stairs for the chorus.

'Roll me, baby. Cure my midnight blues
Roll me, sugar. I got nuthin' to lose…'

He continued up the stairs. Mike Oldfield's *Ommadawn* would calm him down. Bloody fine album, that. Much better than *Tubular Bells*. He hoped Neil wouldn't phone and start burbling on about the Westferries. He hated anyone interrupting when he was deep into an album.

Two minutes later, the phone rang.

Rose called up.

'It's for you.'

'If it's Neil, I'm busy.'

'It's not Neil, it's someone called Roy.'

Roy?

Tom went down to take the call.

'Roy?'

'See Claire, did ya?'

'I caught a bit of it.'

'Ha ha, very cool. Listen, I'm thinking there's a pattern. Kate Bush, Debbie Harry, Claire Cross...'

'You've been talking to Natalie.'

'Yeah, look, I've booked us some rehearsal time. Just the band so we can put some songs together. We'll get her along once we're tight. Then, if she's half decent, we'll form a band around her. You know how shallow the music business is. They'll be looking for the next female singer, and we'll have her.'

'What if she's rubbish?'

'Then we'll shag her senseless and dump her for another bird. I mean the law of averages says we'll get to a decent singer at some point. And if we don't, it'll be a right laugh finding out, eh?'

'I'm not sure.'

'Have a think and I'll get back to you, alright? See ya.'

Tom sighed. Roy was an appalling human being. But he did have a point. Finding the next big female singer could indeed be an interesting challenge. Maybe his musical journey wasn't over yet.

Over the next few days, Tom embraced the celebratory mood at school. Thanks to Neil, everyone remembered to acknowledge Tom's minor role in putting Claire, and indeed Craig, on the road to stardom. The only thing he was struggling with was Roy's carefree attitude to abusing the trust Natalie was prepared to place in them.

Meeting him one evening in the Lord Nelson to work out a plan, he dodged Roy's "we could both shag her" direction and tried to concentrate on the music. That wasn't so easy though, with a middle-aged crooner on the pub's tiny stage belting out "You're Sixteen".

'What is it? Don't you fancy her?'

'Oh she's a looker; no problem there.'

'So what's the problem?'

It was hard to explain to someone like Roy. The two of them shagging the same girl lacked the touch of romance Tom associated with losing his virginity. Besides, the thought of sharing such a precious moment with Natalie then looking round to see Roy grinning at him…

'I've still got a thing for Claire. We talk on the phone at least twice a week.'

'I wanna screw Claire,' said Roy.

'You what?' said Tom, annoyed.

'I wanna screw Claire. I bet she's good in bed.'

Tom felt a fury rising in him. He was going to punch Roy's face in.

'Hey, hey,' said Roy. 'I'm only saying what half a million blokes are thinking. We've all seen her on *Top of the Pops*. Or are you gonna duff up every man who wants to "roll her"?'

Tom was confused. His anger had yet to subside but it no longer had anywhere to go.

Roy shook his head. 'She's gone, mate. Probably shagging all them DJs at *Top of the Pops*.'

'I don't think so.'

'Take my advice. Get over her. What you've got is the kind of thing most blokes can only dream of. Seriously, you could have birds queuing round the block.'

Later, in his bedroom, staring up at the damaged ceiling caused by broken tiles that their landlord had failed to get fixed, Tom pondered the idea of having women queuing round the block for him. It would be okay as long as they liked him, not because they believed he might be able to do them a favour. Of course, there was no evidence he'd be able to do anything for them. He didn't know Phil's Soho contact. He didn't properly know Mr Oily. And Claire hadn't got there by luck. She was a special talent. You couldn't just take someone else along the same route.

On the other hand, Roy had a point. Everyone fancied Claire. Since she'd turned eighteen she seemed to have become even more attractive. She'd been on the telly. She'd done some photo-shoots for magazines and posters. Guys were starting to get hot in the Y-fronts over her. All over Britain, boys would be putting up fresh new posters so that they could flop back on their beds, stare up at Claire and imagine…

He wondered where she was at that moment. The Westferries were playing in the north-east. Newcastle, Durham and a couple of other places. Or had they moved to the north-west? She'd mention in their last phone call something about playing Manchester and Liverpool again. And Sheffield. Had she listened to the LP he bought her? Julian Lloyd Webber playing variations written by his brother Andrew?

Before he went to bed, he listened to the cassette tape he'd made of the album. It wasn't bad. Pretty good, in fact. Especially the theme tune to that new arts programme, *The South Bank Show*. He couldn't think of Julian Lloyd Webber playing the cello on it though. When he closed his eyes, he saw Claire. In a classroom. Playing bloody magnificently.

Hello, cello girl. Where are you now?

"Roll Me, Baby" entered the chart at No. 17. At the same time, Tom was busy moving stuff in his bedroom away from the rainwater dripping through his ceiling and setting up East India, a new band with female singer

Natalie Hiscock. He also watched Claire on *Top of the Pops* – all the way through this time. Not to idolise her but to pick up tips for Natalie. It was hard to deny his feelings for Claire but he was preparing to move on with Natalie, Roy, bass player Jez and a drummer called Tufty. He felt a fraud, of course. All the early indications were that Natalie was about as talented as a turnip. That said, Tom was keen to write some new songs. He just wasn't sure what they should be about. After all, he couldn't write love songs in case Natalie got the wrong idea.

He did try to get to know her better though. He even took her to West Ham, although she wasn't impressed at seeing them lose 2-1 to Wolves. Of course, music was a big factor. He played her tapes of Genesis, Bob Marley and Frank Sinatra to show her different approaches to the vocalist's role. She didn't like any of them.

Even so, Tom was determined to do his best. Who was he to deny her a chance? Then Roy begged him to have a word with Natalie on his behalf.

'She turn you down, Roy?'

'I gave it my best spiel, but she's bullet proof.'

Tom took his guitar round to Natalie's and got her to sing a few songs he'd been practising with the band. Once she got the hang of them, she wasn't too bad.

'Do you think I'm good enough?'

'I think you're good, Natalie.'

'You really think so?'

Tom felt bad. He meant she was good, not great. What she lacked was that extra thing. The thing Phil said Claire had. It was hard to say exactly what it was, this thing, but it was easy to spot when it was missing.

'Maybe we could try a different way to put more of you into the delivery.'

'How?'

'Well, Kate Bush and Debbie Harry have a certain something…'

'I've got tits too, you know.'

'I mean vocals-wise. Claire Cross too. It's like their personalities blend with their delivery. You don't just get the singer, you get… well, you get more.'

'So you want me to get more of my personality into my singing.'

'Yeah. The best aspects, if possible.'

'What's that supposed to mean?'

'Well, for example, you might want to focus on your sunny side. If you were a punk, you'd focus on your angry side. Actually, have you thought of being a punk?'

'Punk's dead. Let's concentrate on my sunny side.'

'Yeah, right, so when you sing "Show You The Way To Go", try to channel Michael Jackson.

'How?'

'Sing like you're enjoying it. You know, happy and sunny.'

'Show me.'

'Eh?'

'You sing it so I can see what you're on about.'

'No, me and Roy are only doing backing vocals.'

'Yeah, but I need you to show me what you mean. You know, show me the way to go.'

Natalie laughed at her own joke. Tom could only gulp. He couldn't sing a love song to Natalie Hiscock. That would be perverse. Still, he was a musician. It came with responsibilities.

He played himself in and gave it his best shot. It was only halfway into the first line that he realised he had no idea how to put his personality into the song. All he could think of was to sing it to Claire. Even though she was miles away. Worryingly, as he hit the chorus, Natalie joined in. It was insane. Had embarrassment had a maximum setting, this exceeded it like a speeding lorry through a shop window. He stopped as soon as it wasn't rude to do so.

'You meant that, didn't you,' she said. 'You've got a thing for me, don't deny it. I can always tell when a bloke's genuine.'

'Er...'

'You want me, don't you, you cocky fucker.'

'Er...'

'It'll be our little song. You know, when we're at it.'

She giggled coyly. He almost retched. She was such a crappy liar.

47. INTEGRITY

Around the end of March, Tom was in the record shop in Chrisp Street Market going through the albums. They were playing the Bee Gees, "Staying Alive" and he found his foot unexpectedly tapping along to it. A bloke came in and asked for Elvis Costello's "I Don't Wanna Go To Chelsea". The man behind the counter joked that he didn't want to go there either. Then he played Buddy Holly. His *Twenty Golden Greats* LP was at No. 1. Tom quite liked it.

A moment later, another bloke came in and asked for the Westferries' single.

Tom glanced at the chart pinned to the wall. It was No. 5. He would have bought a copy himself but it felt too weird to pay to have Claire sing to him.

Natalie came in. She'd been looking at shoes. She patted him on the bum. He wouldn't commit yet though. Not to her or the idea of recording a tape. Not until he was sure they had put everything into the songs.

Later, he took her to the Bridge House to see a good singer – Chris Thompson, who performed regularly with a band at the pub while co-existing as the singer in Manfred Mann's Earthband and enjoying worldwide hits.

Polly was there with a couple of new mates. He wanted Tom to come on the Anti-Nazi League and Rock Against Racism march from Trafalgar Square to Victoria Park. Tom wasn't keen. Neither was Natalie. Finally, they had something in common.

A week later, Tom and Neil sat through *Saturday Night Fever* in the comfort of a West End cinema. It was certainly a good film and the music sat with the story really well. For Tom, the whole dance thing was beginning to make sense. He could understand why people wanted to flock to Cherry's disco at Hackney dog track, or that new place up by Mile End Station. He didn't particularly want to join them, but he could see the attraction.

Outside the cinema, the fever subsided. It was snowing.

'Maybe Natalie could be a disco singer,' said Neil.

'I don't think so. You have to believe in what you're doing. Natalie's a fraud. She has no passion. For music, I mean.'

'Stardom, eh?'

'Exactly. She only wants to be famous. She'd sing Gregorian chant if she thought it would get her on *Top of the Pops*.'

It didn't help that The Westferries were No. 3 in the charts.

'Not much of a match, is it. You don't like her and she's only using you.'

'I just feel I have to give her a chance. Even if it's just a chance to prove to herself she's not good enough.'

'You should never have got involved, Tom. If you send a tape to that bloke who helped Claire, you'll look a right idiot.'

'I know. We're getting to the point where we'll have to though, or she'll castrate me.'

'Does her dad get involved at all?'

'What, in the castrating? He will if I upset his precious daughter.'

'Well, you've managed to fight her off till now.'

'Natalie and Nat Hiscock…' Tom shook his head.

'Speaking of Nats,' said Neil, 'I bought my mum Nat King Cole's LP for her birthday.'

'Nice.' The fifties crooner's collection had reached the top of the album charts. 'Maybe Natalie could sing "When I Fall In Love".'

'Don't be alone with her if she does. It'll only go one way after that.'

It was the penultimate Sunday in April and Tom was in the rehearsal studios at Furze Street. This had to be among their final attempts to make some magic because pressure was building to hire the recording studio in Islington. Not that the cost was a problem – Nat Hiscock was happy to stump up the cash to fund his daughter's rise to the top.

While they were waiting for Roy, the talk varied between the previous day's National Front St George's Day activities, Brian Clough's Nottingham Forest winning the league and the fact that Tom had bought two albums: Genesis' *And Then There Were Three* and Bob Marley's *Kaya*. Natalie was most taken by the fact that the Westferries' single had hit No.2.

When Roy arrived they didn't waste any time in getting down to business. Natalie sounded better than before with the band drowning out some of her flatter notes. What also helped was her removing her jean jacket to reveal a tight, almost see-through white T-shirt. With no bra to spoil the view, the band warmed to her like never before. They only had three songs that suited her voice, so they ran through them a few times. To Tom's ears, there was no noticeable special element, but Jez and Tufty were full of praise and, in fairness, Natalie looked stunning. Tom worried about a lack of integrity, but guessed he was in a minority of one. Natalie's body would undoubtedly take an audience's mind off her vocal shortcomings and lack of personality.

Later, at home, Tom helped Ted by testing him for an hour on his Knowledge of London runs in readiness for an appearance at the Public Carriage Office. That done, he skipped off to the Waterman's Arms to meet Neil. Disappointingly, Neil had invited Polly, who seemed to be there solely to urge Tom to attend the Trafalgar Square rally and march to Victoria Park for what he was calling the Carnival Against The Nazis.

Tom wasn't so sure, but Polly reminded them of the ten-year-old Sikh boy who had been stabbed to death locally. Surely Tom would come on the big march? He couldn't let racists go round killing little kids. Could he?

'I'm going,' said Neil.

'Really?' said Tom.

'I'm going with someone new.'

'Anyone I know?'

'No,' said Neil, blushing. 'I don't think you've met Nadia. She's a squadist.'

'What's that – Dr Who's latest enemy?'

'A squadist is a special member of the SWP. I met her when Polly and me were up Brick Lane the other week.'

'You never said anything.'

'I wasn't sure if she wanted to see me.'

Tom was annoyed. Anyone arriving from the planet Neptune would instantly spot that Neil and Brenda Brand were made for each other. They were just too shy and lacked the oomph to really give it a go. Polly allowing Neil to team up with an SWP type was throwing a leg of lamb to a wolf. Neil would just get chewed up then dropped.

Neil had a flyer for the event. Tom Robinson, the singer they had seen in the Bridge House yonks ago would be headlining the concert at Victoria Park. There was talk of the Clash playing too. It didn't sound too bad.

'Okay,' said Tom. 'Count me in.'

'Good man,' said Polly. 'Who wants a drink?'

Around 11:15 p.m., just as Tom arrived back home, Natalie phoned to ask how much longer before he decided on a recording studio date.

'We're getting there. We don't want less than a hundred percent, do we?'

'Will we rehearse again next Sunday?'

'Ah, no, I'm going on this march and rally thing. Trafalgar Square and Victoria Park. The Tom Robinson Band are playing.'

'I'll come.'

'Really?'

'You can stay at my place afterwards.'

Tom felt the pressure building again. Would he turn Natalie down? *Could* he turn Natalie down? After all, what would integrity count for if she was wearing that tight white top?

48. THE RALLY

It was the last Sunday in April and Tom was only just recovering from the depressing events of the day before – a trip with Neil to Upton Park, where they watched West Ham lose 2-0 to Liverpool and get relegated.

Now he and Neil were with Natalie, Nadia, Polly, Barry and Sangheeta at Trafalgar Square surrounded by yellow banners and red placards, listening to Rock Against Racism and Anti-Nazi League speeches. It wasn't Tom's ideal day out, but he wanted to make the best of it.

The political speeches were well received but dragged on a bit. Tom wanted to get to the bit where they marched. Then they could get to the bit where they watched some bands in Victoria Park. Then he could go home. But would he go home to Ted and Rose, or home with Natalie? That was the question occupying his thoughts.

Even so, he still managed to get into a conversation with someone going on about music changing Britain. Yet again, he found himself pointing to the album charts, which currently featured a top five of Nat King Cole, Saturday Night Fever, Genesis, Wings and Abba. The singles chart was topped by the Bee Gees "Night Fever".

'Hardly the stuff of revolution,' he pointed out, which made Oz laugh.

The biggest disappointment was the Westferries failing to reach the summit. "Roll Me, Baby" had slipped to

No.5 and would soon leave the chart. Still, to peak at No.2 with your first single wasn't to be sneezed at. Certainly, he would ram that point home when he next spoke to Claire.

Of course, Anti-Nazi League member Polly banged on about it being Britain's first ever political music festival. Neil was full of it too, now that he had a Socialist Worker squadist girlfriend. Tom was finding it hard to take on board the change that had come over his best mate in the past week. Neil was now possessed of a vision. Typically, it was Nadia's vision. Worse still, he was also possessed of the latest fad for permed hair and looked a total wally. But there could be no denying the transformation – it was a sort of growing up, a stretching out, a reaching for something further and possibly higher. Since meeting Nadia, Neil had become engaged in The Struggle. Nadia was so unlike uncommitted Brenda. She was a nouveau cockney; born in Bucks, reborn in Bow, where she shared a squat in Tredegar Square with five other post-student socialists and anarchists. It was a pity. Tom had grown to like Brenda a lot.

'Look, the paint mob,' said Nadia.

'Who?' said Tom.

'They organised the painting out of NF graffiti on the railway bridge by Bow Road police station.'

'What for?' asked Natalie.

'Because it was there,' said Neil. 'It was a bit dodgy, too. Apparently, a comrade had to be held over the side with the police sitting at a window just a couple of yards away.'

'A comrade?' queried Tom, feeling the communist tag to be a bit heavy for Neil to be throwing around.

'They were all there at Lewisham last summer, too,' said Nadia, filled with pride.

'Who did they have at Lewisham?' asked Natalie.

'What?'

'I said who did they have at Lewisham? What bands?'

Nadia was aghast. 'Lewisham was a stand against the Nazis!'

'You've said all that already. But who played?'

'No-one played,' said Neil. 'Lewisham was the SWP taking on the NF and the police.'

'It was amazing, Tom,' said Nadia. 'We linked arms and held a line up by Clifton Rise. There was an almighty riot.'

'I know,' said Tom. 'I was there.'

Once the march set off, Neil found the time to give Tom all the details. He'd been up Brick Lane with Polly to leer at the NF and scour the record stalls for Hawkwind, Led Zep and Pink Floyd bootlegs. Nadia was one of the lefties selling the *Socialist Worker*. Taking a pee break, she found herself reaching for the door of the Seven Stars at the same time as Neil, who was holding a dog-eared Hawkwind *Live Strangeness In Dusseldorf '76* album. He said 'ladies before gents' and she told him that Dave Brock represented an outmoded sci-fi tinged apolitical post-hippy daydream. Neil pointed out that it was Bob Calvert, not Dave Brock who wrote most of the lyrics these days, and that there was nothing apolitical about seeing government as a conspiracy. Unperturbed, Nadia pointed out that Britain was in need of a revolution and that it was only by workers uniting against the ruling elite that the world could become truly free. They both argued their corner so nicely that Polly saw to it they continued their debate over a shandy, with Neil offering prog rock as a valid alternative to the Establishment's take on music, as well as a guide to living in spiritual harmony with the planet. He didn't mention that he liked

Fleetwood Mac and the Eagles too. In return, he learned that the real action was taking place right there on the corner of Brick Lane and Bethnal Green Road every Sunday morning between the SWP and the National Front.

'The fact is, Tom, if we don't stop them soon, they'll become Britain's third biggest party.'

'It's certainly a concern, Neil.'

'That's why Nadia's a squadist. Lewisham changed her life.'

'Had I been nicked, it would have changed mine too,' said Tom.

Natalie chimed in. 'How about getting a number eight from Liverpool Street?'

'Marching is a symbolic act,' said Nadia. 'Getting on a bus is not.'

It was reasonably clear that Natalie and Nadia had polar opposite world views.

'Look at the police around you,' said Nadia. 'There's nothing they can do. This is the kind of power the oppressors fear.'

'Yeah,' said Polly, 'think of the Nazis on the corner of Brick Lane, knowing there's, what, a hundred thousand of us coming for them.'

'Maybe two hundred thousand,' said Nadia.

'Probably not *that* many,' said Tom. 'And we're not coming for them – we'll be marching straight past so we can see The Clash and Tom Robinson play in Victoria Park.'

'Tom, look around you,' said Nadia. 'All these people aren't here to listen to music.'

'Yes they are. That's why it's called Rock Against Racism. We all hate the Nazis but we're here for a gig and this march is the admission fee.'

'No Tom,' insisted Neil. 'No. We're here because young Asian people are being beaten up and murdered by right wing scum. That's why we're here. We're here to stop it.'

Tom shrugged. It was a fair point. 'Yeah, sorry, Neil. You're right. That *is* why we're here.'

Then Nadia started a chant that would grow and ring back along the Strand around Trafalgar Square and down into Whitehall, where the Prime Minister would no doubt hear it above the gentle drone of Radio 4.

'Black and white unite! Black and white unite! Black and white unite!'

'Scruffy lot, ain't they,' said Natalie, as if the disarray of bad clothing, bad hair and weird smells were a personal rebuff to her Marks & Sparks pink blouse and neat bob courtesy of Alan of Mayfair's Hairstyles (Poplar).

For Tom, marching along The Strand with thousands of Anti-Nazi League supporters was a *kind* of life-changing experience. Not because of the passions arising in him at the thought and feel of all that power directed against the fascists, but because he finally accepted that he couldn't sleep with Natalie Hiscock.

He was grateful. If he'd had any lingering doubts that a relationship could be based solely on physical attraction, Natalie was dispelling them. He knew she didn't like him. Sex was the price she was prepared to pay to get on in life. Not that he had a heartfelt view on it. It was *her* body, after all. It was just that she could gain an undeserved advantage, a bit like cheating in an exam, and he didn't like it.

'This is giving me a headache,' said Natalie. 'And my feet don't half ache.'

Tom knew she wouldn't leave his side. The Westferries' chart success ensured it. She was desperate to follow in Claire's footsteps, even if it meant, for now, following in the Anti-Nazi League's.

He even tested her, by moving away to be with Barry and Sangheeta. He had barely begun to ask Sangheeta about life at the London School of Economics when Natalie appeared at his side.

When they eventually turned into Bethnal Green Road tensions rose. They would soon be passing the corner of Brick Lane where the NF would be out in force.

'Let's hope it stays quiet,' said Tom. 'I don't fancy a mass punch-up.'

As they neared the spot, the sight of many Union Jacks filled him with pride. Why did the NF have sole ownership of the national flag these days? Why didn't the Left adopt it too?

It was eerily quiet as they passed the solid-looking wall of Old Bill that hid the NF supporters. Only their flags could be seen, fluttering in the light breeze.

'They're nothing,' said Neil. 'They're nobody. The days when we run from the Far Right are over. We've got Nadia and the SWP squadists to thank for that.'

Tom could hardly believe this was Neil Sullivan.

'Bunch of wankers!' yelled Nadia.

Tom winced. He didn't want a bottle coming his way. It would never hit Nadia; it would hit T. Alder esquire.

Nadia didn't seem at all troubled.

'When you can get over a hundred thousand people out, you've won the point,' she said.

Tom couldn't help thinking that in the last Greater London Council election a similar number went out – to vote for the National Front. He also couldn't help thinking he needed to put Neil and Brenda together, as Nature had obviously intended. But how? Would it be a case of waiting for Nadia to dump him and then setting them up? He could get Neil out for a drink, but where would Claire be when he needed her? After all, he'd need someone to shore up Brenda's side of the equation.

By the time they arrived at Victoria Park, the area in front of the stage was packed. This was due mainly to the thousands of Anti-Nazis who had shirked the long march and headed straight for the venue to claim the prime spots.

'Come on,' said Polly. 'I can get us backstage.'

It took ten minutes to get twenty yards but they made it through security on Polly and Oz's say-so. There, they learned that people were coming from all over Britain. Forty-two coachloads from Glasgow, fifteen from Sheffield, an entire trainload from Manchester. For Tom, having 100,000 people gather together for a single cause – *Black & White Unite* – was undeniably impressive.

A girl smiled at them.

'Poly Styrene,' said Nadia. 'X-Ray Spex singer.'

Tom watched Natalie's nose turn up. Then some cool blokes barged past him.

'The Clash,' said Nadia. 'And Jimmy Pursey.'

'So the Clash are cool again, are they?' said Tom.

'The Clash have always been cool,' said Polly.

Tom wasn't arguing. It was just that the hundred grand they'd received from CBS had some people calling them sell-outs. Personally, he couldn't see the point of remaining poor in oblivion. If you play a handful of gigs and someone offers you a huge pile of cash, in what state of insanity do you say no?

'This could be good,' said Sangheeta. 'I think this could really be something.'

'I think you're right,' said Tom.

Polly meanwhile greeted a mate who looked like he'd been sleeping in a bush.

'Good march?' said the mate.

'Amazing,' said Polly. 'Any trouble here?'

'Nah, all quiet, Poll.'

Tom learned that the ANL had posted a number of supporters on the stage, to sleep there overnight and ensure local NF activists didn't set fire to it. He also found himself drafted into moving cables and sound equipment. It was getting close to time. The first band would be on soon.

He ventured onto the stage. He'd stood on a stage before, of course. He'd played to, what, a hundred people? Here there were a hundred thousand.

Oz joined him.

'Shame you're not playing, Tom.'

He was glad he wasn't. Well, not *glad*.

'Part of me would love to be the bloke with the vision. I mean I've got the passion for music, I'm just not sure I've found the best way to express it.'

The performers they had been loitering with soon took their rightful places in front of the appreciative crowd. Whether it was X-Ray Spex's "The Day The World Turned Day-Glo" or The Clash with Jimmy Pursey belting out "White Riot", the crowd's response was noisy and abundant.

Then came Steel Pulse with a reggae vibe that seemed to carry everyone off to somewhere much sunnier than Victoria Park under grey skies. Maybe it was this warmer vibe that made Natalie snake her arm around Tom's waist and whisper in his ear.

'I want you.'

Tom felt the torment rise in him again. Could he let his first time be with someone he despised?

The Tom Robinson Band came onstage at half-past five. Although the authorities had allowed the concert to take place, it was on the strict understanding that it ended bloody early.

'They're good, aren't they,' said Tom.

'Might chat him up,' said Natalie, eyeing Tom Robinson.

'He's gay,' said Tom.

Natalie looked miffed.

It was a short but good set then everyone piled onstage for a rousing, singalong of "We've Got To Get It Together".

Sangheeta was singing along and crying.

'You alright, Sangheeta?' Tom asked.

'Yeah,' she said, through the tears. 'There's a hundred thousand people here and they're all on my side.'

For Tom – that was the moment he completely got it. This *was* worthwhile. Britain might not have witnessed an issue-motivated concert before, but surely it would do so many more times in the future.

After the singing faded away and people began to leave, Tom and his friends decamped to the Alexandra pub for a pint. Then it was a case of resisting Natalie. Or not.

Later, at Natalie's flat, Tom pondered the day's events as he watched her pour two glasses of Blue Nun and get out her records. If only he could be like The Clash and Tom Robinson, writing songs people liked.

Natalie put half a dozen singles on the stackable turntable. The first to drop and play was Britain's number one, "Night Fever".

She sang it directly to him.

He tried to take it all in. The wine, the Bee Gees, the lights down low, Natalie. After all the speeches and marching and political stances at the park, was he now about to swap ideals for sex?

'You're not gonna turn me down, are you?'

Tom found he couldn't reply because her mouth had clamped onto his.

'I… I have to get up early tomorrow,' he managed to say.

'No, you don't, babes. It's a Bank Holiday.'

'Oh yeah.'

Monday, the first of May would in fact be, for the very first time in Britain, a public holiday. Not that everyone was behind it as a day to enjoy. Its unavoidable link with the May Day celebrations in Moscow's Red Square had some Brits reaching for their Union Jacks and calling it the Devil's Work.

'Ooh I love the Bee Gees,' Natalie uttered.

In fairness, Tom found her soft-carpeted floor very inviting. And her breasts were quite magnificent. Soft and firm at the same time. Her bum was also pretty fab.

It was probably the hardest erection he'd ever had. Well, Natalie knew what she was doing. As the next single dropped onto the deck, she rolled onto her back and invited him on top. The moment had come. Destiny awaited. The needle hit the groove. He readied himself to enter her. And Claire Cross started singing.

'*All I think of is you…*'

It was all a bit of a blur after that.

49. THE SHOEBOX

The following Saturday morning, ringing Grandad's doorbell, Tom was in a good mood. He had a party to go to that evening and, thanks to a phone call to Midge, he was going to sort out Neil Sullivan's stupid love-life. However, waiting a little too long on Grandad's doorstep, his mood began to turn from expectancy to concern. He reached into his pocket for his key just as a neighbour emerged from next door.

'They've taken him to hospital again.'

Tom puffed his cheeks.

Half an hour later, he was at Grandad's bedside at the London Hospital in Whitechapel. The poor old fella had come over faint and fallen down. Luckily, he'd only grazed his head.

'I got out of the chair too quick, boy. Should've taken me time.'

'Yeah, well, don't do it again, Grandad. Your head might've damaged the furniture.'

'Ha, cheeky so-and-so. So what are you up to? Any big plans?'

'I'm going to a party tonight. Some bloke I know has got a new flat.'

'Sounds like fun. And how's that band of yours? Soon be bigger than the last one, eh? That'll show 'em.'

'Claire's talented, Grandad. She deserves to make it. We're trying another singer now – Nat Hiscock's daughter, Natalie.'

'Nat Hiscock? You wanna be careful messing around with his little girl. He'll chop your legs off.'

'Natalie's twenty-one, Grandad. She's more than capable of handling herself.'

Indeed, had Claire's voice not intervened, she would have handled him too.

'Yeah, well, best of luck, Tom. You deserve it. Very patient boy, you are. How's school?'

'Oh, I'm busy revising Shakespeare. I expect you escaped all that in your day.'

'What, Shakespeare? Well, I never did A-levels, but we did our bit. *A Midsummer Night's Dream.* Lysander and Hermia. "The course of true love never did run smooth"…'

'Well, he got that right.'

Grandad laughed. 'I loved it, boy. I'd go back tomorrow if I could.' But he started coughing and the nurse came over to suggest he needed to rest.

Outside the ward, she stopped Tom.

'Could you do me a favour? We're keeping your grandad in overnight just to make sure his head doesn't fall off.'

Tom was alarmed.

'That's a joke,' said the nurse. 'Now there was a bit blood on his shirt, so…'

'You want me to get him a change of clothes?'

'That's the ticket.'

On the way out, he phoned Rose, but there was no answer.

Tom entered Grandad's flat and paused. It was still and quiet and he could hear himself breathing. There was a faint mustiness in the sir. Damp, probably. Always a problem in these old Georgian properties. No wonder the council were always looking to knock them down in favour of modern housing. Not that Tom liked modern housing. The old places had something going for them that you couldn't quite measure. Character, he guessed.

He entered the bedroom and paused once more. He felt like an intruder. Even so, he located the socks and underwear in the old chest of drawers then opened the wardrobe to get a shirt. To the side of the shirts were two shelves for odds and bits. On one was a lidless old shoebox full of papers.

Tom took out a shirt. The shoebox was none of his business.

Although…

What if Grandad passed away one day? It would be handy to know where he kept his important documents.

He took the box and placed it on the bed. Sitting down beside it, he sighed. He couldn't really go through Grandad's stuff. It wasn't right. And yet… what if there were things in there that related to the family?

No, he didn't want to know about the family. Okay, yes he did, but he didn't want to cause anyone any pain, including himself.

He wondered. What if he took just a quick peep to satisfy his curiosity? Just a quick glance to make sure there were no vital papers or photos?

The first thing he picked out was an insurance document. Then a receipt for the telly. Then a marriage certificate. Grandad's from… he had to double and triple check the date, because the wedding at All Saints Church, Poplar was only five months before Ted was born. So his nan, aged twenty, had been pregnant out of wedlock and had clearly undertaken the part that led to it as a teenager.

It hadn't been so long ago that Tom had assumed it was randy teenagers of the 1970s that got up to mischief. Now he could see that randy teenagers weren't too bothered about which decade they happened to live in.

He found himself holding an envelope. Not an official one. Grandad's name and address were scrawled on it in blue pen. The envelope had been opened so Tom took a peek. It was a handwritten note. He couldn't quite read it in the envelope so he took it out.

Dad, why have you written? I told you not to contact me.

His heart thumped.

Harry *did* respond to Grandad's letter.

Tom had tried hard to put all this behind him, but he hadn't succeeded. Deep down, he had never really been able to give up on the truth. But what if it was too hurtful?

He struggled with his options. If he read it, he'd have his real dad's voice in his head. Or at least the tone of it. If he didn't read it, the bloody thing would haunt him forever.

He delayed a decision by looking in the shoebox. Bunched together were some old photos. Obviously not ones Grandad wanted to put on display. There was one of Tom and Danny when they were three or four. In what kind of messed-up world did that have to remain hidden?

Of course, Tom understood that Grandad would have removed photos of Danny as technically he was no longer part of the family – even though Grandad would have known that Danny was still his grandson, albeit via Harry. It must have hurt him to take them down, but Tom supposed having photos of Danny on display would have upset Rose.

He flicked through a few more until he came to a

black and white photo of a young man. Was this his real dad? There were similarities, mainly around the eyes.

He returned to the letter.

Dad, why have you written? I told you not to contact me. I don't want to hear any news about anyone or have you stir everything up again. My kids don't know the past and it will stay like that. They've done nothing wrong. DON'T WRITE TO US AGAIN.

He checked the envelope. Enclosed was Grandad's letter to Harry, still in its own envelope, torn in two – clearly to show that it had absolutely not been read.

He wondered. Had Grandad left it in the shoebox so that, if he did peg out, the family would know he tried to patch things up?

A key rattled in the front door lock.

Tom put the two halves of Grandad's envelope together to reveal Harry's address. The fear, excitement and possibilities made his hands shake. At last he knew where his sister lived. And not just his sister. Harry had *kids*. Plural.

He put the letter in his pocket and the shoebox in the wardrobe just before Rose came in.

'Oh! You gave me a fright, Tom.'

'Sorry.'

'Grandad's neighbour phoned. Been trying to get me while I was at the shops. I phoned the hospital and they said you'd been up there.'

'He's okay, mum. He grazed his head when he fell. It's nothing serious.'

'I wasn't sure if anyone thought of getting him a change of clothes.' She eyed the things Tom had laid out on the bed. 'Right, so he'll need trousers and a cardy.'

'Mum?'

'Did he have a coat up there? Probably best if I take one. Just in case.'

'Mum?'

'What?'

'Before you go…'

He showed her Harry's note. Her look suggested she knew where this was heading. Then she sat on the bed to read it while Tom watched her.

'I wonder what possessed your grandad to write to him.'

'I asked him to.'

'Oh.'

Tom got the shoebox out again and placed it on the bed by Rose.

'Tell me about Victoria.'

'Oh God, I only came round to get some clothes.'

'I want to know everything.'

Rose sighed – then gave him Harry's note and started looking through the box. A moment later, she handed Tom a photo.

'She must have been, what, thirteen? Fourteen?'

Peering into the black and white face of his real mother as a young teen, Tom felt as if he wanted to reach back in time and protect her.

'No one meant for you to get hurt,' said Rose.

'Why does everything have to be so complicated?'

'It's not. Ted's stupid brother got my bloody daft sister pregnant and had to marry her. Then he got a girl I was supposed to be looking out for pregnant, so he had to vanish before my bloody stupid dad killed him for bringing shame on the family.'

'Well, maybe not complicated, but not great either.'

'No, not great. But Vicky was younger than you are now when she had you.'

'Yeah, I suppose so.'

'It still might've worked out, but… well, after she'd been married to Harry a few months he made sure it went from bad to worse. I mean she knew he was up to no good. We all did. What we didn't know was him being up to no good with Jean. When that came out it was agreed that Harry would disappear and give Vic a divorce. Then we found out Jean was pregnant and wanted to keep her baby and… well, it was a terrible business.'

Tom could imagine it was.

'What happened with me?' he asked.

'Vic fought to keep you – gave our dad a bloody nose, but… she knew it would tear me apart to give you back. I wish that wasn't the case, but it was. Anyway, Norman, thank God, comforted her. Of course it was a surprise when she fell pregnant again – I mean before her divorce came through. She and Norman had to move away and pretend to be married until they could tie the knot officially, on the quiet, like.'

Tom hadn't known that. All these teenagers getting into a mess. Didn't they have rubber contraceptives back then? He supposed they did, but could imagine, in the heat of passion…

'It shouldn't really bring shame on a family, should it,' he said.

'Different times, Tom. It was a real stigma back then. It's all changing now, thank God. As far as my dad was concerned it was more shame than anyone could bear. He was such a proud man, see. From Narrow Street to the Tower of London, he was someone you went to if you had something that needed sorting out. You didn't go to the police or the social service people – busybodies, he called 'em. I mean he wasn't the type to let emotions get in the way of what to do about Harry's babies.'

'It must've been hard for you, too.'

'Me? Well… it'd been a living nightmare since the miscarriage. I used to fall apart seeing mums outside the school gates. Then God, or Fate, or whatever-you-like got involved and Vic was expecting again. I mean everything changed then. And, well, everyone liked Norman. Such a smashing fella. Reliable, if you know what I mean.'

'The opposite of Harry.'

'Oh, chalk and cheese. He'd liked Vic for years – you know, before Harry swept her up.'

'Poor Norman.'

'Yeah, but thanks to him, Vic grew to accept the situation. Well, what with them starting their own family… Jean was a different story, of course. That's why Danny was always likely to be temporary under our roof. She just wanted her son back and to get on with her life. Very independent is Jean.'

Tom could see that Rose had suffered enough losses. Not just Danny. She had lost a sister, Sarah, to pneumonia during the War. She lost another sister, Vic. She lost her friendship with Jean, who was like a sister. She lost her mum and dad. She was probably worried about losing Ted to Elsie Sullivan.

Rose put the box aside and seemed to become lost in thought. For a moment, the room was still like a photograph. Then Tom put the box away and Rose got the rest of Grandad's clothes together.

'You can hear Harry if you want,' she said. 'We've got a tape.'

'What?'

'Ted kept it. There's a reel-to-reel thing…'

'What, the one on top of your wardrobe?'

'There's some tapes in a box. Look for the Spitfires.'

'Right…' He knew the box. To think it had been up

there all this time without him giving it a thought.

'Well, I'd better take this lot up to Grandad then.'

'Thanks, Mum. I hope you don't think I'd ever swap you and Ted for Harry.'

Rose tried without success to hold off the tears. When Tom hugged her, she didn't feel like a parent in his arms, more like a child.

When she recovered, she ruffled his hair, like she used to when he was little.

'Go and see Norman,' she said. 'Tell him you know about your mum. He's got something for you. From Vic.'

Tom's heart raced and his stomach flipped over. He didn't know what to say.

Once Rose had left with Grandad's clothes, he tried to gather his thoughts. Would he go round to Norman? Or go and listen to Harry's tape. And what about Lynn? Would he write to her? What if Harry intercepted the letter?

He paced the floor. What about using a John Bull printing kit to stamp "From the Girl Guides" on the back? No, Harry might open all her letters. And what if she wasn't in the Girl Guides? And what about Jean? She only lived at the other end of Poplar High Street.

He went round there. He stood outside her place. His finger hovered over the doorbell. But he found he couldn't press it.

50. SATURDAY NIGHT FERVOUR

It was meant to be a celebration. Thanks to Polly, Oz had secured a fourteenth-floor, two-bedroom, hard-to-let flat in Stepney and was having a house-warming party. But standing in the front room with a can of lager in his hand and Motown blaring out, Tom's head was too full of other things to get into it. What would he do about a certain torn envelope and an address in West London? What would he do about seeing Norman or listening to Harry's tape or dealing with whatever Vic had left for him? And would he see Jean or bottle out again like he had earlier?

He was at Oz's with Neil, Brenda, Midge and, of course, Polly. Neil, looking unconvincing in a Status Quo denim outfit, said Nadia would be meeting them there later.

'Been to any good football matches?' a woman asked Tom. He recognised her and the two women she was with from a party at Cassland Road over the Silver Jubilee weekend.

He shook his head. 'I'm a West Ham fan, so no.'

Oz had welcomed them with news that he'd signed up to become a trainee social worker with Tower Hamlets Council. Tom was really pleased for him. Oz was a grounded sort; he'd do well.

Neil was more interested in the flat.

'Two bedrooms *and* a view of the City…'

'Yeah,' said Polly. 'No-one wants to live up high.'

'It's amazing,' said Neil.

'Maybe we should apply for one,' said Polly. 'They've got hundreds all over Bow, Poplar, Stepney, Wapping...'

'Maybe,' said Tom. He wasn't all that sure. Most of the hard-to-lets were above the seventh floor, so he'd be at the mercy of urine-stained lifts – if they were working. The ground floor flats in the scheme seemed to be really old places that came with a free weekly burglary.

Midge nudged him and raised her eyes. Of course – their mission.

'Excited, Neil?' he said. 'Maybe you could get a flat with Nadia.'

Neil sighed. 'Nadia's not coming. We split up.'

'What?'

'I couldn't find the right moment to tell anyone.'

Tom put on a sad look.

'Never mind, Neil.' He glanced at Brenda, looking nice in a lime green dress with her hair in a neat bob. 'All's not lost.'

He knew they'd split up, of course. As ever, Polly knew everything on the left-hand side of their social lives and had reported Nadia running off with a lecturer from Camberwell. That's why Tom had invited Midge – with strict orders that she got Brenda to come too.

Strangely, it had been a confused phone call at first: 'Hello Midge, it's Tom Alder. I need a really big favour. There's this party in Stepney...'

'Oh Tom, I really like you. Seriously, I do, but I've got a boyfriend. I mean he's a bit of a useless lump but—'

'Midge, I need you to help me with Neil and Brenda.'

'Oh.'

The only fly in the vino now was Brenda not seeming too keen to talk to Neil. Clearly Tom and Midge had their work cut out.

Typically, Oz's party had plenty of political talk. Polly quickly got busy recounting his presence among the thousands at the Altab Ali murder protest march. Tom couldn't fault his passion. People couldn't go around knifing tailors just because they were Asian. The trouble was that some of the people carrying out these attacks were the same blokes who hung around local pubs having a laugh. People knew them, knew they were violent, knew they were killers. But those old East End values of not telling the police about stolen T-shirts also held firm here. The death of a twenty-five year old Asian on his way home from work? Nobody had anything to say about it.

Even as Tom thought that, Polly was moving on to the local election results. He wasn't impressed.

'What are you on about?' said Neil. 'Labour won in Tower Hamlets. Sixteen thousand votes.'

'Labour's the problem,' said Polly. 'It's become the Establishment. People need to understand the SWP offers the real alternative.'

'They got 300 votes,' said Neil.

Polly ignored him. 'The NF have to be massively defeated.'

'They got 3,000 votes,' said Neil. 'The Tories got 4,000.'

'Neil, they had more candidates, you pillock.'

'I was only saying…'

'Who did you vote for, Tom?' Polly asked.

It had been Tom's first election. Uncertain of anything, he'd plumped for the Liberals. That is, until he entered the voting booth to find that the Millwall ward only offered a choice between Labour, the Conservatives and the National Front – none of which he fancied.

'I didn't vote. I meant to.'

Tom was too distracted. He wanted to leave, to go home, to go to bed, to sleep. But he caught Midge eyeing him from across the room. She look great in a revealing low-cut black dress, although he wondered if she might be overdoing things seeing as they were only there to sort out Neil and Brenda. Then he realised – that's why she was eyeing him. He signalled his understanding. Neil Sullivan was his best mate and he deserved better than some half-arsed effort.

A moment later, he was pulling Brenda away from some bloke with glasses and a tweed jacket and placing her between himself, Midge and the wall so she couldn't escape.

'Why won't you speak to him?' he asked.

'Who?'

'I think he means Neil,' said Midge.

Brenda glanced in Neil's direction. 'I don't want to be seen as desperate.'

'Don't be daft,' said Tom. 'We're all mates.'

'Why did he have to go out with that Nadia?'

Tom sighed. Why indeed? But then he realised he knew the answer.

'He had no choice, Bren. Nadia was a decisive girl. The sort that can take someone like him and iron out all the doubts. You know, decision-making, that sort of thing.'

'Can't he make his own decisions?'

'Yes, but they're usually the wrong ones. I mean he's not eighteen till July.'

'Nor am I.'

'No, but you're a girl. You grow up quicker. I'm right, aren't I, Midge?'

'You're right, Tom.'

'See, Neil's a typical boy and typical boys are pretty

stupid, especially when it comes to girls. We usually make the wrong decisions. It's not our fault. Aren't I right, Midge.'

'You're right, Tom.'

'I don't know…' said Brenda.

'Take control of the situation,' said Tom. 'Tell him you want to go out with him. Believe me, he'll be all yours. I'm right, aren't I, Midge?'

'Yep – definitely advice worth following.'

Brenda glanced over at Neil again.

'I'm still not sure.'

Roy arrived and grabbed Tom away.

'What's the crumpet situation?'

'You sound like Sid James, mate – which would make me Bernard Bresslaw.'

'Any spare birds around then, Bern?'

'Yeah, actually… those three women over there. They might be talking about abortion rights or something, but don't let that put you off.'

Roy looked over and seemed to see possibilities.

Tom tried to get back to Midge and Brenda but Polly came over to greet Roy, thereby stopping both from moving away.

'Alright, Roy? I see that GLC ban on music's still causing trouble.'

'Yeah, well, obviously I don't hold with bans.'

'The Stranglers can't perform in London. How ridiculous is that? Just because Hugh Cornwell wore that T-shirt on stage. It was eighteen months ago, for Chrissakes.'

Tom appreciated Polly's point. The Stranglers singer and guitarist had worn a Ford logo shirt, except it said "Fuck" not "Ford". It was definitely a vindictive punishment on the part of the council.

'You can still see them,' said Roy. 'I saw them in a pub in New Barnet calling themselves Johnny Sox. They play as the Shakespearos too.'

'Yeah, well, it's time we organised a fightback campaign.'

Roy looked bored. 'Yeah… 'ere, anyone see Joyce McKinney in the *Mirror*? What a girl. Bondage, oral sex, fur-lined handcuffs, a *Joy of Sex* manual. Imagine it…'

Tom found it impossible not to – thereby justifying Fleet Street's long-running pre-occupation with her kidnapping of a former Mormon boyfriend for sex and her subsequently jumping bail and fleeing abroad.

'Naked on the front page, too,' said Roy. 'That was 7p well spent.'

'Well, the bloke didn't want any of it,' said Polly.

'They're calling *her* a weirdo,' scoffed Roy. '*He's* the weirdo.'

Roy pulled Tom aside.

'Listen, how do you fancy playing a holiday camp in the summer?'

'A holiday camp?' Tom wasn't sure.

'Yeah, a holiday camp – full of birds.'

'Full of families, surely.'

'Yeah, but there's always a bunch of birds clogging up part of the dancefloor. I mean we know a genuine pop star. They'll be all over us.'

Tom had to admit – there was a certain attraction to having loads of women after him. Is that how Harry used to see it? The man whose genes he'd inherited. Did you play guitar, have tons of sex, and never worry about the consequences? Was that the way forward?

He made his excuses and tried to get back to Brenda and Midge, only they were now with the three Cassland Road women. Tom switched to Oz, who was by the balcony door singing along to "Walk Away, Renee". They exchanged nods and Oz indicated some clean glasses next to a small cask of beer.

Tom finished off his can of lager and helped himself to half a pint of... a dark liquid. He sniffed it and Oz laughed.

'It's what I'm into these days,' said Oz. 'I joined CAMRA – the campaign for real ale.'

Tom frowned and then tried the ale. It lacked the fizz of lager but it wasn't too bad.

'We've been served enough slop in the pubs,' said Oz. 'Time to get back to real beer.'

'Where d'you get it?'

'A guy called Pat from Hackney. He went to India and came back with a heavenly calling to brew beer. Don't ask me how it's connected. He just started up an outfit called Godson's. It's the first new brewery in London since forever. He reckons it could start a whole new approach. You know, by-pass the big boys.'

Tom drank some more and felt he could get used to it.

'The music's good, Oz.'

'I'm a secret Motown fan,' said Oz with a conspiratorial wink. 'Brought my records over from my parents.'

'I quite like all that "Reach Out, I'll Be There" stuff. Classic party music.'

It didn't last. The single ended and someone put the *Saturday Night Fever* album on.

'This is still cool,' said Oz, nodding away in time.

But Tom's mind was switching from music to Oz's new social work job.

'I hear Tower Hamlets has a lot of children in care,' he said.

'Oh hundreds, Tom. Hundreds and hundreds.'

'Really?' Tom was amazed. 'I didn't know it was that many.'

'More than any other local authority in Britain. Imagine it – all those kids stuck in children's homes. It's not likely to change all by itself either. They were telling us on the induction course that some of the poor so-and-so's just yoyo in and out, in and out.'

Tom was grateful he'd never shared their fate.

'They're trying different ways to address it,' said Oz. 'It's not easy though.'

'Will you be involved in that?'

'Yes, I'll be working out of Bow Road for the Foster Care and Adoption team.'

The words Foster Care and Adoption made Tom's blood run cold.

'Sounds good, Oz.'

'Basically, it's finding families for unwanted kids rather than stuffing them all into long-term care. You should see some of these rotten old places we use. There's one children's home out past Romford – bloody enormous sprawling thing with hundreds of kids. It's like we don't know the Victorian era's over.'

They chatted for a bit about the Victorian East End and pre-War social conditions until some bloke joined them, yapping on about sweeping away the old ways in music. Tom didn't like him barging in so rudely. He was also completely fed up with people who still thought like that.

'The only thing we need to sweep away is musical fascism,' Tom said pointedly. 'We don't have to ditch the old stuff. We just have to make sure there's room for the new stuff too. I mean we can all like the charts nowadays in a way we couldn't a few years back. Look at the singles. Rod Stewart, Johnny Mathis, the Bee Gees, Patti Smith,

Ian Dury, Blondie, The Stranglers, Elvis Costello, Tom Robinson, Thin Lizzy, Blue Oyster Cult, Manfred Mann's Earth Band – that's what's been achieved. It's not about shutting certain people up, but giving everyone a voice. See, out of that lot you're free to take your pick – so embrace the stuff you like and don't waste your time hating the stuff others like.'

'Nicely put,' said Oz.

'Yeah, well, I see what you're saying…' said the other bloke.

But Tom was, for the first time in his life, publically on the warpath. And he didn't care who heard him.

'Take the album charts. *Saturday Night Fever* at the top – good. We've also got the Stranglers, Ian Dury, Tom Robinson, the Buzzcocks, Blondie, Kate Bush, Genesis, Jethro Tull, Rainbow, Fleetwood Mac, AC-DC, Pink Floyd, Van Halen, Steve Hackett, Bob Marley, Abba, Wings, ELO, Frank Sinatra, Nat King Cole, Elvis Presley…' He took a breath. 'It doesn't need fixing because it ain't broke.'

The bloke nodded and fled. Oz laughed. Tom felt liberated.

'Music's my politics, my religion, Oz.'

'Oh, I can see that, Tom.'

Oz was called onto the balcony by a couple of his friends just as Midge came over.

'Neil's busy talking to Polly, not Brenda.'

Tom was fed up with the whole business. It didn't help that Brenda was talking to some boring thirty-year-old with a comb-over.

'I'll sort him out,' said Tom.

'Give him a minute,' said Midge. 'Polly's in full flow. You'll only get trapped.'

'Right. Okay. So…'

'So, we might as well chat for a minute.'

'Yeah.'

'So… are you playing the Docklands Summer Dance this year?'

'No. That's never going to happen again.'

'You were good last year.'

'Well, we… hang on, didn't you turn up *after* we played?'

'Ye—es… and no. I got there just as you started. I knew it was you and… well… I just stood at the back. I mean I was going to leave but…'

'What are you on about?'

'Nothing. I mean you and Claire looked so… you know. Then I thought, sod it. You know, as you do. Occasionally. Kind of thing.'

'Midge, I have no idea what… hang on, Polly's moving off. You go and rescue Brenda.'

Tom hurried over to Neil.

'How's it going with Brenda?'

'I'm just preparing myself mentally,' said Neil, taking a long breadstick from the small buffet table.

'Oh, for God's sake, go and dance with her.'

'How?'

'You go over there and move your legs about.'

Neil took the tiniest nibble off the end of his breadstick.

'What if I have to chat her up?'

'She's already your mate.'

'No, but… to go out with her, I mean.'

'Look, if you're worried she doesn't fancy you, then attach yourself to something exciting.'

'How do you mean?'

'Just say you really fancy going to that exciting thing.'

'What exciting thing?'

'How do I bloody know?'

'Do you think she'd be excited by kendo?'

'Kendo?'

'It's a Japanese martial art with long sticks.'

Tom grabbed the breadstick off Neil and smashed it over his head, shattering it and leaving Neil with wheaty dandruff. 'Forget bloody kendo! Take her to a museum or something, you twit.'

'Not Oriental combat then?'

Tom sighed. Then he marched over to Brenda and Midge.

'Brenda, Neil's in love with you.'

'Is he? He never said.'

'Bren, what do you like at the moment? Any crossover with Neil?'

'Dunno.'

'She loves *Saturday Night Fever*,' said Midge.

'Amazing,' said Tom, 'so does Neil!'

'She's also excited there's another John Travolta dance film coming out.'

'*Grease*, of course. Neil can't stop singing "You're the One That I Want".'

He could see Brenda was keen to dance. Well, Neil wasn't going to pile in all by himself.

He went over to Neil. 'It's dance time,' he said, grabbing him and pulling him over to Brenda. He stepped away to leave them facing each other like John Travolta and his girl.

Unlike John Travolta and his girl they shuffled their feet and smiled shyly at each other.

The *Saturday Night Fever* album was on the Bee Gees' track "More Than A Woman". Annoyingly, it made Tom think of Claire. He looked to Neil, trying to give him "look cool, not gormless" signals. Then on came Yvonne

Elliman's "If I Can't Have You".

Another song to drive home his separation from Claire. Was this album doing it on purpose?

'*Saturday Night Fever,*' said Midge. 'Brenda's obsessed.'

'Maybe she'll take him to Cherry's then. You know it?'

'Yeah, Hackney dog track. The disco there plays all this kind of stuff.'

Tom watched Neil with Brenda. Thank God they were warming up now. In fact, they were both singing. She was nodding… and nodding some more… and smiling some more… and her eyes were lighting up. Good job Neil wasn't a total dipstick, otherwise he might have turned and given Tom a thumbs-up.

Neil turned and gave Tom a thumbs-up.

What a total dipstick.

'So, Midge – mission accomplished.'

'Yeah, which means we've got a couple of hours to kill.'

'Yeah, so what revelations will you be springing?'

'That's not fair, Tom. I was just told your Aunt Rose adopted you to give Vic a second chance and I stupidly assumed you knew. I'm really sorry. I would never hurt you.'

Tom took in her genuine remorse. She had such a lovely, caring demeanour.

'Midge, it's me who should be apologising. You never did anything wrong.'

'Tom… call me Michelle. Midge is from when I was little.'

'Michelle. Yeah, it's a nice name.'

'So… Tom… we seem to have misplaced the party spirit.'

'Yeah, look, I'm sorry I took you away from your boyfriend on a Saturday night.'

'Oh, no problem. No problem at all. In fact, now I think of it… I mean now I'm here with you…'

'Maybe we should go out.'

'Yes!'

'Me, Claire, you and your boyfriend – when Claire's around.'

'Yes… that's… a good idea.'

51. VOICES FROM THE PAST

The next morning, Tom rang the doorbell and waited. His stomach was churning. In his head, a sentiment was tumbling over and over. It went along the lines of "someone needs to sort this bloody family out."

The door opened.

'Hi, I'm Tom Alder.'

'I know who you are, Tom. Has something happened?'

'Sort of. I've been looking into my family, my real family… it is alright if we talk?'

Jean raised an eyebrow. 'Well, you're a bold one. Nothing like my Danny said.'

'Is he in?'

'No, he's out.'

'Is it alright then?'

'Yes. Come in.'

Tom liked Jean and Danny's place. It was small but uncluttered. The front room had a black leather two-piece suite, the walls were white and, apart from a red rug, the floors were plain varnished boards.

Jean made them a cup of tea and then sat facing him. To Tom, it felt like an interview, although he wasn't quite sure who was doing the interviewing.

'I found out Aunt Vic was my mum.'

'Right. Must have come as a shock.'

'A bit, yeah. Thing is, I know Harry was… well, is my dad. And I know he's Danny's dad too.'

He tried to gauge how Jean felt about hearing it, but she just nodded. He was relieved. There was always the outside chance she was still having mental problems. Talking to her though, he was sure she was quite together.

'Okay, Tom. Let me spell it out for you. Harry got me pregnant... and Ted and Rose took my baby away. Do you know how I feel about that?'

'Er...' This wasn't so good.

'I feel... that it's all so far in the past, we should all be getting over it. I don't hate anyone because I appreciate now that a sixteen-year-old girl in 1960 wasn't going to be allowed to keep a baby.

'So you don't hate Rose then?'

'Vic and Rose were like big sisters to me. Rose did what she thought was for the best. Between you and me, she had as many problems as I did. Never got any help for it though so she was always going to be worried – panicky, even. About losing you, I mean.'

Tom could see that now – Rose's heavy drinking, bouts of tears and the pills from the doctor – it had been going on his whole life. He supposed it explained Ted's need to discuss things with Elsie Sullivan rather than Rose. He could imagine it: Ted and Elsie chatting... a brief mention of Tom's adoption... Micky Sullivan ear-wigging...

'I heard Rose and Vic's dad was involved,' he said.

'King of the walk, he was. Everyone looked up to him. He was mates with my dad and when they decided Rose should have Danny, it wasn't like I could ask them to reconsider.'

'No...'

'These days I'm a proud mum. I've got a nice flat, a decent job in a shipping firm in Aldgate... Back then I took an overdose because the world was just spinning around in my head, not making sense. Now, I see that it still doesn't make much sense but I can look after my tiny bit of it.'

Tom nodded. 'I'm sorry you went through so much. Rose misses you. She considers you family.'

Jean put her tea down.

'Did she say that?'

'Yes, she did.'

He wondered if Jean might take the reins from him now. He hoped so.

'He was just a boy, really.'

'Who, Harry?'

'All the girls fancied him. I mean I'd seen him around when I was growing up, but there was this special day. It was my sixteenth birthday and I was feeling like a proper adult – you know, as you do at that age. He was married to Vic, of course, and she was seven months gone with you, so I supposed he'd ignore me, but… well, no. Next day he's telling me Vic was a mistake and I was the one for him. I believed him. I even ruined your homecoming by telling everyone Harry and me were lovers.'

'Wow.'

'Yeah, I dropped a bomb there, eh? I think Harry was hoping we might keep it a secret.'

'Well, you were young.'

'Later, there was talk of me having an abortion but it was illegal back then. I mean there was this woman, Poison Ivy, who got rid of unwanted babies, but… well, there was this poor girl in our street, Angie. Seventeen, she was; thought she was going to marry the boy, but… anyway, they sent her to Ivy and poor Angie bled for ten days. I mean the police were invited round eventually but no one said a word. They wouldn't grass, see. I mean there's all this talk of me needing an abortion and there's all of us going to poor Angie's funeral. Well, my dad and Rose's dad got together and came up with their plan.'

'For Rose to have Danny.'

'I told them I would never give up my baby. I was waiting on Harry's call. In my mind he was setting up a flat for us in West London. Obviously, I never heard from him and... I tried to do myself in.'

Tom sipped his tea. The ten seconds of silence that followed felt like an hour.

'I have to be going,' he said. He didn't really, but he was keen to get away so he could think properly. 'Why don't you phone Rose? She's practically your older sister.'

Tom headed for the top end of Westferry Road. Reaching the bus stop though, he wasn't sure he wanted a swift return home. Instead, he walked south until he could cut through the Quarterdeck Estate to Alpha Grove and Tiller Road. There, he climbed the stairs to the Glass Bridge over Millwall Dock. He stopped halfway to look across the quiet waters of the outer dock to a forklift truck moving stuff outside McDougall's Flour Mill on the far quayside.

He worked back nine months from his birthday. The fourth of October gave him the fourth of January. What if he'd arrived a few days late? He could have very likely been conceived on New Year's Eve, 1958 or the early hours of January the first, 1959.

He recalled catching Ted and Elsie Sullivan in mid-grope at a New Year's Eve party in 1966. Was that the way the Alders liked to see in the New Year?

He crossed the bridge and, in one final delaying tactic, headed to Island Gardens to commune with the river. Even then, his mind was wandering westward.

Lynn, who's there with you? Another sister? A brother?

Back at home, he took the old reel-to-reel into his bedroom. There was a bit of dusting-off to do but it looked in good nick. Once he was happy it was in working order, he took a tape marked: "The Spitfires March 1959" and placed the reels on the spindles.

March 1959. Vic would have been two to three months pregnant with him. An unmarried teenager. She must have been scared.

He took a breath. It was a strange sensation. He'd experienced many emotions when it came to music, but never fear.

Click.

Guitar. Jangly. Low amplification. Drums. Bass coming in… Vocals.

It was Harry singing. Tom didn't recognise the song, although it was a breezy rock 'n' roll number that sounded like a hit. Harry's voice was pretty good. He sang with complete confidence. The band were good too but Harry the vocalist was in complete command.

As the song ended, Harry laughed. Tom laughed too, but only for a second. Then the lump in his throat got in the way.

Ted stepped into the room.

'He played a 1957 Hofner semi-acoustic. Maple veneer, brunette finish. No cutaways. Single pick-up. Brand new – nicked out of the docks.'

'You know your stuff.'

'Recorded in the Lord Nelson, that was. Everyone loved him.'

'He did wrong, dad.'

Ted smiled sadly. 'I know.'

'Good band though.'

'Thanks.'

'What, you mean…?'

'The Spitfires wasn't Harry's band. It was me and Nat Hiscock's. I played drums.'

'What? Really?'

'It was me who put Harry in the band, it was me who encouraged him, it was me who brought young Jean to the pub as a sixteenth birthday treat, it was me who encouraged her to ask for Harry's autograph as a bit of fun… wrecked a lot of lives, I did.'

'It wasn't your fault, Dad.'

Ted looked out of the window.

'He was my little brother. I was proud of him. He had this talent, see. I mean you could just sense it, but… if I hadn't encouraged him, Jean wouldn't have fallen under his spell and none of this would have happened.'

'Shame he didn't get called up for National Service,' said Tom. 'That would've sorted him out.' He didn't really know if it would have, but he wanted to show his support for Ted.

Ted turned to face him.

'They'd started easing up on it by then… 1957, I think. Started to let the younger ones off. It wasn't all it was cracked up to be, Tom. I know I go on about it but that's only because I had to do it. I mean when Rose was having the miscarriage, I was in Scotland peeling spuds for two hundred men. I mean, honestly… the moment she needed me most, I was five hundred miles away for no good reason.'

Ted went downstairs. Tom soon heard the kettle being filled. He went down after him. Rose was there, all ears and eyes. It didn't seem a good time to continue the conversation, but there was one question still bugging

Tom.

'Why did gran buy me a guitar? Wouldn't it have reminded her of Harry?'

'No, she loved music,' said Rose. 'All the family played: piano, banjo, mouth organ…'

Ted patted her on the shoulder. 'She saw everything that happened as a problem with Harry, not music.'

Tom understood. His nan was right. How could there be a problem with music?

Having phoned ahead, Tom cycled round to Norman's. It was a strange ride. Familiar streets but with an eerie feeling, as if he were in some weird 1950s sci-fi film. Fear rose in his chest. Had Vic left him a letter? If so, what would she say to him? Did he actually want to know? Well, yes, in a part-desperate, part-terrified kind of way.

Norman welcomed him. He looked edgy while he made them a cup of tea. Terry was up in his bedroom listening to music – Steely Dan, by the sound of it. Jack was in the front room, playing with Lego. Tom sat at the kitchen table knowing that his phone call had changed everything.

Norman put their mugs on the table then pushed the kitchen door to.

'Right then…' he said.

Tom didn't know where to start. 'I've known a little while. I mean I didn't want to spoil… I mean…'

'You have every right to feel angry, Tom. It can't be easy to find out this sort of thing. All I can say is Rose… well, everyone involved only wanted… I'm not sure any of us got it right, but there you are.'

'What did you make of Harry?'

'Harry? Couldn't stand him. He always had a smile, but

he didn't care about anyone other himself. I knew what he was up to behind Vic's back. He used to brag about it in the pub. What's worse is a lot of the gormless blokes admired him. Bloody envied him, some of them. Like he was… well, he was your dad, so I've probably said enough.'

'Women liked him then?'

'He knew how to turn on the charm. I mean women don't get to see that, do they – him turning it on and off and then bragging about how he did this one and how did that one. I was crazy about Vic before Harry showed up, and I was there after he went. And I'll be honest with you, Tom, that day he went, while everyone was all tears and talk of murder – that was the happiest day of my life. I knew I'd get Vic back, see. I wanted to take you on as well, but… well, things moved on and it wasn't to be.'

'You must have loved Vic a lot.'

'She was everything to me. I won't marry again, that's for sure.' Norman retrieved an envelope. 'From your mum. Before you open it though, Vic was worried you'd never feel part of this family. So…' He took a photo album from the side and placed it on the table. 'Why don't I leave you a minute. All that tea goes straight through you, don't it.'

Norman left his full mug and went upstairs, leaving Tom with the daunting task of opening the album.

The first photo was one he knew. "Tom aged three months". It was a copy of one Rose had. So was "Tom 6 months" and "Tom first birthday". He was beginning to worry that this was no more than a copy of his own family album. But then, as he turned the pages, it began to change. "Vic, Tom and baby Terence, Island Gardens 1961". Terry looked tiny. The next photo was "Vic and Tom at Vic's favourite view". It was Vic holding him, aged two, by the railings in Island Gardens with the Old Royal Naval College across the river.

Emotions rose in his chest. He had to gather himself.

Next came "Vic, Tom, Norman, Terry – London Zoo, 1963." Tom had to stretch his brain cells… because he did have a vague recollection of it.

Then came "Vic and Tom (4th birthday)" and "Vic, Tom, Norman, Terry, Millwall Park, 1964". There were at least a hundred photos. All with Vic and Tom, along with Terry and Norman, and, a bit later, Jack. Some with Ted and Rose too. These were all photos where Vic had been looking after him, or visiting for a birthday or Christmas or whatever. Now he thought of it, Vic always had a camera in her bag.

What he was looking at was a made-up family album…

No! It wasn't made up. What he was looking at WAS his family album! As much as the one Rose and Ted kept. Vic had NEVER forgotten her first baby. Looking through, he could see he'd lived another life without realising it. Years from now, anyone studying it would see one thing shining through the Kodachrome pictures: a loving family.

Norman came downstairs. As the kitchen door opened, Terry whizzed by into the front room.

Tom tried to say something but he couldn't get the words out.

'You take after her,' said Norman. 'She wanted to mend the family. You've finished her work and I know she's up there somewhere looking down, very proud of you. Now come and meet your brothers. Properly, I mean.'

An hour later, Tom rode up to East London Cemetery. It was a lovely spot, just as Norman had said. During the funeral, he'd been surrounded by people wearing black. Now he was in open space with a few sparse visitors and the invisible dead.

'It's me,' he said. 'Tom…' He studied the headstone. It was quite plain with minimal details. 'I've got your letter.'

He held it, but was reluctant to read it – as if it might change things in a way he wouldn't want. Even so…

My dearest darling boy,

Tom, by now you will know the story of your birth and the mistake I made in not fighting harder to keep you. My only comfort is the caring parents I left you with and thanks to God the chance to see you every week as you grew up. I want you to think about all those auntie kisses on the cheek and silly presents I bought you and I want you to know now they were given by a loving mother.

I hope you liked seeing the family album. I always kept it updated and when I was alone I'd get it out and talk to you about the fun times we had together. I hope those times aren't all lost to you and that some of them have stayed with you.

I hope, one day, you will find it in you to forgive me. Finally, could I ask you a favour. Please keep an eye out for Terry and Jack. They look up to you.

God bless and may all the good fortune this world has to offer come your way. Better late than never, Tom.

All my love
Mum

Tom folded the letter and put it away.

'Of course I forgive you… I love you, Mum.'

Then he dropped to his knees, unable and unwilling to stop the tears from falling.

52. DOING THE RIGHT THING

For Tom, early June was very much about last-minute revision for his A-levels and an interview at the town hall for a place on the junior entrants' scheme. In the wider world, the papers were saying that a general election might be held in the autumn if Jim Callaghan's minority Labour government continued to struggle. Polly wanted them out but Tom didn't get it.

'You'll let in the Tories, Poll. I mean you don't seriously think Britain would vote for an SWP government?'

'No, but what I see now is a defeated Labour Party turning Left. Then we could take the Tories on and wipe them away forever.'

'Says who?'

'It's obvious. If Labour moves left, it'll carry the working class vote with it.'

There was no arguing with Polly. He was dead certain.

Once the exams were upon them, the world seemed to shrink away to nothing. Tom didn't even watch much telly – apart from the World Cup, with live games coming on late at night from Argentina. He and Neil watched a couple of them in the pub. And in the middle of it all, Grandad died. A kind of asthma attack related to his emphysema. Tom felt terrible and could only hope that Grandad was back with the old gang now.

The funeral was just before his final exam. It was a

quiet affair. Much of the talk was about the docks. One of Ted's mates reckoned the new firm on the graving dock behind Preston's Road was doing very badly and wouldn't last. Ted briefly mentioned nationalisation and how repair yards needed to be treated separately, but given the occasion, his heart wasn't in it. Tom was part-there, part in the Roman world of *Coriolanus,* part in the pre-War days when his grandparents first met.

The funeral aside, Ted and Rose were getting on better than ever, thank God. Rose was happier now that Ted had given his blessing to her working part time in the chemists. She was also very pleased when Jean phoned her out of the blue. They were now seeing each other again. She thanked Tom on both counts.

Ted was generally happier too. With the Knowledge of London progressing nicely, he now had the prospect of being a London cab driver when the docks closed. Very timely too, what with Northfleet Hope opening at Tilbury: a huge new container terminal that would finally kill off the comparatively small West India and Millwall Docks. Ted and his docker mates were holding out for ten grand to quit. That way, those on the Knowledge would be able to buy their own cabs and have some change left over for their building society accounts. Of course, it was a different world from those old photos of ships packed along the quaysides. It had been a slow, suffocating, terminal decline, much like Grandad's final years.

After the exams, Tom found it impossible to relax. He'd been wound up tight for too long. His brain was still hyper-active and if he tried to slow down, something kept nagging at him suggesting that there had to be something he was meant to be doing. He felt he'd done okay in all three subjects and was happy to let the gods decide his fate now. Neil was also confident. Polly too – even though he'd spent his weekends protesting against the National Front up at Brick Lane. Danny was so confident he didn't have to say he was confident; it just poured out of him. Brenda was also confident, but uncertain of what she might do. Barry was hopeful of following Sangheeta to the LSE.

Then came the World Cup final, with Argentina beating Holland to lift the trophy, the final recording session with Natalie and the band, the worryingly sagging ceiling, rotten thanks to unchecked water ingress, and the Westferries' second single, "Hot Summer Nights". It was the week's highest new entry, straight in at number twelve. Soon after came Natalie's phone call, which set up a meeting that would most likely prove to be somewhat challenging.

It was a bright morning and, with Ted and Rose at work, Tom had the house to himself. He was in the front room, which doubled as his bedroom pending his bedroom ceiling being repaired. He was listening to a tape Neil had given him. Kraftwerk. *The Man Machine.*

Roy would be round in a couple of hours – once he'd finished moving some gear for some shady bloke he knew down at Tilbury. Thanks to Roy's constant prompting and the fact that Claire was away on tour, Tom was packed and ready for a Kent seaside holiday camp. He had no intention of becoming a Harry or a Roy but he was looking forward to a couple of months' of fun playing pop hits in a band called the Shoreliners.

With too much time on his hands, he checked his clothes bag again. And his guitar. He wouldn't need his little amp as they would use the house gear.

Natalie's car pulled up outside.

This wasn't going to be easy. The recordings simply weren't good enough. Roy had gone back and overdubbed a couple of songs but it didn't really help. Natalie had nothing special to offer. She wasn't terrible. She just wasn't interesting. Tom had decided to tell her the truth.

He let her in and smiled. A fake smile. The best he could do. She was attractive and oozed sex appeal. But it wasn't enough.

'Natalie, I'm not sure the tape is good enough.'

'We don't know that. Not till the bloke in Soho's heard it.'

'Yeah, but you can't bother people like him with tapes that aren't good enough.'

'Hey, don't get all excited. When he hears it, he'll like it.'

'Look, we really can't—'

She clamped her lips to his. A massive waft of Charlie perfume filled his nostrils. Then she pushed him into the front room/bedroom, reached for his dressing gown, which was draped over an armchair, and pulled out the belt.

'Fancy a bit of Joyce McKinney?' she said.

'Um... no.'

'No?'

She pushed him backwards, onto the bed where she whipped his trousers and underpants off. He felt exposed. Not that she was looking. She was too busy getting her own clothes off.

'Natalie, I can't take advantage of you like this.'

'Shut up,' she said flopping onto the bed and sending another hurricane of Charlie up his nostrils. He wondered – did she bathe in it?

'Um...' His blood was pumping, her legs were opening and Claire was in Germany.

'Come on then.'

Nat Hiscock came to mind. If he found any man at it with his precious daughter, he'd remove said bloke's goolies with a rusty Stanley knife.

'Are you sure I haven't put you in a situation you'll regret?'

'Don't be silly. I fancy you.'

He was ready, of course. He would happily push into her. It would feel wonderful. It would be quick, probably. A rush. A release. Relief. All the pent-up frustrations of adolescence purged wholesale into that beautiful body. 'All done?' she would say, as if he'd been decorating her lounge. And he would roll off and regret it down to the smallest atom in his soul.

That aside, he was only human.

'Well?' she said.

He stared at the peeling wallpaper, once pristine, long since stained by pollutants. Of course, the guilt had to stop. It wouldn't be wrong. In fact, making love to Natalie would be *very* right. Claire was never coming back to him and he'd been left with no choice.

And yet...

'Come on, Tommy-boy.'

He tried to keep a clear head.

'I wanna feel you inside me.'

This had to be the right decision.

'Tommy-boy...?'

'No,' he said.

'No?'

The phone rang.

He grabbed his beltless dressing gown and went into the hall to answer it.

'Hello, Tom speaking,' he said, pulling on the gown.

'Hello, handsome.'

'Cl…' He reached to the front room door and pulled it to. 'Claire?'

'Listen, I reckon we've waited long enough, don't you?'

What?

The hall began to feel hot. He let his gown fall open.

'I'm at home. All by myself. Come round.'

'I thought you were on tour.'

'Our management rescheduled a few things and I've got a couple of days off.'

The front room door opened to reveal Natalie, starkers.

'My dad's outside.'

What?

The doorbell rang. Tom almost dropped the phone but managed to whisper into it.

'Can I call you back?'

53. CERTAINTIES

Somewhat unhelpfully, Nat let himself in.

'Alright, Nat?' said Tom, trying to conceal both his panic and his privates. 'Wasn't expecting to see you here.'

'Arranged it with Ted to look at that ceiling upstairs. Natalie here?'

'Natalie?'

'Her car's outside.'

'Yeah, she's in the loo,' said Tom eyeing the closed front room door, behind which Natalie was hopefully yanking her knickers back on. 'Literally just arrived.'

'Gonna discuss album covers, are you?'

'Er, yeah. Let's go to the kitchen. We need to talk.'

'You wanna finish dressing first?'

'Oh, yeah. Sorry. My bedroom's in the front room.'

'I know. That's why I'm here.'

'Look, let's put the kettle on first, eh?'

In the kitchen, Tom was grateful for the noise the kettle made.

'So… you've come to fix my bedroom ceiling.'

'I know Bernie the landlord. I often do jobs for him.'

'Bernie, yeah. Never actually met him.'

'Shrewd bloke. Comes from Shoreditch, but he's got properties round here, Barking, East Ham, Forest Gate…'

Natalie appeared at the door, looking super-cool and smelling of a fresh coat of Charlie.

'Hello all.'

'Hello, princess,' said Nat. 'Is he looking after you?'

Natalie glanced at Tom. 'We have an understanding, Dad.'

Nat turned to Tom. 'What you've got there is talent. You handle her right and you'll be doing yourself a favour.'

'No, I'm definitely…'

The doorbell rang.

Now what?

Tom went to answer it.

'Alright?' said Roy. 'I got away earlier than I thought… You just got up?'

'I'll be with you in two minutes.'

As Roy returned to the car, Natalie grabbed Tom's arm.

'So when are you seeing the bloke up Soho?'

'Er…'

She leaned in close. 'Or do I tell dad you've been taking advantage of me.'

'What?'

'You know he went to prison once. It wasn't for selling dodgy gear. He stabbed a bloke.'

'Look, the tape's at the recording studio. I'll phone them. Get them to pass it on. Okay?'

'Okay.'

Natalie left. She seemed happy enough. Tom got dressed and grabbed his guitar and things, leaving Nat to assess the work in his bedroom. A moment later, he was getting into Roy's Austin 1100.

'I'm giving the go-ahead for the tape to go to Soho,' he said.

Roy pulled a face. 'What for? Natalie's boring. It really annoys me.'

'That we wasted our time?'

'No, that I never got to shag her.'

As they pulled away, Tom rolled down his window and planted his arm on the ledge. Roy nudged his passenger.

'Got a nice pay packet from my mate. Twenty notes for three hours' work.'

'Shame he can't give you more than a day's notice about containers accidentally bursting open then.'

Roy laughed, full and throaty with the hint of hoarseness of a young regular smoker.

'Now,' he said. 'This is what we're gonna do – play in a naff band, drink free booze and shag loads of birds. Got it?'

'Yeah,' said Tom. Manchester Road looked alien somehow. Life itself felt awkward.

'We, my son, will be racking 'em up by the dozen.'

'Yeah.'

'A different bird every few days. Think on that, Tom.'

He did. It was how his family fell apart. Okay, so Roy would make sure his women were on the Pill – probably. No, Roy wouldn't care. He'd see that as their problem. Tom sighed. He didn't want to interfere in other people's lives. And he didn't want to be a moral judge either

Up ahead, the Blue Bridge loomed large. What of Claire? She wanted to see him. What if she was waiting for him right now, preparing to say, 'Tom Alder, I love you', unaware that he was heading for Kent? And what if, after a few hours, she gave up on him and fell in love with someone else? What kind of grim tragedy would that be?

'Drop me here, Roy.'

'What?'

'Anywhere here.'

'You bottling out?'

'Just drop me here.'

'What's the matter?' said Roy, pulling over. 'We'll have more women than we can handle.'

'I'm just wondering… you know… if we shouldn't all be looking for someone…' He wanted to say "someone who might love us" but he knew Roy would bust a gut laughing.

Roy laughed anyway.

'You're pathetic. You could have shagged that Natalie but you weren't man enough.'

Tom got out and retrieved his stuff from the back seat. Roy's tone softened.

'If you change your mind, come down. But be quick. They'll bring in another guitarist and there won't be anywhere to stay.'

'Have a good summer, Roy. Tell all the girls you launched Claire Cross. I mean, who's to know?'

'Well, I was gonna do that anyway, you pillock.'

'Rock on, mate.'

He closed the car door. Roy called through the open window.

'You too, Tom. Use it wisely.'

Tom watched the car roar off over the bridge. Roy would soon be up to the East India Dock Road and through the Blackwall Tunnel, heading for Kent and a summer of music and nookie. It wasn't the worst outlook in the world.

Hauling his stuff, he crossed the road. Reaching the bridge, he stopped and stared out across the Thames. It wasn't just Claire on his mind.

He put his things down and took out the letter he'd written for Lynn. Her name and address stood proud on the white envelope in his best handwriting. Would sending it just be another wrecking ball through his family?

He knew the words by heart.

Dearest Lynn

Apologies for writing as I've been told your family don't wish to see me or know me. I'm Tom Alder, your eighteen-year-old brother, and I can tell you my heart is very heavy with the knowledge that I have a sister I've never seen (a sister! How brilliant!)

Anyway, just in case what I've been told is incorrect, my address and phone number are at the bottom. We don't have to become a family or anything if you don't want to but it would mean a lot to meet you. Our brother Danny feels the same way, although he doesn't know I'm contacting you.

All my thoughts and best wishes,

Your loving brother

Tom Alder

Was it really a good idea? Could he trust Fate to turn this the right way for him? What was the right way anyway? He leaned against the railing feeling uncertain. He needed to find a way forward. A way where there was hope of sorting things out without causing people pain.

A tugboat on the river sounded its horn. It was one of Ted's mates. Tom waved. Then he wondered about life and family and friends and politics and music and nothing. And Lynn called to him, or at least the breeze coming across the docks behind him might have carried her voice from west to east. He wished he could talk to her.

Lynn? What's for the best?

The wind got up. The letter fluttered in his hand.

He hesitated at Claire's door. What if she'd only invited him round for a cuppa? That was the problem with seeing

Claire. He was never quite sure of the situation.

He rang the bell and Claire answered almost immediately. Her flushed cheeks and smile told him he wasn't there to drink tea. Archie brushed against his leg. Tom reached down to ruffle his ear but kept his gaze on Claire.

'Well done on the new single.'

'Thanks. I wasn't sure if you were coming.'

'Oh, I had Nat Hiscock round about the ceiling and his daughter going on about a tape.'

She eyed his bag and guitar. 'You haven't moved out, have you?'

'Oh... no.'

In the front room, he tried to air something that was nagging him.

'Look, Claire...'

'Tom, I'm a bit nervous so the less said the better.'

'Oh right. It's just if you've decided it's time we...'

She kissed him and he lost the power of speech.

When he recovered, his nagging feeling came straight back.

'Claire, I not sure I can do it.'

'Oh, don't worry. You'll soon rise to the occasion.'

'No, I mean... I know we said we'd wait...'

'But you didn't?'

'Oh, I did, Claire. Only, it was more by luck than willpower. I mean I wouldn't want us to... you know... if you didn't like the fact I'd been inches away from... you know... with Doops and Natalie. I mean literally inches.'

'Tom, it doesn't change anything.'

'Really? That's great. But... despite what I've said, would it be possible for me to know what I mean to you?'

He instantly felt daft for saying it and began to pull away. But she still had his forearm.

'A few years back, I realised I really liked this boy. He had a friendly smile and nice eyes. He was a bit unsure of life. Tended to exaggerate a bit. But through it all, he was decent and caring. And yeah, he made big, stupid mistakes, but he never set out to do the wrong thing. He always tried to get it right, always tried to be true. And so nothing, *nothing*, has changed about the way I feel. He was always the one I knew I could trust… when I reached this moment.'

The moment hung in the air, like a hummingbird, still and busy.

'Tom, I don't have plans to sleep with loads of men but who knows how things will work out. The first time should mean something. I couldn't bear to wake up hungover in a foreign hotel with someone I barely know. Not the first time, Tom. I know it's not everything you want. I know you want a lot more, but…'

He looked into her eyes. It was as if some magnet was drawing them together. They fell into each other's arms. They hugged so tight Tom thought they might merge into a single being. And he thought back to them standing in the school entrance, with him recounting the legend of Salmacis and Hermaphroditus to Mrs Dorset, and ponytailed Claire watching and applauding him… and he thought back to the party where she threw up over his beloved trainers, and to the cinema date she effectively set up for him and Darbs, and to her standing in as his bass player, and to them writing a song on the hill in Greenwich…

Upstairs, they undressed each other and smiled and kissed and hugged again. Claire smelled of herbal shampoo but her hair was dry. He guessed she must have had a bath a few hours ago and then pondered whether or not to phone him. He didn't want to let go of her because that must have been a big thing for her to think about. Emotion rose up in him and he felt like sighing all the breath from his body. She was so special and fantastic and brilliant and bloody desirable and *she trusted him*.

Claire led him as they lowered themselves onto the bed and she opened up to him and her scent reached him and he could have died right then and died damned happy but she frowned slightly as if she was wondering why he was waiting and so he plunged into her – not so much on top, but the upper half of a whole. Finally, they were together, nose to nose, her wonderful hands resting gently on his back. He drove into her welcoming body, unable to hold anything back and within seconds a dam burst into her.

A moment later, he rolled off and smiled to the ceiling. Everything felt right, whole, complete. Claire rolled over, too, her head now above him.

'Sorry to interrupt, but our moment isn't actually over.'

'Oh?'

And so she showed him exactly what to do. And her response was more powerful than anything he had ever witnessed. He could have sworn the building shook. And after their moment was properly over he just wanted to rush out and start a new religion dedicated to the female of the species.

54. JOURNEYS

A month had passed since Tom and Claire's moment and her career with the Westferries had claimed her once more. That was her life now. Touring and making records. He was so pleased for her. He hoped she became bigger than the Beatles. They would always be the greatest of friends, of course, but the world had turned and things had changed.

Happy in his freshly repaired and decorated bedroom, he held up his two favourite shirts. Which one to choose? The black and white zig-zags or the plain navy blue?

The house was quiet. Ted and Rose had booked a last-minute holiday – a few days in Bournemouth. Their first holiday since 1966. Thankfully, Rose seemed more confident about life. She had even dusted off an old photo of Tom and Danny playing in the garden and another of Vic and Tom taken in Island Gardens with the Old Royal Naval College in the background. She'd put them both on the mantelpiece with a few other family photos, explaining that it "makes a house a home."

Tom liked having the place to himself. He liked to pretend it was his for real. Well, he'd be nineteen in three months' time. Maybe he'd start having friends round to dinner.

He hummed "You're the One That I Want" as he opted for the navy shirt. It would go well with his best jeans but the black shoes would need a polish. No, he couldn't be bothered. They would be fine.

For Tom, the music scene was fracturing again. Brenda was now a music nut, armed with her *Saturday Night Fever* and brand new *Grease* soundtrack albums, and dragging them all over to Cherry's disco at Hackney dog track to do their best John Travolta impressions. Then there was Neil hauling him to the Hole in the Wall pub just over London Bridge where the whole crowd would sing along at the tops of their voices to "Return of the Giant Hogweed" by Genesis. Then there was Polly getting him over to the Marquee Club to see the latest New Wave bands. Then there was the jazz session at Ronnie Scott's he went to with Oz. And not forgetting the tickets he and Neil had for the Thin Lizzy-Sex Pistols hybrid band The Greedies at Camden. Or his promise to himself to get along to a classical concert at the Proms.

In the end, he supposed there were only two types of music. Good music and the rest. He loved seeking out the best stuff now, regardless of style, and was completely switched off to people at Cherry's hating rock music and people at the Hole in the Wall hating disco.

He sat on the bed and took another look at the package Claire had sent – the Westferries first album, *Strings Attached* – and read her note again.

Tom
Track 7. You lovely man, you.
Always special to me.
Claire

He looked down the track listing:

7. A Song For You (Alder/Cross)

Their song. He didn't need to consult the lyric sheet. It was a boy admitting he was no Shakespeare, and they had written it together. Even though he'd read her note earlier, this time it got to him. Imagine showing that around.

Start forming a queue, girls.

He picked up his journal: *A Journey Into Music* by Tom Alder.

He flicked through its pages.

"Sept 1975. I went up to Claire's for guitar lessons. She was so patient with me. So kind. What a lovely girl she is."

"Sept 1976. You could fall in love with a girl like Claire Cross, if you weren't careful. Believe me, I know."

"May 1977. Claire's performance on stage blew my socks off. How does anyone get to be like that? When she sang 'Get A Grip On Yourself', she had the whole crowd in her hand. I think we're witnessing a rocket that's about to take off. I hope we can all cling on when she flies."

He closed the journal. Then, above the title, he wrote very neatly. *Claire Cross:*

Yes, that looked more like it.

Claire Cross: A Journey Into Music by Tom Alder.

He would send it to her. A reminder of how it was at the most special time of anything – when you're starting out.

He was happy. In search of certainty his whole life, he understood that Claire could never have given him what he needed because it would have required her to slow down, to change course – and that would have suffocated her. In the same way, he would have grown unhappy knowing he was holding her back. He was glad their paths had crossed though. Glad with fifty noughts on.

He went down to the front room to wait and his mind drifted back almost three years to a party in a front room just up the road. A battle of wills. Him versus Tony Cornish for a date with Megan Vanderlin. He laughed. Claire Cross had fancied him and he'd failed to notice. But there *was* a God and Tom was grateful for everything that had followed.

Who else was at the party?

Micky Sullivan. Hardly ever seen nowadays, but Neil's twin brother was training to be a plumber. Polly, of course – going to Southampton either to study or start a revolution. Then there was Darbs. He loved working in the City. Apparently, traders earned an absolute fortune. Then there was Cheryl Allbright. It turned out she hated the City and was now training as a nurse. The thought of Cheryl in a nurse's uniform had an effect on Tom, so he switched to thinking of Megan Vanderlin at Warwick University. In a way, it was she who really launched Claire's career. Without her, Tom would never have picked up a guitar. Then there was Sangheeta, now preparing for her second year at the LSE while Barry was looking forward to joining her there for his first. Brenda was going into retail – a job at Harrods, no less, in the book department. She was also going steady with Neil. Then there was Tony Cornish, approaching twenty-one and looking for a more meaningful life. He was engaged to his girlfriend – trainee nurse Cheryl Allbright.

The doorbell rang. Tom checked his watch. Ten a.m.

'Bang on time.'

He opened the front door to a familiar face.

'All set?' said Danny.

'Yeah, all set.'

Heading for the bus stop, they began a journey that would take them to the nearest Tube station and into Central London – two brothers going to meet their sister for the first time. The chosen rendezvous was Covent Garden. They would meet outside the Roxy Club; until a few weeks ago the spiritual home of punk rock – now closed down forever because punk was dead. Apparently, Lynn used to sneak up there from time to time with her mates. Tom had been up there a few times himself and couldn't get over the fact that he might have bumped into her while X-Ray Spex or the Adverts were playing or DJ Don Letts was blasting out reggae.

Right now, he felt more nervous than any date he'd ever been on. He thought back a week or so to his trip to the address on Grandad's torn-up letter. God, he'd got up early that morning. Well, if Lynn really was fifteen, he knew she wouldn't have got off early for the summer holidays like those sixteen-year-olds who had taken exams. She would still have a few days of the term left. And when a girl of around that age came out of the house, he followed her to school. And as she neared the main gate, he paid a kid 10p to give her the letter. When she took it, she looked around, but Tom was hiding behind a car, peering through the windscreen.

Then came the wait.

Oh the agony.

Then, a few days later, the phone rang. He knew it was her. He actually *knew.*

And there was that eternal moment as he picked up the receiver and put it to his ear. A moment crammed with a universe of possibilities.

'Hello, is Tom Alder there, please?'

He'd been hardly able to answer due to his chest tightening and his throat constricting. She must have thought he was having a heart attack. It didn't ease off when he learned he had another sister, eleven-year-old Louise.

His little brother Jack and little sister Louise would both be starting big school in September. They would find him a fair but firm brother. *Learn a musical instrument, do your homework, never be afraid to think big.*

There hadn't been much luck down the years for Alder brothers. Grandad George lost Lenny to a German bomb and a home for disabled children, Ted lost Harry due to rampant hormones, irresponsible lust and bone-headed stupidity. Tom lost Danny to circumstances. But now luck was turning like a tide up the Thames – and for Tom it was a flood tide bringing Danny, Terry, Jack, Lynn and Louise.

As a 277 pulled up at the bus stop, he nudged his brother.

'The older generation's had their go, Dan. It's our turn now.'

'You've done alright, Tom.'

Praise from Danny. He would never get used to it. He wished the best for his brother, of course. Danny was hoping to get into Oxford. Tom felt that if anyone from Poplar was getting into Oxford, it would be Danny.

'What about girlfriends?' asked Danny as they took their seats. 'Seeing anyone?'

'Yeah, a really nice girl called Michelle. Lives by the river in Limehouse. She's going into commercial insurance in September. We went on a first date in 1975 and I asked her a couple of weeks ago if it was time we went on a second. She thought it probably was, so…'

'Two dates? It must be love.'

Tom laughed. They had in fact since been on a third, fourth and fifth date. For Tom, the sixth, planned for Saturday, couldn't come soon enough. There was something about Michelle. She was warm and generous and he wasn't getting the feelings of being on an emotional roller-coaster with enormous highs and lows. It was a much steadier build-up of deep, potent feelings he was experiencing, and he liked it *a lot.*

'Hopefully, she's not a musician,' said Danny.

'She is, as it happens. She gives free violin lessons to local miscreants at a youth centre. There's a scheme where you can borrow instruments. She reckons I should go along too. You know, to give guitar lessons.'

'You should. The fact you know the Westferries – they'd be eating out of your hand.'

'That's what Michelle says. I said I'd do it. You never know, we might discover the next big thing.'

'Too right. The East End's always had plenty of talent. Claire Cross wasn't the first and she won't be the last.'

Mention of Claire Cross would always stir emotions, of course, but Tom had moved on. For Claire, the Westferries' album was doing well. Europe was calling. Japan was calling. America was calling. For him, the local council had called offering a place on their junior entrant scheme. Neil too! Ha-ha! Everything was working out just fine.

Staring out of the window at a clear blue sky, he reached for the fresh pack of fruit pastilles in his pocket. With summer under way and the 277 bound for Mile End Station and the future, Tom Alder had never felt more in tune with life.

THE END

Thank you for reading The Girl Who Lived By The River. If you've enjoyed it, please feel free to leave a review on Amazon. It really helps me get noticed. It doesn't need to be long. A few words would be absolutely brilliant.

Best wishes

Mark

Printed in Great Britain
by Amazon